For Vivian
With my ...

Arlynn K. Freedman
June, 2021

FINDERS KEEPERS!

ARLYNN K. FREEDMAN

FINDERS KEEPERS!

iUniverse books may be ordered through booksellers or by contacting:

iUniverse
1663 Liberty Drive
Bloomington, IN 47403
www.iuniverse.com
844-349-9409

Because of the dynamic nature of the internet, any web addresses or links contained in this book may have changed since publication and may no longer be valid. The views expressed in this work are solely those of the author and do not necessarily reflect the views of the publisher, and the publisher hereby disclaims any responsibility for them.

Any people depicted in stock imagery provided by Getty Images are models, and such images are being used for illustrative purposes only. Certain stock imagery © Getty Images.

ISBN: 978-1-6632-1353-2 (sc)
ISBN: 978-1-6632-1352-5 (e)

Library of Congress Control Number: 2020924155

Print information available on the last page.

iUniverse rev. date: 01/30/2021

To the memory of my husband, Herb Freedman, who, through all the many years of my efforts to write, offered constant encouragement and belief in me.

We supported and were proud of each other, and it saddens me that he is not here to rejoice with me in the publication of this novel. There is a part of him in every page.

ACKNOWLEDGEMENTS

This novel had an extremely long gestation, and would never have been completed without the support and encouragement of valued friends and role models.

Self-doubt is a writer's worst enemy, and I was helped to move past it on innumerable occasions. The very early draft of the work was read by Arlene Mollow, who encouraged me to believe that I might in fact be a writer. Strong and consistent encouragement came from Ruth Rosenfeld and Hope Medel. Dear friend and confidante Marcia Frezza was with me from the beginning. Leah Coblitz sent positive vibes in person and by phone. Members of my book club, which has met steadily for more than fifty years, have waited patiently for a published work to appear. In addition to members Arlene and Ruth, I'm giving a shout out to Shelly D'jmal, Claire Boren, Vicki Portman, and Judy Benn of blessed memory, with thanks to all. In Florida, my writers' group offered extremely useful critiques. Thanks especially to role models Pat Williams, Bunny Shulman, Carren Strock, and most of all, group leader Barbara Bixon, who spent a long and fruitful day in New York with me, guiding my research into police matters.

At International Writers Guild conferences, author Pat Carr believed in my ability, and taught me almost all I know about point of view.

Early on, Lauren Sanders-Jones edited a first draft and helped me shape the story that became *Finders Keepers!* The final draft was honed and fine-tuned with the help of my editor David S.

My sons Mark and David, and daughters-in-law Maryla and Lisa, encouraged my occasionally flagging motivation, and Lisa in particular did some helpful fact-checking for me, giving generously of her time. Many thanks to Reed Samuel, my Publishing Services Associate for his time, help, and mostly his patience as he took me through the ins and outs of producing a published work.

Finally, although this book is dedicated to his memory, I must also acknowledge once more how constantly supportive my beloved husband Herb, of blessed memory, continued to be throughout the long years of struggling to make my dream of publishing a work of fiction into a reality.

CHAPTER

1

It was hard not to stare at Heather the first time I saw her. The tight, curled-in-on-herself posture and the scowl told a wordless story. She had pushed herself into the corner of my waiting-room couch, as far from her parents as possible.

You can drag me to a shrink, her body language said, *but you can't make me talk.* She might have been pretty, but back then it was impossible to tell. Her hair, too black to be natural, was combed into heavily gelled spikes, sticking up at odd angles. Her left eye was obliterated by more hair, which fell almost to her chin. On the right side, the hair had been chopped to the top of her ear, which was adorned with five different earrings, the largest in the shape of a skull. I could barely see one blue eye through the fringe of jet-black mascara applied top and bottom, along with liner that made her look almost bruised. The small face, with a pronounced dimple in the chin, was covered with pancake foundation almost as white as the wall behind her head. Her lipstick was nearly black, extending considerably past thin lips. She was chewing her gum aggressively.

"Hello, Heather," I said, careful to keep my voice even as I extended my hand. "I'm Rachel." The girl shifted in her seat, crossing one black spandex-clad leg over the other, flashing four-inch patent leather heels. She lifted her chin upward slightly but didn't offer her hand, which sported talons, painted black, where nails should have been.

I turned to the parents. I was struck by Stephanie Brody's stiff posture. I didn't spend much time reading the society pages, but

1

even I knew that the woman had a reputation as an icon of fashion, a dictator of taste and trends, and the giver of fabulous parties. That day her back was rigid, hands folded in her lap, legs slanted, ankles crossed. She was coolly beautiful, in the aristocratic style made famous by Grace Kelly. Her champagne-blonde hair fell softly to her shoulders, pulled back at the sides by two gold combs that looked like antiques and probably were. She wore a cashmere sweater set, camel colored, and matching wool slacks. Her jewelry was understated— diamond studs, a heavy gold-braided choker, a fine, thin watch. The only ostentatious thing about her was her engagement ring, which blazed its four-plus carats on her left hand. There were points on the expensive fabrics where the outline of her collarbone and shoulder bones was visible. I guessed that she was in her late forties.

William appeared older—probably closer to sixty. I recognized his face from TV interviews. News director for a major New York TV station, he had been credited for keeping his network at the top of the ratings game. His hairline had receded, but his hair was still plentiful, gray on top, silver at the sides. His business suit was well tailored, the shirt dazzling white, the tie conservative. He had laugh lines around his mouth. I stretched my hand first to Stephanie, then to William, saying as I did so, "I'm Rachel Marston."

"We'd like a word alone with you first," Stephanie Brody said.

"I plan to spend some time with both of you, and some time with Heather, but I'd rather not start that way." I led them into my office. Bill touched Stephanie's elbow lightly, as if guiding her. Heather followed, exaggerating her reluctance as she dragged her feet.

Stephanie and William settled into matching armchairs upholstered in pale blue corduroy. Heather threw herself onto the beige leather couch. In the course of my career as a psychologist, I'd seen many adolescents who didn't want to be in a therapist's office, but Heather's sprawling insolence, one leg thrown over the back of the sofa, one hand dragging limply on the area rug, signaled a major challenge. I sat in my high-backed swivel chair, crossed my legs, and addressed my first remarks to the teenaged girl.

"Heather, I get the feeling you have better things to do than kill an hour in a shrink's office."

"You've got that right." *Good. She can speak.*

"She wasn't given a choice," her mother explained, as if I had for one moment thought otherwise.

"Since you've agreed to come—"

"I never agreed."

"Since you're here," I corrected myself, "I'd like to see if there's anything I can do to help your family with the problem you all seem to be having."

"You can count me out," the girl said. "I have to sit here, but I don't have to say anything."

"Of course you don't. That will be completely up to you. I thought you might want to tell me why you think your mom and dad are giving you a hard time." In my peripheral vision, I saw William reach over and take Stephanie's hand. I silently applauded his effort to communicate both restraint and support with the single gesture.

"I told you, I have nothing to say."

"Okay. I'll start with your mom and dad, and if they say anything you disagree with, or if you want to add something, feel free to jump right in."

Stephanie didn't wait for a question. "Heather's been in therapy before," she said, "for all the good it did. She's been expelled from her third boarding school in a little more than a year. She seems determined to punish us and destroy her life. Your aunt Gloria spoke so highly of you that I thought maybe you'd have a solution. She's a lovely woman." *Oh, right. Aunt Gloria's referral.* "I was at her lovely home several times for bridge. She really knows how to throw a party," Stephanie added.

"Yes she does." I was determined not to turn this appointment into a social call. I studied Stephanie briefly, searching for a memory of her as one of Aunt Gloria's many friends. It had been too long. I couldn't place her. It didn't matter in any case.

"We've kept in touch," Stephanie said. "I miss your aunt. I could always count on her for help on any committee or to share the latest gossip. She has such excellent taste." She tittered at the memory.

"Gloria wasn't the only one recommending you," William added, his tone cool and businesslike. "I did my homework. You have an excellent record. It's our hope that you can find out what's bothering Heather, and help her."

"Who says anything's bothering me, and who says I need help?" Heather interrupted. "Is it my fault that who I am bothers you?"

I turned back to Heather. "It sounds like you're feeling that your parents don't accept you for who you are."

"Are you kidding? They want a clone who'll go to the right schools, wear the right clothes, and date the right boys, so they can be oh so proud in front of all their rich-bitch friends. And instead they've got me."

"And you're your own person. I can see that."

"I dress the way I want to. And I see who I want. If they can't accept it, that's tough."

"What happened at school?"

"Oh, school. They turn out cookie-cutter kids. It's all preparation for the debutante ball and catching some rich husband. Besides, I smoke. They don't like that."

"She broke every rule," Stephanie said. "Stayed out past curfew, ignored dress code, smoked in the bathrooms and in the dorm."

"We want her to have a good education," William said. "Unfortunately our daughter hasn't made the connection between getting into a good college and having a fulfilling life."

"Fulfilling to whom?" the girl put in. "Her?" She stared at her mother. "That's it. I'm through talking."

"You sure are angry." I kept my tone neutral.

"Because they give me a pain in my ass. Anyway, I'm not saying anything else."

Stephanie opened, then closed her mouth.

"Sometimes," Bill Brody said, his voice low and pensive, "it seems to me as though Heather didn't want to be a part of our family from the day we adopted her. Perhaps, in retrospect, it was a bad fit."

"You should've given me back," Heather muttered before clamming up once again.

When I get nervous my hands tingle and feel weak. It happened so often when my husband was dying that I was evaluated for circulation problems. "Anxiety," the doctor had pronounced after I'd gone through all the tests. He'd prescribed Valium. I weaned myself off it with some difficulty and had used nothing since.

"You didn't mention on the phone that Heather is adopted." I rubbed one prickly palm with the thumb of my other hand.

"She's our daughter, who happens to be adopted," Bill said. "I didn't think it was that important."

"How many fifteen-year-olds get to ski at Saint Moritz?" Stephanie asked. "How many have charge accounts at Saks and Bergdorf's? Not that she uses them, mind you. She prefers the secondhand shops downtown, wearing things that have been on God knows who!" Heather rolled her eyes.

"And the character she runs around with," Bill Brody added. "To tell you the truth, he's my biggest concern. I can deal with the way Heather chooses to look, and I'm willing to search for a school she'll be happier in, but that boy really worries me. He's older, he's been in trouble, I'm sure he uses drugs, and I'm afraid he's going to take my daughter down with him."

"You don't understand him at all, Daddy," Heather said.

I stood up. "I'd like to spend some time with Heather alone. Then it will be your turn."

I escorted Bill and Stephanie back to the waiting room and then came back to find Heather still sprawled on the couch. The girl made a great show of chewing her gum, snapping a large bubble as I returned.

"So," I said, sitting down and resting my hands on my knees, "if I didn't have to be here right now, I'd like to be up in the Berkshires looking at the colors of the leaves. Just driving around, you know?" The girl gave an elaborate *Who cares?* shrug.

"Where would you be if you didn't have to be here?"

A thoughtful look crossed the teenager's face. "On the back of my boyfriend's motorcycle."

"Does he like to go fast?"

"Like the wind. But no, I have to be here, getting fixed, so I won't want to ride motorcycles, or smoke, or have any fun at all." She pushed her slim hips firmly into the couch cushion and turned her face away from me.

"Well, I can't drive around in the mountains right now, and you'll have to postpone that bike ride for a while, so why don't we talk about how I can help."

"You can't. Unless maybe you can get them to leave me alone. I doubt it though."

"I get the feeling they're worried about you."

"Worried? They're worried about what their friends think. At least my mother is."

"And your father?"

"He's okay. But it doesn't matter because she's the boss. Anything she wants, she gets. It makes me want to puke."

"Tell me about your boyfriend."

"You wouldn't understand him. Nobody does."

"Nobody but you."

"Right. Frankster and me, we get each other. But like I said, I didn't want to come here, and I've already talked too much." She pressed her lips together and stared at me.

"Okay. I get it. Frankster understands you, and your mom and dad don't. That's got to be hard for you."

"I'm used to it. I've always known that I'm their big mistake."

"Why would you say that?" The girl shifted, squinted, and studied her black fingernail polish. To speak or not to speak? I leaned in a little closer and waited.

"They wanted a kid, so they adopted me—and I had the wrong genes. I mean, I must be like my real mother and father, 'cause I'm certainly not like them. My dad said it: I just don't fit into their family."

I was still rubbing my palm. I began massaging the other one, keeping my hands in my lap while I did so.

"Have you ever told them how you feel?"

Heather snorted. "You're kidding, right? They don't listen to me. Nothing I say is important. I mean, I can't even finish a sentence before one of them is telling me not to be foolish, or to try it their way, or something."

"Maybe I could teach them to listen better."

"Thanks for the offer, but you don't get it. I don't *want* to talk to them. And I don't think they'll want to come back. They want me to come so I can get fixed, and get into the right school, and make friends with all the phonies. They don't want to change anything about themselves. Because they're already perfect."

"Well, nobody can remake you without your participation. But maybe you could use someone to talk to, someone who'll accept you just the way you are."

"I've got the Frankster."

"I know. I meant someone else. I know the Frankster is very important to you, but he's at one end of your life, and your parents are at the other, and there you are in the middle. Maybe it would help to have someone else in the middle with you, someone who can see both sides."

"You mean you."

"For now. Long enough to see if we could hit it off. No matter what your parents want, I don't see my job as trying to change you. Maybe I can help you take a look at what you really want for yourself, without pressure from your parents on one side and from the Frankster on the other. Does that make sense to you?"

"I'm not a mental case. I don't need another shrink."

"Of course not. But you've got people around you giving you a rough time. Maybe I could help you deal with your parents once in a while, if you'd let me."

"You'll see that that's not what they want. They want you to turn me into Miss Deb of the Year. And it's not going to happen."

"That wouldn't be you, would it? But I'm not totally convinced that this is you either. When you're angry, it's hard to know who you really are."

"You're talking shrink language. I hate that."

"You're right. I'll try not to do that." I glanced at my wristwatch. "Now I need to spend some time with your mom and dad. Will you wait in the reception room?"

"I need to use the john."

"Sure. Ask Jan for the key." Jan was my receptionist, my friend, and a jill-of-all-trades. I walked Heather to the door. "By the way," I said, "there's a smoke alarm in the bathroom."

As Bill and Stephanie settled back into my office, I said, "Before I forget, you might want to pick up this book." I pulled a rather thick volume from a crowded shelf and passed it to Bill.

"*Going with the Flow*," he read from the cover. "*How to Make the Most of Your Adolescent's Strengths*. By Larry Tobin, PhD. The name sounds familiar."

"I think I saw him on the *Today* show," Stephanie commented. "He's some kind of guru on teenagers."

"And on teenagers' relationship with their parents," I said. "He makes a lot of sense. You might find it helpful."

"So what do you think, Dr. Marston?" Bill asked. "About Heather."

"First, could the two of you fill me in a little on your early history with her? Has it always been this rough?"

"From the day we brought her home," Stephanie answered. "She cried all night. We had to keep the baby nurse for months. She didn't like being held, and she hated pretty clothes—said they itched. When she got older, she was wild and rebellious. She was more than we'd bargained for—twice the headache and less than half the joy."

"You know," her husband added, "we've been blessed. I've done well, and we can give this child a wonderful start. We adopted her because we realized that we had so much to offer a child. She arrived rather late in our lives—at least in mine. We had very high hopes, but she's rejected everything we've tried to do for her. She doesn't want clothes or trips, and she hated the summer camps we chose, always being sent home early. Now we can't get her to settle down and accept a decent education. Plus, I'm afraid she's headed for real trouble. To say the least, it has been frustrating."

I felt for this couple, especially the father, who wanted so much to be able to share his good fortune with his child. I chose my words carefully.

"You're right that she's vulnerable. But the power struggle in your household isn't doing anything to change that. And since she's not about to suddenly capitulate, the initial change has to come from the two of you." I leaned back and waited, studying Bill and Stephanie for their reactions. They looked at each other. Stephanie stroked the links of her heavy gold choker. She spoke first.

"I'm not sure I understand. We're not the ones who have to change. That should be obvious."

"Yes, dear," Bill said, "but I think the doctor's point is that something has to change, and it has to start with us."

"Can you think of anything you might do differently? Something Heather would notice?"

"I can't think of a thing," Stephanie said.

"Maybe," Bill responded, drawing out the word, "we could begin by not commenting on her appearance."

"But that's condoning her outrageous outfits and makeup," his wife protested.

"Not really," I chimed in. "I suspect that she becomes more and more extreme in order to get a rise out of you. If it doesn't work, it may lose its appeal."

"It is true that every week she does something new and awful," Stephanie said. "She looks like a refugee from *Nightmare on Elm Street*. But I'm her mother. How can I let her go around looking like that?"

"You've been not letting her, but she's doing it anyway. I believe strongly that if something's not working, you might as well try something else. All your critiques of her appearance have only resulted in her finding new and better ways to horrify you."

"That's true."

"Then let's try something different. Bill's idea has merit. Don't comment."

"It will be hard. And I'm not sure I agree. But you're the expert."

"In most cases children who've been brought up with good values eventually straighten themselves out, even if their rebellious stages have been truly frightening."

"We'll hold that thought," Bill said.

"You know, Doctor," Stephanie said, her hand fluttering to smooth the silky blonde fall of hair across her forehead, "it's very important that Heather make some major changes this year. We'll be relocating to Washington next summer. My husband will be appointed to the directorship of the national news desk. By the way," she added, leaning forward slightly, "that information is not yet for public consumption. But this is all confidential, right? There are some fine boarding schools in Virginia. Heather must be capable of being accepted and not being expelled. We simply cannot have in Washington a repeat of what she's put us through in New York."

"It's hard to work with a timetable," I commented. "And the more important it is to you, the more your daughter may have invested in maintaining the status quo. Also, I must tell you," I continued, reaching deep within myself to strike a nonjudgmental tone, "you're not offering much incentive for a young woman with Heather's problems to conform to your expectations."

"I'm not following."

"You want Heather to behave herself, dress like a lady, give up a boyfriend of whom you disapprove, and otherwise stop giving you a hard time so that you can send her away to yet another school."

"Well, of course," William said, his tone that of someone who has blundered a negotiation. "Her greatest incentive should be her own happiness. We want her to have a productive life. College. The right boy. A good marriage."

"Understandable goals," I said, tabling for the moment my concern about these parents' need to put distance between themselves and their daughter. "I'm prepared to start now and see what we can do. I'd like to see Heather weekly and have a conference with the two of you every three weeks or so. But you must understand that I won't betray Heather's confidence unless I feel she's in actual physical danger. So don't expect me to convey anything of what she tells me. I hope that's perfectly clear."

"Don't we have a right to know—" Stephanie began.

"I understand," William interrupted. "You need to gain her trust."

"Exactly. The only reason I want to see you at all is because there will be things you can do to help, and I'll need the opportunity to share those things. If Heather recognizes that I'm acting as her advocate when I meet with you, I think she may accept it. And indeed that is what I'll be doing—advocating for her."

William Brody stood up and glanced at his watch. "You've been generous with your time, Dr. Marston. Feel free to charge us for the extra half hour."

"That won't be necessary. First sessions run long, but from now on the time frame will be fifty minutes. Now I'm going to invite Heather back in for another minute."

When summoned, the girl slouched into the room. "Yeah?"

"I'd like to see you next week without your mom and dad, to continue our conversation," I said.

"I figured I wasn't going to get off the hook. So, big deal. I kill an hour. Just so long as it doesn't interfere with my plans. I do have a life, you know."

"She'll be starting a new school tomorrow," Stephanie said, "here in the city. Living at home, temporarily at least. So give her a late afternoon appointment, Doctor."

I flipped open my weekly planner and made a notation. "The appointment is at 4:00 p.m. a week from today. It was good meeting all of you." To Heather I said, "And I'm looking forward to seeing you again," placing a hand lightly on the girl's shoulder.

"Yeah, well, I guess. See ya."

And the Brody family was gone.

Notes, Mid-October

Power struggle. Heather acting out to establish independence. Angrier at mother. Prognosis uncertain. Adoption issues: added complication.

As I wrote, I glanced at the portrait of Larry Tobin that filled the back cover of his book. I couldn't stop myself from running my thumbnail briefly across the thin lips of the man in the picture. Having finished writing, I found myself picking up the book with two hands and raising it to eye level. I stared for a long moment at the almost handsome face, his eyes as shockingly blue as I remembered. I shook my head, baffled as always whenever I thought of Larry. *How is it possible that the boy I knew turned into this man?* Retrieving my purse from the bottom drawer, I paused, as always before going home, and let my gaze fall on the photograph in a plain sterling-silver frame that was placed at an angle at the corner of my desk. I touched two fingers to my lips and then to the face of the handsome man, wearing shorts and a T-shirt and squatting on one knee, an arm around each of two little boys who were miniatures of him. I shut the lights, locked the door behind me, and left the office for the day.

CHAPTER 2

Dipping into the well of memories of Larry always evoked guilt. Heading home after that first session with the Brodys, I slipped into an empty seat on the subway. With rumble and clatter in the background, I let my mind wander into the past.

I was sixteen. He was a little more than a year older. "Wasn't the movie wonderful?" I said as we exited the Regal Flatbush two blocks from Larry's home. I'd only been in his apartment once, to meet his parents. They were older than mine. His mother retained a trace of a German accent. His father barely spoke. The rooms were small and crowded, the furniture shabby. Introductions were rushed. Larry couldn't wait to get me out of there.

"Sure, if you go for nonoriginal predictability." His tone underlined his scorn. "Of course I knew you'd like it," he went on. "You have many sterling qualities, my dear, but artistic taste doesn't happen to be one of them." Larry liked to pretend that he was a brilliant connoisseur of the arts, fine dining, and all attributes of a lifestyle that neither of us enjoyed. That ended any further discussion of the movie. I switched topics.

"Sandy and Jay want to go out with us Saturday night." I hoped he could tell from my tone how much I wanted that double date.

"Another night with your best friend and the guy whose greatest claim to fame is that he can recite the RBIs of every player on the Mets. Spare me, please."

"But, Larry, I miss being with my friends."

"If you really loved me, being with me would be enough for

you." He pulled me close. "Being with you is all I need to be happy." So many years had passed, and yet I could still remember how my throat closed around a lump and how I'd felt the heat of unshed tears waiting behind my eyelids as I tried to make sense of my boyfriend's need for isolation.

"You don't like anything I like, or any of the people either," I argued. "You don't even like my mom and dad."

"Because they don't like me. They'd like to see me disappear." That was true enough.

"He never smiles," my mother had said as we dried dishes together. "And you don't smile as much as you used to either. Besides, it's impossible to have a conversation with him."

"He's just more serious than most boys his age." I waved a dish towel for emphasis. "He's always thinking. He's going to be somebody someday." Pressed by both my parents to date other boys, I dug in my heels to defend Larry. "Besides," I argued in a quivering voice, "he really needs me."

"But do you need him?" my father had asked. "That's the question."

I shook my head a little at the memory as I stood, grabbing a strap as the train approached my West Fourth Street station. I'd been a precocious sixteen-year-old, already a senior in high school. I knew better than my parents and better than my friends. Larry's consuming need for me and only me was a powerful aphrodisiac that led me to his bed on a snowy Sunday morning when his parents were out of town.

"You are so beautiful," he told me, running his hand, with its long, sensitive fingers, over my stomach. "I know that you're going to leave me one day. And I won't be able to stand it."

I sat up in the bed with my legs crossed beneath me so that I could look directly into his impossibly blue eyes and touch his face. "I love you," I insisted. "We're going to get married one day. After college."

"You'll see," he said, his voice mournful. "You'll go away to school; you'll meet other boys. I'm going to lose you. My life is like that. I never get what I want." He ran long, perfectly manicured fingers through my auburn curls. "Your eyes change color after sex," he said. "Right now they're a rich turquoise. In bright sunlight, they're emerald green. I love your eyes."

I made up my mind right there on the bed. "I'll go to NYU and live at home so we can be together."

The break came three months later. Larry had planned a surprise, dinner at Shun Yen in Manhattan.

"You can't afford this." Larry went to NYU at night, working by day as a bookkeeper in an import-export office. Most of what he earned paid for his tuition and books. He also helped his family financially.

"I saved up. This is special."

We ate overpriced chicken and cashews, and consumed pots of hot tea. Over fortune cookies, Larry pulled a small package from his pocket. Reaching across the table to hand it to me, he gnawed on his lower lip.

"What's this? It's not my birthday."

"Open it."

The ring was a quarter-carat diamond marquis in a plain gold setting.

Sixteen years later, walking home from the subway station on a brisk autumn late afternoon, a few leaves swirling around me, my stomach clutched with the same apprehension I'd felt that night as I looked from the ring to Larry's expectant face.

"Larry, I can't accept this."

"We're going to get married. You said so yourself. So why shouldn't we be engaged? Put it on. Here, let me." He took the small box from me. Reaching for my hand, he slid the ring onto my fourth finger. "There, it fits! Do you like it?"

"I don't know what to say. It's beautiful." I felt tears rise up and close my throat. Larry raised my hand to his lips and kissed it.

We walked together to the subway. "This doesn't change anything," I said. Suddenly it was very important that he understand. "I'm still going to college. We're still going to wait."

"I know, I know." His tone was reassuring. Then he added, "At least I'll know you're mine. I won't have to worry that you'll meet someone else."

"Is that why you did this?"

"I don't want to lose you, Rachel. You're going to college in the fall. There will be men everywhere. Handsome men. Rich men. I don't want you to forget you belong to me."

I stopped walking and stood there on the sidewalk, staring at him. "You don't trust me. You're doing this for yourself." I slid the ring off my finger and placed it firmly in the palm of his hand. "I'm not ready to be engaged, Larry."

"Don't do this, Rachel. I thought you'd be happy. I wanted to surprise you. I want to marry you. I'd marry you now if I could."

"I'm sorry, Larry." Now the tears that had threatened to overflow poured out in earnest. "I'm only sixteen. I'm not ready." I ran ahead of him, going down the subway stairs, and darted into the train that had just arrived at the station and opened its jawlike doors. I cried through all the stations that whizzed by before I got to my own, at Columbus Circle in Manhattan.

At home I flew into the house and ran, weeping, to my room. My mother followed me up the stairs. She sat on the edge of my bed as I sobbed and told her what had happened.

"You did the right thing, sweetheart," she consoled. "College is the time for you to be free."

"He's so hurt," I sobbed. "He always says I'm all he has. Now he thinks he's going to lose me."

"Rachel," my father, who'd entered the room quietly, responded, "you can't sacrifice your life to someone else's need. He'll be all right. He'll survive. This would be a good time to take some time away from him. You've been accepted at Case Western Reserve. I'm hoping you'll go there."

Case had been my first-choice college before I made the decision to stay in New York. My mother's sister Gloria lived in Cleveland, and the college program offered everything I wanted. I gave a long shuddery sob. "I don't know," I wailed. "I don't know what to do."

Larry made the decision for me. "I think I need to go to Cleveland," I told him in one of the fifty phone calls he'd made in the week following the near engagement. "My parents are right. I need a little space now."

"If you leave me, I'll kill myself," he said. I could hear his dry sobbing. "I knew this would happen. I knew it." Right then I knew what I had to do. I remember heaving a deep sigh.

"I hope you don't do that. I'll be really, really sad if you do. It would be a terrible waste. But I'm going to Cleveland." After that conversation, I refused his phone calls. Thinking back, it seemed to me as if I cried for at least a month. *What will become of him? He needs me so much.*

Thoughts of the past had receded by the time the elevator stopped on the eleventh floor of my West Village condominium. As I jiggled my key in the lock, the door flew open, and I was squeezed in a tight hug by one blond, freckle-faced nine-year-old boy, whose identical twin pushed him away, eager for his turn. "Wait. Wait a minute," I protested, laughing, as I bent down for kisses. "I can't hug both of you at once."

"Give your mother a chance to catch her breath," Mrs. Marcus said, appearing in the kitchen doorway, wiping her hands on a floral-print apron. I sank gratefully onto the couch, and the boys flanked me.

"Hard day?" Molly Marcus spoke in the guttural Russian accent of her youth. When the Soviet Union began allowing Jews to leave the prison of their homeland, she had been one of the first to arrive in New York. She had been widowed, childless, and alone. "You look exhausted."

"New case," I acknowledged. "A tough kid. She's going to be a challenge. So, what's for dinner?"

"I made spaghetti and meatballs for the boys. And salad. And garlic bread. Do you want a glass of wine first?"

"I'd love a chardonnay." I kicked off my shoes and tickled Mitch, the twin on my left. He giggled, wiggled, and escaped.

"I am so lucky I found you, Molly," I said as I felt the chill of the wineglass with both hands.

"I have told you many times, Rachel, I am the lucky one. You have given me a family."

"When you walked in the door at the worst time of my life—"

"It was meant to be. When poor Mr. Marston was so sick, and you with four-year-old boys, and going to work besides, you certainly needed my help. And I needed you too. I have told you so many times." Her gaze took in the twins, Ben still beside me, Mitchell buzzing the room with an imaginary airplane. "It is amazing how much they look like him."

"I know." For a moment Neil was a presence in the room as

we both remembered how his vitality had ebbed while he slowly succumbed to the ravages of a brain tumor. "I hope they grow up to be like him in every way."

"They will. You can tell already," Molly Marcus said as she headed back to the kitchen. "They're doing just fine."

Indeed, five years after their father's death, Ben and Mitch were happy, well-adjusted children. As small boys they had asked, "Why did Daddy die?" and "Where is heaven?" Now, at nine years old, they occasionally asked if Neil had liked meatballs and spaghetti, or if he was a really good tennis player, but they had adjusted to the pain of his loss and to life with Mrs. Marcus and me.

Two hours later the boys were bathed, the tomato sauce scrubbed from two round, freckled faces and their teeth brushed, and were ready for story time. I continued a tradition that Neil had only had time to begin.

"Who's going to tell us our chapters?" Ben had asked, weeping, after his father's funeral.

"I will. I promised Daddy that I'd tell the chapters."

Before his illness, and for as long as possible afterward, Neil had climbed onto the lower bunk with both boys and made up adventure stories starring all four of us. "Ben and Mitchell were out in the desert," he would begin. "The wind began blowing, and the sand flew all around, so they couldn't see where they were going. Suddenly, Daddy and Mommy rode up on a giant white horse. Daddy grabbed Mitch and Mommy grabbed Ben, pulling them up on the back of the horse and riding out of the sandstorm and back to the safety of their cave."

Neil had been a much better storyteller with a vivid imagination for preposterous plots and impossible rescues. But I did my best, always including Neil in the stories. There was a chapter every night. Now I joined the boys on Ben's bed, sitting cross-legged and tucking one twin under each arm.

"Where should we go tonight?" I asked.

"Mount Everest," Mitch said.

"Again?" Climbing Mount Everest was one of their favorites. Neil had told it first and embellished it in future tellings. Now I added my own touches. "A big snow cloud gathered on the top of the mountain, and it came down to where Mommy, Daddy, Mitch, and Ben were huddled on a ledge, trying to keep warm. Mommy and Daddy couldn't see Mitch and Ben, and nobody could see anybody else."

"And then what happened?" Ben asked.

"Well." I drew out the word. "Daddy took a great big deep breath, and then he huffed, and he puffed, and he blew that old snow cloud away." It was lame, I knew, but I was better at creating emergencies than I was at finding a way out. Lucky for me, the boys could laugh at my chapter-telling inadequacies.

"Mommy, you're silly." They giggled at the image, and did some huffing and puffing of their own, before I dispensed hugs and kisses and Mitch climbed into the upper bunk.

At 9:30 the phone rang. I was in bed, a copy of the *New Yorker* tossed on the duvet. I'd given up the attempt at reading when my mind jumped to images of Heather Brody and her mother, polar opposites, both in pain. Now it was my own mother on the phone, checking in as she'd done frequently ever since Neil died.

"I started a new case today that reminded me a little bit of us," I said. "A teenager and her mother driving each other nuts."

"We did have our moments," Mom acknowledged.

"The parents want this kid to give up a boyfriend they don't like. Sound familiar?"

"My sympathy is entirely with the parents." I could hear in Mother's dry tone the acknowledgment of our turbulent history. I had eventually developed an appreciation for her many wonderful qualities, but I had a lot of maturing to do before I got there.

"I'll tell you, Mom, this family makes ours look like Ozzie and Harriet. It's going to be a challenge for sure."

"*You* were a challenge. But you turned out okay in the end."

"I assured the parents that there's hope. This girl's adopted, by the way."

There was a small pause, just long enough to draw an extra breath.

"Is that hard for you, sweetheart?"

"It was a long time ago, Mom."

"I still think about her sometimes. I have four wonderful

grandchildren, but there are times when I wonder about the other one, the first one."

"Well, me too," I acknowledged. "But I'm okay. Really." I hoped that was true. We chatted for a few more minutes about Mitch's tennis lessons and about Ben's piano recital coming up in three weeks.

"I'll be there with bells on," Mom promised as we said good night. I picked up the *New Yorker* and tried again to focus my attention on climate change. Giving up, I swung my legs off the bed and walked barefoot to the French doors from which, in the distance, I could see the sparkle of the Chrysler Building. Staring out into a star-filled night and with a crescent moon off to my right, I remembered the night I'd told my parents I was pregnant. My mother had burst into tears and then pulled me into a hug. My dad had clenched and unclenched his fists.

"Your mother will call Dr. Wiener," he finally said. "You'll put this behind you and go away to college, and it will be over."

I pressed myself into a corner of the big old couch, shrinking not so much from my parents as from my misery at having disappointed them, and my despair about the limits of my choices.

"I don't want an abortion." I was, after all, the girl who'd brought home wounded birds and stray kittens. "It's fine for some people, but not me. I can't do it." I felt tears streaming down my face.

My father, who had been perched at the edge of his black leather Barcalounger, jumped up. "You're not going to sacrifice your life at seventeen."

"Michael, calm down," my mother said. "I want to hear what Rachel has to say."

Dad confronted me: "What do you plan to do, marry that boy? give up college, a career? You're finally getting over him, and now this? Think about what you're saying, Rachel."

"I can't talk to you." I ran upstairs, slammed the door and threw myself on my bed.

"What about adoption?" I asked timidly and tentatively the next night.

"You'd still have to have the baby. What about college? You leave in three weeks. Don't you think it would be better to wait until you're ready to have a child? This one is a mistake. Don't let it ruin what should be the happiest time in your life." My mother twisted her wedding ring as she spoke.

"I was thinking I could go for the first semester and then take off the spring semester and have the baby. Maybe I could even stay with Aunt Gloria and take some classes. And then I'd let some good family adopt it. But at least it would have a chance."

My mother sighed deeply. "It wouldn't be my first choice for you," she said. "But I'm not going to force you to have an abortion, and I don't think your father will either. You have to make that decision for yourself."

We decided not to tell anyone about the pregnancy, not even our closest friends and family. The only one who'd been let in on the secret was my older sister, Annie. "If you don't want Larry to find out," Dad had warned, "then you can't tell anyone at all. People talk. It will get out."

I definitely didn't want Larry to know. "He wouldn't want me to give it up," I told my sister. "He'd want to marry me—right now. It doesn't feel right not to tell him, but he just can't find out."

"So you know for sure you don't want to be with him?"

"It's such a relief to be free from him, I don't want to say or do anything to let him back into my life."

I never moved into a dormitory in Cleveland, choosing instead to stay with Aunt Gloria in the upscale suburb of Pepper Pike. My aunt was the polar opposite of her sister, my mother. It was sometimes difficult to believe they were related. My mother was quiet, introspective, and intellectual. Our den at home was filled with her books, many of them nonfiction, with an emphasis on history. She rarely wore makeup, and when she did, it was just a touch of coral on her lips and a dash of mascara to lengthen her blonde eyelashes. She favored wool slacks in winter and cotton blends in summer, and usually had a cardigan thrown loosely over her shoulders. She stayed at home when Annie and I were young, and when I reached junior high school age, she took a job teaching European history at Barnard College.

Aunt Gloria, on the other hand, while very kind and welcoming, was very busy with her active social schedule, which on any given day might include golf, or bridge, or a workout with her personal trainer at the gym. She loved nothing more than beads and sparkles. She thrived on parties, whether she threw them herself or was a guest. She had a closet filled with silk cocktail dresses and cashmere slacks and sweaters. There was a vanity table in her bathroom that would have been the envy of a Hollywood star, with makeup brushes and a variety of blushes and lipsticks displayed on the mirror-topped surface. She had hairdresser and manicure appointments every week and loved changing her style, one week showing off a French twist, the next week toying with blonde ringlets tossed over her shoulders. There was a parade of elegant women who always seemed to be arriving or leaving. Gloria threw great cocktail parties and brunches. She had a great sense of humor, an easy laugh, and boundless energy. If I hadn't been so wrapped up in my own personal tragedy, I'm sure I would have loved being her houseguest. As it was, I spent a lot of time in the chintz-and-lace guest room with sounds of gaiety drifting up the curved staircase.

Aunt Gloria had been married more than once. I never knew husband number one, from whom she was divorced when I was very young. I had a vague memory of number two, whose name was Harry. He had a mustache that tickled, sparse hair, and a Porsche. Gloria was now married to Uncle Reggie, a cosmetic surgeon whom she had met while getting her generous breasts lifted. Uncle Reggie was happy to welcome me as a guest in his household. He used to take my chin between his thumb and forefinger and compliment me on my bone structure.

"You have a perfect oval face," he once told me, turning my head left and right as he appraised my appearance. "Beautiful eyes, and a very nice trim figure." He liked to tug a little at one of my auburn curls and watch it spring back into place. I was a few inches taller than he, and although my impulse was to push him away, I allowed the occasional inspection of my attributes, out of courtesy to Aunt Gloria. "You should hold up well until your forties," he told me once, "but if your mother is an example, you'll need me, or someone like me, to maintain that youthful beauty when you're older." Aunt Gloria was always nearby, smiling and encouraging. It was hard for me to imagine her growing up in the same household as my serious, astute mom. And I knew my mother had chosen the better man. My dad was an attorney for the city of New York. He was the handsomest man I knew—and the smartest too. The mayor relied on him, and had been to dinner at our home. We lived in a different universe from Aunt Gloria and Uncle Reggie. I spent my exile at Aunt Gloria's home, observing from the sidelines like a visitor to a foreign country. She was sweet and kind and supportive, but I missed my family and my friends, and I longed for my life to be normal again.

By Thanksgiving I was wearing big man-style shirts and bulky sweatshirts. I came home from Cleveland for the holiday, and my pregnancy was hardly discussed. It was easy to attribute my weight gain to the infamous "freshman fifteen."

"Rachel, Larry's on the phone," my sister said as we were clearing the holiday meal from the heavy oak table that had been my grandmother's. "What should I tell him?"

Heavyhearted, I went into the kitchen and took the phone.

"I wanted to wish you a happy Thanksgiving," Larry said. "I miss you."

"Happy Thanksgiving to you too. How have you been?"

"Miserable. I need to see you." I glanced down at my stomach, protruding beneath my mother's gingham apron.

"It's not a good idea, Larry."

"Why not? Please, Rachel, just for a little while. Have a cup of coffee with me. I need to see you."

"No, Larry. I don't want to see you."

"It's because you still love me. Give me another chance, Rachel. I've changed."

"Don't do this, Larry. I can't see you. I am so sorry." I gently placed the receiver on its hook, sat down at the kitchen table laden with leftovers and dirty dishes, and wept into my hands. My mother came in and reached down to embrace me.

"Annie told me he called. You didn't have to talk to him."

"Yes I did, Mom. But don't worry, I didn't tell him anything. I said I couldn't see him. I'm fine."

Less than two months later, I was sitting in a rocking chair and waiting for a nurse to bring the baby to me. My sister, Annie, was sitting in the visitor's chair nearby. I'd been given a choice, and although my parents advised against it, I'd decided to see the child before turning her over to the strangers who would raise her. My mother and father had opted not to meet this first grandchild, and Annie had volunteered to come to Cleveland and stay with me until the baby had been returned to the nursery.

The baby was brought in by a motherly nurse named Mabel Johnson who'd been sweet to me since my admission. "Here you are," she said, laying a bundle wrapped in pink and white in my lap. "I'll be back in a few minutes. It's best not to stretch it."

I looked down at the child in my arms and sighed deeply. "I need a little time alone with her, Annie. Please."

"Are you sure?"

"Yes. Please."

Annie left. "I'll be right out here if you need me."

I began to rock, pushing the chair with my toe.

"It's going to be all right, little one," I crooned. "You're going to have a wonderful mommy and daddy to love you and take care of you. You're going to have a great life." I bent and touched my cheek to the baby's exquisitely soft one, feeling one of my tears moisten the delicate skin. I dried the baby's face with my thumb.

"I'm going to call you Julie, even though your new mommy and daddy will give you another name. But you'll always be Julie to me because you're my little jewel." I shuddered from the force of my sob. "And maybe someday when you're all grown up, we'll meet each other again, and I can tell you how much I love you and how hard it is to do this." I raised the baby up against my chest and rocked her back and forth, back and forth. Through it all, little Julie slept, tiny blue veins tracing a pattern beneath translucent eyelids.

Mabel returned, too soon, and Annie followed her into the room where I sat, my baby folded to my breast, rocking.

"It's time, Rachel. I'll take her now." My arms tightened. I pressed the small bundle against my body.

"It's easier if you just let go. Believe me, hon. I've been through this before."

Annie came to stand behind me as I slowly stretched out my arms and let Mrs. Johnson gently lift the baby from them. Annie's hands pressed firmly on my shoulders, squeezing support and compassion into me. She would soon be married, and our closeness would be tested by separation. But right then, she was my strength and lifeline.

Mabel Johnson walked out of the room, little Julie resting on her shoulder. I looked up as the baby opened her electric-blue eyes, and it seemed as if she looked right into my face. Black ringlets bobbed as the door swung shut and the infant disappeared.

I slipped on a pair of scuffs, souvenir of a holiday with Neil spent at the Savoy Hotel in London before the twins were born. I couldn't bring myself to throw them out. The soles were torn, and the terry cloth was no longer white. Still I clung to them and the memories they represented. Padding into the kitchen, I opened the refrigerator, scanned the contents, and closed the door without choosing anything. I sat down, elbow on the table, chin in my hand. I hadn't thought of little Julie for a while. Her birthday would be coming in January, and I would send myself a bouquet of flowers, a sentimental ritual I'd begun almost sixteen years ago. "I hope," I whispered into the night, "she's as happy as Ben and Mitch are." Thinking of my twins made me smile. Slipping into their room, I discovered that Mitch had kicked his Batman quilt off as usual. I stood on the edge of Ben's bunk in order to reach Mitch, tossing his covers back over his sprawled body. I smoothed Ben's blanket for good measure.

I hope someone does that for Julie, I thought as I headed back to bed.

CHAPTER

3

On a late October morning, my first client was at ten o'clock. When I stepped onto my sixth-floor terrace, the first chill of autumn brushed my face, so I dressed in my favorite toast-colored flannel blazer and my most comfortable shoes. I welcomed the walk to work on a crisp fall day.

I breathed deeply and hummed softly on my way uptown. I thrilled to the pace and the energy of the city. I watched in awe as a bicycle messenger wove in and out of Sixth Avenue traffic, and I waved to a jackhammer operator, who shut off his noisy machine for a moment so that I could hear his whistle of appreciation. I reached my office building before I knew it.

"Hey, Shorty," I greeted the disabled Vietnam vet who'd operated the coffee concession near the elevators since long before I was a tenant.

"Hello, Doc. Walk to work today?"

"Sure did. Gorgeous morning. Doing any better with that leg?"

He rubbed the place where the prosthesis joined his thigh. "Still having some problems with it. It was fine for a long time, and now it's hurting again. Oh well." He shrugged, handing me my coffee, with half-and-half and sweetener, just the way I like it. "What can you do? I may be limping around, but I can still enjoy a beautiful day."

"Way to go, Shorty!" *The man's an inspiration.* I rode up to floor 10 in the elevator, taking my first careful sips of the piping hot brew.

In the office I hung my jacket, eased into a reception room chair, and greeted Jan, my receptionist and friend.

"Celia Hunter canceled," Jan informed me. "She was called back for a second audition. She's hoping to get into that off-Broadway thing she told us about."

"No other messages?"

"Nope. If you're thinking about the Brody kid, she hasn't canceled. Yet."

"Well, the day is young. I'm not placing any bets."

By 4:05 it appeared that Heather would be a no-show for her second session. At 4:15 she sauntered in, sprawled herself on the waiting room couch, and popped her gum. I maintained a neutral silence as I showed her into the office.

If the previous week the girl had resembled a witch, this time she seemed determined to be mistaken for a prostitute. Her black skirt was little more than a scrap of material barely concealing her crotch. She wore fishnet stockings and the same impossibly high heels she'd had on at her first visit. Instead of a shirt, she wore a bustier, black with crisscross laces, which squeezed her little chest into a semblance of cleavage. At some point during the past week she'd dyed the strange chopped hair a vivid carrot red.

"I wasn't sure you'd come," I said.

"I don't know why the hell I'm here." She kicked off the ridiculous shoes and stretched out on the couch, feet up on the furniture arm closest to my chair. Both stockings had holes, and two black-painted big toes peeked through at me.

"So why do you think?"

"Dunno." She accentuated the word with a shrug. The small, tightly laced bosom swelled slightly, then retracted. "Nothing better to do, I guess." I waited. Heather looked at the ceiling. Then she examined her fingernails, chewed absently at a cuticle, and returned her gaze to the molding over her head.

I felt a minute tick by, then two and three. The absence of sound became palpable. I kept my hands loosely folded in my lap. My legs, in their wool-blend forest-green slacks, remained crossed at the ankles. I listened to my breathing as I continued to wait.

"What'd you do to my mom?" Heather's voice was a monotone; her face, a mask of indifference. She addressed the question to the seam between ceiling and wall.

"What do you mean?" I was careful not to change my posture.

"She didn't say one word about my clothes or my hair all week long. That's a record, I think. What'd you do?"

"I didn't do anything. Just told her what she was doing wasn't working, so she might as well stop. I mean, it's not magic, Heather, just common sense."

"I told her that plenty of times."

"Well, maybe she needed to hear it from somebody else. So how do you like yourself as a redhead?"

"Oh, great! My mom finally lays off talking about how I look, and now you're going to take over." Heather swung her legs onto the floor and groped with one naked toe for her shoes.

"It sounds like you'd rather not discuss your taste in hairstyles. That's fine. I was just wondering if you dyed your hair because you like it or because you thought your mother wouldn't."

"Because I like it, of course." The little smirk that flashed across the girl's face told a different story.

"That's good. The person you have to please is yourself."

"Yeah, well, I please myself. Okay?"

"Your taste is quite different from your mother's."

"My mother's taste is whatever the president of the Philharmonic wants it to be. Or the director of the Museum of Modern Art. Or the chairman of the theater guild. She'd have no idea what she liked if she didn't get her cues from the crowd she hangs out with."

"How does that make you feel? When you think she's not being authentic?"

"Authentic?" The girl emitted a harsh, mocking laugh. "My mother's a paper doll. A mannequin. I can't stand her or her friends. And if I dress like she wants me to or act like she wants me to, then that makes me as phony as she is. Does that answer your question?"

"Sure does. So how's it going at the new school?"

"It sucks. I knew it before I walked in the door. But at least it's here in New York and I get to see the Frankster."

Easy does it, I cautioned myself as I thought about how to take advantage of this opening. I leaned forward a little.

"Tell me about him."

"He'd do anything for me," Heather said, her tone tight with teenage intensity. "He's really sweet when he's with me. He says I bring out the best in him."

"Does he have family?"

"Not really. He's got me. He says that's enough. And he's enough for me too." *Shades of Larry Tobin. The old Larry.* I uncrossed my ankles and recrossed them the opposite way.

"Your father told us he's afraid Frank uses drugs. Is that a problem for you?" I kept very still, knowing that this was the moment when she might bolt. Heather stood up and took a few steps toward the door.

"I really need a smoke," she said.

"Not in here. Sorry." The girl looked at the door, then at her watch, a clunky metal affair that was too big for her narrow wrist.

"The point is," she said, standing closer to the door than to the sofa, "I don't use drugs. I wish he didn't, but he does, and it's not my job to control him." It was the most revealing speech she'd made.

"I'm glad to hear it. What does the Frankster think about your hair?"

"He's cool with it. Listen, I can't stay. I just remembered something I really have to do." Before I could react, she was out the door. There were still fifteen minutes left in the session.

I caught up with her as she tossed a prewritten check onto Jan's desk. "Next week, same time?"

"Yeah. Okay. Bye." Heather burrowed in her large leather sack for a pack of cigarettes. Hand on the doorknob, she said, "I sure know how to pick 'em."

"Pick what?"

"Mothers. Both of them." She twisted the doorknob, flung open the door, and was gone.

Notes, October 26

Vulnerable. Angry. Values clash with mother. Doorknob statement exposes hurt and anger at biological mother.

My hands were really bothering me. The weakness and tingling was almost painful. *Damn! Why does this kid have to be adopted? I'm going to have to get a grip!* I closed the Brody file and locked it, along with those of my other active cases, in the bottom drawer of my desk. I pulled my purse from the same drawer and stood up just as the phone rang. Hearing my sister's voice always brought an involuntary smile. I happily greeted Annie, who was calling from across three time zones.

"I've got a few minutes before the kids get home," Annie said, "so I figured I'd give you a ring. Finished working?"

"Yep. Just finished up some paperwork." I shut down the computer and watched the screen darken before closing the lid. Sliding my rolling desk chair back, I stretched, clenching and unclenching my prickling fingers. "I saw a teenager who's furious at her mother. She cut out of the session before the end. I don't know if she'll be back."

"That takes me back. Do you remember when Mom disapproved of your girlfriend? What was her name?"

"Audrey. I remember I came into your room and sat on your bed, and I was so mad, I think I tore your pillowcase." I leaned against the end of my desk and then hopped up on it, crossing my ankles and swinging my legs so that my heels knocked against the wooden base. "'Audrey will never be an asset to you.'" I did a pretty good imitation of our mother's tone, half lecture, half concern.

"I just didn't get why it was always about what someone could do for me and never about what I could do for someone else."

"She only wanted the best for us, Rache."

"Yes, but you could take it. I couldn't. It always wound up in an argument."

"Well, thank God you got over it."

"I used to think that all Mom cared about was what other people thought. Do you remember how she and her bridge group would sit around and pass judgment on everyone and everything?"

"I remember how you hated it. You used to say she had a superiority complex."

"Kind of like this kid I'm seeing now. She's so scornful of her mother. Funny thing is I really like this girl."

"Surprise, surprise," Annie said. "Reminds me of you at that age."

"The family is a referral from Aunt Gloria, believe it or not. She probably saw the similarities and wanted to give me a taste of my own medicine. It would be a very Gloria thing to do."

We both chuckled at the image of irrepressible Aunt Gloria stage-managing the encounter.

"Do I hear Brendan and Kim in the background?" My twelve- and fourteen-year-old nephew and niece were home from school. I glanced at my watch. It would be 3:30 on the West Coast.

"I'll have to go in a minute."

"Annie? Before you go, can I ask you something?"

"Shoot."

"Do you think Julie's happy?"

"Julie who?"

"My baby Julie. You know. Do you think I made the right decision back then? Do you think she's happy?"

"Oh, sweetie, what brought that on?"

"This kid I'm seeing—she's adopted. Her father said it was a 'bad fit.' What if Julie got a family that was a bad fit?"

"I think that almost never happens, honey. The agencies know what they're doing. Rachel, maybe you shouldn't be seeing this family. Can you handle it?"

"I hope so, Annie. Like I said, I really like the girl." *Can I handle it? Can I really?* My left thumb traced a circle pattern around the fingers of my right hand. I had slid off the edge of my desk and was now walking around the room with the phone tucked under my chin. "You know, I still see her face, that tiny little face with the blue eyes looking at me as the nurse carried her out of the room."

"Oh, sweetie."

"It's not that this new client is adopted. I've worked with adopted kids before. It's that she's adopted and so unhappy. That kind of gets to me."

"It's stirring up old stuff for you. That can't be a good thing."

"I'll try not to get too involved. She's just another rebellious teenager after all. Love you, Annie. Thanks for calling."

I tried to imagine what my former supervisor, Estelle Garner, would advise if I told her about Heather Brody.

"Have you achieved closure about your own baby?" Estelle would certainly ask.

"I think so," I'd answer.

"Then you should be okay. But you'll need to monitor yourself closely."

I sat down again, rested my elbows on the desk, and supported my chin in my two hands. A sigh escaped. The weakness and tingling in my hands was an early warning signal. Involuntarily I rubbed them again.

On the subway I brooded. Had Heather really been placed in a family that was a bad match, one that couldn't meet her needs? Did that happen often? *Let it go, Rachel. Your own life is quite enough for you. Enough about Heather.* Rule number one for mental health professionals: Leave the clients in the office. My two healthy, happy boys waited for me at home and needed all my attention. Still, I tried to rub feeling back into my tingling fingertips as I thought about the vulnerable adopted child who felt unwanted and unloved.

CHAPTER

4

Heather was a tough nut to crack. She didn't show up for the next session. I called her mother to ask for her cell phone number.

"Can I give her a message?" Stephanie asked.

"No, I need to speak with her. It would help if I had her mobile phone number."

"Is she coming to her sessions?"

"I can't discuss it with you, Mrs. Brody. I need to speak with Heather."

"She didn't show up." Resignation colored Stephanie's voice gray.

"Mrs. Brody, may I please have Heather's cell phone number?" Finally she gave it to me. When I hung up, I spent a few minutes chastising myself for not getting Heather's number directly from her and having to call her mother.

"Oh yeah, right," Heather said when I reached her. "I forgot. Sorry."

"Can we reschedule?"

"I s'pose." The following week she was ten minutes late. She looked different. Her hair, still flaming red, had begun to grow back. She had encircled her eyes with black liner and was wearing bright red lipstick, but the pancake makeup and the solid black attire were gone. She wore a floor-length skirt made of layers of flounced white organza. A pink bodysuit with long sleeves clung to her slight torso. I was pretty sure she was wearing a bra.

"I can't handle a whole session without a cigarette," she said as she entered my office and flopped on the couch.

"Maybe we can make a deal."

The wings of her eyebrows came together. "What kind of deal?"

"If you show up on time, we can take a five-minute break halfway through. Would that help?"

"I s'pose. But if I have to go all the way down to the street to smoke, I'll need more than five minutes."

"Okay. Seven minutes."

"What about today?"

"You were late today."

"Yeah, but we didn't have the deal yet."

"Okay. A short break today, but you'll stay until five o'clock." And so Heather and I negotiated our first contract. While repeatedly and pointedly glancing at her oversized watch, she reported that she'd been experimenting with styles of dress and makeup. "You said something last time about pleasing myself," she told me, "and I decided that I didn't feel like being a biker chick every day."

"Great skirt," I ventured. "Where'd you find it?"

"The Goodwill has a neat thrift shop over on Tenth. People give away stuff they've hardly even worn! I have lots of things from there. Can I take my break a little early? I didn't have time for a last drag because I was late."

"Five more minutes. How are things at home?"

"Still can't get a rise out of my mother. It's like you cast a spell on her or something."

"Do you miss her comments?"

"Like, *duh*. Hardly. But it is weird, you know. If she's not criticizing something, she has nothing to say to me at all."

"Can you think of anything you'd like to say to her?"

"Oh, sure. Like, 'Hey, Mom, did Mrs. Van Felt wear her new diamond broach to the museum's Belle Epoque Ball? How many carats is it anyway, Mom? Six? Seven?' I mean, can you see me having that conversation?"

I allowed myself to smile. "Well, no, not *that* conversation. But, you know, all these things your mother's involved in—it's my guess that some of them must be about charity. If you'd ever like to open a conversation, you might ask her about the causes she supports." I assessed her reaction. No eye-rolling, no overt dismissal. She wasn't falling over with enthusiasm, but I thought she might be listening.

"It's only one idea, of course. I'm sure you could think of other topics if you wanted to."

"I'm cool with us not talking. I'm talking to you, right? That's about all I can deal with. Can I go downstairs now?"

"Go."

She did come back, but the session was effectively over. The interruption I'd agreed to was going to be an impediment, but I couldn't very well go back on the bargain I'd just made. I'd just have to find a way to work around it. I wondered why I'd made an arrangement I wouldn't have offered to any other client. I knew I'd have to be careful and monitor myself more closely. Heather had really gotten under my skin.

For the next several sessions any gains we made could be measured in millimeters. Heather showed up regularly and on time, careful not to lose the privilege of her cigarette break. I stayed alert for any tiny crack into which I could wedge a psychological shoe. Her choice of outfit was always a surprise.

"Keeping up the wardrobe experiment, I see," I said when she showed up in a purple crocheted vest that fell from her shoulders to her ankles. She wore a floppy black velvet hat with a garish purple flower. She'd turned the brim of the hat so that the flower was dead center on her forehead.

"Yeah."

"What kind of reactions are you getting?"

"From who?"

"Anyone."

"I don't give a shit. Excuse the expression. I please myself. You said—remember?—that I should please myself."

"Sounds like you're having some fun trying on different looks."

"I s'pose." That was all she'd give me before her cigarette break.

"When you get back, we'll have twenty minutes left," I said as she headed for the door, her ubiquitous leather pouch slung over a fragile shoulder. "Think about how you'd like to use that time while you're having your break."

So it went, like pulling teeth. When she came back, she talked about her boyfriend, how misunderstood he was, how her parents refused to understand. I listened and said little. There was less overt hostility, which I counted as progress.

Stephanie and Bill Brody came in after the third session with Heather.

"I definitely see a change," Bill reported. "Heather seems calmer, not so ready to pick a fight. And she's looking better. Not quite so—how should I put it?—outrageous."

"She actually asked me what we do with the money we raise from the museum ball," Stephanie informed me. Inwardly I cheered. *Right on, Heather!* "I told her we have a scholarship program for art students."

"How did she react?"

"Oh, she said 'Neat' or something like that. It was the longest conversation we've had in months."

"Whatever you're doing, Dr. Marston, please keep doing it," Bill said.

"A lot of it is what you're doing. By not being critical, you're opening up space for a new relationship to develop."

"I'm reading that book you recommended," Stephanie said. "You know—Dr. Tobin. He says we should take notice of her talents and be quietly encouraging. Those are his words, 'quietly encouraging.'"

"And what have you noticed?"

"We think she's creative," Bill said. "First of all, she's trying out all these new looks."

"Some of them are truly hideous," Stephanie put in.

"True, but sometimes she doesn't look bad. Different, but not bad. I have to say it takes guts for her to go to school wearing all those outfits. And I think she has artistic talent. She left a doodle pad lying around, and her sketches look kind of professional. So we're thinking of looking for a school in Washington that has a strong art program."

Stephanie brought up the subject of Frank and his negative influence on Heather.

"I think that one's going to take care of itself," Bill predicted. "We'll move to Washington, and it'll be out of sight, out of mind."

Notes, Mid-November

Some progress observed in both H. and parents. All three receptive to new approaches. H. initiated brief conversation with mother. Parents noticing creative talent. BF still an issue.

Heather missed a session because of strep throat; we had no meeting Thanksgiving week; and time melted, as it always seemed to do before the holidays.

"I thought maybe I should try out a blank slate," Heather told me the week before Christmas. "You know, tabula rasa."

Indeed it was difficult to recognize the girl settling into my office. She wore no makeup, not even lipstick and blush. She'd had her hair cut very short in an obvious effort to even up the lopsided creation she'd been sporting. It was styled severely at a length that just brushed the top of her ears. The heavy hank that had fallen over her eye was gone, replaced by a wispy fringe of bangs. And the color had changed again. It was dark again, but this time it was brunette with a few reddish highlights. I guessed it might be close to her natural color.

I could see her eyes, undisguised by hair, mascara, or false lashes. They were large, almond shaped, and strikingly blue. With no makeup, the spray of freckles across the bridge of her nose was obvious. The new haircut revealed the heart-shaped outline of her face. She looked young and very vulnerable.

"So how does it feel?" I asked.

"Naked. And dumb. I don't know why I did it."

"So this isn't comfortable for you. Not the 'real you'?"

"No way. I even went to my mother's stupid hairdresser and asked him to dye my hair back to its natural color. He made me have a hot oil treatment. Said my hair was all dried out from too much dye."

"When did you do all this, Heather?"

"Yesterday after school. I mean, I really feel dumb. This haircut—it's so butch."

"The nice thing about hair is that it grows."

"Yeah, but I'll probably go out and get a wig until then. The Frankster couldn't stop laughing when I saw him last night. Wouldn't go out with me. We just hung around his place."

"Sounds like the Frankster's another one who cares what people think."

"He says he doesn't give a damn, but yeah, I guess. Why else wouldn't he take me out?"

"How did it make you feel?"

"Oh, you know. Pissed off. For about a minute. But it was okay, staying in with him. Anyway, I got into this thing about trying out different looks, and I've been doing it for a while now."

"So how's it going?"

"Kind of fun. I show up at school, and the teachers and the kids never know who I'm gonna be that day. One day I wore a teeny little skirt and high silk stockings that went up to the middle of my thighs. And a little sweater with a bare middle."

"How was that?"

"Sexy. And chilly. I froze." I laughed and was rewarded by a smile, which lit up the child's face. Her eyes twinkled, and I discovered a pair of dimples in her cheeks. Then, as if remembering where she was, she reorganized her face into its usual pout.

"You're very pretty when you smile."

"Yeah, well, I haven't got much to smile about. You know, during all this costume party stuff, my mother didn't say one word about my clothes, even the day I dressed in the skirt and sweater she bought me. That day she opened her mouth and then closed it again. But then she wished me a good day at school. I guess she liked it."

"Did you like it?"

"No!" The tone was vehement. "I felt like one of those prissy debutantes from my last school. But I figured if I was doing an experiment, I should do it right."

"Tell me something, Heather. Did you notice that people treat you differently when you wear different kinds of clothes?"

She snorted. "Of course they do. It just proves how superficial people are. They think you are what you wear."

"Or maybe they feel more comfortable with people who seem to be more like them. Have you noticed that about yourself, or the Frankster, that you trust people who look and dress like you?"

"I guess." Heather's tone was guarded.

"So is there some group of kids at school whom you'd like to know better?"

"I'm a loner. I'm just putting in my time there. I don't need any of them."

"You don't want to have friends?"

"Nah. I travel solo. Except for the Frankster."

"And the friends the two of you have together?"

"They're a bunch of losers. We hang out with them, but they're not my friends."

"If you were to have a friend, what would she—or he—be like?"

"If. If. How do I know? Creative, I guess. Arty. Nonjudgmental. And loyal. Especially loyal. Once I have a friend, they're, you know, a friend for life. None of this 'here today, gone tomorrow.' My mother's friends, they flit, you know? They compete with each other. They'd cut each other's throats if it suited their purpose."

"I can see that you're creative. All these different outfits—you have a real flair. What else do you do that's creative?"

"I sometimes paint. But I usually just paint over it—blacken it out, you know? My stuff isn't any good. You wouldn't like it. Too morbid."

I crossed and recrossed my legs. "Why do you think your art is morbid?" Heather was silent for a moment. Her eyes shifted, studying a spot on the ceiling.

"I don't know. It's what comes out. I don't think much about what I paint. I just make brushstrokes. Dark, swirly brushstrokes."

"Still, I'd like to see it someday. If you feel like it. I bet you could discover a couple of people you could like and who would like you. Artists, poets, people with real values."

"I'm glad you think so. Can I go now? We never took my cigarette break, and I can't wait to get home and put some makeup on. See ya."

"Happy holidays, Heather."

"Oh yeah. Happy holidays."

Notes, late December

H. taking risks exposing more of her inner self. Less angry, more communicative. Some well-guarded self-esteem emerging, especially around her assessment of her own loyalty and recognition of her artistic ability. Possibility exists for shift from destructive to productive modality. Parents "playing to her strengths" (to quote L.T.).

CHAPTER
5

I took the boys to Playa del Mar for our usual winter vacation. All of us looked forward to the tropical sun, the water sports, and a break from our New York routine. I also looked forward to spending time with Eduard Montvale, a divorced dad from Montreal who came to the resort over the holidays with his nine-year-old daughter Clarisse. Mitch and Ben liked Clarisse, and I liked her father. I spotted them at dinner the first night. He seemed as pleased to see me as I was to see him. We agreed to meet for a nightcap after the kids went to bed.

Eduard helped me to remember that I was a woman. "You are so beautiful," he told me. "I love the green-gold of your eyes and that rich auburn of your hair." He pulled gently on one of my corkscrew curls, smiling as it sprang back and caressed my cheek. He ran an index finger lightly down the bridge of my nose. "Clearly your own," he teased. He was a plastic surgeon, so he appreciated the fact that my straight, narrow nose hadn't been shaped in an operating room.

I wondered if his compliments seemed more genuine because of his sexy French accent. Eduard had recently divorced his third wife (Clarisse was the child of wife number two). I knew that he and I would not share a future, but I welcomed a vacation dalliance.

The five of us might have been mistaken for a family. The three children cavorted on the beach like siblings, while Eduard and I had leisurely breakfasts on his patio, walked hand in hand on the beach, and relaxed with books and magazines on lounges by the enormous pool. I found the no-strings-attached, "same time next year" nature of our friendship to be liberating.

I lay on a cushioned lounge at the beach, watching the three children adding packed sand to the top of their tower. Without conscious intent, I found myself thinking about Heather Brody, who was skiing at Saint Moritz with her parents. She had come close to admitting that she was looking forward to the trip.

"It'll be okay," she told me. "I don't see them all day long. I ski the expert slopes. There's a couple of guys who usually show up, and I ski with them. I have dinner with my parents and that's about it." I was optimistic about Heather. She'd made good progress in the nearly three months I'd been seeing her. I smiled at the memory of her makeup-less face at our last session. *The kid has guts.* Estelle Garner's voice interrupted my thoughts. "That girl is taking up too much space in your head," she would caution. *Here I am, on vacation, thinking about a client. Enough!* I rolled onto my belly and held out the suntan lotion to Eduard, who applied it to the backs of my thighs. Warmth surged through me. My thoughts of a tropical evening with my handsome Canadian served to expunge Heather from my mind.

We returned to New York hours ahead of a winter storm that alternately awed me with its pristine beauty and made me long for the silhouette of a palm tree against a cloudless sky, the pungent aroma of suntan oil, and the broad hand of the sexy man who'd smoothed it on my back for the past ten days.

I stood at my window watching impossibly large flakes curtaining the city street, remembering my time with Eduard and willing myself back to the real world. This would have been my first day back to work and the boys' return to the routine of school, homework, and piano and tennis practice. The twins rejoiced at the unexpected extension of the holiday. I would have preferred to plunge into my schedule, catch up with my clients, and trade vacation stories with Jan. Jan would be all ears when it came to details about Eduard Montvale. She was the only person other than my sister to whom I would confess both the intoxicating pleasure of being romanced by a suave gentleman and the certainty that Eduard was an escape from reality who would never be a part of my life during the other fifty weeks of the year.

"Good for my ego. And for my libido," I'd tell her, and we would chuckle together. Jan would describe her family's foray into the world within a world that was Disney World. And then it would be back to business as the New Year began its relentless ticking away of minutes, hours, and pages on my pristine appointment calendar.

It had been Jan who'd made the calls, checking to see if any hardy clients intended to venture out into the year's first blizzard. It seemed everyone in New York was tucked away, drinking cocoa, with no intention of braving the elements. "Clean sweep," Jan reported by 10:00 a.m. "I've rescheduled everyone for later this week, except Heather Brody. She came home from Switzerland with a relapse of her strep throat. Her next appointment's on the eleventh."

It was a day for a marathon Monopoly game, played with much entrepreneurial glee and ultimately won by Mitch. I had an unexpected opportunity to finish the P. D. James mystery I'd begun on the last days of my vacation. In the end, I decided that the extra transitional day was beneficial. By the time the plows had thrown off the streets' white blanket and the sounds of city traffic once again provided a steady background music, the glow of Playa del Mar had faded to pleasant memory and my internal metronome had picked up its beat to match the pace of the New York winter.

The next morning, the boys were bundled up, despite their protests, in layers of winter wear. I pulled on the red wool beret knitted for me by Neil's mother, wrapped myself in my lamb's wool coat, and slid my hands into leather gloves as I prepared to face the cold and head off to work.

The week or two immediately after the holidays were busy ones for me. When New Year's Day had passed and the longest and coldest stretch of winter lay ahead, feelings that had been denied or ignored pushed their way to the surface. That's when my phone began ringing.

I could well understand the power the holidays had to reincarnate old pain, evoking sadness, longing, and sometimes anger. I felt restless myself. I stared out the window at the city below as if perhaps something out there awaited me, if I only knew what—or where.

My natural optimism inevitably came to the rescue, however, and I plunged into the New Year, meeting new clients, reconnecting with some old ones who needed an emotional booster shot, and picking up my regular caseload where I'd left off before Christmas. Focusing on my clients' concerns left little room to dwell on my own. The image of Eduard Montvale receded to a warm memory that left a smile on my lips but only a trace of the heat that had coursed through my body when I was with him.

On the ninth of January, I stopped into Bella's Bouquets, the florist shop a block from home. I didn't have to contemplate my choice. It had been sixteen years. "Pink roses," I told Bella. "A dozen. Please deliver them tomorrow." Julie would be Sweet Sixteen. *Happy birthday, sweetheart.*

The next day I filled my prettiest vase with water and clipped the thorny stems. I stayed home from work, as I did every January 10, to celebrate Julie's birthday and to remember the perfect little round face and the dark blue eyes that stared at me as she was carried out of my life. I unlocked the privacy drawer at the bottom of my bureau and took out the pink cloth journal that I'd hidden under my silk scarves. I kept a pen inside the cover. I closed my bedroom door and sat on the edge of the bed. I flipped through the pages. Each entry was dated, and each one began with "Dear Julie." I'd written to her for the first time a week after leaving the hospital. "I hope one day you'll understand," I wrote, "that I wanted to bring you home with me, take care of you, and raise you, but it wouldn't have been fair to you. You're going to have parents who can give you everything I can't. You're going to have a wonderful life. I hope one day you'll learn that I love you very much."

I wrote to Julie every year on her birthday. I wrote to tell her that I'd met Neil, that we got married, and that she had twin brothers I hoped she'd meet one day. I wrote when Neil died. I told her that Mitch played piano and Ben loved tennis.

Now, I wrote:

Dear Julie, today is your sixteenth birthday. I'm imagining a party that your mom and dad are giving you with all your friends gathered around. I see you wearing a corsage of pink roses. I see your dad taking pictures and your mom straightening your sash and looking at you with a great big smile. I wish I could be there too. Happy birthday, Julie.

As the second week of work approached, I found myself thinking about Heather Brody. How had she managed the holidays in France, I wondered. On the eleventh, when Jan appeared at my office door at 4:00 p.m., her expression was warning enough. "Batten down the hatches," she said. "Stormy weather ahead."

Indeed, the girl's face was a black cloud as she paced the perimeter of the reception room. She spun on a heel at my approach. It was clear that on this day Heather's demons were in control. It was white makeup and deep black eyeliner again, black leather and fishnet stockings, death's-head earrings and black talon fingernails. This was the Heather of our first meeting, not the girl who'd made so much progress in the last few months.

She preceded me into the office, her movements half swagger, half vamp. If it didn't so clearly indicate how troubled she was, I might have smiled at the child's efforts to appear nonchalant. But I dared not allow my lips to twitch. Instead, I settled into my chair and waited. Heather blew a large gum bubble then slowly sucked it back into her mouth, cracking it bit by bit. Finally she made the decision to sprawl on the couch.

"You seem upset," I ventured when the girl remained silent, glaring a challenge out from the deep holes of her eyes.

"Very observant. You get a gold star." Another bubble, then another series of pops as she withdrew it.

"Talk to me." I leaned forward slightly, resting my hands on my knees. "You can tell me."

"What's the point? There's not a damned thing you can do. I go to France like a good little girl and don't mess up their precious vacation, and I try to figure out what they want and give it to them, but in the end it doesn't mean a thing."

"Something happened. What?"

"Oh, just the same old. Actually, it's what didn't happen. Yesterday should have been special, you know? I wasn't looking for a present or anything. I mean, they give me enough stuff, y'know? But I thought maybe we could do something together, the three of us. I guess being with me for ten days at Saint Moritz used up their parenting quota or something. Because it turned out they were busy last night. A big theater benefit. So they didn't plan anything for us."

"Yesterday meant a lot to you. Why was it so important, Heather?"

The girl was off the couch, pacing again. She balled up her hands. I had an image of the long, sharp black nails digging into her palms. "No big deal, right? Just my birthday. I mean, that can't compare to a theater benefit, can it? Not that they forgot. They gave me my present." She pulled at the ubiquitous black pouch and dragged a battered wallet out of it. She reached inside and pulled out a piece of paper, which I realized was a check. Heather waved it at me.

"Here. You want it? I sure don't. Take it." She stuffed it into my hand, throwing herself back down on the couch in the same movement. My mind was spinning. I had a sudden image of the vase of pink roses that stood on the piano at home, their petals just beginning to open.

The check, crumpled in my hand, was made out to her, for a thousand dollars.

"Neat gift, right? 'Here's some money, darling. Have a nice time. Happy birthday.' You might as well keep it, Rachel. If you don't, I'll give it to the Frankster, and he'll just put it up his nose."

"Your birthday? Yesterday was your birthday?" I heard the words, which sounded inane in my ears. Yet I hung on the girl's response.

How amazing. Heather has the same birthday as Julie. And she's the same age. How could I have missed that? I glanced at the file, which was open on my desk. There it was, right next to her name and Social Security number: DOB 1/10. The Brodys had filled out the paperwork before coming into my office that first day. I'd gotten caught up in their family drama and never even looked at the forms.

"Yep. Sweet Sixteen, and been kissed a few hundred times, I guess. No big deal—not to my mother and father at least. They had important stuff to do, y'know?"

I fought to regain control of my racing thoughts. *Coincidence,* I told myself, the silent word in my head severe and forceful. *Pure coincidence. There must have been dozens of little girls born that day who were given up for adoption. Dozens at least. Probably more.* The tingle in my hands felt like a thousand hot pinpoints. I forced myself to look down at the check I held.

"This is a lot of money." *Stupid, idiotic statement of the obvious.*

"No kidding! Give me a pen and I'll endorse it over to you.

You can buy your kids a helluva belated Christmas present at FAO Schwartz. Really, I mean it. Where's a pen?"

"No. No, Heather. I can't take this."

"I'll give it to the Frankster. I swear."

"I'm not sure that would be my choice, but it's yours to do with as you wish. I can't take it from you though. Thanks for the offer, but I can't." I looked up in time to see the tough little face crumble as tear tracks began to cut through the pancake makeup on her cheeks.

"Why can't they just love me, Rachel? Frankster loves me. He wanted to give me a special gift last night. He wanted to give me my first cocaine high."

"Did you accept his offer?"

"Believe me, I was tempted. I was so fed up with Madame Stephanie and her wimpy husband, I thought to myself, *What the hell?* But no, I didn't. I wanted something, but that wasn't it."

I realized I'd been holding my breath only when I felt myself let it out.

"Good girl," I said, breathing out. "You're your own person, kiddo. I'm proud of you."

"At least someone is." I could see that Heather was calming down. The tight muscles were relaxing. The foot in its impossibly high heel stopped its incessant tapping.

I fought and lost a brief internal struggle. "So you've had a birthday. Sixteen. You're growing up." I heard myself babbling, so I cut it off short. "Where were you born, Heather? Here in New York?"

The girl raised her eyes to look at me, confusion on her face.

"No, not here," she said slowly, stuffing her gum into her cheek with her tongue. "Ohio. Why?"

"Where in Ohio?"

"Excuse me, Rachel, but you're acting weird. Why do you want to know?"

"Oh, you know. Your birthday. Just curious. Another bit of information that makes you who you are. Where in Ohio?"

"Somewhere around Cleveland. Beechwood, that's it. My dad worked there before I was born. But we moved to New York when I was a baby. I don't remember Cleveland at all. Are you okay, Rachel? You look funny."

I felt a chill and shivered, a violent convulsion that caused me to wrap my arms around my chest. Just as quickly, heat coursed through my body. My hands tingled. My head throbbed. I pressed the spot between my eyebrows with my two middle fingers.

I was staring at the child's small face, clown makeup streaked with tear tracks, eyes hollow inside their heavy black outline. *My God, my God* bounced from wall to wall of my skull. It took a huge effort to pull myself back to the session, to the unhappy girl in front of me, who was now showing more concern for me than for herself.

"Rachel?" Heather's expression registered alarm. "Rachel, are you sure you're okay?"

"No, no, I'm fine. I felt a little dizzy for a minute, but it passed. I'm really proud of you, Heather. You were angry and upset, but you didn't take the easy way out. You have a lot of character."

"I'm no angel. I've smoked plenty of pot. I just think it stinks that I'm finally trying to be the kid they want, but they still don't want to spend time with me. It's like I can't win, y'know?"

"I know it feels that way. It might help if you made a real effort not to see it as personal. In other words, it's not that they don't want to be with you but that they get caught up in all this stuff they've made commitments to do, and then they're in a bind."

"Nice try, Rachel. But this was different. My sixteenth birthday. They shouldn't have made commitments on my birthday. Anyway, I'm feeling better. I probably won't give the money to the Frankster. Maybe I'll just tear it up. Or save it. I don't know."

She stood up, smoothing the scant leather skirt, running her fingers through the hair that was beginning to grow again. I stood with her.

"I never asked you how the ski trip went. Did you like Saint Moritz?"

"My cousin Chester came with us. He's okay. A little young, but okay. I spent most of my time with him. It was fine. I like to ski, and I got new skis for Christmas. I won a race." For a brief moment, her face lit up. Beneath the makeup, she seemed like any brand-new sixteen-year-old talking about her winter vacation.

Impulsively I reached out and put my arms around the girl, feeling as I did so the points of her shoulder blades, the fragility of her slim waist. I squeezed, then stepped back and held Heather's shoulders for an extra moment.

"Happy birthday, sweetheart." As I reached to open the door, I saw the dark eyes swimming with unshed tears. And then Heather was gone.

"Oh my God," I said aloud as I closed the door behind her. I dropped onto the couch, which was still warm from Heather's body. "Oh my God."

CHAPTER

6

I don't know how long I sat alone in my office. Jan poked her head in, took one look at me, and asked if I was all right.

"I'm fine. Go on home. I need to finish a few things." She left after wishing me a good night. I sat at my desk, resting my aching, too heavy head in my hands. My thoughts didn't progress much further than *Oh my God.* Eventually I forced myself to stand up, pull my coat from the closet, and lock up on the way out.

I walked, head down, deep in thought, through the twilight. Few people were out on this cold January early evening. I knew I couldn't walk all the way home. Unable to face the clamor and congestion of the subway, I hailed a cab. I'd have to go home and behave in front of the boys as though my life had not been rocked. But meanwhile my thoughts remained locked in the past, a past whose images were imprinted as clearly in my mind as though it had been yesterday, not sixteen impossibly long years ago. The chill I felt had little to do with the icy temperature. It was a cold that came from deep within me. I huddled in my down coat, knowing that neither fluffy down, nor a warm fire, nor a blazing sun would have the capacity to warm me on this night.

Oh, I would find out if more than one baby girl born in Beechwood, Ohio, on January 10 had been adopted. *There have to be others,* a stern, strictly rational voice in my head insisted. But I knew with my heart, absolutely and incontrovertibly, that Heather Brody was Julie, the child whose birthday I commemorated every year with pink roses.

As the cab wove through the end of rush hour and the start of theater traffic, my thoughts tumbled over each other. I found myself jumping randomly from one realization to the next. In one moment I was elated at the thought that in the whole wide world, sixteen years and five hundred miles from where I'd left her, I had found my child again. My next thought, crowding in upon the first, was that this child, to whom I'd promised a better life than I could provide, was miserable with her affluent family. I swallowed hard at the lump that rose in my throat at that particular irony.

I could not avoid a reality that pressed against my confusion. By the time the taxi rolled up to the doorway of my building, I had acknowledged that I would have to give up this case. I could no longer treat the child or advise the parents. I was suddenly, astonishingly, an interested party. I tried to imagine what would happen when I told the Brodys that I could no longer work with Heather. The truth, of course; I'd have to tell them the truth. They'd thank me for my honesty, and that would be it. It would be over. Surely they wouldn't tell Heather that the therapist she'd come to trust was her birth mother. No, they'd take her out of treatment, and I wouldn't see any of them again.

In the morning, I told myself, groping for a bill to pay the cabbie, finally tearing my mitten off with my teeth and pulling out twenty dollars, I'd call and ask for a meeting with the Brodys. The sooner, the better. This was not a professionally gray ethical area. I couldn't delude myself into pretending there was another solution. I'd give up the case and encourage the Brodys to continue Heather's treatment with a therapist of their choosing. I was sure they wouldn't be asking me for a recommendation. Once they knew who I was, they'd want to distance themselves from me as quickly as possible. I wondered if they'd even let me have a session to say goodbye to Heather. I doubted it.

I was half through my third glass of cabernet when I remembered Aunt Gloria. *She did this on purpose!* I stood up suddenly, sloshing a bit of the red wine on my sleeve. *How could she do this to me?* I began to pace. I headed toward my small desk, my eyes on the telephone. I would call her and demand an explanation. What did she imagine she was doing? I reached for the phone but didn't pick it up, turning on my heel and circling back to the couch, and then to the desk again. What was I going to say to her? I wanted to scream. Again I turned my back on the waiting phone. Back at the couch, I used a cocktail napkin to pat dry the coffee table where some wine had spilled. I sat down and picked up my glass again, staring into its depths briefly before taking a deep sip. My racing mind was beginning to slow. This was, after all, Aunt Gloria. She had never been a deep thinker. She read paperback mysteries and watched nighttime soap operas. Sometimes it seemed as if she were trying to live in a soap opera of her own creation. She probably thought she was orchestrating a wonderful surprise. She had socialized with Stephanie Brody. She would have known when the Brodys adopted their daughter. Somehow Aunt Gloria figured out that Heather Brody was the baby I had given up. She'd stayed in touch with Stephanie after the Brodys moved to New York. How perfect, my aunt must have thought, that I could meet my child, and help her, even though I didn't know who she was. How wonderful the reunion would be when Heather was old enough and all could be told. This was my mother's flighty younger sister who delighted in arranging blind dates with the children of her friends, who loved giving creative and unusual gifts, and who rejoiced at what she thought of as her cleverness. But I couldn't call her, couldn't tell her that her secret had been exposed. She would tell someone. She wouldn't be able to stay quiet about it. She might even tell Stephanie Brody. I wasn't ready yet. I needed to think. I needed to prepare myself. And if there was any telling to be done, I was the one who had to tell it.

It was a night in which sleep, when it came, was punctuated with dreams in which I tried desperately to hold on to something precious. It was never clear just what I held, wrapped in a pink blanket in one dream, tucked in a large black leather bag in another. The wind whipped it out of my grasp, or I misplaced it and ran, searching frantically. In the dream that finally awakened me, my father appeared, saying, "Give it back, darling. Give it back."

By 5:30 I gave up any pretense of sleeping. I reached into my bottom drawer and drew out the little pink journal I'd kept faithfully for the child I knew I would probably never see again.

I've found you. They named you Heather.

That was all I could bring myself to write. I locked the book away. By 7:00 I was showered and dressed. By 8:00, when I waved Ben and

Mitch out the door, lunchboxes and book bags in hand, I knew I would not call the Brodys that day.

I was about to enter a world of pretense and half-truths, a world in which I was a stranger. As I pulled on my coat and gloves, I glanced at my drawn face in the round hall mirror and said aloud for the first time, "I can't do it." The words had the ring of a decision made. The agonizing pros and cons were over. The shoulds and shouldn'ts no longer tortured me. Calm settled over me. Molly Marcus watched me brood over my coffee cup. "Problems, Rachel?" she'd asked. "Can I help?" In that moment another decision was made. I realized I would confide in no one about my discovery. Not Molly, not Jan. I desperately wanted to be held, comforted, told that it would be all right, but this was a secret I couldn't share. In fact, if it were at all possible, I would try to forget it myself.

But of course it would not be possible. Already, as I recalled Heather's features, I saw Larry's eyes, bluer than blue, his high forehead, and his shock of wavy black hair. I saw my father's dimpled chin, which had been inherited by both of Annie's children but not by my own twins. Heather's straight nose and thin lips might have been my own. But most of all I recognized the hostility with which Larry had faced the world years ago. *Like father, like daughter,* I thought, barking a short ironic laugh. There was no doubt in my mind that this was Larry's child.

I knew, even as I vowed that it would not matter, that every time I looked at the girl, I would be reminded that this was my Julie, the child I'd turned over to others to raise. She was just beginning to trust me. I was helping her to acquire some control, to exercise judgment, to think about consequences. I'd given Heather reason to hope that she might be happy someday.

To give up my daughter a second time felt like—no, it *was*—abandonment. It meant walking away from the same child twice. And no matter the consequences personally or professionally, I simply could not do it.

Nor could I tell Heather who she was. She was too young and not nearly stable enough to come face-to-face with the mother who'd given her up, leaving her to be raised by parents who she believed neither loved nor wanted her. I had planned to submit my name, when Julie was eighteen, to one of the organizations that helped adoptees find their birth parents. If the girl had any wish to locate me, she would be able to do so. But she was still a minor, and her parents were having trouble enough coping with her. Now was not the time.

I vowed, as I taxied to my office, leafed through a magazine I didn't read, and waited for my first client of the day, that I would take this development one day at a time. *No one will be hurt as long as I'm the only one who knows.* And then, *Rachel, you know you're rationalizing.* I would exert every effort to be sure my words and actions were the same as they would have been if I'd never made the incredible discovery. *And anyway,* I reminded myself, *the Brodys will be going to Washington soon. I just have to make it through a few months, and then they'll move, and by then I will have been able to help Heather.*

I could hear Estelle as clearly as if she were sitting opposite me. *Think it through, Rachel,* my friend and advisor would say. *You know you're on very shaky ground. You can't ignore the fact that this could blow up in your face. You know the Ethics Committee would never condone this decision.* Estelle would never pass judgment, but she would not encourage my plan either.

It may be less painful in the long run to be open about this right now, she'd say. *You know how destructive secret keeping can be.* And I, acknowledging the wisdom of her words, would find myself helpless to do anything differently, which is why I wouldn't be calling Estelle.

Later in the day George Rosenberg, my lawyer and friend, confirmed what I knew in my heart. I'd called him on behalf of "a client," asking him to find a contact in Cuyahoga County and determine how many children born on January 10 sixteen years ago had been adopted. Once children of other races and boy babies had been eliminated, he found that there had been only one relevant adoption in the entire county for the date in question: Baby Girl Green, records subsequently sealed.

I knew I had to talk to someone. Sure, I'd intended to keep my decision secret from the world. But the knowledge I carried was so heavy, and my heart and mind were in such turmoil, that I had to share the burden of my secret. And indeed, I realized, there was someone who had been there from the beginning who would know what I was going through, someone who loved me, someone who was far enough away and would not be drawn into the complexities of the lie I'd chosen to live. I picked up the phone and dialed the area code for Malibu.

"Hello, Annie," I said, my older sister's voice reassuring the moment it came through the wire. "Do you have some time?"

Annie had understood. She had, in rapid succession, experienced the same wave after wave of emotion as I had. Here was someone who could share my joy, my sadness, and my amazement at the incredible coincidence that had brought my daughter and me together so unexpectedly.

"I've decided to go on seeing her, Annie," I said, feeling a vast relief at confessing the unorthodox thing I was about to do.

"Oh, honey," Annie said. I could imagine the two vertical lines between my sister's eyebrows puckering into a frown behind the round frames of her glasses. "Do you think that's wise?"

"Probably not. I don't know. At first I was going to tell her parents and give up the case. But I can't do it. I just can't. There's only one thing I can do, so I'm doing it."

Annie didn't spend time trying to dissuade me from a course of action I'd already determined. "Call me when you need to talk," she said. "Anytime, day or night."

"I love you, Annie. Thank you." There was now one other person who knew what I was doing, and that knowledge gave me the security of a handrail on a steep and treacherous stairway.

Why can't I be satisfied with what I have? I asked myself that evening as I listened to Mitch play a Chopin etude and helped Ben draw a map for his current events project. *These are my children, and they're wonderful boys. They remind me so much of Neil. They are the legacy of his short life.*

Likewise, I realized, Heather was predominantly her father's child, but Larry's legacy was, sadly, more negative than Neil's. I sat in front of the TV, the boys in bed, staring at a magazine program I wasn't really seeing. Instead I was seeing Heather, full of heat and anger, ready to cast the worst possible light on anything she thought might threaten her. *How like her biological father.* I remembered the angry young man I once thought I loved.

I had given up this child once, imagining a privileged childhood filled with love, laughter, friendship, and all the advantages money could buy. If I could have chosen only part of the package for my baby daughter, I would have picked the love, laughter, and friendship. Instead, the child had received only the material part of the wish list. Now fate, disguised as my aunt Gloria, had brought me a second chance to help steer a direction for my unhappy child. I resolved to give it my very best shot.

CHAPTER

7

"Our apartment got sold." It was early May. The treetops of Central Park, visible in the distance from my windows, sprouted the rich green leaves of spring. I'd known this day was coming, but still I felt a sinking sensation as Heather said the words. She sank onto the couch in my office and leaned forward, her arms wrapped around her knees. "We're moving this summer, and I'm just another piece of furniture to be dragged along." She stared at the swirl pattern in the oriental rug. "No one asks me what I want."

So soon? How can I let you go so soon?

"What *do* you want?" I leaned forward and she looked up at me, her blue eyes dark and smoldering.

"I know what I *don't* want. I don't want to move. I don't want to go to some fancy new school. I don't want to leave Frank. He's a pain sometimes, but he cares about me."

"It sounds like you're having trouble saying goodbye." My hands rested loosely in my lap, but my thumbs pressed each of my fingertips, trying to ease the tingling that felt as if a thousand needles were pricking the tender skin.

I appraised my young client. She wore no makeup. The dark hair had grown to nearly chin length and was caught up in a black ribbon. Over the months that we'd been together, Heather had gradually developed a style that was uniquely her own. She favored long skirts and high boots. She liked vests of all types, silk or crocheted, leather or woven. She had an array of body shirts in a variety of colors. She wore black only when she was upset. Today she was upset.

"Why should I have to say goodbye?" Heather demanded. "Because they say so?"

"They're your parents. You're a minor. Where they go, you go. I know it's rough."

"Great. I knock myself out to be what they want, and now they snap their fingers and that's it. Rachel, why can't things just stay the way they are?"

Why indeed? I wish I could freeze time and keep you here in this room with me.

"I was just starting to think I could fit in somewhere. There's this girl in my art class; her name's Chrissie. She kind of digs my painting, y'know?"

"Tell me about her." As Heather described Chrissie, I allowed part of my mind to wander, recalling the sessions that had led up to this one.

I'd sat week after week opposite that child in transition, whose eyes one day glowered with hostility and another day swam with vulnerability.

"They're hopeless," she announced on one visit, throwing her hands out, palms up in a gesture of futility. "They have no clue about what's important."

"What do you think is important?"

"Peace. Global warming. Hungry children."

"And you don't think your parents care about any of that?"

"Oh, sure they do, when they're not wining and dining with the Beautiful People. Which is practically never."

A week or two later, Heather was subdued. "I'm worried about Frank," she said. I took quiet notice of the use of his given name.

"What's troubling you?"

"All he talks about is getting his hands on a lot of money. He calls rich people parasites and says the wealth should be spread around."

"A lot of people believe that," I ventured. "The Socialist Party is all about redistributing wealth."

"Yeah, but I think Frank might be planning to do his own personal redistribution."

"You mean something criminal?"

"I don't know," she said. "I'm just worried."

She brought me one of her paintings, rolled up and held together with a rubber band. It was an abstract. "Tell me about it," I encouraged her.

"I just painted what I was feeling."

"And what were you feeling?"

She pointed to the upper left quadrant of the canvas, gray-black streaked with vivid yellow and orange. "Stormy, I guess."

"Yes, you captured that very well. What's this part?" The bottom right corner was smaller and brighter than its counterpart. The brushstrokes had created a shimmering blend of bright shades with rays of color emanating from a hot-pink center. It was the yellows and oranges, reaching out in undulating waves, that reached upward, piercing the darkness above.

"Hope?" she asked, trying out her interpretation on me.

"Oh, yes, I can see that. It's really quite wonderful, Heather." After that session I sat alone in my office, long after Jan had gone home, and basked in the warmth of proud parenthood.

When I emerged from my reverie, Heather was still talking about Chrissie, unaware that my concentration had lapsed. "She asked me to sit at her lunch table," she was saying.

Bless you, Chrissie, whoever you are.

"So you've made a friend."

"I wouldn't go that far," she was quick to assert. "But still, it was kinda nice."

"And now you have to leave."

"How unfair is *that*?"

"Very." My heart hurt for her, but it was my job to help her recover and move on. "Do you think Washington might be an easier adjustment for you than some of the other changes of schools were?"

"I won't know anybody."

"That's the bad news and the good news, isn't it?"

Heather gave me a long look, the dark wings of her brows forming a V as she puzzled over my enigmatic statement.

"What do you mean?"

"Well, it's hard to start over, that's for sure. But you're not bringing your past along with you either. You can be anyone you want to be. You're getting a fresh start!"

"But you won't be there." This was new. It was the first time Heather had ever indicated that these sessions had meaning for her.

"Before you leave I'm going to give you my cell number. If you ever want to talk, I'll be only a phone call away. Meanwhile," I said, holding back a powerful longing to gather her up and squeeze her in a bear hug, "think about who you want to be when you start your new school in September."

"I'm not sure I know what you mean."

"Just think about it. We'll talk more next time."

I wrapped my arms around myself as I watched her leave, that ubiquitous black leather bag slung over her shoulder, looking like too heavy a load for her slight frame. I remembered the furious rebel with the death's-head earrings, the white pancake makeup, and the black talons pasted onto her fingers who had stormed into my office seven months earlier. She still had a long way to travel, my little girl, but she'd already come so far.

Notes

H. displays anger, covering fear at move to Washington.
Willing to show vulnerability; more willing to listen.
Final sessions will focus on preparing for the move.

A few days later, Stephanie and William Brody sat opposite me, having responded to my request for an appointment.

"We're quite pleased," Bill Brody said. "Heather can still be sullen and difficult, but she's toned down those god-awful outfits, and her hair and makeup show signs of improvement. Whatever you're doing seems to be working."

"Have you told her you're pleased?" William and Stephanie glanced at each other, then quickly refocused on me.

"I think I mentioned it," William said. "We've been afraid to say anything."

"I told her I liked her hair one day last week," Stephanie remarked, "but all I got back was a shrug."

"It's a start. Heather's a kid who needs lots of positive feedback, but only if you mean it. She can spot a fake compliment at fifty paces."

"It's so difficult," Stephanie said. She fiddled with the strap of her Gucci handbag, then set the bag down on the floor next to her seat. "I want so much to be proud of her, and she does so little to encourage me."

"I understand you've sold your condo and are making plans for Washington."

"We have." Stephanie warmed to a subject with which she was comfortable.

"We'll probably move in July," William said. "We're house hunting." I did a silent lightning calculation. *Less than two months. Six or seven sessions at most.*

"What have you decided about school?"

"We've been discussing it," William said. "We can see that Heather's making an effort. We're thinking about letting her make the choice—a private day school or boarding school."

"Frankly, I'm scared to death," Stephanie put in. "It's true she's been a little more presentable, but she's far from a joy to have around. There have been times since Heather's been at home that *I've* wanted to run away. My first choice would be boarding school, but if you think it's important that she stay at home—"

I found myself with jaw clenched and hands carefully folded in my lap, fighting to hang on to the illusion of objectivity and professionalism.

"I think it's important that Heather feel wanted and loved," I said carefully.

"Then why does she provoke us so?" William asked. "I still don't understand."

"It's hard to say. She seems to be testing you. How much can you take? Can you love her with a ton of white makeup on her face? Can you love her in spite of the friends she chooses, the language she uses? She's very hurt, and she's afraid to get close, afraid to trust you. So she lets you see only the tough, hard part of herself."

"Look, Dr. Marston," William said, glancing at the slim gold and leather watch he wore, "if you can keep the progress going, I think we can invite Heather to stay home if she prefers."

I turned to Stephanie. "What about you? You're at home more than your husband. Are you willing to give it a try?" Stephanie met my gaze.

"I'll try," she said, "but Bill thinks she should continue her treatment. And I agree. Oh, you'll be pleased about this. I called Dr.

Tobin—you know, the one who wrote that book? I saw him on TV again last week and I was quite impressed. Did you know the book's still at the top of the charts? He has a waiting list, of course, but his receptionist felt that when we arrive in Washington, he'll be able to squeeze Heather in."

I hoped my shock didn't show in my eyes or the muscles of my face. Once again anxiety flowed into my fingers. I held my hands in my lap, rubbing one, then the other.

"Really? I'm surprised. With all that TV exposure."

"Well, so was I." Stephanie sat up a little straighter. "But I mentioned who we were and the responsibility Bill would have with the network, and it seems to have opened the door."

"I'm sure when the time comes you'll help ease the transition for Heather," Bill said. "Perhaps you can speak with Dr. Tobin and bring him up to speed on the issues and where you are in the treatment."

"Of course. I'll do whatever I can." My voice sounded strong enough in my own ears, belying my trepidation. In search of steadier ground, I went on. "If you're going to invite Heather to live at home with you next year, I suggest you do it soon. If you wait to see how she'll ultimately turn out, you'll lose your chance to let her know you love her and want her in spite of everything."

"We've given her so much," William said as he completed writing his check and turned to leave.

"She doesn't need material things. Just show her you love her and trust her." I held the door for them as they left.

I sank into the chair Stephanie had vacated, trying to envision the moment when I would introduce myself to Larry Tobin as Heather's therapist. I closed my eyes. My mind refused to go there. And the further complications did not bear thinking about. That Heather was being treated by her biological mother and would soon transfer to the care of her biological father, who had no idea that this child existed, was all too much.

"My first choice would be boarding school." I clenched my fists as I recalled the words of the mother to whom I'd turned over my baby. I should have found a way to keep her. Of course I knew how impossible that would have been, but I'd promised my Julie a happy life, and she'd wound up as the child of an overprivileged social climbing couple who had little time and even less patience for her. *You could have tried harder, dammit.*

Too soon, I'd have to give up even the tenuous, once-weekly contact that had miraculously allowed me a chance to give something other than my DNA to my child. How I wanted to hold on. I felt like the rancher in some B movie, clutching the foreclosure notice that will ruin him.

My mind jumped from one distressing thought to another. *How am I going to handle William Brody's request? It's one thing to make a rash decision that involves only me.* But what if I helped the family transfer to Larry? *It would be wrong,* the voice of reason indicated. *Wrong because I know the truth. Wrong because it would compound what I've already done. Wrong because if any of them ever found out—but they'll never find out. And besides, Heather needs a skilled therapist. Larry has a national reputation. And her parents respect him, so there's a good chance they'll cooperate. It's the logical choice.*

I shook my head so hard that I could feel my curls bounce. *Why shouldn't Larry treat Heather? He's the best, or so they say.*

I don't know how long I sat there, the two sides of myself locked in combat. *He's her father. He can't be her therapist.*

He's their choice. He's the best. He doesn't know he's her father.

Yes. No. Yes. No.

But there was something, more feeling than thought, more instinct than either of those, that nibbled and gnawed at my ability to reason. I'd be turning my daughter over to someone with a connection to her, even if neither of them would ever know it. If I couldn't see my little girl all the way to a healthy adulthood, then perhaps her father, transformed somehow into a warm and caring human being, could finish the job. *Sure, I know it's wrong. But it feels incredibly right.*

Two weeks later I sat at my desk, deep in thought, when Jan came in to say good night.

"Aren't you leaving?" she asked. "No one's coming in tonight, right?"

"Right. I have some paperwork to finish up. See you in the morning."

"Okay. G'night. Kiss the monsters for me."

I flipped open my laptop and stared at the cursor blinking white against the blackened screen. In the past two weeks, I'd composed several versions of the letter I knew I had to write, but I had hit delete each time.

At first I thought I'd dictate a brief note to Jan informing Dr. Tobin that I'd been treating a client who would be transferring to his care. I'd sign it Rachel Marston, leaving out the middle name, which would otherwise give away my identity. I'd be just another therapist, referring just another client. That was the safe way to honor the Brodys' request. It's what I would do if I'd never known him except by reputation.

Instead, I brought up a blank compose screen on my email program, filled in the address I'd gotten from his website, and began another version of the letter.

Dear Larry,

You must be quite surprised to hear from me after so many years, but not nearly as surprised as I was recently when I learned that you are practicing psychology. By great coincidence, it is my profession as well. I've since discovered that your praises are being sung to the rafters. I'm very pleased that you're doing well. I bought your book after your last New York lecture (I was in the last row), and I think it's wonderful. I've recommended it to several clients.

Which brings me to the point of this letter. I've been treating a young girl, age sixteen, and I've had collateral contact with her adoptive parents. The work has been going well, but the family is moving to Washington before the end of summer. It will be a vulnerable time for the youngster, what with severing old ties, adjusting to a new school, etc.

She came into treatment very angry and somewhat self-destructive, and I'm afraid she could regress without ongoing high-quality treatment. The parents have already been in touch with your office and have been advised that you will see their daughter, whose name is Heather Brody. I fully concur in their choice of therapist and would like to provide whatever help I can to assist in the transition.

There's a lot of water under the bridge between us, and I hope that this professional contact doesn't stir up too many unpleasant memories for you. If it does, I'll send you a case summary; you'll need not worry about having direct contact with me. On the other hand, I'd be pleased to touch base with you again if that's your preference.

Once again, congratulations on your book and your phenomenal success. I think it's terrific!

All the best,
Rachel (Green Marston)

I sat a few minutes longer, staring at the screen until the words blurred and faded into the background. *You don't have to send this,* I reminded myself. *This may possibly be the worst idea you've ever had.*

I assigned the letter to my draft folder and shut down the computer. I retrieved my purse and groped for my keys as I walked to the door. I hesitated as I crossed the threshold, ready to lock up and head for the elevator. Instead I pivoted, went back to my desk, and booted up the laptop again. *No more 'should I or shouldn't I?'* I retrieved the email, and with more pressure than was absolutely necessary, I pushed Send.

I tried to imagine him reading the letter. He'd probably wait until the end of the day, as I did, to check his emails. Perhaps he'd pour tea from a thermos as I sometimes did. Most likely he'd stretch his long legs under his desk, pushing back that renegade lock of hair as he did so.

What would he think after all these years? He'd been bitterly angry with me at the end, accusing me, not unjustly, of leading him on. I'd refused his phone calls, refused his desperate plea to see me one more time when I was seven months pregnant. He thought I was being gratuitously cold and cruel. I'd let him think it.

Perhaps he won't respond. That wouldn't surprise me. A lot of years have passed, but then again, I hurt him very deeply.

I won't write again, I decided. If he were to decide not to reply, I'd have my answer.

But his response came so swiftly that he must have answered by return mail. And it was anything but cold and distant. Its tone was much more in keeping with the man he seemed to have become than with the boy he'd been seventeen years ago.

> Dear Rachel,
>
> Great to hear from you. What a surprise! Lots of memories, most of them very pleasant. I'm writing this with a smile on my face.
>
> I see you've married. Wonder what else has been going on in your life. I'm in New York often. Would welcome a meeting with you. Let's get together, discuss your client, spend some time catching up on us.
>
> Great hearing from you. Hope to see you soon.
>
> Larry

CHAPTER

8

The weeks ticked on. The whir of air conditioners could be heard from the street as I walked home from the office each day, sometimes wilting even in the coolest clothing I could find. My letter to Larry had been written and responded to, and now I waited for the day when I would see Heather for the last time. My sessions with her had a roller-coaster-like intensity as Heather struggled with the thought of leaving New York.

"Have you visited Washington yet?"

"Yeah. It's okay, I guess. We're going to live in a real house with a pool and a tennis court. And grass. It's not really in Washington. It's in Virginia. Arlington."

"That'll be a change."

"I guess so. But I don't know. I guess I'm just scared."

"Of course you're scared. New beginnings are scary as hell. But they're also opportunities."

"I suppose."

"For a fresh start, I mean. For example, who do you want to be in Washington?"

Heather looked puzzled. She was silent for a moment. "You asked me that before. I don't get you," she said.

"I mean, the girl who walked in here a few months ago or the young woman sitting here today?"

"They're both me. Different parts of me."

"What parts?"

"The mad part—and the okay part, I guess."

"Great!" I flashed her a beaming smile. "So which Heather is going to Washington? Or, more precisely, which one do you want the kids at your new school to meet?"

Heather shared a small smile of understanding. "I guess the okay one?"

"Is that a question?"

"Not really."

"Good. I just wanted you to see that you have a choice."

Heather leaned forward. "You know," she said, "I didn't want to come here."

"I know."

"I figured you'd be like my parents and my teachers and that guidance person at my last school, telling me what to do. But you never did that. You always let me feel like I had a choice."

"You always did."

"I know. And when it's my choice, not theirs, then it's okay. Know what I mean?"

"Sure."

"I'm really going to miss you."

"I'll miss you too." *Oh God, you'll never know how much.*

"I don't feel ready to stop seeing you. I feel like I'm just in the middle of something. And now I have to move and meet all new kids, and you won't be there anymore."

"First of all, you're welcome to call me. I'd love to hear from you." I cleared my throat once, then again. "But I understand that your parents have chosen a colleague of mine who practices in Washington, a really good therapist. I agree with you that this is not the right time to end your treatment."

"Someone else new? I don't know. I'm not great with new situations. Who is she?"

"It's not a she."

"A guy? Oh gosh, I don't know. Is he cute?" She giggled.

"That's a pretty subjective thing. I know he's good at what he does. And his specialty is kids your age. He can help you get through all these changes."

"Is it okay if I think about it?"

"Sure." I hoped the Brodys had learned enough about their daughter to let this decision be Heather's. Pushing her too hard now would make the issue of continuing treatment a fertile field for another power struggle. Heather would make the right choice, I was quite sure, if her parents weren't too obvious about how much they wanted her to make it.

Next time, and then once more, and Heather would disappear from my life—again. Only this time there was Larry, unsuspecting Larry, so ready to renew old ties, to accept my client in treatment. *This is not right,* I thought, knowing as I thought it that I would take no steps to undo what I had started. I showed Heather out, and the girl gave a small salute as she left. I moved swiftly to the window and watched for a glimpse of her as she came out on to the street many floors below. Returning to my desk, I picked up the phone.

"I've done it again, Annie," I said. Talking to Annie when I was troubled felt like settling into a soothing bath, allowing the warm water to ripple over me, relaxing my tension, calming my nerves. I had told Annie months earlier that Larry was now a successful therapist. We had shared our amazement, and Annie had even joked a little about how such a transformation might have occurred. "Maybe he fell on his head," she'd said, and we'd chuckled together. But I had not yet shared with Annie the news about Heather being treated by him once she moved to Washington. As much as I cherished the open relationship I had with my sister, as much as I knew I could tell her anything, I'd hesitated to confess what felt like a fit of insanity. Now it was time.

"Heather's moving to Washington in two weeks," I said. "Her parents chose Larry Tobin, of all people, to continue her therapy. And I agreed."

"Oh, hon," Annie said, trepidation riding on her tone of voice. "You couldn't have changed their minds?"

"I probably could have, but I didn't."

"I'm sure you had a good reason. But it seems—"

"Foolish? I know. I went back and forth a hundred times. The parents wanted him. I could have headed them off if I'd really wanted to. But he's good, Annie. Really good. He understands kids. And Heather is so much like he was back then."

"Still, Rachel, you're deceiving him. Isn't that a risk? For everyone?"

"What if I'd never found out, Annie, never knew who Heather

was? There'd be nothing wrong with what I'm doing. She's done so well. She's become warmer, more trusting, able to express her feelings. She even told me she's going to miss me! I'm sending her to the best therapist I know so she can continue making progress."

"Honey, aren't you rationalizing? Just a little?"

"Probably. There's something I can't explain—won't even try—but it feels right to me. Like she belongs with him. He'll take care of her now that I can't. I know it's not rational. It's just how I feel."

"Okay. You made the decision. I hope it works out for everyone. Now you have to let go of it. And let go of Heather. Or try. Focus on those two great kids you have, and get your life back to normal. Promise?"

"I'm trying, Annie. But there's something else. I wrote to Larry when I knew he was going to see her, and he wrote back. He wants to see me—professionally, I mean, to discuss the case. He sounded so glad to hear from me. Now I'm thinking about him more than I should, wondering how he could have changed so much, remembering how he was and how Mom and Dad hated him. Remember?"

"Oh yes, I remember. I wasn't his number one fan either."

"And I felt so sorry for him and so needed by him. And the way all of you told me how wrong he was for me just pushed me closer to him. That old adolescent rebellion thing. So what if I ruin my life? It's *my* life."

"But in the end you knew you'd be miserable with him. You made the right decision. Is it a good idea to let him back in your life again? It will only stir things up for you."

"I'm a big girl now. I can handle it. And besides, he really does seem so different. Like there's another person living in his skin."

"Possession, maybe?"

"That's about as logical as any other explanation. Well, I'm in it now, Annie. We'll see. The hardest thing will be saying goodbye to Heather. I want to kidnap her, take her home to meet her brothers, and never let her go again."

"I know, I know. Call me as often as you need to. We'll talk."

"It helps so much, Annie. Thanks. And thanks for understanding and not lecturing me."

"You don't need any lectures. You're a bright woman. Everything

I could tell you, you already know. Just consult your head before going with your heart, okay?"

"I haven't been doing enough of that lately. But it will all work out, as long as nobody knows any of this except you and me." I made a kissing noise and hung up, sighing deeply as I did so. *Thank God for Annie.* I scooped up my purse and shut off the lights as I went home for the night.

Shouts greeted me as I let myself into the condo after my brisk two-mile walk downtown. Ben and Mitch, and Billy from across the hall, were crouched in various positions around the TV screen. Mitch was guiding an animated figure through a maze of villains and obstacles, with much verbal encouragement and warnings from the others. "Watch out," Billy screeched as the figure appeared to be blown to bits and then reemerged, bouncy as ever, on a new screen.

"Hi, I'm home," I said in a singsong tone of voice.

Ben glanced up. "Hi, Mom," he managed before turning back to the set. Mitch sat, tongue between his teeth, concentrating intently. I ruffled his blond curls with my fingernails, and he nodded his hello.

Mrs. Marcus was in the kitchen, her ever-present cup of chamomile on the table as she turned a page of the latest Danielle Steele.

"Hi," I said. "Any good?"

"Oh yes. The best one yet." Molly stole a last glance as she closed the book.

"Did the boys eat?"

"They tried to wait for you, but they were starved. Yours is in the oven."

"Great. I'm starved too. Everything okay around here?"

"Ben skinned his knee in the park, but he's all fixed up. Nothing a little bacitracin can't cure."

I hadn't told Mrs. Marcus about Heather. We respected each other's privacy. Although Molly clucked and fussed over me as though I were one of the children, she didn't pry. As I sat at the kitchen table, savoring a perfectly grilled chicken cutlet and chunks of Dijon potato salad, I considered telling the motherly woman the whole story—considered and then rejected the notion. I wanted my baby, and Molly

Marcus couldn't give that to me any more than could Annie or anyone else. Why talk about it?

Ben flopped noisily onto his chair. He leaned on his elbows, spread wide on the tabletop, watching me eat.

"Guess what, Mom!"

"You're getting an A-plus in math?"

"No. Guess again."

"You're getting married?" I teased him with my eyes.

He giggled. "You're silly. Want me to tell you?"

"Okay."

"I'm starting pitcher in Saturday's game."

"Wow! That's great! What time does it start?"

"Two o'clock."

"I'll be there. Who're you playing?"

"The dumb Hawkeyes. No problem. I want to pitch against the Cards."

"They're number one?"

"Yeah. And we're number three. If I pitched and we won, I'd be a hero."

"Well, maybe you'll get a chance." I savored these moments one-on-one with my kids, sharing and intimate. Little League wasn't exactly the major interest of my life, but it was important to the boys, especially Ben. I was aware that many of my sons' confidences, hopes, and fears were revealed to Auntie Mol while I sat in a steel-and-glass tower listening to the innermost thoughts of strangers. I shook off my brooding concerns about Heather to focus on Ben. He was the twin who most reminded me of Neil. Although the boys were identical, Ben held his chin at a certain angle, squinted his eyes when deep in thought, and more than Mitch, approached the world as his personal playing field.

Mitch had other qualities that tugged at my heart. He was introspective, less sure of himself than his open, carefree brother. "Mom, do you think I should?" he'd ask, trying to decide whether or not to go on a campout with his Pueblo troop.

"It could be fun," I'd answer. "What's your concern?"

"What if I hate it?"

"What if you do?"

"Well, it's only one night."

"That's true."

"Maybe I'd have a great time. And if I don't go, I'll never know."

"There's that."

"I guess I should try it."

"Okay. What do you want to pack?" Mitch eventually reached the decision I would have chosen for him, but he was more like me in his initial anxiety and indecisiveness.

Now, as Ben slid off his chair and went back to the TV, I forced myself to avoid falling into another reverie about Heather. *You're blessed, kiddo,* I reminded myself, tuning in for a moment to the sounds of raucous laughter from the living room. *Snap out of it.*

Heather's last appointment was on a humid, gray Wednesday, rain sprinkling from the sky. The sidewalks had felt steamy as I stepped out of my building, and in rare submission to my mood and the weather, I'd allowed Joe the doorman to hail me a cab. In my office, the conditioned air had felt blissfully frigid as I leaned back against the soft leather of my desk chair and contemplated the day ahead. It would take all my professional discipline to focus on the clients who preceded Heather, but I was determined not to cheat any of them of an attentive, caring therapist. Heather would come in at 4:00, and I would spend a final hour with the girl who would never know that she was bidding a final goodbye to her birth mother.

Jan greeted me as she entered, a cardboard container of coffee for each of us in a brown bag. "Hi. You must have cabbed in. You look too cool."

"How observant. Right as usual. I'd need a shower now if I'd walked. Any messages?"

"Dan Avery canceled. Job interview. He'll see you next week. The copy machine serviceman will be here around two o'clock. I'll deal with him. And Mr. Brody called, left his work number. Call him around noon, if possible."

William Brody answered promptly when I gave my name to his secretary. I imagined him in his corporate aerie, windows behind him bringing the panorama of New York into his world, glossy expanse of desk with a picture of the elegant Mrs. Brody in a classic frame.

"Thank you for returning my call," he said.

"Of course. What can I do for you?"

"I'm aware that today is Heather's last session. I want to thank you for the excellent job you've done with her."

"It was Heather who did the work, Mr. Brody. Changing oneself is very difficult. She deserves a lot of credit."

"Yes, well, of course, I give her all the credit in the world. But you clearly knew what buttons to press. I just wanted to say thanks and to let you know I wouldn't hesitate to recommend you in the future."

"I appreciate that. You have a very special daughter, Mr. Brody. She has a great deal of potential that she's just beginning to get in touch with. I'll miss working with her."

"She told us she'll miss you too," he responded. "In fact, it's one of the few times she's ever shared her feelings with us."

I felt the pulse in my throat slide upward and threaten my speech. I hesitated.

"I hope she'll follow up and see Dr. Tobin," I said. "He has a wonderful reputation. I believe he can help her to consolidate her gains and move forward."

"I hope so too," Heather's father said. "But I'm afraid to push her too hard."

"I wouldn't force her," I advised. "But a little gentle encouragement might help, as long as she knows the choice is hers."

"Well, thank you again, Dr. Marston."

"I want you to know that you or Mrs. Brody, or Heather, can call me if you feel the need. Good luck in Washington."

"Thank you. Goodbye."

I sat motionless after I hung up. *He's not so bad. There's hope for that family.* I smiled a little bit as I allowed myself to realize that I'd made a difference in my child's life. I remembered my grandmother who had lived by maxims and spouted clichés for every occasion. "Fate moves in mysterious ways," Grandma used to say.

"Right, Gram," I said aloud as Jan buzzed to signal that the next client had arrived.

I had clients at one and two o'clock. "I'll be back," I told Jan at three, and headed for the elevator. I needed a walk. Heather would be in at four, and I was so unready to face my last session with her. The sidewalks were sending up waves of heat. I darted into a Starbucks and ordered an iced cappuccino. Holding the sweaty paper container in both hands, I sank into a leather chair and stared into space. At 3:50 I headed back to the office, feeling as if I had lead weights attached to both my feet.

Heather was waiting. As I came in, she wiggled her fingers at me in a hello gesture.

"It's early, but come on in," I said. "It'll give us a few extra minutes."

She looked lovely. She wore off-white palazzo pants with a muted floral pattern in shades of soft brown. A darker brown T-shirt with a rounded neckline was covered by a long vest that matched the pants. She had on short off-white lace-up boots with a small heel. Her hair, longer now, was caught up in two gold combs, and her makeup was all peach and coral with just a touch of light brown eye shadow. Her earrings were crafted of silver and a beige material that looked like stone.

I remembered the tragicomic parody who'd paced angrily around my office on that first day. "Wow," I said. "You look fantastic!" Heather beamed her pleasure and pirouetted, arms stretched at her sides.

"I wanted you to see another Heather before we said goodbye."

"Do you like this Heather?"

She hesitated for a minute. She grasped the tip of her tongue between her teeth while thinking. "Yeah. I guess so," she answered finally. "My folks are taking me out to dinner and the theater tonight, sort of a 'say goodbye to New York' thing, and I feel like"—she paused to find the words—"like I fit in, y'know? And what's really strange is, I'm looking forward to it."

"Why is that strange?"

"Because they're … you know, my parents. I mean, they never much wanted to be with me, and I certainly couldn't see myself hanging out with them. But this is kind of … nice."

I gazed with satisfaction at the young woman who sat, so poised and mature, in front of me. *Miracles do happen.*

"I gave Chrissie my cell phone number, and she said she would friend me on Facebook. She said I should post some of my paintings on there. So when I get to Washington, I'm going to sign up." Her smile was bemused, one eyebrow raised. She lifted a shoulder. "Who would've thought I'd get into something like Facebook?"

I was having trouble staying focused. I couldn't take my eyes off the poised, pretty sixteen-year-old heading out for an evening of dinner and theater with her parents. My mind kept jumping back to that first appointment, what, nine months ago? Long enough to gestate a child.

"I said goodbye to Frank last night," Heather said. "He told me I could stay here in New York with him. He lives with a bunch of other kids in an old apartment in Brooklyn."

"What did you tell him?"

"I said, 'I don't *think* so'! I guess I might have considered it once, when I thought I didn't have anyone but him. But now his lifestyle really doesn't appeal to me. It's so, I don't know, scruffy. Still, I feel really bad for him. 'Cause he really doesn't have anyone but me."

"Sometimes we just outgrow people," I remarked. "You move on with your life, and the other person stays in the same place. It's not anyone's fault. It just happens."

"I s'pose. I'm just afraid he's going to mess up if I'm not around to help him."

"Heather, would you let me take your picture?" The idea had suddenly jumped into my mind, and the words were out before I had time to think.

"Sure."

I pulled my cell phone from my purse and aimed. Heather threw an arm across the back of the couch, lifting her chin and offering me an authentic dimpled smile. I took the shot, and another for good measure.

"Thanks. Too bad I don't have a before picture." We shared a laugh.

"Can I take one of you, and you can email it to me?" she asked.

I loved the idea, but I hesitated. What would Stephanie think if Heather were to display a picture of her therapist on her bureau? Actually, I decided, I was beyond caring. I handed her the camera and leaned forward, hands on my knees, smiling broadly into the lens.

Heather handed me her email address, scribbled on a scrap of paper, along with her check. It was time.

"You've worked very hard in here," I told her. *I will not cry!* I cleared my throat.

"Y'know, sometimes that other girl—the one from the before picture—comes back."

"Of course she does. She's part of you too. She's you in a bad mood. But, you know, you've learned that you have choices. You don't have to act on those feelings. You can if you want to, but you don't have to."

"I guess that's what I'll remember most about you, that you helped me see that I have choices."

Heather was moving toward the door. I felt paralyzed. My child was walking out of my life. I flashed back to the moment when the nurse carried her out of the room and the little newborn face turned and seemed to look at me.

"Would you mind if I gave you a hug?" I didn't wait for her answer; she was in my arms. Warmth surged through me as she squeezed me back. *This is not okay. I can't hide my feelings. It's probably a good thing that she's leaving.*

"Thanks again," she said, stepping out of the embrace. And she opened the door and was gone.

CHAPTER
9

I hesitated outside the entrance of Soeur et Frere, a small French bistro near Lincoln Center. It was one of my favorites, not too far from my office. The email I'd received from Larry a week earlier had made my pulse jump. The subject line had said simply, "Meet me?"

In NYC Nov. 7–11. Can we meet for dinner?

How about the ninth, anyplace you wish?

It had been several months since Larry had indicated that he was willing to meet me. I thought perhaps he'd decided in the interim that it wasn't a good idea. Now there would be another step in the drama that had become my life. I was about to see my child's father for the first time in seventeen years.

Jean-Claude, the *frère*, greeted me and took my coat. I liked the role reversal that this brother-and-sister team represented. Jean-Claude played host, while his sister, Marie-Elene, concocted simple but fabulous food behind the scenes.

"Dr. Marston, *bon soir*. The gentleman is waiting for you. Please, follow me." Near the back of the room, I saw Larry stand up.

There'd been no question of my refusing this invitation. Larry was my only link to my daughter. I would meet him wherever and whenever he wanted.

I'd had a rough time since Heather left for Washington. *I will not obsess!* I had commanded myself. *It's over!* I threw myself into parenting the twins in ways that felt, at times, a little frantic, a bit overdone.

In August we'd gone to the Jersey Shore, to a familiar and comfortable clapboard rooming house near the ocean at Bradley Beach. I built sandcastles with my sons; I tossed their Frisbee; I helped first Mitch, then Ben, bury his brother up to the neck in damp sand. I swam with them, and when it rained, I sat on the porch and played marathon tournaments of Sorry and Monopoly. And I willed my conscious mind not to return to the last time I'd seen my oldest child.

I had emailed the photograph of me that Heather had taken with my phone camera. It had taken me half an hour to compose a brief message to go with the picture. I'd finally settled on "Good luck in Washington. I know you'll make wise choices. Warmly, Rachel."

She'd written back. "Got the picture. You look great. Thanks. Heather." I'd stared at the computer screen, willing it to give me a few more lines, a couple of words, a little information.

As the summer days wound down, I told the boys their chapter and kissed them good night. Then I took out Heather's picture, safely tucked away between the pages of the little journal. *Keep up the good work, sweetheart. I miss you.*

Now I was about to get my first real news since the day four months earlier when she'd walked out of my life for the second time. And I would satisfy my curiosity about Larry Tobin. He would finally be more than a glossy picture on the back cover of a book, more than a seventeen-year-old memory. I offered a little wave as I followed Jean-Claude to the table.

As I approached, Larry reached out and grasped both my hands.

"We meet again," he said. And then with a small chuckle he added, "Excuse the cliché.

"I'd know you anywhere," he told me as he helped me get seated.

Of course I recognized him instantly from his photograph. But he too seemed largely unchanged. A shock of black wavy hair still fell over his forehead, covering his left eyebrow. I remembered how that renegade wave would fall over his eye. He was always impatiently pushing it away. His cheekbones remained well defined. There was no hint of jowls or any extra pounds. His lips were thin, forming a straight, neat line. His eyes were still strikingly blue. Heather's eyes were the same intense blue. But one thing was different. The eyes of the teenaged boy I knew had been probing searchlights. They seemed always to be reading me, questioning me, as though looking for some flaw. Crinkles at the corners of these adult eyes suggested humor and kindness. The new, added ingredient was warmth.

A cooler stood next to his seat, and he waved over a young woman server. "I took the liberty of ordering champagne. It is, after all, a reunion. But if you'd rather have a cocktail—"

"No, that's fine. Champagne's great." The cork popped; the wine foamed. Larry filled my flute and then poured San Pellegrino, from a bottle resting in the same cooler, into his own glass. He raised his glass. "To happy endings," he said. We clinked glasses and sipped.

"Tell me about Heather," I said.

"What an interesting young woman. She told me quite a lot about her work with you and what a hard time she gave you in the beginning. She says you helped her a lot. She also let me know she wasn't at all sure if she wanted to work with me."

"Have you met her parents?"

"Once. They're very involved in breaking into the Washington social scene. Especially the mother. Dad's really busy taking on his new responsibilities at the TV station. I get the sense they want Heather to adapt, cooperate, and not give them grief."

I smiled. "You've got that right. How's Heather doing with her self-esteem?"

"Up and down. You can tell right away when she's down on herself. It's written all over her. In fact, if she comes in wearing black, I can guess before she says a word. But she told me that she learned about making choices from you, and it helps her to get over her bad spells. You did really good work with her, Rachel."

I leaned toward him. He put his elbows on the table, folded his hands under his chin, and moved an inch toward me as well.

"Do you know if she's painting? Has she made any friends?" I knew I sounded too interested.

"She likes her art teacher. Sounds like a good mentor for Heather. She told her she has real talent. She hasn't talked much about friends, although she did say she enrolled in Facebook."

"Larry, do you think she's going to be okay? Do you think she's going to make it?" He didn't answer immediately. He gazed at me for what seemed like a long time. The twitch of his lips betrayed amusement.

"Do I detect a little case of countertransference, counselor?"

"I guess so." *Good. I'm glad he used that word. Countertransference explains my overinvolvement.* "I do tend to identify with my teenage girl clients, especially those having difficulties with their mothers." I chuckled. "And that would be all of them."

"I can certainly understand. Don't forget, I know something about your teenage years. And your mother."

"My main problem with my mother was you."

"Right. And one of Heather's main problems is her mother's feelings about her boyfriend Frank. You know about Frank, I'm sure."

"The Frankster. Oh yes, I know. Does Heather stay in touch with him?"

"I think they have some contact. She's very protective of him."

Larry cocked his head to the left, those blue eyes still watching me intently. "I think the transference is somewhat of a two-way street."

"Meaning?"

"Heather seems to have cast you in the role of good mother."

I felt a flood of warm pleasure. I touched my hot cheek with the back of my hand, masking the gesture by fluffing my hair. "We were making good progress. Too bad it was interrupted."

He smiled again. The warmth that crinkled the corners of his eyes was so opposite what I remembered that it startled me. "If she'll give me half a chance, I'll try to finish the job."

Now that we'd both acknowledged my more than normal interest in this particular client, I bombarded Larry: "Does she stay in touch with Chrissie? Does she still carry around that huge black bag?"

He laughed. "Her security blanket. If ever she comes in without it, I'll know our work is just about done." He made a temple of his fingers, touching the two pointers to his lower lip. "Anyway, Rachel, I'd really like to catch up on the last seventeen years of your life." I leaned back in my seat, struggling to shift gears.

The fresh-faced young woman who'd poured my champagne approached. "My name is Betsy. I'll be your server," she announced. She refilled my flute.

"Give us a few minutes," Larry told her. "Do you want to take a look at the menu?" he asked me.

I knew the fish was excellent here, although I had little interest in food at the moment. After a brief consultation, we agreed to share a dozen oysters and a chopped salad. I settled on sole meunière. He opted for Chilean sea bass. He gestured to Betsy and gave our order. Once she disappeared, he put his elbows on the table and leaned toward me. "Tell me," he said.

"Well, you know I went to college in Ohio," I began. I filled him in briefly on the undergraduate years and my decision to focus on psychology. The birth and subsequent adoption of my first child, our child, was not part of the story.

"And so I went to Yale for graduate school, and I met my husband before I earned my degree."

"Tell me about him." I paused while Betsy produced our oysters and set us up with plates and cocktail forks. We each speared an oyster and dipped, he into a shallot vinaigrette, I into delicious cocktail sauce.

"Yum," I said, licking sauce from my lips. "So, about Neil. He was a wonderful man."

"Was?"

"He died five years ago."

"I'm so sorry." Young Larry had perfected a poker face. The mature man opposite me allowed compassion to shine through his eyes, while one of his hands reached for one of mine.

"We had a few really good years. And wonderful twin boys." I rummaged through my purse and brought out the photographs I always carried in a special leather case. Larry could see my personal history in a few pictures: a formal wedding shot, I looking up adoringly at my new husband; a group shot of Neil and me, each of us holding a two-year-old blond boy; and the boys' latest school picture, their hair slicked back, Ben serious, Mitch grinning, freckles standing out.

"They are adorable. How old?"

"They're almost ten."

"They're the image of him."

"I know. They're like him in many ways. They're wonderful boys."

"Where do you live?"

"We bought a condo in the West Village while I was pregnant."

"Do you enjoy your work?"

"I do. It was a good choice for me. Isn't it amazing that we wound up in the same field? Why did you become a therapist?"

"It's a long, long story." He gazed at me; it seemed as if he were deciding how much he wanted to say. Right behind him Betsy appeared. Our oyster shells disappeared, and Betsy was holding our salad, neatly divided in two portions. Larry lifted a fork but held it in the air as he spoke.

"The year we broke up," he began, "my mother died."

"I'm sorry." I'd met his mother only twice. She was very thin and had a perpetually worried look. She spoke with a European accent, and on both occasions she had a flowered apron tied around her waist. She seemed to be grateful for my presence in her son's life. "I liked her."

"She had pancreatic cancer. It was over very quickly. So then it was my father and me. And he just sat in that old leather recliner and read his newspaper and smoked his cigar. We never spoke. So I went to work every day and went to school every night, and began hanging around after my last class with a group of seniors from the art department. We'd go out for a few beers, and then I was invited back to one of their apartments, where there were drugs." He paused and stabbed at his salad. Realizing I'd been holding my breath, I let it out and began eating.

"It's not a pretty story," he went on. He ate a few more forkfuls of salad before speaking again. He cleared his throat, and his brow furrowed. "I got heavily involved. Mostly cocaine, but other stuff too. The guys I was with, they seemed to be able to handle it. Me, I got hooked. I was out until one or two in the morning. I'd get home; my father would be snoring in the chair. I'd wake him up and send him to bed, and then I'd conk out for a few hours. I flunked that semester. Eventually I lost my job."

"Oh, Larry."

"I'll be honest. Back then, I blamed you." He put up his hand to stop what I was going to say. "I don't anymore. In fact, I know that you did what you had to do, and it all worked out in the end. But I was very bitter at the time. Actually I was bitter about everything. So anyway," he said, scooping up the last bits of salad, "I had no job, I had no money, I started dealing drugs, and I got caught."

"I had no idea."

"I could have gone to jail. Almost did." He folded his arms across his chest in a gesture that reminded me, eerily, of Heather. "By that time I couldn't afford a good lawyer, and my father wouldn't even return my phone calls. But the judge mandated me into a treatment center instead and gave me probation."

Realizing that I'd been holding my breath again, I gently blew it out between my lips. I shook my head as though the movement might help my confused thoughts and feelings to settle into place.

"Something happened at the treatment center that changed things for you?" I slid the salt and pepper shakers an inch to the left, moving them closer to each other, then farther apart. I adjusted the napkin on my lap.

He nodded. By then our fish was in front of us, growing cold. "I'm not going to try to explain it," he said, "because I don't understand it myself. But I was forced to face myself there, every day. I was called arrogant. And I was, much as I didn't want to admit it. I wasn't allowed to hide behind a pseudointellectual facade. I wanted to walk out, but the alternative was prison. The treatment was going to cure me or kill me. It cured me."

"Apparently." I smiled at him.

"One day during group therapy, I broke down and cried, and it felt like I'd never stop crying." He ran the fingers of both hands through his hair, combing it back, holding his head for a moment as though to steady it. "Somewhere along the way I'd learned how to feel. And that's what works with the kids I treat."

"What happened when you got out?"

"I became a drug and alcohol counselor. I got some scholarship help with recommendations from my sponsors at the treatment center. I started working on the outline for my book while I was treating substance abusers. As I got more experience, I expanded the material. Eventually I was able to go on to get my PhD. The material that became my book was developed for my thesis." He glanced at his watch. "Coffee?"

We ordered, cappuccino for me and espresso for him.

"So that's my story," he said, rubbing lemon peel on the rim of his espresso cup.

"Wait. You have to bring me up to date. Are you married?"

"I was. Briefly. While I was doing the drug counseling. It didn't work out."

"Were there children?"

"No kids, and that's my greatest regret. I would have liked to have had a son or daughter while I was young. I had an old father. I didn't want to be one. Oh well." He spread his hands out and shrugged. He signaled Betsy for the check. "Nobody gets everything they want. And I've been lucky. I should be dead now, the way I was going for a while." His smile radiated acceptance and serenity.

"Excuse me for just a minute." I stood and aimed myself toward the restroom. Once there, I sank into the small upholstered chair near the makeup mirror and dropped my head onto my knees. I felt my secret turn over in my belly, where once I'd carried the child Larry longed for. Hot tears, which had been threatening, finally spilled. I sat for several minutes until my eyes had dried. I splashed water on my face, applied fresh lipstick, and returned to the table.

When the check arrived, Larry said, "I'll see you home."

"Not necessary. Your hotel's just a couple of blocks away. I live way out of your way. Hail me a cab." I was glad he didn't protest. We stood together on Columbus Avenue, waiting for my taxi.

"It was really good to see you," he said. "To catch up on your life. I enjoyed the evening."

"Me too." A Yellow Cab swerved to the curb. I slid into the back seat. "Good luck with Heather," I said as Larry closed the door.

"Thanks. I'll be in touch." The cab moved out into the thinning traffic heading downtown. I leaned my head back against the cracked and weathered vinyl, closed my eyes, and let out a deep and shuddery sigh.

CHAPTER
10

A few weeks later, I was sitting on a hard wooden bleacher, an arm loosely around Mitch's shoulder, watching Ben skate energetically over the hockey field. This was my reality, the stocky towhead waving as he grinned at me and his twin sitting next to me, face smeared with mustard. In front of us, Dan Miller leapt to his feet. "That's my boy Scotty!" he shouted. At the sound of the proud father's voice, the noisy arena faded, and it was Larry whose face I saw clearly, Larry who had longed for a child. He might have been a beaming father praising his daughter for her starring role in the school play. I imagined his blue eyes flashing with pleasure and pride.

The crowd cheered. Mitch, next to me, shouted, "Awesome, Ben!" I looked up in time to see Ben acknowledging shouts and cheers from the crowd. Damn! I missed it! He'd made a goal while I daydreamed.

I thought of Larry again as I walked home briskly on a clear night in mid-December. My mittened hands were stuffed in my pockets. I lifted my face, enjoying the feel of crisp air against my cheeks. It had been a good day. A couple who'd been about to separate when they first came to me had reconciled, and this had been their final appointment.

"We're going to have a baby," Melissa had announced.

"We're thinking of naming her Rachel if it's a girl," Dave had added. "After all, if it wasn't for you, there'd be no baby. Hell, there'd be no marriage." He was puffed up with the image of himself as Dad. Remembering, I smiled. And then I heard the echo of Larry's words:

"Mostly, I'm sorry we didn't have a child."

Oh, Larry, what would you say if you knew you had a daughter— if you knew she sat in your office every week and told you her secrets? I wish I could tell you. But how can I? Sixteen years lost to you in the life of the child you wanted so much. I can never tell you.

Stop it! I can't keep doing this to myself. I'll go crazy! I picked up my pace and walked on.

I had a dinner date with Alan Cook as the holidays approached. Alan was a writer I'd met more than a year before. He'd been playing tennis while I was watching Ben's lesson on the next court. He'd come by to tell me that he was impressed by Ben's natural form. We'd chatted for a while and exchanged numbers, and we'd been dating sporadically ever since. When Alan was struggling with a plot transition, he didn't call me. "I won't inflict myself on you when I'm preoccupied," he told me. But at other times he was a good companion. We enjoyed the same books and plays; we both liked sushi and great pasta; and when we made love, he was gentle and considerate. Between dates I rarely thought about him.

At dinner that night, Alan asked, "So what do you think, Rachel? Will the new plot twist work?" *Oh my God, I didn't hear a word he said.* In my reverie Larry was telling me that Heather thinks of me as the Good Mother.

"I'm *so* sorry, Alan. My mind wandered for a minute. I'm working with this really depressed young woman—"

He put up a hand, cutting off my fabricated excuse. "It's okay. I was wondering if you thought it rang true that Suzanne could forgive Peter after he betrayed her so badly."

"You can make it believable. You're such a good writer." I reached out and squeezed his hand, forcing myself to focus on Alan and his plans for the novel he would write after this one.

After dinner he gave me a playful squeeze. "My place?"

I hesitated. I imagined myself lying naked on Alan's dark brown suede comforter, but the face that hovered over mine was Larry's. When had I begun to think of him that way? It had been all about Heather. When had it changed?

"Would you mind terribly taking me home? It was a lovely evening, but I guess I'm just tired."

"Sure." Alan patted my hand and released it. I was grateful for the ease I felt in this relationship. He seemed genuinely okay with an abbreviated, asexual evening.

"Thanks for understanding," I said.

He kissed me lightly at the entrance to my building. "No problem. I'll call you."

That night I lay in bed, fighting against the image of myself in Larry's arms. The boy he'd been merged with the man he'd become, and my body grew warm as I remembered his passion and attributed it to the handsome psychologist who'd sat opposite me and grasped my hand. *No. I have to stop this!* I threw off the cover and sat up. Larry was history, not current events. *We have a professional friendship. This can never work. I have a secret I can't share. It would always be there, coming between us. Just forget about it!* I flipped my pillow to the cool side, plumped it up, and stretched out again.

The night passed slowly. I'd reach the precipice of sleep when a jolt of sexual longing would surge through me, rousing me and leaving me restless and uncomfortable. Larry, I recalled as I sat at the kitchen table at 4:00 a.m., had been tensely wired, all heat and light and hungry, raw sensation. How would he be today? The serene, self-possessed man would be gentler but would still possess knowledge of my sensual core and how to awaken it. *It wouldn't take much,* I thought with a weary chuckle. *I'm turned on, and he's not even here. Not in person anyway.*

The next day I shook off the lethargy of a sleepless night and took Ben and Mitch to their favorite skating rink. Ben was the stronger, faster skater, but Mitch had grace and form. They both loved the sport. I sat on the bleachers, turning pages of the *New York Times Book Review.*

Larry's book had just come out in paperback and had earned a paragraph in the New and Noteworthy section. "A sensitive and loving approach," it said, "to guiding your child through the pitfalls of the teen years. Dr. Tobin brings the voice of reason to an emotionally draining challenge."

I should call and congratulate him. I looked up to see Ben reaching down to pull Mitch, who'd fallen, back up to his feet. They skated off together. I smiled and waved. Before last night I wouldn't have hesitated to call Larry. "I saw the mention in the *Times*," I'd tell him. "I'm sure the book will go right to the top." But now the sleepless night and my fantasy of his hands on my body was fresh. *Keep your distance. You don't want to go there.*

I felt as if I'd conjured him up when Jan buzzed me the next day. "Dr. Tobin is on the phone. Do you want to speak with him?"

"Sure." I punched the blinking light on my phone.

"Larry! You must have read my mind. I wanted to call and congratulate you on the 'new and noteworthy' mention."

"Thanks. I was pleased. Want to celebrate with me? I'm in New York."

My mind said no, but my mind was not the operative force.

"I'd love it. What time?"

"A little on the late side, I'm afraid. About eight o'clock. Let me pick you up at home." This time I hesitated, drumming my fingers on the wooden desk. He didn't mention Heather. This was a date. There was a faint buzzer going off somewhere in the back of my consciousness. I squeezed the sides of my temple together and ignored the warning.

"Fine. You'll get a chance to meet the boys." After giving him my address and home phone number, I hung up the phone and shook my head. I pulled my curls back from my face and held them at the crown of my head as if to make a ponytail, letting the hair fall back to my shoulders. From the time I learned that Heather was my daughter, I hadn't made a single decision that I could deem wise or rational. I consistently overruled the sensible thing in favor of instinctive desire and need. I was like an intermediate skier who has taken a wrong turn and is suddenly careening down an expert slope, exhilarated and terrified—and totally out of control.

I answered the doorbell at 8:00. I'd chosen a cashmere dress of the softest sea-foam green. I'd looped a couple of gold chains around my neck and attached my diamond stud earrings. I had stood an extra minute in front of my full-length mirror, satisfied that I had remained slender and that my body still looked much as he would have remembered. My mouth was dry, my hands, uncharacteristically cold. It wasn't difficult to catch his look of appreciation as I welcomed him.

"Come in, Larry. Let me take your coat." Mitch and Ben, in pajamas and robes, were fresh from their bath. They looked up from the TV screen.

"Boys, I'd like you to meet an old friend, Dr. Tobin. Larry, these are my sons, Benjamin and Mitchell."

Larry smiled at my formal etiquette, so obviously a camouflage for my nervousness. He walked to the front of the couch and offered his hand to each boy in turn. Following my lead, he said, "How do you do, boys? Pleased to meet you."

Ben sized him up with a long, slow scrutiny. "You knew my mom before now."

"Yep. When we were both much younger." Larry was relaxed and cheerful.

"So how come this is the first time you're here?"

"Ben!"

Larry put up a hand to stop me. "It's okay. Good question," he said, smiling down at the boy. "We live in different cities," he explained. "I'm from Washington. Your mom and I kind of lost touch with each other. It's good to see her again. Are you the hockey player?"

"Right. In winter. I play Little League ball in the summer. Do you like baseball?"

"I'm a fanatic."

"Maybe we could go to a game sometime," Ben ventured. Larry had passed some kind of test.

"That would be great. And you're the pianist," Larry said to Mitch. "I hope you'll play something for me."

I glanced at my watch. "We haven't got time right now. We have to get going."

"Do you like Chopin?" Mitch asked.

"My favorite."

"Okay, next time."

"Gotta go. Nice meeting you, guys," Larry said.

"Right. See ya." Ben had turned his attention back to the TV.

"Bye," Mitch added.

As Larry eased my coat over my shoulders, he glanced at a

photograph on the wall unit, surrounded by books. "It's amazing how much the boys look like their dad. They're nice kids. I'll bet you're proud of them."

"They're everything to me."

Mrs. Marcus came in from the kitchen, untying her apron.

"Larry, meet our guardian angel, Molly Marcus. None of us could make it without her." She made a dismissive gesture.

"You'd be fine. Have a good time." Turning to the twins, she said, "Okay, boys, bedtime."

In the elevator I turned up my collar and pulled on the creamy leather gloves Jan had given me for Christmas. As we stepped out into the cold, a cab pulled up and Larry settled me inside, leaning forward to give the driver the name and address of a well-known seafood restaurant in the Village.

"I'm sure Neil would have been a great dad," he said. "But that's not always the case. Remember my father? His bitterness poisoned my soul. I used to think it would have been so much better if it were just my mother and me."

"I do remember him. I can see him sitting in that chair in front of the TV with an angry look on his face. I thought he was mad at me."

"He wasn't. He wasn't mad at me either. It took me years to figure it out, and more years to forgive him. His parents didn't know how to show their love, and neither did he. His scars never healed, and he left me with quite a few of my own."

"Speaking of parenting," I said, hoping the segue seemed natural, "how's Heather Brody doing?"

"I've scaled her back to once every other week. She's made some positive moves. She's found a group of friends who seem to have some balance—not too brainy, but not self-destructive." The cab pulled up in front of the restaurant. A few minutes passed while we entered, checked our coats, and settled in at our table. Larry picked up the conversation seamlessly.

"Heather seems to be making it at this school. First-quarter marks are due in a couple of weeks, and she doesn't think she's failing anything."

We gave our orders. Both of us decided on the sea bass prepared in parchment.

"How about the parents?" I asked when the waiter had disappeared. "I'm sure you've discovered they can be tough."

"Oh yes. They're putting forth some effort, but it's hard for them. Especially when some social obligation conflicts with a need of Heather's. 'You have to understand, Doctor,' Stephanie told me on the phone last week, 'it's very important that we establish ourselves in this new area. That takes effort. Surely my daughter is old enough to understand.'"

I smiled at Larry's ability to capture Stephanie's nuances and cadence. "And does Heather understand?"

"You know Heather. Her first inclination is to put the worst possible face on anything. 'She couldn't care less about me. Well, fine, screw her too.'"

Thank you, Grandpa Tobin. Here we were, Larry and I, sitting in a lovely romantic place discussing the trials and tribulations of our daughter's teenage years. Only we weren't raising her, and Larry had no idea that he was her father. *Oh God, what a minefield. We could all be blown up if I take a single misstep.*

Our food arrived. Looking down at my plate, I touched the base of my throat, where my pulse felt rapid and fluttery. I doubted that I could swallow. I cleared my throat.

"She's got such a tough exterior," I said, "but she's so vulnerable. Push everyone away, and then you can't get hurt."

"That's true, of course. But her anger doesn't last as long and doesn't seem so bitter. I think she's starting to let her guard down a little. She's beginning to realize that she can take some risks and survive."

"I wish I could have worked with her a little longer. You should have seen her when she came in for her last appointment. She was going to the theater with her parents. She looked like a cover girl for *Seventeen*. What a change!"

"Well, she responded to you. This move has been hard for her, but she's managing. I think you can take a lot of credit for that."

At last we changed the subject, speaking at some length about a van Gogh exhibit that was touring the United States. I'd seen it at the MoMA, and Larry at the Hirshhorn.

We lingered over coffee until I noticed the time. "It's late," I said.

"I know." Larry stood and helped me up. "We'll both be bleary-eyed tomorrow."

"It was worth it. I had a lovely evening." A cab pulled up as we emerged from the restaurant. *This is unreal,* I thought in the taxi. As we approached the Washington Square Arch, Larry asked me if I'd like to walk the last few blocks.

"Good idea." It was cold but not windy, and there was a full moon. Larry reached for my hand, snug in its leather glove.

"There was a time," he said, "when this was my vision of the future, you and I, at the age we are now, walking hand and hand together."

"I know. Once I thought so too. My grandmother would say, 'Man plans and God laughs.'"

"I've learned the hard way to be grateful for each day. Right now I'm grateful for this moment."

"Me too. It's been a lovely evening, Larry." We reached my building, and he rode up the elevator with me. Outside my door he took my shoulders and drew me into a hug. We stood for a long moment, embracing through our coats. He held me against his chest, and I put my arms around him. He bent his head and gave me a light kiss.

"Good night, Rachel." As I turned my key in the lock and stood in my doorway, he waved to me from the elevator.

I had a powerful need to talk to Annie. It was still early enough in LA. Kicking off my shoes, I stretched out on top of my flowered comforter and reached for the bedside phone.

"I've been out with Larry," I told her. "This is the second time. The first wasn't really a date, but I think this one was."

"You couldn't resist finding out what happened to him, I suppose." I knew she was suppressing an urge to tell me I was nuts.

"It's an amazing story. And he really has changed. He's as totally transformed as anyone I've ever known."

"And how did he accomplish this miracle?" It was probably just as well that I couldn't see her face.

"He had a drug addiction. It's a really long story, but in recovering from that, he learned a lot about himself, and he turned himself inside out. And it's not phony."

"Honey, you're not getting involved, are you?"

"It feels right being with him. We had a great evening tonight. But I can't get carried away, because of Heather. Even if I wanted to carry this further, I can't. I can never tell him the truth. Annie, he told me how much he regrets not having a child. He'd never forgive me for keeping her a secret, for letting strangers raise her." I struggled not to burst into tears. Annie picked up on the quaver in my voice.

"Rachel, I'm afraid you're going to let yourself get hurt again. It's great that he seems to have changed so much, but I remember what he was like when he was angry. So cold, distant, unapproachable. Did all that just go away? I don't think so."

"I know. I know. That's what I keep telling myself. I've been off-the-wall lately, ever since I found out who Heather is. Y'know, Annie, I'm pretty good at helping my clients reconnect with their brains when they do crazy, impulsive things. But I can't seem to do it for myself."

"Probably because all this brings back the strongest feelings you've ever had. Breaking up with Larry, giving up your baby. You're reliving all of it. Just be careful, honey. It would be much easier for you if you could just walk away."

"I know. And I'm trying."

"I love you, baby."

"Me too you. Good night."

CHAPTER

11

"I took a chance you'd be free." It was a bitter January afternoon. Jan had called in sick with the flu. Heather stood framed in my doorway, her large black leather bag slung over a frail shoulder. She had no appointment. I jumped out of my seat to greet her, sending my chair rolling back against the wall.

"Come in. It's good to see you." I masked a qualm of concern. Heather was heavily made up with dark eyeliner top and bottom and too much blush. Her jeans, tucked into tan suede boots, were skintight, and her pink sweater was cut too low, hugging her body like a lover. She settled into the couch, throwing a leg casually over the arm.

"So, how've you been?" she asked. She wasn't in the client role now—more like the reverse.

"I'm fine, Heather. And you?"

"Good, really good. Things are working out, Rachel. Washington's not so bad."

"What brings you to the city?" I glanced down, checking to make certain that the thumping of my heart was not visible beneath my shirt.

"I'm still off school, and Dad had to fly in for the day. He had the company jet. I asked if I could catch a ride, and he said sure. I told him I had things to do. And I did."

"Such as?"

"Oh, catching up with some old friends?"

"You mean Frank?"

"Of course. I really missed him." That explained the clothes and the makeup.

"Have you seen him yet?"

"Yeah. We had lunch. My treat. We went to the Hard Rock."

I monitored myself, determined not to let concern or disapproval creep into my voice. "And how is he?"

"Messed up as usual. He's on probation, and if he slips up, he's a goner. He's eighteen now, you know, so he's looking at the slammer if he screws up."

"How does that make you feel?"

"Crappy. Hey, you're being the doc now. I know the signs. This is a social call, y'know? I've got a shrink back home."

I permitted myself a smile. "Caught me. Force of habit, I guess. Did you call your friend Chrissie?"

"Not this trip. Maybe next time. Anyway, I just wanted to say hi and thanks. You're the other friend I wanted to see."

"I'm glad you did. And you're very welcome. When are you going back?"

"I'm taking a cab to LaGuardia from here. Which reminds me— can I use the john?"

"Of course." I walked with her out to Jan's desk and gave her the key to the women's room. "You know where it is. Come say goodbye before you leave."

I returned to my desk and sat, fingers together steeple fashion, resting my forehead against the tips. Intuition told me that Heather was troubled. But she was right. *I have no business involving myself again as her therapist. I've done my part, and now she's Larry's client.* What I truly wanted, of course, was to involve myself as her mother. And that wasn't going to happen.

Heather came back, swinging the key on its chain from her index finger. In the few minutes she was gone, she'd transformed herself into a fresh-faced, wholesome teenager. The heavy makeup was gone, replaced by tones of peach and pink lightly and deftly applied. In place of the revealing sweater was a simple crew neck, charcoal gray, and a short strand of pearls. The jeans were the same, but the sweater covered more of them.

"Ta-*da*," she announced, throwing her arms wide and delivering a little bow. "I'm off to meet my daddy."

"Quick-change artist, I see." My tone was neutral.

"Yep. No need to get Pops all worked up. He thinks I went shopping with a girlfriend."

Coming out from behind the desk, I held out my arms. Heather allowed herself to be lightly embraced.

"I'm really glad you stopped by. It's good to see you. And it gives me a chance to wish you happy birthday. Just a few days from now, right?"

"I can't believe you remembered. Wow! Yeah, well, thanks. Bye." Heather hoisted the large black leather bag and was gone.

I had forty minutes until my five o'clock client was due. My paperwork was piled on the corner of my desk—case notes to write and insurance forms to fill out, the bane of my professional life. I didn't even make a dent. Instead I stared into space, mentally writing and discarding scenarios in which I revealed myself as Heather's mother. *I'm not her therapist anymore. Maybe I could tell the parents and ask permission to tell Heather. No, that would never work. She's not ready to hear it, and anyway, Larry would find out. It would be a total mess.*

The image of the nurse taking my little Julie out of my arms and carrying her out of my life came back, as it did often, with the vividness of a much more recent incident. Once again the baby's blue eyes seemed to stare at my face before the door closed and she was gone.

Maybe I could have a hypothetical conversation with Heather. "What if your biological mother wanted to meet you?" I could ask her. No, I have no right to do that. Let it go, Rachel. I glanced at my watch. *Enough! My next client will be here any minute.*

Ben and Mitch were exuberant and loaded with boy power when they greeted me that evening. I hugged each of them a little more tightly than usual. I rested my cheek on Mitch's head, breathing in the scent of his hair.

"I love you guys. I hope you know that."

"What's the matter, Mom?" Mitch stepped out of the hug and studied my face. I turned up the corners of my mouth.

"Not a thing. God, it's good to be home with my kids." Ben threw his arms around me and squeezed hard. "So what's for dinner?"

"Aunt Mol made burgers and fries. We waited for you."

The evening passed with the twins outshouting each other as they described a playground brawl involving their friend Bobby. I just listened, which was all that was required of me. Later we did homework together. Then I stretched my imagination for yet another chapter at bedtime.

It was almost 10:00 p.m. when the phone rang. I was sipping spearmint tea and catching up on the morning's *New York Times*.

"Hi." Larry's deep voice made the single word seem like a heavy drop of warm honey.

"Hi yourself. How've you been?"

"Good. Incredibly busy, but good. Listen, I have a question. Do you ever get down to Washington?"

"Rarely. Why?"

"I'd love to show you the town, and I have tickets for the symphony in three weeks."

"It sounds wonderful. And it's so nice that you'd ask me. But I don't know. It's difficult with the boys and everything. We have so little time together."

"Why don't you think about it? We have a little time to decide. I'll check with you in a few days."

"Okay. We'll see. It's a lovely invitation."

"So, how's everything?"

I spoke before I had a chance to think. "I had a visit from Heather today. Unexpected. She just waltzed into my office and curled up for a chat."

"Interesting. You really made an impact on her."

"I guess I did. But I got a little worried. She was dressed the way she used to, before you met her: skintight jeans and sweater, too much makeup. And she let me know she'd been with her boyfriend, the kid she calls the Frankster. I have no doubt she spent the afternoon in bed with him."

"Sounds like she needed to touch base with her old support systems. Him. You."

"Some support system. Him, I mean. Larry, you know that boy can destroy her."

"Whoa, Rachel. You may have lost a little perspective here."

I stopped myself. I should never have said anything. I was as transparent as a glass of water.

"You're right. I guess she really got to me. I do worry about her."

"Well, you know, I think we've got to trust Heather's basic instincts." Larry's voice was soothing. "She'll have some slips. We all do. But if we panic, we're not handling it much better than her parents, you know?"

"I do know. And thanks, Larry. It was good to talk to you. I guess I thought you should know about this. But really, it was more fear on my part, and you've helped me deal with it."

"Good. I'm glad. And you'll think about coming down to DC?"

"I will. And thanks again."

My tea had grown cold in its mug, but I sipped it anyway, staring into space. I struggled against the knowledge of how much I wanted to go to Washington, and then I stopped struggling and acknowledged it. I tried to block my recognition of my growing feelings for Larry Tobin, and then I stopped blocking them.

Okay, Rache, so you're totally bowled over by how special he is. I finished the last few drops of tea and stared into my empty mug as though the dregs might provide an answer to my turmoil. *So he soothes you and comforts you and you want to fall into his arms. You're not going to do it, but it's okay to feel it. He really is an incredible person.*

I rinsed my mug and left it on the drainboard. I looked in on the twins, pulling up their covers and giving each one a light kiss on the top of his blond head. Entering the bathroom, I stripped off my sweater and slacks and adjusted the shower, wanting it as steamy as I could stand it.

It would be so wonderful to go to Washington. The water sluiced between my breasts. I watched it swirl down the drain. *Forget it. You're going to do the only thing you can do. Get some distance. Keep this relationship professional.* I toweled myself dry and chose my coziest pink flannel pajamas.

Warm under my down comforter, I flipped channels with the TV remote. I wanted *Law and Order* or *CSI* or *Bones*. On any given night I could lose myself in the distraction of fictional murder. Tonight there were only reruns of the repeats. Giving up, I turned off the TV and shut off the light. As I waited for sleep, I mentally packed my sexiest nightgown in the garment bag I would take to Washington.

CHAPTER
12

The Acela sped south. I sat with an unread book open on my lap, remembering my goodbye to the boys that morning as they left for school. We'd shared bear hugs. "See you Sunday night," I promised as they entered the elevator. I'd rarely left them overnight, and then only for a professional conference. I rolled my shoulders forward as a chill of guilt shot through my chest. Crossing and uncrossing my legs, I imagined Larry greeting me at Union Station. Warmth replaced discomfort. I envisioned the smile of greeting and the pleasure that would glow in his eyes and brighten his face. I leaned back and allowed myself to enjoy the moment. *You're asking for trouble.* "Oh shut up," I said aloud. Three people in neighboring rows turned to look at me.

Molly Marcus had waved me off earlier. "We'll be just fine," she assured me. She'd baked chocolate chip cookies; the seductive smell permeated the apartment. The boys would be distracted by sweets, games, and a visit from Billy next door, who was invited for a sleepover. The next two days were mine.

I'm going to hear the symphony. I'm going to have a grown-up weekend. In my luggage, side by side, were flannel and silk, jeans and a cocktail suit. I was prepared for anything. I was prepared for nothing.

The sound of the train on the tracks mesmerizing me, I dozed. I hadn't been sleeping well. Tea at 2:00 a.m. was becoming almost a ritual. Anticipation vied with anxiety whenever I began to examine the decisions I'd made—the decisions I was continuing to make. *If I dig this hole any deeper, I'll be in China,* I'd thought the night before, warming my hands on my teacup, imagining the following day. Now Amtrak was delivering me, with soothing sounds and alarming speed, headlong into the weekend.

An hour later a conductor offered his hand as I swung down from the train at Union Station. Fast-moving crowds surged around me. I pulled up the handle on my wheeled bag and scanned the platform. *So many people, and everyone's in a hurry.* Then I felt a strong, steady hand at my elbow.

"You made it!" I looked up to find those kind eyes smiling down at me, their corners crinkling with pleasure. Larry took my hand and reached for my bag. He led the way, and soon we were in a warm taxi. He leaned forward.

"Ritz-Carlton," he instructed the driver. Then he draped his arm loosely around my shoulders. I turned and smiled at him.

"I'm glad you came," he said. "It's going to be a great weekend."

"I'm glad I'm here." Anxiety, so constant a presence that it had felt like part of my body, slipped away as though I were shedding a heavy, uncomfortable coat. After all, there was no turning back now. The cab inched forward into the stream of traffic.

A vase of pink and white roses sat on the bureau in the comfortable suite Larry had reserved. The attached note read, "Welcome to Washington. Larry."

"They're beautiful." I buried my face for a moment in the soft petals. "This was so thoughtful of you."

"Glad you like them. I tried to remember. It's been a while, you know. It was pink and white, right?"

"Absolutely. Was and still is. I'm impressed. And very pleased."

"We have an eight o'clock reservation for dinner. There's time for a drink if you'd like."

"That would be great."

"I planned a quiet dinner for the two of us tonight," he said as I settled into a comfortable banquette in the cocktail lounge of the hotel. "I thought we'd see some sights together tomorrow, and in the evening we have the concert."

"I'm really looking forward to it. I haven't been to a concert in ages."

"I'm looking forward to the entire weekend. I've been remembering how it was when we were together. Remember when we'd drive up to the Catskills and hike for the day? We'd pack lunch and just enjoy the outdoors and each other."

"I remember. Those times were so—what's the right word? Pure. Blue sky, clean air. We didn't fight then."

"It's as close to happy as I can remember being back then. When the bitterness wore off and I thought of our time together, I pictured us up there in the mountains with our backpacks."

We interrupted our conversation to listen to the poignant music of *Phantom of the Opera* playing in the background. I leaned back, stretched my legs, and studied Larry. His profile remained unchanged, except that his hairline had crept back a bit, exposing two parallel horizontal lines etched into his brow. High-hats in the ceiling accented the silver strands of hair that glinted among the dark ones. His nose was slim and straight. When I focused on his lips, I remembered how they had once felt. My own throbbed in response.

As though reading my mind, he leaned over and said, "At this moment you look exactly like the sixteen-year-old girl I fell in love with."

"Must be the lighting. A little magic. Do you suppose everyone in here is twenty years older than they look?"

"I can't speak for anyone else, but you look terrific. I used to imagine what it might be like, you and I meeting again later in life. I don't think I ever really got over you, Rachel." Meeting his gaze, I struggled for a response. I laid a hand softly over his.

"There's something about one's first love," I finally said.

"I think it was more than that."

"Perhaps. But we've traveled such a long road since then. Neither one of us is the same anymore. My life now is all about raising my children."

"What a challenge, raising two boys without a dad."

"You can say that again! But they're such good kids. Neil would be very proud of them."

"You think of him often." It was a statement.

"Every day. I remember the lovely times we had together. But mostly I think of him in connection with Mitch and Ben, how like him they are. Ben has his energy, his athletic ability, his sense of humor. And Mitch has his logic, his rationality, his good common sense and his talent with words. And of course they're the image of him. So, yes, Neil is always present."

"That's what's been missing for me, Rachel. I had warm feelings for my wife when we married. I thought I was in love with her, and she thought the same, I'm sure. But what we shared was fondness, a certain sexual attraction, and respect. At the end, the fondness and respect had largely disappeared."

"That's really sad, Larry."

"Well, I don't dwell on it. At least not often."

Our empty glasses sat in front of us. We had declined refills. Larry picked up the check, put down some bills, and held my chair for me. "I think you should go up and get some rest." He walked me to the elevator. "See you at 7:45," he said, squeezing my hand.

Upstairs, I slipped out of my jeans and sweater and lay down on top of the quilted spread. I wiggled my toes and rested my arms under two of the pillows. *How easy he is to talk to. How understanding he's become. How kind and open and giving. Maybe I saw a hint of this man in the boy he was back then. Maybe that's why I was attracted to him.* It was hard to keep my eyes open.

The red numbers on the clock radio showed 6:50 when I woke up. A corner lamp shed the only light, glazing the room gold. I hadn't meant to fall asleep. Now I'd have to rush. I unpacked, hanging a dress and my slacks. I lifted a nightgown carefully from its nest of tissue. It was pencil-thin midnight black, the softest silk I'd ever felt. It was slit up one side to the hip. I'd bought it two weeks ago, even while still fooling myself into believing I might not make this trip. The saleswoman had smiled as she folded the tissue around the delicate fabric. "It's lovely," she told me, "and you have the perfect figure for it."

"I hope so. I really hope so." I slid the gown into the top drawer of the bureau alongside a small pile of underclothes. I had also brought floral pajamas and my reliable pink flannel nightie. I was prepared for anything.

Sitting on the edge of the bed, I phoned home, knowing that the boys would be finished with dinner. Ben ran to my room while Mitch stayed in the kitchen so that I could talk to both of them at once. They regaled me with the day's events.

"How's Washington, Mom?" Mitch asked.

"Great! We have to come here together soon. There are so many things to see."

"Have fun, Mom," Ben chimed in. "Are you going to call again?"

"Of course, silly. Around this time tomorrow." I blew and received a dozen kisses before replacing the receiver. I showered, put on makeup, and dressed in the red knit two-piece outfit I'd selected for this first evening. Red always gave me an extra glow. My hair was longer than it had been when I first saw Larry in November, the curls falling softly to my shoulders. I fastened one side with a gold comb, leaving the other side loose. Once I sprayed Trésor behind my ears, I was ready.

Larry called from the lobby a few minutes later. "Shall I come up?"

"No, I'm all ready. I'm coming down." He took my arm as I stepped out of the elevator.

The Sequoia restaurant overlooked the Potomac with a stunning view of the Kennedy Center. The crab cakes were as good as any I'd ever had. I felt myself tingle with excitement and anticipation.

"I haven't been to Washington for years," I said.

"Well, wait until you see what you've been missing. I'm surprised you never came to a clinical conference here."

"There was always some reason I couldn't make it. Primarily Ben and Mitch. Now that they're a little older, I feel better about leaving. I did take them to one conference a couple of years ago. It was on Cape Cod, and they had babysitting arrangements. The kids loved it."

"I go to that conference every year. It must have been a different week."

"That's when I first saw your name on a program, and I dismissed it. In my wildest imaginings I didn't think it could be you." He smiled his understanding. I noticed the twinkle in his eye, the easy humor that seemed to rise effortlessly, as though he were saying, *Isn't it fantastic that things worked out this way?* I grinned back at him. "I'm glad I was wrong," I admitted.

We slipped into shoptalk and discovered that we shared a great deal of our professional philosophy. Neither of us believed in keeping clients in treatment for extended periods. "My clients are relieved to learn that they won't be coming forever," he said.

"And I've found that clients do more work when they know they have a limited time. We must have read the same books." I dipped a crust of French bread into a bit of sauce left on my plate.

Larry reached for my hand. "It's so good to have you here. I feel as though the years have rolled away. I'm twenty again and I'm out with the prettiest girl on campus."

"This book was supposed to be closed forever," I said. "Marriage, children—you weren't supposed to be in my life."

"Some books just beg to be reread. Hey, wanna share a crème brûlée?"

I was aware of the subtle intimacy of our two spoons slicing through the creamy dessert. I could tell that he felt it too. It was a married gesture, sharing dessert.

"Remember the time I saved enough to buy twofers for Broadway?" Larry said suddenly. "We saw *Les Mis* and went to Lindy's for dessert."

"That cheesecake!" I started to laugh.

"I wanted to be a big shot, so I insisted we each have our own."

"They were the most enormous slices of cake I've seen before or since."

"You ate about three bites."

"And I insisted on taking the rest home—for you, of course. I think I embarrassed you to death."

"Probably. I was sensitive enough back then. Doggie bags weren't couth."

"So now we've grown up enough to know we share dessert. Chalk one up to maturity."

We held gloved hands as we waited for a cab.

The hotel doorman bowed his welcome as we exited the taxi and entered the lobby.

"Would you like an after-dinner drink?" Larry asked as we approached the lobby bar.

"I don't think so." I hesitated, feeling the flutter of decision time somewhere in my belly. There was still time, right this minute, to clarify that I was here as a friend, to share pleasant reminiscences and professional camaraderie. I could keep the compartments of my life from overlapping more than they already were. I could play it safe, or I could give in to the intense pull of my attraction to this man, an attraction first felt eighteen years ago. I gazed at the planes of the face I'd once known so well, older now and firm in the promise hinted at long ago. The chin jutted slightly, but what had once seemed aggressive now appeared decisive. There were humor lines around the eyes that had so seldom smiled at me. The hand that held mine felt secure rather than imprisoning.

"Would you like to come up for a while?" I asked.

"Sure." We were the only ones in the elevator. As it sped upward, I could feel my pulse in the tips of my fingers. At the door to the suite, I handed Larry the key.

I dropped my coat on a chair and went to the window, gazing at the unique tableau that was Washington at night. I felt, rather than saw, Larry come to stand behind me.

"It's a beautiful city," I said, turning to look at him. He took my face in both his hands. Holding me with melting gentleness, he bent and kissed my lips. I stood very still, feeling that moving a muscle would destroy the moment. As his kiss lingered, I turned my body into his. He dropped his hands from my face and drew me close. I reached up and felt the muscles of his back beneath the jacket of his suit. I pressed him into me, running my hands up and down the length of him, suddenly more eager for closeness than I'd been in years.

He dropped his lips to the hollow between my throat and my shoulder. "Oh God, Rachel. You feel so good."

"Mm." I struggled with the button of his jacket, and he obliged by shrugging out of it for me. Now it was only the cloth of his fine white shirt that separated me from the warmth of his skin.

His hands moved over the fabric of my suit and then under it. His lips kissed a trail down my throat. Soon his clothing and mine intermingled at our feet, and still we stood at the window, high above the city, stroking and feeling, letting our touch awaken the sensory memories of two young kids ablaze with a passion that knew no reason or limitation.

We couldn't stop touching, even as we found our way to the other room, to the large bed. Light from the living room cast a warm glow and cut a slice across the plane of quilted spread. Larry's thigh was illuminated, as was the curve of my breast. He cradled me with one arm, his hand in the tangle of my curls as he held my head close for his kiss. His other hand traced patterns that were familiar to both of us as he rekindled the fire in special places that I'd almost forgotten I had.

"Remember?" he whispered.

"Oh yes." My fingertips were exploring everywhere. He still had the dimple in his buttock that had fascinated me the first time I'd discovered it. And here was the little nick on his knee from a childhood fall. The thin ray of light illuminated a few silver hairs in the curls on his chest. I kissed him there, lingering to feel the soft brush of his chest hair against my face.

When he moved his hand slowly from my breast to my stomach, to the hidden spot that always trembled when he caressed it, and farther down to the warmth between my thighs, I was enflamed instantly. I groaned softly as he touched me; the waves of passion would not be held back. He held my eyes with his own as I submitted to the most powerful physical sensation I could ever recall. When at last it subsided, his kiss was deep, long, and loving.

I smiled at him, a smile of pleasure and fulfillment. "I feel sixteen again," I said. I rested my hand against his belly. My fingers crept lower. I explored around the base of his erect penis.

"It feels as though we've never been apart."

"I know. Isn't that a little scary?"

"It's wonderful." He turned to lay the length of himself on top of me, supporting his weight on his hands above my head. I moved side to side, feeling his chest against my breasts, his stomach touching mine, his legs and mine pressed together. When he moved to enter me, his hands came down beneath my buttocks and raised me up to meet him. I was ready, and I joined with him in a rhythmic rocking that gathered speed as it gathered heat. I was pure physical being, incapable of thought or feeling other than the increasingly heightened sensations that poured through me, lavalike. The soles of my feet tingled. I raised them up to rub them against the muscles of his calves. I knew that my lips felt swollen, my pulse pounding in them. I turned my head to kiss him, catching his lower lip between my teeth. He responded, drawing his tongue in and out of me, in and out, until I gasped from the intensity of the matching sensations above and below. I knew he would come in the moment before he did so. As his climax began to ebb, mine rolled forward. When the power that held us captive subsided at last, we lay together, arms around each other, wordless. I listened to his heartbeat, as fascinated as though I'd never heard the sound before. He moved his hand over my hair, over my brow. He ran a finger around the outline of my lips, and I drew it into my mouth lazily. Gradually I became aware of the sounds of the city far below us. Through the partly open door I saw a sliver of light in the next room and our clothes in a tumble on the floor. I turned my body into his and threw my arm across his shoulder. I felt his light, dry kiss against my cheek just before I fell asleep.

The fluorescent face of the alarm clock glowed 5:18 a.m. when I opened my eyes. The living room light had been turned off, and the cool linen sheet had been drawn up around my shoulders. At some point during the night Larry had been up, but now he lay beside me on his stomach, one arm under his pillow, the other dangling off the bed. His breathing was slow and rhythmic. In sleep, the lines of his face smoothed out. He looked not much older than the boy I'd known. I felt a wave of tenderness for that unhappy boy and for the excellent man he had become.

Now, in the darkened room, I came face-to-face with my dilemma. I wouldn't walk away from Larry, not if he still wanted me. I wanted him with an urgency I hadn't felt since the early days of my marriage. But my lies and my secret could turn this fledgling happiness to cinders.

I remembered the power of Larry's anger, its scalding intensity. If he knew that I'd given birth to his child and never told him, all his love and tenderness might become seething rage. Surely that knowledge had the power to reawaken his cynicism and fury. And I'd compounded the sin by sending Heather to him, never telling him who she really was. Working with her, he saw how unhappy the girl had been in her adoptive family. He could blame me for everything. He probably would.

I didn't want to lose him now. The risk was too high if I were to tell him the truth. I'd had enough pain and loss. I didn't want to take the chance.

I lifted my head and flipped my pillow over, staring at the crown molding. *But if I don't tell him, it will always stand between us. And if Heather seeks us out when she's older, or if he finds out some other way, it'll be worse.* I ran the fingers of both hands through my hair, spreading it out on the pillow. *Oh God, I don't know what to do.*

Two voices debated inside my head as Larry slept, peaceful and unknowing, at my side.

He's changed. He'll understand how bad things were between us back then and why I did what I did. He'll be shocked, but he won't condemn me. I have to tell him.

My pessimistic side responded: *Maybe he'll understand, but maybe he won't. What's the harm in going on just as I've been doing? Try to forget about it myself, and don't say anything. Larry will stop treating Heather soon. He and I will make a new life together. The subject never has to come up.*

If I'm going to tell him at all, I have to tell him now.

I don't have to tell him at all.

I threw off the cover and headed for the shower. There was no answer to this riddle. I simply didn't know what to do.

The hot needles of water stimulated my skin until the maddening circle of my thoughts was quieted. The force of the shower rained on my head. I massaged shampoo into my hair as if to drive all insoluble dilemmas from my mind forever.

Only when I'd stepped from the shower, wrapped in the fluff of a luxurious terry robe, did I remember the nightgown lying in its tissue paper nest. I smiled at the irony. It had not been missed. Sliding the drawer open quietly, I lifted out the black silk gown, careful not to rustle the paper. I raised my arms and shivered with pleasure as the cool fabric slid down my body, which was still hot from the shower. I rubbed the towel vigorously once more on my damp curls and slipped back into bed. The sun was shedding a pink glow on the drawn curtains when I stretched out beside Larry, pulled up the blanket, and closed my eyes again.

I sensed him looking at me before I opened my eyes. When I did so, I saw him propped on one elbow, smiling down at me. Feeling happiness swell in my chest at the sight of him, I smiled back.

"Good morning," I said.

He reached out and fingered the delicate strap of my nightgown.

"So," he said, his tone mockingly accusing, "you little hussy! You planned all this!"

"Not exactly." I arched and stretched, catlike. "But I did consider the possibility."

"Oh, you did?" He bent and kissed my lips, a cool and lazy kiss. "Well, I must admit, so did I."

I moved into his embrace, and we made languid love, as though we had nothing but time. At one point he whispered close to my ear, "I've missed you." I tightened my embrace. We were content to stroke and explore, to allow the time to stretch until neither of us could hold back, and then to submit to the passion that swept us up and held us captive. As I lay there, some unknown span of time later, my head on his chest, feeling his hand softly caress my hip, I knew that I would not tell him.

CHAPTER
13

We breakfasted in the suite on fresh strawberries, croissants and jam, and dark, rich coffee. I dressed in slacks and a sweater, and then we drove to Larry's Georgetown home so that he could change his clothes.

He lived in a town house, three stories of austere good taste, dark woods, and endless rows of books. His bedroom was on the top floor with an extension that served as an office. A wide rosewood desk faced a large window that looked out onto the street. Across the room a deck hung over a small enclosed garden.

Dark brown carpeting, springy and plush under my loafers, contrasted with white-painted walls. Larry's bed was covered with a simple beige spread. Pillows in browns and beiges lined the solid oak headboard. A special intimacy passed between us as I stood in the doorway and looked into the room where he had slept so many nights alone.

A long, handsome bureau filled most of one wall. A flat-screen TV sat on the left end, facing the bed. Larry opened the top drawer, drew something out, and handed it to me. I recognized it at once. It was a snapshot we'd asked a stranger to take as we hiked in the Catskills the last spring we were together. I remembered that day as a time of rare tranquility. We'd been alone, and Larry had been at his best, free of tension, enjoying having me to himself. We'd wandered off the trail and discovered a secluded grassy cove that seemed to be a million miles from civilization. I was pretty sure I'd become pregnant as the sun was setting that afternoon.

"I'm touched that you kept this all these years."

"It was the happiest I can ever remember being," he said simply. "Then or since." He took the photograph from my hands and placed it gently, almost reverently, on top of the dresser.

He changed clothes quickly, and we headed out to be a couple of tourists. When I confessed that I'd never seen the Newseum, we decided to spend most of our time there. Larry had only been there once, and both of us were fascinated by the exhibits. We sat in a mock newsroom, tried out a teleprompter, and saw the control rooms that orchestrated the news shows. We stood on the long terrace overlooking Pennsylvania Avenue and imagined the famous parades and corteges that had passed by the spot. The day flew.

In the small coffee shop we ordered tea and sandwiches. We were silent for a few minutes, each lost in our thoughts.

"You know," Larry finally said, "when I got your email, I started talking to myself. 'Now Larry,' I said, 'she's got a different last name. She's married. It's been almost seventeen years. Don't get carried away.' But I couldn't help it. I kept thinking, *What if? What if there could be a second chance for us?* I tried not to let myself believe it, but it was there. I couldn't make it stop."

"And I couldn't stop thinking about how I'd hurt you and how much you must have despised me. It was hard sending that email. But I was glad you were going to work with Heather, and I thought, *Maybe enough time has gone by. He's probably married and has forgotten all about me.* I never expected to see our picture in your bureau drawer."

We left the Newseum and took a leisurely walk on the Mall. My small brown leather glove was encompassed in his larger black one. Our arms swung companionably as we walked past the National Archives and the Smithsonian Castle toward the Washington Monument. "It's so impressive," I murmured.

He smiled at me. "It's quite a town." He pushed back the cuff of his glove to glance at his watch. "We'd better be getting back," he continued. "You'll want to rest before dinner."

An hour later, I called Ben and Mitch.

"I miss you, Mom," Ben said.

"When are you coming home?" Mitch asked.

"Tomorrow night. I'll be there to tuck you in. What did you guys do today?"

"Aunt Mol took us to the Museum of Natural History," Ben answered.

"Again?"

"Yep. We saw those giant dinosaur bones again. And we went to the planetarium, and we had lunch in the coffee shop."

"And we went to the park for a little while," Mitch added, "but it was too cold, 'specially for Aunt Mol. We took a taxi home."

"Sounds like a good day."

"It was. Are you having fun too, Mom?"

"Lots of fun. Larry and I went to a museum that's all about how people learn the news. It was really interesting."

Mitch said, "Auntie Mol said we could stay up late tonight. We're going to watch a video and make popcorn and everything."

"Sounds fun. Have a good time, but remember, it's a special treat, not a regular thing."

"We know," they answered in chorus. "Bye, Mom."

As always, talking to the boys put a smile on my face. When Larry called from the lobby, I headed down feeling confident and ready for the evening.

"Something's wrong here," he said when he saw me. "How come I got to be thirty-six and you stayed sixteen?"

I lifted my head to be kissed. The kiss lingered as though neither one of us could break the magnetic attraction of my lips to his.

He pulled away first. His lips clung even as he drew his head back to look at me. "Ready for a great evening?"

"I can't wait."

"There's a little Italian place a couple of blocks from here. Let's get a quick bite." We walked to the neighborhood spot, where the proprietor, who knew Larry, led us to an intimate booth replete with red-and-white checkered cloth and Chianti bottle with a candle dripping wax over its woven holder. We laughed a lot as we shared pasta and salad.

The concert hall was filled to capacity as we slid into our seats. The low hum of hundreds of conversations contained a crackle of anticipation. This was a long-awaited program with guest conductor Michael Tilson Thomas and soloist Nina Postolovskaya. I was especially looking forward to the second half of the concert, when the brilliant Russian pianist would play Rachmaninoff's Second Piano Concerto.

The beautiful hall darkened, the music began, and it soon encompassed us. I settled into it as though it were a blanket of cashmere. I turned off thought and all senses except sight and sound. Barber's magnificent adagio played to all my newly awakened emotions. I was startled by a hot track of tears spilling down my cheeks. Larry reached over to touch my face with his handkerchief.

"It's beautiful, isn't it?" he said as we applauded fiercely, along with the rest of the madly appreciative audience.

"I never realized how beautiful. I guess I'm hearing it differently tonight."

"Me too."

I was enthralled by the grace of the conductor's movements, half hypnotized by the bows of the string section moving as one, lost in a reverie that was half images conjured by the music and half amazement at the reality of sitting here beside Larry. Sooner than I'd expected, we were applauding again, and then standing to exit for the intermission.

Larry took my hand and led me to a couple who were heading our way.

"Rachel Marston, I'd like you to meet my very good friends Sharon and Ed Silverman."

"Nice to meet you." Ed offered his hand. "Wonderful concert, just wonderful! I've been waiting months for this."

"Ed could give up just about everything in his life except his music," Sharon said.

"Not quite everything." Ed ruffled her hair. "And if I were asked, I'd probably keep the kids too."

"But it's obvious that you love this," I said.

"Understatement," Sharon said. I saw the subtle thumbs-up gesture she made to Larry and the broad smile he gave in response. She spotted someone at the far end of the lobby and, pulling Ed in her wake, went to greet an acquaintance. "Back in a minute," she said over her shoulder.

"Dr. Tobin. How are you?" Larry and I turned toward the cultured female voice.

"Mrs. Brody. And Mr. Brody. Nice to see you."

"And Dr. Marston. This *is* a surprise."

"Hello, Mrs. Brody. How are you?"

"Excellent concert, isn't it? Thomas is in fine shape. I spoke with him earlier. At the cocktail reception? The man's busier than ever. What a talent!"

"It sounds like you've made a fine adjustment to Washington," I said.

"It's a wonderful city. I hardly miss New York at all. Except for the shopping, of course. And I fly up once or twice a month for that. It was a good move for us."

"Absolutely." William Brody moved forward to join the conversation. "I'd say we've all come through the move with flying colors."

"I assume that means Heather too?"

"Thanks to Dr. Tobin here. And you too, of course. Naturally she has her ups and downs. But don't we all?"

"It's quite unexpected to see both of you together," William Brody said. "It gives us an opportunity to thank you both at once. Heather appears to be coping much better than she once did. And we're coping better with her."

"Thanks for sharing that," Larry said.

"We're both pleased that she worked so hard and did so well," I added. "The credit is really hers, you know."

"Of course. Well, enjoy the rest of the concert." Stephanie wiggled expertly manicured fingers, and I inclined my head in response.

"What's the story with them?" Sharon had reappeared, curious. "That's Stephanie and Bill Brody, isn't it? They seemed to know both of you."

"They knew Rachel in New York and me here," Larry said. "Interesting coincidence."

"Rather la-di-da, wouldn't you say?" Sharon struck a pose.

"Sometimes," I said, deliberately vague. The lights flickered. We headed back to our seats.

Postolovskaya walked on stage with Tilson Thomas. The applause filled the hall and seemed to go on forever. Finally there was a universal hush as the pianist arranged herself on the piano bench, Thomas raised his baton, and the strains of Rachmaninoff's Second Piano Concerto erased thought. I lost myself in the music and in the awareness of Larry beside me. It wasn't until later that I would dwell on the unique experience of Heather's biological and adoptive parents chatting together while only I knew the reality of how we were all connected.

Sharon invited us to join her and Ed for coffee after the concert, but Larry and I declined at the same moment.

"Why am I not surprised?" Sharon said, a low chuckle in her voice. "Have a good night, you two."

Larry and I became so engrossed in each other's lips and hands in the privacy of the elevator that we weren't aware that the door had opened until it closed and we were returned to the lobby. The elderly gentleman who entered found me giggling and Larry grinning. "Must be an entertaining ride," he commented as he punched in his floor number.

"Most definitely," Larry said, one hand resting on my rear, which he stroked through the thickness of my coat.

It were as if the music had lit a demanding fire in each of us. I felt wanton and insatiable. Sheets and quilt were in our way; we kicked them to the floor to mingle with our clothing. It was a night in which we awoke twice to touch and hold and ignite each other. It was a morning in which we slept while sunlight streamed through the sheer curtains and the Do Not Disturb sign kept the housekeeper from knocking. When we finally smiled at each other, the clock read 10:50.

"Let's go out for brunch," Larry said. "We have to talk."

"And somehow we never seem to talk in here."

He made a phone call and secured a table at the Lafayette in the Hay-Adams Hotel. We went to his town house, where he changed into a turtleneck and sports jacket. It was after twelve when we were seated at the well-known restaurant.

"I don't want you to go back," Larry said. I looked at his earnest face over the rim of my mimosa glass.

"I know. If I had no responsibilities, I'd just stay."

"I watched you walk out of my life once. There's an eighteen-year-old in me who doesn't want to let you out of my sight."

"You know, Larry, we're just getting to know each other again."

He reached for my other hand. "I know you. I've always known you."

"It's been a magical weekend. But real life beckons."

"I want to be part of that real life. We have to see each other again, soon."

"I'd like that. It would be lovely. But you're here, and I have to be in New York, where my boys are—and my work and my life."

He pulled his hands free and folded them across his chest. "So you're saying you might disappear on me again?"

"I don't want that. But it's not going to be easy."

"But it could happen." The look he gave me was so long and penetrating that I couldn't maintain eye contact with him. "I want to lock you up and never let you go," he said.

"Part of me wishes you would. But I have to go back."

"I love you. It's a miracle that you came back into my life." He leaned across the table and kissed me softly.

As we left the restaurant and walked through the lobby of the storied Hay-Adams Hotel, Larry turned to me. "Can we at least talk hypothetically?" he asked.

I smiled. "Sure."

He led me to a sofa in the lobby, opposite the check-in desk. "*If* it works out that we get back together, I may be in a better position to move to New York than you would be to come to Washington," he said. "I'm doing more lecturing and writing and less treatment these days."

"*If* it happens, we'll figure it out." I smiled at him and touched his face.

The lines on his forehead grew closer together as he searched for clues in my eyes. "I feel as if it already happened. Now that there's a possibility that we'll be together, I can't imagine anything else. It's like the past seventeen years never happened."

"I have ten-year-old boys to prove that they happened. And I have to put them first, Larry. You do understand that?"

"I want to spend more time with Ben and Mitch. What are you doing next weekend? I can stay at the Park Lane and we'll dedicate the weekend to the kids."

"Perfect."

Memories of the short, idyllic time with Larry ran through my head like a movie—an X-rated movie—as I settled down for the train ride home. Feeling my face turn hot, I touched my cheek, glancing around to see if any fellow passengers noticed the blushing woman who was smiling at nothing.

I'm alive again! Funny that I hadn't realized what was missing until it showed up. The replay of the incredibly sensual moments was almost as enjoyable as the original had been. I crossed and recrossed my legs, shifting in my seat as I recalled the sensations I'd experienced. I wanted to have those feelings again. Soon.

CHAPTER
14

By the time the taxi pulled up outside my condo, I'd shaken off the spell of the weekend and couldn't wait to feel the boys' arms around my waist and my neck. I called to them as I opened the door of the condo.

"I missed you *so* much," I said, meaning it, as Ben and Mitch assaulted me with their enthusiastic welcome home. I smelled their newly shampooed hair and received wet kisses and a bear hug that nearly knocked me over. They were full of questions.

"Boys, boys," Mrs. Marcus said, "give your poor mother a chance to catch her breath. She only just took her coat off."

"So, Mom," Ben said a short time later after I had finished the nightly chapter and was tucking him in, "this guy Larry, you knew him a long time ago, right? Before you met Dad?"

"Yes, sweetie, long before I met Dad. Once we even thought we might get married."

"So how come you didn't?" Mitch asked from the lower bunk.

"It just didn't work out. I guess there were some things we couldn't agree about. Anyway, I'm glad I married your dad. And I'm glad I have you."

"Is Larry going to be your boyfriend again?" Trust Ben to get right to the point.

"It's possible. We had a really nice time this weekend, and he's coming to New York on Friday so we can spend more time together."

"What about Alan?" Mitch asked. "Isn't he your boyfriend?"

Good question. "Alan's a good friend. I hope he'll always be a good friend. I know you guys like him a lot." This was proving harder than I'd thought. I hadn't realized how accustomed the kids were to the status quo, even Alan with his on-again, off-again role in my life.

"Will you be going to Washington a lot? To see Larry?"

"I'm not sure yet, hon. We'll see. But next week he'll be here, and we'll all have some fun, okay?"

A duet of okays closed the subject.

During the week I daydreamed whenever I could. Frequently my memories brought weakness to my thighs. I'd never been so preoccupied with sensual thoughts. Now there was little else on my mind but the possible changes my life would undergo.

Washington or New York? Moving the family would be monumental. But Larry said it wouldn't be necessary. How would letting Larry into our lives affect the boys? They'd been my sole focus for so long. And Heather—what about Heather? What if she needed him and he wasn't there for her because he was here with me? Could I continue to keep the secret if Larry and I were married? *Wait a minute. You're* way *ahead of yourself, Rache. We're having a fling. Enjoy it and stop thinking so much!*

That was the point at which I always forced my mind back to the present—to my next client or Ben's dental appointment. I couldn't let myself dwell on Heather.

Let it go, Rachel. Just let it go!

"Your eyes are the eyes of a woman in love," Jan serenaded me, off-key, one morning. I laughed in response.

"In like," I amended. "Maybe even in lust. Believe me, I'm not falling off the deep end."

"So who's rushing you? Take your time. And while you're at it, enjoy yourself. You deserve it!" Jan had been with me from the beginning, through Neil's death and the tough times that followed. She knew me well.

"Oh, I intend to enjoy it," I assured her. "Believe me, I intend to enjoy it!"

Surprisingly, my work didn't suffer. I seemed to go into a kind of alpha brain wave state when I was with a client. My concentration was total. During the week I heard, several times, "Great session, Rachel. Thanks so much." It was while traveling to and from the office, or late at night when the boys were in bed, that I allowed myself free rein to remember the weekend and to think of the future. That future was tenuous at best given the huge secret that loomed between us. For now, though, I pushed those thoughts aside and imagined a life with Larry, knowing all the time that my denial was almost as big as the secret itself.

Jan's eyes twinkled when she handed me a message after my last client had left on Friday. "Call me at the Park Lane when you're free—room 1106." She went back to her desk. I punched in the phone number even before she closed the door.

"Hi. I didn't think you'd be here so soon."

"I cut out early. Are you through for the day?"

"Yep. I'm all yours. Yours and the boys'."

"How about joining me here for a drink, and then we'll go get the kids?"

"Be there in fifteen minutes."

"I'm outa here," I told Jan. "Have a good weekend."

"You too," she cooed. As she closed the door behind her, I reached for my purse and headed out. I tapped one impatient foot as I waited for the elevator.

At the hotel, I climbed the stairs to the second-floor bar, adjacent to the hotel's dining room. Larry was waiting.

"It was a long week," he said as we nibbled mixed nuts. It was dark and quiet. Only a few tables were occupied by people engaged in Friday night conversation—businesspeople wrapping up last-minute business before the weekend, a couple of tourists planning the next day's activities.

"I got through it with the help of some very pleasant memories."

"Me too. But we can't live on memories. I want to begin looking forward, not back."

"I hope so." I reached across the tiny table to lay a hand on his arm. A waitress arrived with my gin and tonic and his virgin Bloody Mary.

"I want Ben and Mitch to like me," he said.

"How strange, with your record of working with kids, that you'd worry about that."

"They aren't just kids." He put down his glass and combed his hair back from his forehead with his fingers. "They're your kids. That makes it a whole other ball game."

"I know. If it's any help, you're off to a good start."

"Really? How so?"

"They think you're neat. Your offer to take them to a game didn't hurt."

"Great. Too bad we have to wait until spring."

"I told them about us, that we almost got married once."

"Excellent. The fact that we have some history will reassure them."

"It feels like you're someone brand new in my life."

He leaned toward me and kissed me lightly. "I know." He drained his glass and picked up the check. "Onward! To the boys!" He reached for a shopping bag that he'd placed at the side of his chair.

"What's that?"

"Oh, just a little something for the boys."

Two identical round faces watched from the window as we approached. Ben grinned as he threw open the door for us. Mitch wore a thoughtful expression as though he were searching for something. Larry put the paper bag on the floor of the guest closet and hung up his coat.

Molly had made an old-fashioned dinner straight out of her Eastern European past. There was steaming chicken soup fragrant with dill and rich with noodles and matzo balls bobbing above the golden surface. The roast chicken was plump and brown, and awaited Larry's carving skill. There was noodle pudding, and carrots and peas, and her special cranberry applesauce. She had, with forethought born of experience, roasted several extra drumsticks. Ben and Mitch indulged in old jokes about multilegged chickens, which they found hilarious. Soon they were waving the bones, stripped bare, and fighting over the wishbone, their smiles now shining in rings of grease. Shyness had vanished, and they interrupted each other, vying for Larry's attention as they told him about school, friends, and their activities.

After a dessert of homemade apple pie, a perennial Molly Marcus favorite, Larry pushed back his chair and put both hands on his stomach.

"I can't breathe. That was absolutely delicious." He left the table for a minute and returned with the shopping bag. In no time there was the rustle of gift wrap being torn. The boys held up their presents. Larry had bought Mitch a recorder, and soon he was tooting into it, practicing covering the holes with his fingers and doing a remarkable job of figuring out the instrument. It was the first time he'd ever seen one.

Ben held up a massive book on baseball history with color photos of all the famous players and pages of statistics. He flipped the pages reverently.

"You should be able to find out anything you need to know in there," Larry said.

There was one more package, which had both their names on it. Mitch pulled off the paper and revealed the board game Clue.

"I took a chance. Do you have this one?" Larry was answered with a resounding double no.

"Want to play?"

"Will you teach us?" Mitch never took anything for granted.

"You bet. It's a great game."

Everyone helped clear the table. Larry had the twins' and my rapt attention as he explained the fine points and strategies of Clue. All vestiges of polite guest manners disappeared as the boys settled into the game. "I'm gonna win," Ben announced.

"Not!" Mitch responded. They were teasingly familiar with Larry.

"I bet you bought us this game because you wanted to play it," Ben said.

"You're right," Larry responded easily. It seemed as if he'd been part of the family for years. There was a sense of completeness to this relaxed evening with my children and the man who so obviously wanted to be their father. I didn't glance at the clock until almost 11:00. The game had finally been won, with many gestures of victory and power, by Ben.

"To bed, monsters," I commanded.

"Can we have our chapter, Mom?" Mitch asked. I glanced at Larry.

"I usually tell a story," I explained. "It's a short one."

"By all means. Can I listen in?"

The chorus of "sure"s came from all three of us. Pajamas were donned hastily, and soon I was sitting on Mitch's bed while Larry stood quietly across the room. I resurrected an old Amazon River favorite, deliberately including Neil in the adventure as I always did. Cheers erupted when Daddy saved us from the piranhas. As I climbed off the bunk bed, I gave each boy a kiss on the forehead. Larry spontaneously held out his hand, and both Ben and Mitch shook it.

"You were so wonderful with them." I curled up next to Larry on the couch. "You spoiled them a little, but I forgive you this time."

"You tell a mean adventure story. I'm impressed. Could you tell how nervous I was?"

"I could've sworn you do this every day!"

"Is it too late for you to come to the hotel for a while?"

"Thought you'd never ask." I knocked softly on Mrs. Marcus's door. "I'm going out for a while. The boys are asleep."

"No problem. Have fun, and don't worry. I'm here."

At the hotel we left the drapes open. Only the sheer curtains covered the windows, allowing the lights of Central Park, and the headlights east and west through the park, to spread their shimmery glow. I'd packed nothing, needing nothing as I slipped out of my wool dress and went to stand beside Larry.

"I haven't been so sexually obsessed since we were teenagers," I confided, running my hands over his bare back and down to his hips and buttocks. "I couldn't wait for you to get here."

His appreciative laugh sounded like velvet, deep in his throat. "I love you. I never expected to say those words to you again. I love you." The words turned into caresses, into liquid heat in which I gladly would have drowned. Below us the headlights became sparse as the city began to wind down from a long, hard week. I lay in bed on the eleventh floor of the Park Lane, stroking Larry's chest in easygoing circles. *I can trust him. It feels safe. It feels right.*

I stilled the voice that echoed a frightening response: *Yes, but can he trust me?*

Larry came to New York every weekend in February. We slipped into a rhythm that worked for us. Evenings were ours. We enjoyed a reunion at the hotel every Friday night. Sometimes we ordered room service and only got out of bed to open the door to the waiter. Other times we sampled the best of New York's wonderful restaurants.

"Do you remember how I'd save up for a Chinese meal?" Larry asked as we maneuvered our chopsticks at Nobu, enjoying the exotic and expensive oriental food.

"You always knew you would be successful someday." I dipped a delicate slice of salmon sashimi into a special tangy sauce.

"I thought I'd be a hotshot Wall Street broker or the CEO of a Fortune 500 company." Larry shook his head. "Who knew I'd make it as a therapist and a writer? Back then I thought therapy was for psychos. That's what my father believed, and I had no reason to think otherwise."

Sometimes we went to the theater or a concert. But most of our attention was focused on Ben and Mitch. Larry embraced his project, that of winning the hearts of my sons.

As planned, we catered to Ben and Mitch. *New York Magazine* under Larry's arm, we found everything the city had to offer for children.

"Want to go ice-skating?" Ben asked hopefully.

"Sure."

I felt a swell of emotion in my throat as I watched Larry take my boys' hands, one on each side of him, and skate away across the rink at Battery Park City. They skated back to me, all three of them beaming. "Let's rent you some skates," Larry suggested. I surprised myself by agreeing. It had been years, and I was no athlete. But soon his strong arm was around my waist and my movements matched his as we circled the perimeter, following the boys.

Ahead of us a little girl skated alone. She wore a puffy wool hat with a pom-pom on top. Two brunette pigtails swung as she moved from side to side. She was bundled in a pink down parka and matching ski pants. She turned to wave at someone sitting on a nearby bench, and suddenly she was sprawled on the ice, one pink leg bent under her.

Larry smoothly disengaged from me, checking quickly to make sure I had my balance. He skated over to the child, reaching her before her mother, who wore no skating gear, arrived on the scene. Larry lifted the girl, standing her carefully back on her feet.

"Are you okay?" Larry balanced on one knee in front of the child. "I'm fine. Thanks."

The mother put her arm around the child, guiding her to the sidelines. "Thank you so much," she said over her shoulder to Larry.

"No problem," he replied, grabbing my mittened hand and skating off with me to catch up to Ben and Mitch. "Cute little kid," he commented.

That's how he'd look after a daughter. If he had a daughter. Stop it, Rachel. Just stop it!

"Can we get pizza?" Mitch asked as we untied our laces and blew warm breath onto cold hands.

"Great idea!" Larry appeared to be reveling in the activity. Whenever I looked at his face, he was smiling, deep laugh lines and crinkling eyes displaying a side of him I'd almost never seen.

As he bit into a slice of crispy pie with pepperoni, he told us, "I never got to do this when I was a kid."

"Didn't your mom and dad take you skating?" Ben asked.

"Oh, they weren't very athletic. And they liked to stay warm." I reached out and squeezed the hand that was not manipulating another bite of pizza into Larry's mouth.

A bit after that, Larry helped me get the boys settled down.

"It's amazing," he said later as we sat up in bed, sheets and blankets pulled up over our naked bodies. "I feel so connected to you and the boys." We'd been together for four weekends, each one more fulfilling than the last.

"I feel it too." I turned to face him, resting on one elbow, resisting for the moment the urge to touch him. "It seems so natural. It was a wonderful day. The boys are incredibly comfortable with you."

"Remember, so far it's been all fun and games and presents. The first time I have to read them the riot act, they might not feel so generously accepting."

I touched his face as I laughed. "I have a hunch that they'd welcome having a father to keep them in line."

"Do you mean that?"

I realized late what I had said. My words hung in the room. The word *father* echoed. Larry's blue eyes deepened as he searched my face. I don't know how long I waited, afraid to answer, afraid not to.

"I mean it. They'd welcome it, and so would I."

Larry stood up and moved to my side of the bed. He reached for my hands and pulled me onto my feet beside him. He pressed himself against me, chest to breast, stomach to stomach, thighs to thighs. It felt as if he wanted to absorb me into himself. He took my face in his two hands and kissed me, a deep and lingering kiss. Finally he took my shoulders and held me away from his body. He drank in my face with his eyes. "Were going to be together, aren't we?"

"Yes. We're going to be together." He hugged me again and stroked me as we sat down on the edge of the mattress. We made love again, gently, saying with our caresses that we knew we had time, endless time.

Afterward Larry got out of bed and rummaged in a bureau drawer. He was back in a moment. As I lay there watching him, he dropped to one knee next to me.

"Will you marry me?" He took my hand and slid a two-carat marquis diamond on my finger. I reached over and flipped on the bedside lamp. The jewel sparkled up at me.

"It's so beautiful." My voice was a whisper. "It's perfect."

"I love you."

"Me too you. I still can't believe this."

"Believe it. It's happening. But you haven't answered me. Will you marry me?"

"Yes. Yes, I will marry you."

He sealed my promise with a long, luxurious kiss. "We have to make some plans."

"I know. We will. Soon."

As I waited for sleep to overtake me, my joy was interrupted by a sobering thought. *This has to work. The stakes are so high.* Now, as if my own risk weren't great enough, I was gambling with my precious sons' happiness. If I were to lose Larry, they would lose him too. And they'd already lost so much.

CHAPTER

15

I woke up, startled, at 3:00 a.m. *I've got to get home!* I began groping in the dark for my discarded clothing. Larry sat up. "What're you doing?"

"I've got to go home. It's so late." He switched on the lamp.

"Don't go. Stay here with me."

"I can't. The boys will be up early. They'll be scared if I'm not there."

He came around to my side and gently pressed my shoulders until I was sitting on the edge of the bed.

"We'll get up early and go together. We have important news to share with them."

"But—"

"Mrs. Marcus will hold the fort. We'll call her first thing in the morning. Go back to sleep."

"You didn't say you weren't coming home," Ben accused as we came through the door. "How come you didn't come home?"

"It was late, and I was tired. I stayed over with Larry."

"Oh. Hi, Larry."

"Hi, kiddo. Where's your brother?"

"Somewhere around. Mitch, Mom's home. Larry too." Mitch rounded the corner, half a corn muffin in hand and crumbs on his chin.

"Hi. Where were you?" he mumbled around the edges of the muffin.

"She stayed with Larry." Was I imagining the emphasis in his voice? *They're ten years old, for heaven's sake!*

"Listen, you guys, I'm starved," Larry said. "Do you think Mrs. Marcus has an extra one of those muffins?"

"She's got a whole breakfast for all of us. Mitch just couldn't wait—as usual!" Ben led the way into the kitchen, where the center island held a buffet of lox, cream cheese, tomatoes, and onions, along with a basket of bagels and a platter of assorted muffins. On the counter next to the sink, a full pot of coffee sat on its hot plate.

"Hallelujah!" Larry reached for the coffeepot and filled a mug for each of us. He swiped a dab of cream cheese over half a bagel and pulled up a chair. Molly Marcus surveyed the scene from a corner of the kitchen, arms folded under her bosom. She wore the satisfied look of a mother whose flock is feasting on her bounty. The smile of gratitude I gave her was meant for the breakfast and for her covering for me. She nodded. Words were unnecessary.

"Sit down with us, Mrs. Marcus," Larry said, pulling out a chair for her.

"Oh no, that's okay. I ate already."

"Please. Rachel and I want to talk to all of you." She wiped her hands on her apron and sat.

Mitch set down his glass of milk.

"What's up?" Ben asked, just before wrapping his mouth around his bagel and taking a huge bite.

Larry and I looked at each other. He gave a small nod, deferring to me.

"What's up," I said, "is that Larry and I discovered that we love each other and we're going to get married."

"Yay!" Ben cheered.

"I knew it!" Mitch said.

"That's wonderful news. Congratulations," Mrs. Marcus said, smiling broadly.

"Thank you. We're really happy."

"You haven't known me very long," Larry said, "but I have to tell you guys that I can't wait to be part of this terrific family."

"We think you're cool," Mitch said.

"Where are we going to live?" Trust Ben to get to the heart of the matter.

"Excellent question," Larry acknowledged. "We're still talking about that."

"Would we have to live in Washington?" Mitch asked.

"Not necessarily. Would that be a problem for you?"

"It could be fun," Ben volunteered.

"Yes, but all our friends are here. And our school. And my piano teacher. And your tennis coach. And—"

"Whoa! Let's not panic. This isn't going to happen right away," I said. "We have time to talk about all the pros and cons."

"What if one of us wants New York and the other one wants Washington?" Mitch, the worrier, asked.

"Let's be clear," I responded, "you guys aren't the ones who are going to make the final decision. Larry and I will listen carefully to everything you have to say, but then we'll decide."

"What if one of you wants New York and the other one wants Washington?"

Larry reached over and put his hand on Mitch's shoulder. "Trust us. We'll work it out. Anymore questions?"

"Are you going to be a strict dad?" Ben asked.

"Can we call you Dad?" Mitch wanted to know.

"After we're married you can call him Dad," I said. "And does he look strict to you?"

"Firm, maybe," Larry said. "I don't know, guys. I guess we'll find out together. I've never been a dad before."

"Poor guy," Mitch said. "Never been a dad before, and then he gets us!"

"Double trouble," Mrs. Marcus put in.

I enjoyed watching Larry eat. He had an extra half a bagel and drank prodigious amounts of coffee. Eventually he patted his still flat stomach. "That was delicious!"

"I have to call my sister," I said, pushing back from the table. "She should be awake by now."

Annie answered on the second ring. "How did I know it was you?" she asked rhetorically. "Everything okay?"

"Great, actually. Annie, I'm going to marry Larry."

I was walking around the living room, the phone tucked under my chin, punctuating my news with elaborate hand gestures.

"Oh, Rache, you sound so happy. I just hope you know what you're doing."

"This isn't the Larry you once knew, Annie. All the tension and anger is gone. This is who he was always meant to be. I really, really love him." My hands reached out in a gesture of supplication.

"When is this going to happen?"

"Soon. We want it to be soon. Larry says seventeen years is long enough to wait."

"Don't you think you should take a little more time, be really sure?"

"I am really sure, Annie."

"How is he with Ben and Mitch?"

I touched my heart with my right hand then juggled the phone so it wouldn't crash to the floor. "Absolutely wonderful. We just told them the news, and they're thrilled. Annie, please try to be happy for me."

"I am, sweetie. Of course I am. You know me—just an old worrywart. I'm concerned that you're carrying around this huge secret."

"Can't talk about that right now. Just don't worry. It's going to be fine. I hope you'll come to the wedding."

"Wouldn't miss it. You can count on it. Have you told Mom?"

"She doesn't know anything about any of this. I have to tell her, of course. I just don't know where to start."

"I'm having her over for dinner tonight. Do you want me to tell her?"

I could feel the relief right down to my toes. "Oh, Annie, that would be such a help! Just tell her about Larry, nothing else, okay?"

"Of course."

I felt a tug of sadness when we hung up. I wanted Annie here to share everything, to help me pick my dress and the menu for the wedding supper. I really missed her, more than I'd realized.

"She was thrilled," I reported when I returned to the kitchen. The boys were helping to clear the table, and Larry had retrieved the Clue game from a cabinet and was setting it up.

"She must have a doubt or two," he said.

Ben swiveled his head toward Larry. "Why would she?"

"Well, I was going through a not-so-nice stage of my life when I knew your aunt Annie before. I wouldn't be surprised if she didn't like me much back then."

"Is that why you and Mom broke up?"

"That's why, kiddo. But I learned my lesson. You've got to be a nice guy if you want to be with someone as terrific as your mother. So I developed my 'nice' muscles. And I won her back in the end, just like in the movies."

"I can't imagine that you were ever not nice," Mitch said.

"Trust me, I was as not nice as they come."

We settled into a companionable Sunday afternoon at home. The boys and Larry played Clue and Sorry, and several games of War, while I worked on the *Sunday Times* crossword. I must have sighed my contentment because Larry looked over at me and grinned. By mutual consent we ordered a pizza delivery, adding the mushrooms Larry liked and eliminating the pepperoni Mrs. Marcus hated.

"When do we get to go to Washington?" Ben asked, wiping the remnants of his second pizza in two days from his mouth.

"Anytime your mom says," Larry answered.

"Next weekend?" the boys asked in unison.

"Why not?" Cheers followed, along with the chant, "We're gonna go to Washington, we're gonna go to Washington," until Mrs. Marcus stepped in and shooed both boys out of the room.

Too soon Larry was holding me in his arms for a lingering goodbye. We made no effort to hide our affection from Mitch and Ben, who amused each other with mugging and pantomimes of kisses and hugs. "Bye, guys," Larry called, smiling his male-to-male understanding of all that mushy stuff before walking out the door.

"Do you think Dad would've liked Larry?" Ben wore an atypical serious expression. I could read in his eyes the loyalty issue tugging at his conscience.

"I think he would have liked him a lot. I think he'd want you to have a dad, and me to have a husband. He'd want it to be the right person. He'd trust the three of us to pick the right person."

"Yeah, I think so too. He'd probably be relieved that we're going to have Larry around." Ben wrapped his arms around my waist and leaned his head on my chest. "I love you, Mom."

My throat tightened. "I love you too, Benjy. And I want both of you to know that even though I love Larry too, there'll always be time and love enough for you two. Don't you ever worry about that."

Larry and I fell into a pattern of talking on the phone after the 11:00 p.m. news. I'd be under my comforter, makeup scrubbed off, flannel nightgown keeping out the winter chill. I always warmed to the sound of Larry's voice. We talked about everything and nothing, each of us reluctant to sever the connection. Often our conversations went on for more than an hour. Larry would hear my voice droop, and he'd say, "You're falling asleep. Good night, sweetheart."

"Good night. Love you." I'd drift off while replacing the receiver in its charger.

On the Wednesday night after his visit, Larry said, "By the way, I saw Heather Brody today."

I sat up a little straighter and clutched my quilt. "I thought you saw her every week."

"No, she was phasing out, coming in only occasionally. It was her choice, and I went along with it. I hadn't seen her for several weeks."

"But she came back."

"Not willingly. Her father forced the issue. Apparently there's been some backsliding, at least according to the parents' standards."

"What happened?"

"She was seeing a boy from her class. It hadn't gone on for long, but she seemed pretty happy about it. He broke up with her and started seeing a girl she thought was her best friend. You know Heather. It doesn't take much to bring out her cynicism."

The pang of sympathy I felt for Heather's hurt was mixed with a large dose of worry. "How did she react?"

"Her grades took a nosedive. And according to her dad, she started to dress and wear makeup like in the old days—tight sweaters, fake lashes. You know. You've seen her like that."

"Is that how she looked when you saw her?"

"Sort of a modified version. Just short of crossing the line."

"So what do you think? Is she in trouble?"

"Hard to say. She wasn't forthcoming. Talked a lot about that

boy in New York, the one she calls 'the Frankster.' He might have
faults, but at least she could always depend on him—that kind of
thing. Didn't want to talk about her feelings of betrayal." I wrapped
my arms around myself and squeezed. Mentally I sent a reassuring
hug of compassion to my hurting child.

"Did she agree to see you again?"

"We scheduled another appointment. It wouldn't surprise me
if she canceled or no-showed. It only works when she wants to be
here—and this time it's just another one of her parents' unreasonable
requirements."

"Keep me posted," I said as neutrally as I could manage. Larry
switched the discussion to plans for the kids' weekend in Washington—
the National Air and Space Museum, the FBI tour, the White House.

"They'll love anything you plan. They're most interested in getting
to know you."

"Me too. Listen, Rachel, should I make a hotel reservation? Would
you like to stay at the house? I have plenty of room."

"Of course we'll stay with you. I just assumed that."

"I wish you could see the smile on my face."

"I can't see it, but I can hear it. Can't wait till Friday." That night
I didn't fall asleep as soon as I put the phone down. I lay awake and
thought about Heather. I wanted to physically punish the boy, and the
girlfriend, who'd caused my daughter pain and set back her progress.
Damn, damn, damn! Outside my window the sky was turning pink
before I dozed off.

Larry turned Washington into a huge playground for Ben and
Mitch. He listened indulgently to their excited rendition of the plane
ride, glancing over their heads occasionally to bestow a warm and
welcoming look onto me. How wonderfully he fulfilled my major
requirement, that of being a loving father to my children. After
five years of watching families doing things together, feeling like
an outsider with my nose pressed to the windowpane, I reveled in
the knowledge that my boys would have a dad, that we would be a
complete family too.

Hand in hand, Larry and I trailed behind Ben and Mitch as they explored the museums and the history of the capital. I tantalized myself for the hundredth time with the thought of telling him about Heather. Again, as I'd done all the other times, I dismissed the thought with a tiny shake of my head. Mitch and Ben would be his as much as mine, and maybe someday, if Larry felt the need for a biological legacy, we might create another child together.

The boys loved Larry's three-level house. They raced up and down, calling to each other over balconies. Ben slid down the banister, whooping as he went, skidding to a halt just before banging his butt on the post at the bottom. "Great house, Larry," he said, hopping off like a cowboy dismounting his favorite horse.

"Glad you like it, Ben. And I'm glad you're not having a problem feeling at home."

"Hardly," I commented.

Their stomachs filled with hot dogs, fries, Coke, and chocolate chip cookies, the twins watched an ancient *Star Trek* on TV and went to bed without protest afterward.

Much later I relaxed in Larry's arms, filled with calm in the aftermath of love, savoring the safety I felt, the warmth of the down comforter, the faint aroma of aftershave mingled with the musky scent of recent sex. My boys slept the exhausted sleep of youth in a nearby room. There was a completeness that I hadn't felt since the night before Neil received his diagnosis. This was a new beginning. This was right!

On Sunday we were tourists once more. We took the mandatory White House tour and also visited the FBI Crime Museum. At the Smithsonian National Museum of Natural History, the boys were fascinated by the exhibit on evolution. The International Spy Museum intrigued them. All too soon we were gathered in the food court of Union Station, allowing Ben and Mitch to pick their dinner from any booth they wished.

"I wouldn't mind living in Washington," Mitch said as we settled into our seats on the Amtrak train that would take us back to New York.

"What if we stayed in New York?" I asked. "How would you feel about that?"

"Fine," Ben answered. "We've got all our friends, and my tennis coach, and Mitch's piano teacher."

"What about Aunt Mol?" Mitch wanted to know. "If we went to Washington, would she come too?"

"I can't answer that, sweetheart. She has to do what she thinks best."

"If she can't come, then I think we should stay in New York," Ben said. "What would she do if she didn't have us?"

And vice versa. "It'll all get sorted out," I promised. "Larry and I will keep you posted, okay?"

"Sure, Mom," Mitch said. "I hope we can stay in New York though."

"Me too," Ben added. "But Washington would be okay, as long as we're going to have Larry. He's great."

"I think so too, sweetheart. I really do."

My cup overfloweth. I would not allow fear or worry to spoil this perfect moment.

CHAPTER 16

I couldn't resist unzipping the garment bag and gazing at the dress. The skirt was made of shimmery gold silk, and the matching jacket had a light appliqué of beads that sparkled around the square neckline and cuffs. I'd be wearing it as I walked down a flower-lined aisle, hopefully in the garden (weather permitting) of the Belle View Inn, overlooking the Hudson, on the Sunday before the Fourth of July, six weeks away. I smoothed the silk and smiled as I closed the bag and the door of my closet.

I'd thought decision-making would be hard. I'd imagined trade-offs and compromises, and difficulty planning what would be best for the boys. Instead, one solution had flowed easily into the next. We would stay in New York but look for a larger place. Larry would keep his Washington town house for now. We'd been there with the boys twice in the last two months. Larry would use it whenever he returned to DC for business. In fact, he had left early on this Monday morning to meet with a couple of families he still monitored on a monthly basis. Heather was on his schedule as well. He would attend a dinner tonight and would be back tomorrow evening.

He had begun using the conference room in my office suite as he worked on his new book and prepared for half a dozen speaking engagements lined up over the next three months. I tried hard not to be distracted when I knew that he was sitting at the long table, pecking away at his laptop, on the other side of the wall behind my head.

We decided to keep things simple for Mitch's and Ben's sake. I would continue to work. Molly Marcus would stay on with us. She was thrilled to have a man to fuss over.

Amazing! Larry had been integrated into my life and my family as seamlessly as if there had been a place-saver holding open the spot that he would fill in our world.

"Good morning," I sang out to Jan, tossing my light jacket on to the coatrack with a lucky shot.

"Hi. Are you on your own today?"

"Larry went to Washington. He has a couple of clients and a dinner meeting. He'll be home tomorrow."

"How are the arrangements coming along?"

"The invitations have been mailed. My sister's coming with her whole family. She's bringing my mom. Everything's coming together."

"Rachel, Stan and I are so happy for you. Nobody deserves this more than you do."

"Thanks, Jan. You've been such a great friend through everything." I'd asked her to stand up with me at the ceremony, along with my sister and Molly Marcus.

"You know you're glowing?"

I touched my face with the back of my hand. "I know. So who do we have today?" Jan handed me a printed schedule.

I had four clients lined up. At 3:00 p.m. I had a final session with Edna Masters, age sixty-three, who'd come in after losing her husband. I'd seen her for three months, and she felt that she no longer needed our weekly sessions. She was quite altered from the disheveled, depressed woman who, at her first appointment, had reached for the box of tissues before opening her mouth. She had found a part-time job and had gone back to her bridge club.

"I don't know that I'll ever get married again," she said. "I don't think I could ever find another Max. But that's okay. I can still have a life—a different one, but a good one. And I have my children and grandchildren."

"You never know, Edna. I'm living proof."

"That's true. Of course, you're a few years younger than I am, dear. But we'll see. Anyway, you've been a great help. I thought I'd gone over the edge when Max died, and you dragged me back." The farewell was warm. Edna reached out to embrace me and wish me luck.

She was the last client of the day. I jotted a few case notes and prepared to leave early.

"Go on home," I prodded Jan. "It's too beautiful to stay in the office."

"Thanks." She switched off the computer with no further encouragement. "See you tomorrow."

I was retrieving my jacket from the coatrack when the door opened.

"Oh, you were leaving. Sorry."

"Heather!" She stood in the doorway, gaunt and waiflike. Her eyes were surrounded with black liner. She wore no other makeup. She had no coat, and the off-the-shoulder ribbed white sweater showed the lines of her small braless breasts, also making her collarbone and long neck seem especially vulnerable. Her fingertips were in the pockets of her jeans, which were too tight to accommodate the rest of her hands. My heart sank. I felt a confusion of emotion that turned my hands ice-cold and, seconds later, made my face feel as flushed as though I'd developed a fever. I was so glad to see her, and she was so obviously in distress.

"Come on in." I tossed my jacket back on the rack.

"You sure?"

In two steps I was at her side. I took her hand and led her into my office. "Please. Sit down."

"I really don't want to hold you up. I mean, I didn't have an appointment—"

"It's good to see you." She sank into the well-worn chair, curling one leg under her. I sat opposite, leaning toward her, waiting. My left thumb rubbed the palm of my right hand, where the tingle of anxiety that I hadn't felt for months was suddenly present.

Heather gazed around the room. Her eyes rested on the Renoir print, on my diplomas, on the basket of dried flowers on a corner table. She moistened her colorless lips with her tongue. She said nothing. I waited. I wanted to pace around my office, but I didn't dare move. My right thumb rubbed my left palm. In the silence, I was aware of her soft breath, her chest expanding and contracting beneath the white sweater.

"I don't know why I came," she said finally. "I shouldn't have come."

"No. You should have."

"You're not my shrink anymore."

"True. But I'm always here for you if you need me. I told you that before you went to Washington."

"Washington." Heather's tone held in it a world of cynicism. "What a great place—for my mother, that is."

"What do you mean?"

"Snob City. She's found her true home at last. Do you believe she's found more things to do in Washington than she did in New York?"

"And how about you? How are you doing there?"

"Lousy." She shifted in her chair, pulling her other leg up so she was sitting Indian style. "I tried, Rachel. I promise you I did. But I'm just not like them. I don't like them, and they don't like me."

"Did something happen?"

"It was okay for a little while. I was the new kid. I tried to dress like them and act like them, and it was working, I thought. I had a couple of friends. My mother even approved of them. *That* felt strange! And there was this boy I liked."

I massaged my hands against my knees. "So you got off to a good start."

"Yeah, but it didn't last. Y'know what the real problem is? Loyalty! They might have more money than God, but they don't know the meaning of loyalty."

"Someone was disloyal?"

"Not just someone. This boy Jon, whom I liked and who I thought liked me, and my friend Chloe—one day they just start going together. Nobody says a word to me. And when I get pissed off and tell them I think it stinks, they look at me like I just landed from another planet. I mean, I felt like a freak! Like there's this game going on and I don't know the rules. At least before, I knew the rules. It might not have been the nicest game in the world, but I knew how to play it."

"It really hurt," I said. *Oh God, I want to hug you. My poor baby.* I folded my arms across my chest, squeezed hard, and concentrated hard on staying in my professional role.

Heather stood up and walked to the window. She stared down at the street and spoke without turning to look at me. "You know the worst part, Rachel? I liked him so much that I let him, y'know ... I did it with him. He's the only boy I ever slept with besides the Frankster. What an idiot I am!"

I couldn't help myself. I joined her at the window and lightly draped an arm over her shoulder. We stood together, silent. She half turned her body, bent down slightly, and laid her head against my chest. I felt the heat of her tears through the silk of my blouse. I patted her back and stroked her hair. I hardly dared to breathe. It seemed as if the moment froze in time, although surely only seconds passed. She lifted her head, and I led her back to her chair.

"Are you okay?" She nodded, wiping away a tear with the side of her finger.

"How long ago did all this happen?"

"About two months ago. My dad sent me back to Larry—you know, Dr. Tobin? I guess he thought I needed my oil changed or something. Bent out of shape? Go see your shrink. But I didn't have anything to say to him. I mean, he couldn't fix it, could he?"

"Maybe your dad thought it would help to talk about it."

"I didn't want to talk about it. I wanted to forget about it. My folks were just upset because I stopped caring what I wore to school. I mean, what was the point of trying to be like those kids if that's what they were like? Do you get what I mean?"

"Of course I do."

"So there I am, thoroughly bummed out down there in DC, and my good buddy Frankster is similarly bummed out here in New York. So I came up to see him."

"Do your parents know you're here?"

Her smile was a slow smirk. "How did I know you were going to ask me that?"

"Because you know it's the right question. Do they?"

"Of course not. They're in LA at some big benefit – world hunger or something. I told the housekeeper I was staying at Chloe's. She'll never check. And if they decide to call me—which I seriously doubt— they'll call my cell phone. I could be anywhere. So I'm cool. Unless, of course, you decide to rat on me."

I uncrossed and recrossed my legs. "You don't make it easy for me, you know. I've always maintained your confidentiality, but you really do push it."

"Sorry to be so much trouble."

"Let's forget about that for now. Have you seen Frank yet?"

"Sure. As soon as I got here. He's waiting for me back at his place."

"So what's going on with him?"

"Same old, same old. Keeps talking about getting a real job, but it doesn't happen. But he sure was happy to see me."

"I worry that one of these days he's going to get you in trouble."

"I don't think I care. He's the only person in the world who really accepts me for myself. I'd rather be in trouble with him than lead this nice, clean lonely life with friends who make nice one minute and cut your throat the next. The Frankster's a mess, but he knows what loyalty is. You should have seen him when I walked in the door."

All my fingers had pins and needles running through them. I folded my hands in my lap and rubbed hard. Then I reached across the space between us and touched Heather's knee, letting my hand rest there. "Would you think it was corny if I told you I care a lot about you?" The girl smiled at me, and for just a moment she looked as old and wise as Father Time.

"It's not corny, Rachel. But—don't be offended, please—it's not very relevant either. I mean, look, I've got parents who forget they have a kid unless I do something outrageous. No brothers or sisters. Aunts and uncles and grandparents who think I'm nothing but a problem. Well, my aunt Marilyn's okay, my father's sister. But I don't see much of her. She's in Chicago. My uncle Greg and my mother's parents think my parents' biggest mistake ever was adopting me. I think so too. I've been a pain in the ass to every teacher I ever had, and the only girlfriend I ever had stole the boy I like. And then there's this nice lady"—she nodded her head toward me—"who was my therapist for a few months a year or so ago, who says she cares about me. I mean, I believe you. But you're supposed to care about me. That's why my parents paid you."

I opened my mouth to respond, but for the moment, I couldn't. I found myself mute in the face of the devastating cynicism of this seventeen-year-old. No words of mine were going to convince her that my concern was other than professional—no words except the ones I couldn't say. It was pointless to try.

"Heather, how come you came here today?" I finally said. "I'm glad you did, but I'm not sure I understand why."

"I guess because you never judged me. I mean, even the Frankster judges me—calls me a Goody Two-shoes because I won't snort coke with him. I just wanted to see you, that's all."

"Do you want some feedback on what you've told me?"

"You mean, do I want to hear you tell me I'm making a big mistake? Not really, but if you must, you must."

"I think I must. I've always been straight with you, and I always will be."

"So go ahead. Shoot."

"I think you surprised yourself when you discovered that you could be accepted by the kids in Washington, that adapting to their way of looking and acting could work for you."

"But it wasn't real. It was me acting."

"I know that. You hadn't been doing it long enough for it to become real."

"Okay. So?"

I found myself sitting at the edge of my chair. My feet were flat on the floor, close together. My upper body leaned in toward the girl, every muscle tense with my need to get through to her.

"So you learned that you can make it in a world where kids study, go to service clubs, plan for college. But then you had a big disappointment, and now you're ready to give it all up."

"Because it's not worth it to be like them. What's more important, Rachel, nice clothes and no curse words or real values like love and loyalty?" Heather's face and tone were intense as only a teenager's could be. I felt her eyes boring into me, challenging me to offer a reason to resume the life that had caused her so much pain.

"I think you ran into a couple of kids who weren't worthy of you, sweetheart. But I think it's a mistake to blame a whole class of people. I'm sure there are kind, caring kids at that school too."

"I tried, Rachel. I really did. You can ask Larry. He thought I was doing great. So did my folks. As long as I looked and talked the way my mother thought a young lady should look and talk, she was satisfied. But that's not my world."

"So what are you saying, Heather?"

"I want to come back to New York. I want to be with the Frankster. Maybe I can help him, straighten him out. He needs me."

"Or maybe he'll take you down with him."

"Maybe." She lifted one shoulder dismissively.

"Heather, I think you should go home."

"Where's home, Rachel?" She uncurled herself and stood up. She flipped open the top of the well-worn black bag and groped inside. "What do I owe you?"

"You don't owe me anything. This was a visit, not a session. By the way, I have some news that might interest you."

"Oh yeah? What?"

"Larry Tobin and I are getting married."

"Really? No shit!"

"You brought us together. So let me take this opportunity to thank you."

"My two shrinks, married to each other. That's a blast! Well, lots of good luck, or whatever you say to a bride. And thanks for listening. I know what you want for me, Rachel. I just don't think I can do it. Not right now."

"Just be careful, honey. Listen, is there a phone number or an address where I can reach you?"

Heather smirked. "'Fraid not, Rachel. I'm just one of eight million in the naked city. But don't worry. I can take care of myself." She walked out of the office, leather bag slung over a fragile shoulder, her hair swaying with her walk. She seemed as vulnerable as a young fawn in a predatory forest.

I reached for the back of my desk chair and sank into it. Elbows on the table, I rested my chin on folded hands. The joy I'd felt this morning as I planned my coming marriage was wiped from my mind. "Oh, Larry," I said aloud, "what are we going to do about our girl?"

CHAPTER
17

I walked home, oblivious to traffic noise, shopwindows, or weather. I imagined Heather's Frank, his dirty, smelly, rough hands with blackened fingernails touching her, pressuring her to join him in drug-induced ecstasy. I feared that this time she might give in. *What should I do? I can't call her parents. She'll never trust me again.* I needed Larry's calm, steady common sense, but he was far away in Washington. Lost in troubled thoughts, I was surprised when I arrived at my building. I had no clear idea of how I'd gotten there. The sun hung low over the skyline of New Jersey. It would be another beautiful day tomorrow. *Where will Heather be tomorrow? Will she be okay?*

The boys were noisy and rambunctious. My nerves felt frayed. I longed for time alone. I sank into the floral couch, settling my shoulders and upper back into the softness of the double cushioning. I made myself listen as they took turns reporting the day's events, interrupting each other. Ben pushed Mitch.

"Cut it out," I snapped at him. I really wasn't in the mood.

"Guess what's for dinner, Mommy? Meatballs and rice!" Mitch's eyes danced in anticipation. "Aunt Mol made it specially for me. Because I asked her to."

"Big deal," Ben mocked. "She was gonna make it anyway."

"Listen, you two, I need to rest before dinner. Ask Aunt Mol to hold off for half an hour. I'm going to take some aspirin and lie down."

"But, Mom, I'm hungry." Mitch's pitch rose to a whine.

"Then eat without me. It's okay. I'm not very hungry." As I headed for the bedroom I could hear the argument that broke out on the merits of eating immediately or waiting for me. I sprawled on top of my bedspread, not bothering to take off my dress or my shoes. I stared at the ceiling, which offered no clue as to what to do about Heather. I knew that I should try to get in touch with Heather's parents. I still had Bill's cell phone number in my smartphone. I also knew that if I called her folks, she would never walk into my office on her own again. I got off the bed and groped in my medicine chest for the aspirin bottle. I'd made up the headache as an excuse for stealing some quiet time, but now, as I went back and forth over my limited options, it had become real.

I looked at the digital clock on my cable box: 7:15. Larry would be sipping ginger ale at the cocktail hour before his dinner. It would be hours before I could tell him of Heather's visit and ask his advice. I didn't want to think about where Heather was at this hour or what she might be doing. Rubbing my temples with my fingertips, I pushed myself off the bed and headed for the kitchen to have meatballs and rice with my boys.

It was 10:30 when Larry called me. I was in bed, trying to focus on CNN, waiting for the phone to ring. "Miss you," he said. The warmth in his tone was warm milk to my nerves. "The dinner was boring. I sat through the talk and thought about our honeymoon." We'd decided to fly to Paris and wind up in Cannes. "It's getting close."

"I can't wait either. Larry—"

He interrupted me. "I had this wild idea just before I called. Are you ready for this?"

"Sure."

"I thought maybe we should invite Heather Brody to the wedding!"

I felt my eyes widen. My mouth opened. No sound came out.

"Rachel? Are you there?"

"I'm here." My mind flailed for a response. *Where did that come from?*

"So, what do you think?"

"How weird that you should mention her tonight," I finally said. "I saw her today. She came to the office."

"So that's where she was. She no-showed her appointment with me."

"She's not in good shape, Larry. That breakup with the boy in Washington, the one you told me about, has really set her back. She came to New York to see Frank. She looks like hell. Her parents don't know she's here."

"No big surprise. Last time I saw her, she was headed toward something like this."

"I'm afraid she's going to do drugs with that boy."

"Did she tell you that?"

"No. But she said she didn't care much." I swung my legs off the bed and sat on the edge. I realized I was rocking a little bit.

"You're walking a fine line, sweetheart. She's still a minor, and a runaway, and we know where she is. On one hand you could make a case for informing the parents."

"What's the other hand? That's what I can't figure out."

"She came to you freely. She wasn't dragged. I think she wanted to resist temptation. She wanted to borrow your strength. Why would she walk into your office if she'd made up her mind to go to hell in a handbasket?"

"She said it's because I never judged her."

"And you didn't judge her now. That's what she came for, and that's what she got."

I stood up and padded barefoot to the window, where I raised the blind and looked out onto the quiet street below. "How does that affect my responsibility to inform the Brodys?"

"Let's wait a day or two. I'll call the Brodys to touch base. I'll ask how Heather's doing. I'll ask if I can talk to her. If they tell me she's disappeared, then I think we have to let them know she was in New York today talking about Frank. But let's play to her good judgment. If she's holding her own, refusing to do drugs, then our vote of no confidence could push her over the edge. I mean, she wasn't threatening suicide or saying she'd never go home."

"That's true." Feeling the tightness in my back start to relax, I let out a long breath. "You always make sense, darling. Thank you."

"So what do you think about my idea of having her at our wedding?"

"I'm not sure," I said, vying for time. "Is it a good idea to mix our professional and personal lives that way?"

"Sure. She's not the average client. We wouldn't be planning a wedding if it hadn't been for her."

"Funny, I told her that today. She was blown away that we're getting married."

"Another thing—given the hard time she's having and her low self-esteem, I think it will be a boost for her to know we want her there."

What could I say? I most definitely did not want her there among the guests, unaware that she was watching her biological parents marry each other. The one secret I couldn't share with Larry would be there reminding me all day long.

No! Don't ask me to do that. I can't do that. And I can't tell you why.

"It's a lovely idea," I said, slipping back into bed and pulling the cover up to my chin. "Leave it to you to think of it."

We'd had a wonderful time planning the wedding. We decided to speak the traditional vows, adding a few personal comments to each one. We'd chosen music we both loved, the beautiful piece "Somewhere in Time" instead of Wagner. The best moment of all had come when we were talking about our attendants. The dinner dishes had been cleared, and Larry and I lingered at the kitchen table, sipping tea and munching Mrs. Marcus's delicious biscotti.

"Annie will be my matron of honor, of course," I told him. "And I've asked Jan and Mrs. Marcus to stand up with me. They've been with me through thick and thin." I transferred a crumb from my finger to my tongue. "What about you? Will you ask Ed Silverman to be your best man?"

"I have a better idea." He called out, "Ben, Mitch, come here for a minute." They trouped into the kitchen and perched on stools at the center island.

"What's up?" Ben asked.

"I'm in need of some assistance. Do you guys know what a best man is?"

"It's some kind of wedding thing, right?"

"It's very important. The best man makes sure the bridegroom gets dressed on time and gets to the wedding. He makes sure the groom doesn't lose the ring. He stays close by in case the groom needs anything. It's a big honor."

"So who's your best man gonna be?"

"I was hoping the two of you would be my two very best men."

"Wow!" Mitch jumped off the stool and threw his arms around Larry's shoulders. "I accept!"

"Me too!" Ben hugged Larry, and then I hugged all of them, the group of us making a tight little circle in the middle of the kitchen. Mrs. Marcus stood nearby, chubby arms wrapped around herself, beaming.

Larry gently moved the boys away from his body so that he could look at them. "I'm so lucky that when I found your mother again, she had the two of you. You're like a terrific bonus I didn't expect." Mitch and Ben grinned at each other. I leaned over and wiped a smudge of barbecue sauce from Ben's face.

"We're lucky too," Mitch said.

That had been a wonderful evening. When the boys were tucked in, Larry had reached for me. His touch had enflamed me instantly, as it had that first night in Washington. "Never leave me again," he said into the hollow of my throat. "I couldn't bear it."

"I'm not going anywhere." I'd let the tips of my fingernails graze his chest, where his shirt opened in a *V* and a few curly grayish-black hairs peeked out.

Now, as I imagined my joy at standing with Larry under a canopy in that beautiful garden, my children flanking us, I would have to envision our daughter among the guests, unaware of her blood tie to us. The secret that was never far from my consciousness would be there in person, reminding me of my many deceptions as I married her father.

The following Tuesday Larry poked his head into my office a moment after my 2:00 p.m. client had left. "I'm almost finished with the draft of my book," he reported. "I'll be really glad to get it into my editor's hands before we leave on our honeymoon." He came in and sat on the couch, patting the seat next to him. I stepped around my desk to join him.

I'd read the chapters as he finished them. The topic was children of privilege. That was also the working title. We had talked at length about his theory.

"Kids who get too much, too soon," he said, "value nothing. They don't know what it means to anticipate something, to work and save for it. If they don't have immediate gratification, they're angry and frustrated." It was an ambitious project, a how-to for parents on raising children with healthy values. He used a laptop to write, but frequently I'd come into the conference room to see him gnawing the yellow paint off a lead pencil, his brow furrowed as he tried to work out the fine points of a chapter.

"It's going to be an important contribution to the literature," I said now. I snuggled closer to him. "I love having you right here at the office. It's nice to look up and see you in the doorway."

"You know, I'm going to be pretty busy when we get back from our trip," he reminded me. "I know they're planning another lecture tour along with the TV appearances and book signings."

"We'll miss you. But it's what you do. If you hadn't written the first book, you and I never would have met again."

"That reminds me. I spoke to Heather this afternoon. Stephanie Brody appreciated my call. She told me she's not particularly happy with Heather these days, but she seemed okay when they returned from Los Angeles. She's been going to school regularly. Stephanie seemed totally unaware that Heather had been in New York."

"She's totally unaware, period," I muttered.

"So I asked to speak with Heather, and she came to the phone and congratulated me on our wedding. She had no problem telling me she'd seen you. She probably guessed that I already knew. So it was the perfect opportunity for me to invite her to be there. She was thrilled. Obviously we'll have to invite her parents too. You don't mind, do you?"

So my daughter was really going to be a guest at my wedding. *Well, Rachel, you'll just have to deal with it.* I made my lips form a smile. "Of course not," I lied.

The weeks leading up to our wedding day had the comfortable sameness of routine. I continued to see clients. All but the most self-absorbed of them found time during their sessions to tell me how pleased they were at my newfound happiness. I received a few gifts. Unlike some therapists, I accepted small tokens of appreciation from clients. As my marriage approached, I was given a picture frame, a porcelain candy dish, and a cookbook autographed by the author, who was my client's mother.

The weather was outstanding. Comfortable temperatures and abundant sunshine marked May and early June. Larry and I wore light sweaters as we attended a junior tennis tournament that Ben had a good chance of winning. He was looking more and more like a miniature professional, spinning aces across the net, grunting as he slammed the ball. He seemed to be everywhere at once. We sat in the stands with Mitch. Larry's beaming face spoke even louder than his cheers. Ben and Mitch were his sons too. I knew that Neil, wherever he was, had blessed this new father who had come to take care of his boys.

The next day was Mitch's piano recital. We switched gears and sat with a dozen other parents as the children, ranging in age from five to fourteen, played their assigned pieces with intense concentration. Ben fidgeted as we waited for Mitch's turn. "Mitch is better than those guys," he whispered to me.

"Sh!"

Larry was relaxed, handsome in a white silk open-collared shirt and gray slacks, his long legs crossed at the knee. He leaned back and focused as if this were a concert at his beloved Kennedy Center. When Mitch came to the piano bench, Larry straightened slightly. Mitch's gaze swept the audience, looking for us. Larry gave a small nod of acknowledgment. Mitch played his Chopin nocturne flawlessly, a performance surprising for his age level. The audience showed their appreciation with vigorous applause. The pride I felt was reflected in the swell of Larry's chest and his broad smile. *God, it's good to have him here with me.* My facial muscles stretched in a grin. I reached for Larry and rested my hand on his arm. *Yes. He's real! I'm not a single parent anymore.*

Two days later we decided to walk to the office together. My first client wasn't until 11:00, so we had a leisurely breakfast and strolled down Seventh Avenue, enjoying a pristine early June day. We held hands and swung them gently back and forth. My steps felt as light as my heart.

The serenity of the morning was shattered the minute we pushed open the office door. Jan looked up from her desk and said, "Thank God."

"What's wrong?" Jan's face told me, before she spoke, that there was a client in crisis.

"William Brody called three times. He insisted I call you at home, but you'd already left. I tried texting, but you didn't answer. He said he'd talk to either one of you."

"Did he say why he was calling?" Larry asked.

"Heather's gone. She left a note. Mr. Brody said that it sounds like she's not coming back."

CHAPTER
18

"Get him on the phone," I said, more brusquely than I'd intended.

"I'll grab the extension." Larry went into the conference room and came back holding a portable phone.

Bill Brody was a man who did not lose his composure, and he was calm now, but his voice had an alarming razor edge.

"When Stephanie and I came downstairs this morning, we found a note. Apparently our daughter has had enough of Washington."

"Okay, Bill, try to take it easy," Larry said. He spoke in measured, calming tones. "She's done this before, right?"

"She's taken off overnight once or twice, but never with a note. It sounds like she's never coming back. Good God, she's only seventeen."

"Bill," I said, "can you read us the note?"

"I have it right here. It scares the hell out of me." There was the sound of paper rustling. Larry sat with one hip on the edge of my desk. I had the portable phone; I paced.

Dear Mom and Dad,

I'm writing to say goodbye. I know you'll think I'm ungrateful for everything you've done for me. Maybe I am. I only know that I can't pretend to be your perfect daughter. I'm not perfect, and I'm not even your daughter. If you're totally honest with yourselves, you'll admit that adopting me was the biggest mistake of your lives. We're nothing alike. I must be like my biological parents. I just don't fit into your world. You can believe it or not, but I'm really sorry. I would have liked to make you happy, but I just can't. Anyhow, I'm tired of trying to get the kids to like me. I'm tired of trying to get *you* to like me. I'm going back to where I'm liked for being who I am, and where I'm needed, which is certainly not in Washington. If you'll accept this and not try to get me back, we'll all be happier. I'm a burden you've been dragging around for seventeen years. Give yourselves and me a break. And have a nice life.

Heather

"She's going to Frank." My voice sounded like a groan in my ears.

"I know," her father replied. "Do either of you have any idea how to find her? She's on your turf now or will be soon."

"I don't even know his last name," I answered.

"You know, Bill," Larry put in, "it's going to be hard to hold on to her if she doesn't want to be held."

"I realize that. But how can I accept her living that lifestyle? Doing drugs? Getting pregnant? From everything I know of that boy, he's a pig! She's seventeen, for God's sake. Don't I owe her something? I'm her father!"

"You're right," I said. "You have to try. You have to report her missing. Let the police circulate her picture in New York. Tell them everything you know that can help them find her."

"I'm doing all that. I thought maybe there's an outside chance she'll walk in your door. She feels close to you, Rachel. And she respects you, Larry."

"Certainly if she shows up here, we'll do everything we can. How's Stephanie holding up?"

"Stephanie? Instant migraine. She took two Fiorinal and went to bed. By the way, I'm leaving for New York in an hour. I just have to clean up a couple of things on my desk that can't wait. I'll be staying at the Plaza."

"Okay," Larry said. "Hang in there, Bill. She may rethink

the whole thing and be back in a day or two. Meanwhile we'll do everything we can to help."

Larry hung up the phone and sank into my corduroy chair. "If she wasn't at risk before, she is now."

"I know. If only I'd gotten more information last time she showed up. A name, an address—"

"She wasn't about to give you any leads. It's not your fault."

I walked to the window and stared down at the street, willing a thin, dark-haired girl with a big black pocketbook to enter the revolving doors just beyond my vision. I rubbed my tingling hands on the rounded wood of the sill. "She's out there somewhere. Oh, Larry, I am so worried about her."

He came to me and drew me close with an arm around my shoulders.

"That's your good heart, darling. Remember, in the long run clients will do what they will do. They make the decisions, even when those decisions are destructive."

"But she's just a child." I kept my voice low because my words threatened to emerge as a wail.

"She's a tough, streetwise child. Look, she's had the benefit of a good home and good schools. There's a good chance that at some point she'll be ready to give up this behavior. But it looks like she wants to run with Frank for a while."

I turned on my heel to face him. "Larry, we have to find her." He took a step back and studied my face.

"This one really got you, didn't she?"

"I guess she did. She's got such potential. And I worked so hard. So did you."

And she's our girl, Larry—yours and mine!

"Heather and her mother were never able to make a connection. That's part of the problem."

"Stephanie." I couldn't keep the scorn from my tone. "Instant migraine. Probably thinking about how her friends will talk."

"C'mon, let's get out of here for a few minutes. I need coffee." He steered me toward the door. I had forty-five minutes before my first client.

"If Heather Brody shows up or calls, hang on to her," I told Jan. "We'll be downstairs at the coffee shop, thirty seconds away."

But Heather didn't show up or call. I brooded into my cappuccino. Larry ran out of encouraging remarks. "I guess I'm more used to this than you are," he commented finally. "I've worked with a lot more adolescents, and many of them were drug abusers. Despite our best efforts, not all of them straighten up and fly right. For some of them the thrill is living on the edge, daring their parents and authority to set limits on their rage. You always regret it, but you get used to it. If you don't, you can't do this work."

Thanks a lot. I didn't say it aloud. "She's held out for so long against the drugs. Frank wanted to give her cocaine on her sixteenth birthday. She was very angry at her parents that day, but still she didn't give in."

"Well, let's hope she finds that strength again." Larry patted my hand and stood up to pay the bill at the register.

"Damn!" I said as we waited for the elevator.

"I know, darling. I know."

I got through the day by turning my attention to my clients. Work had pulled me through when I lost Neil, and it was still my best defense against worry and grief. In my ten-minute breaks, I envisioned Heather, her black leather bag slung over her shoulder, entering some darkened hallway in a frightening part of town. And then I went back to work.

I want to tell him. I need to tell him. But I imagined the look of betrayal I would see in Larry's eyes, his disappointment with me, his grief over the lost years with his only child. I pressed my palms against my knees. I shook them as though drying them without a paper towel. The numbness and prickling remained constant.

Once again I stood at the window, staring at the vastness of the city. "Heather," I said aloud, "come to me. I'll help you. We'll help you." I dawdled until after 6:00, pleading an overload of paperwork. I sent Jan and Larry home. I pushed a ballpoint around my desk, writing a few case notes, doodling a lot. Looking down at what I'd done, I saw my blotter filled with fancy curlicue letters that read, "Heather Tobin." I tore off the page and ripped it methodically into miniscule strips.

She's not coming. Lacking the will to walk the three miles home despite the beauty of the mild spring night, I hailed a cab and fell back, exhausted, against the cracked vinyl.

Larry and I spoke with Bill Brody that evening. He was just finishing a late room service meal when we called. "No luck so far," he reported. He had taken Heather's junior class picture to the police precinct nearest her old haunts and also to the one in the district where they had lived, on the Upper East Side.

"I received commiseration, but not much else," he said. "They promised to keep their eyes open, but I'd be a fool to think my daughter is their top priority. Especially since she left of her own free will."

"Technically, she's a runaway," Larry reminded him. "They're obligated to help locate her."

"Have either of you remembered anything at all that might help?"

"I've been racking my brain all day," I answered. "The only thing that might help is that Frank owns a motorcycle. Maybe he belongs to some kind of cycle club or something like that."

"It's a thought. I told the police about the bike. I even described it—the one he was riding when we lived here. It was parked in my driveway once. I made sure that was the first and the last time."

"Listen, Bill," Larry said, "you've given her all that you could. And she's got street smarts she learned from her friends. The combination is going to work for her. She'll do some things she's going to regret later on, but I think she'll be okay in the end."

"I hope you're right, Larry. I wish I could talk to her for five minutes. And find the right words."

"Can you come to the office tomorrow?" I asked. "Maybe we'll think of something if we all sit down together."

"Sure. What time?"

"Around eleven o'clock. I have two morning clients and then nobody until two o'clock."

"Maybe we'll have news by then."

"I sure hope so," Larry put in.

At 3:00 a.m. I abandoned all hope of sleep. Larry lay next to me, snoring lightly, one arm dangling over the side of the bed. He was a therapist whose client was having a crisis. I was a parent whose child was in danger. I drifted from the window, where I saw occasional

headlights—people finding their way home in the wee hours, people with homes to go to—into the kitchen, where I hovered over the tea kettle to catch it before it had a chance to whistle. I sat at the kitchen island, wrapped in chenille, drinking chamomile as the sky lightened.

At seven, Larry padded into the kitchen. I was making toast and pouring juice like an automaton. The sounds of Ben and Mitch getting ready for school resounded from the back bedroom.

"Get any sleep?" He took the coffeepot to the sink and began measuring water.

"Hardly any. I'm thinking of taking a car and driving through the neighborhoods where she might be."

"Needle in the proverbial haystack." Larry scooped coffee into the filter.

"Better than sitting around doing nothing."

"Honey, you've got to detach. She's got parents. The police are looking for her. We can't do anything else."

"I know. Dammit, I know." Ben and Mitch charged into the kitchen, grabbing juice and downing it in what seemed to be a single swallow.

"Slow down," Larry said. "Sit down."

"And quiet down," I added. "Sorry, guys. I didn't get much sleep.'

"I dread seeing Bill Brody today," I said as we poured our second cups.

"He needs our support, Rachel."

"I know. I'm just not looking forward to it. He's in pain, and I can't help."

When Bill arrived at the office, his face was drawn, his eyes hollow. We sat at the conference table in Larry's office and went over the desperately few facts we knew that might help us locate Heather. At 1:00 Jan poked her head in and asked if she should order sandwiches. We all agreed half-heartedly. Larry and I listened as Bill reviewed the rocky history of Heather's childhood.

"I don't know what went wrong," he said, supporting his forehead with two fingers. "Once I got used to the idea, I was rather keen on being a father. Stephanie and I went out and had the shopping spree of our lives getting ready for the baby. She had the perfect layette, the prettiest, most feminine crib, dolls, toys. It was a new project for Stephanie. She threw herself into it with the zest she has for anything she takes on. Only the best would do."

"I guess neither of you had much of an idea what was involved," Larry said.

"Hardly." Bill took a long drink of iced tea. "She cried all the time, from the minute we brought her home. We hired a nurse for two weeks. We kept her for six months. Stephanie was literally afraid to be alone with the child. She started off trying to smother her with kisses and cuddles, and the baby just screamed. Poor Stephanie was helpless. She'd give a few pats and then thrust her over to me or to the nurse. Heather must have been two weeks old when Stephanie said, 'I give up. I can't do anything with that child.' And she's been saying it ever since."

"What about you?" I asked. "Did Heather respond better to you?"

"I think she did. Yes. I'd hold her and rock her, and the screams would taper off to those deep shuddering sobs that broke my heart." He gazed over our heads, his face softening. "I remember how she pushed herself back to look into my face. She had these incredibly long black lashes, and there would be a tear there, caught on a lash; the sun would hit it, and it would sparkle like a diamond."

"She must have been a very beautiful baby." My voice was softer than a whisper. Larry gave me a long look. Clearly he sensed that my reaction to Bill's story was emotional. He felt for my hand under the table and gave it a squeeze.

"Oh, she was. And Stephanie loved to dress her up. But Heather hated ruffles and lace, even as a tiny girl. I guess those frills itched. When she was about two, she'd tear at the little puffy sleeves with the ribbons and say, 'Off, off,' until we had to give up and dress her in soft cotton T-shirts and little jeans and sneakers. I think that's when Stephanie began to lose interest."

"Her little doll wasn't so doll-like," Larry said.

"Exactly. I'm not blaming Stephanie. She tried. It was just a terrible personality fit. She didn't know what to do with the child. I blame myself for giving in to Stephanie the way I always did. In my heart I knew that a child wasn't right for us. And I knew that Stephanie was too immature and spoiled to be a mother. She needs to be pampered and catered to, not to do that for someone else. I guess I hoped that having a child would encourage her to grow up. All of us suffered for my mistake—Heather most of all."

"Bill, it's pointless to blame yourself," Larry said. "You had no way of foreseeing the outcome. You did your best to give Heather what she needed."

"Thanks." The tight thin line of Bill's mouth indicated that he had not accepted Larry's absolution. He pushed away a paper plate that held the barely eaten remains of his sandwich. "I'll be in town for another couple of days. If I learn anything, I'll call you."

"Same here," I said. "Good luck, Bill. Call us if you need to talk."

Somehow that day passed, and the next day, and the next. Bill called to report that he had learned nothing and had to return to Washington. Twice Larry and I took the car out of the garage and rode slowly through the streets of Hell's Kitchen, Spanish Harlem, and the ungentrified sections of the East Village. While Larry drove, I scanned the faces of the young people who lived on the streets, looking for the familiar rebellious chin, tangle of dark hair, and beaten-up black leather bag over a fragile shoulder. I was unable to recognize my child among the teeming life of New York's dark side.

CHAPTER

19

New York City had swallowed Heather, and there was nothing I could do. I had more in common with Bill Brody than I had with Larry: Larry was concerned about his client; Bill and I were worried sick about our child.

Meanwhile, my life moved forward with an intensity that, mercifully, left little time for brooding. Suddenly it was mid-June. Annie would be arriving in a week with my mother. Her husband and kids would follow a few days before the wedding. I put in extra hours with clients, helping them to prepare for my absence. I carried stacks of files into the conference room, where Larry was diligently typing away on his laptop. Determined to stay focused, I caught up on case notes and insurance forms, all the necessary but hated paperwork that was part of my job. Occasionally Larry would reach out and rest a hand on my knee or, taking a break, would stand up, stretch, and then bend at the waist to deposit a soft kiss on my lips.

On a beautiful summer weekend Larry and I traveled to the inn, checking on the accommodations for my family and finalizing the wedding menu. We stayed for dinner, testing the choices we'd made, chicken marsala or stuffed flounder, and finding them more than satisfactory. Afterward we went on to the terrace where our cocktail hour would be held. The sun was a red ball sinking behind the Palisades, reflected in the shimmering waters of the Hudson.

"It's going to be a beautiful wedding," I said, leaning into him as the crown of the sun disappeared from view.

"We could have gone to the municipal court and been married in the judge's chambers, and it would have been beautiful to me."

We squeezed condo-hunting into our free time. We were looking for more space than my current home provided—an office/guest room, perhaps a garden hidden from the street, maybe a building close to the gym we both used. The few places we liked were breathtakingly expensive.

"I'm going to sell my Washington place," Larry said as we considered a sunny duplex with all the room we needed. "If you sell yours, and if my book does well—"

"I think we should wait," I said. Larry's brow furrowed a bit; I remembered that he didn't take disappointment well. "We have everything we need for now. We can take our time." He used to be a pouter, and I hoped his day, and mine, wouldn't be ruined because of his disappointment. His dream when we were young had been to amass a fortune. I know he hoped to live this way someday.

He glanced wistfully behind him as the agent locked the door. I patted his hand as we headed for the elevator. "Give it time," I said. "We'll have it all."

Back at the office, Larry disappeared into the conference room. I greeted my next client. Foster MacCutcheon had sought me out in the aftermath of his divorce. He'd discovered that the younger women he pursued didn't satisfy him, and he was increasingly missing the comfortable relationship he'd shared with his wife of twenty-seven years. He sat, as always, unnaturally erect, in a gray three-piece suit, paisley tie, and white shirt, still crisp at 2:00 p.m.

"It sounds like you're wondering whether you made a mistake," I ventured.

"Maybe the biggest of my life. And the thing is, I have no idea whether Regina would consider giving it another go. I mean, I cast her off like used clothing."

My intercom buzzed at that moment. Jan only interrupted a session for emergencies involving the children or another major crisis.

"Excuse me just a minute, Foster." I reached for my phone.

"Rachel, I've got Bill Brody on the line. He says it's urgent."

"Okay. Thanks." I turned to Foster. "I've got to take this call. Would you mind waiting in the reception room for a few minutes? I'm really sorry."

"No problem." Before he was out the door, I'd stabbed the blinking light on my phone.

"Bill? It's Rachel."

"Heather's been arrested."

"What? Where? What happened?"

"I don't have details. That boy dragged her into something. They were arrested together. Listen, Rachel, I'm on my way. I'm stuck in a traffic jam at Dupont Circle. I'm going to miss the three o'clock shuttle. I don't want her to be alone. Can you go down to the criminal court and be there for the arraignment? It's at 100 Centre Street. I'll be there as soon as I can."

"Of course. I'll leave now."

"Oh, and Rachel, I called my lawyer. He's supposed to meet me there. His name is Gerald Cook."

"Bill, she's alive. Whatever happens, we've found her."

"I know. That's the good news. I'll see you at the courthouse."

I yanked open my bottom desk drawer and dragged out my purse. I threw open the door to my office. There was Foster MacCutcheon, his straight back not quite touching the chair, hands on his knees.

"Oh, Foster. Listen, I've been called out of the office. An emergency. Forgive me."

"Quite all right, Rachel. It happens, I'm sure, in your work as in mine."

"Right. No charge for today, of course. Jan will give you another appointment, for tomorrow. No, let's be safe and make it the day after tomorrow."

I pivoted to face Jan, who sat behind her desk, attentively waiting for instructions. "Please set Mr. MacCutcheon up with an appointment for Thursday. And cancel out the rest of my day."

"Got it." I knew she wanted to ask questions. She kept silent like the true professional she was. I was grateful.

"Thanks. I'm out of here. Sorry, Foster." I raced down the hall, punching the elevator button just as an elevator car arrived. A heavyset woman emerged. I stepped into the car and uttered a silent prayer.

Taxis whizzed by, off duty or already taken. It seemed like forever, although probably it was no more than two minutes, until a Yellow Cab swerved to the curb. I was able to slide in and tersely give the address. Thank goodness the driver, who had an unpronounceable name, chose not to engage me in conversation. I didn't care to comment on why I was rushing off to criminal court or what I expected to find when I got there.

I dug in my bag for my phone. My numb fingers struggled to dial accurately. Larry answered his cell phone on the second ring.

"Good timing," he said. "My meeting just broke up. Jim thinks the new book's going to hit the top ten in the first week. What's up?"

"I'm on my way downtown." I filled him in on Bill Brody's call and his request.

"I'll meet you there," Larry said. A small fraction of the tension in my neck and back went away.

At the courthouse I passed through security and was directed to the room where arraignments were held. In the hallways just outside the double doors, men and women in business attire, probably attorneys, were engaged in conversation with their various clients, whose dress ranged from torn jeans and grunge, to skimpy skirts and five-inch heels, to overalls and work boots. Minutes crawled as I anticipated how Heather would look and thought of what kind of trouble had brought her here. I knew one thing for sure: the trouble had Frank written all over it.

Heather was not among the group in the corridor. I tugged on the heavy door and let myself into the courtroom. The wood benches held small groups of people scattered throughout the room, speaking among themselves in whispers. At the front of the room, a female judge, whose age I guessed was somewhere in her fifties, towered above the room from her high perch. She was speaking to a lawyer who stood at a table along with his client, a young woman wearing a long black skirt and a bright red V-neck sweater. I couldn't hear the dialogue.

I scanned the room for Heather. Had she arrived here, I wondered, from whatever police station she'd been taken to? I wasn't sure where I should wait. Would she be brought directly into the courtroom?

Should I stay in the hall and see if I could recognize her lawyer? I glanced at my watch. *Is Bill on the plane yet?* I willed him to hurry. I stood up and went back to the corridor, still uncertain about where I should be.

A slim, silver-haired man in dark blue pinstripes waved credentials at a uniformed guard. "Gerald Cook for Heather Brody," he said. The guard indicated a hallway perpendicular to the one we were in. As the lawyer headed in that direction, I hurried over to him.

"Mr. Cook? My name is Rachel Marston. I'm-I'm-I'm a friend of the Brody family. Bill's been delayed. He asked me to be here for Heather."

The attorney shifted his attaché case to his left hand and extended his right hand to me.

"Pleased to meet you. Do you know anything about the circumstances of Heather's arrest?"

"Nothing. Except that she was with her boyfriend when it happened. I'm positive he was the instigator of whatever happened. He's older than she, and he's been in trouble before."

"Good information. The first thing I'll do is move to have the cases separated. When is Bill expected to arrive?"

I glanced at my watch again. "I'm hoping he's on the shuttle right now. He was having trouble getting out of Washington."

"Well, when he shows up, tell him I'm here and that I'm with Heather. I'd better go find my client." He headed down the hallway the guard had indicated.

I waited in the hallway, watching for both Bill and Larry. I wondered distractedly who would arrive first. As Larry came through the heavy outer door, I felt my body surge toward him. He acknowledged me with a wave as he came through the security archway, collecting keys and cell phone with one hand while embracing me around my shoulders with the other.

"Have you seen her?"

"Not yet. Bill's lawyer is with her."

"Is Bill here?"

"On his way. I hope he gets here before the arraignment."

"Do you know what happened?"

"Only what I told you on the phone. She could be in serious trouble."

"But she's okay. At least we've found her. She's here in this building."

"You're right. That's the good news."

"We'd better go in and sit down." I followed him as he pulled open the door to the courtroom. We found seats in the second row, directly behind the defendant's table. The judge, whose nameplate showed "Hon. Adrienne D. Marshall," was admonishing a defendant, while his lawyer, a young man significantly smaller than his client, stood by. The prosecutor, whose nameplate read "Beth Arnold," was a slender young woman wearing a navy pantsuit and a pale gray silk blouse. To my right, in what I assumed served as the jury's box, there were two women and three men, either staring glassy-eyed from boredom or fidgeting nervously. A uniformed guard entered the box, leading Heather and Frank, gesturing to them to sit. I gasped when I realized that they were handcuffed. I waved, hoping to catch Heather's attention. She either didn't see me or ignored me. I half turned in my seat, hoping to see Bill walk in, wanting to wave him over to join us. So far there was no sign of him, but I saw Gerald Cook as he strode down the center aisle and appeared at our side.

"Have you spoken to her? How is she?" I whispered after introducing him to Larry. The attorney slid into the row and sat next to me, on the aisle.

"She's distraught. Her main concern seems to be what's going to happen to her boyfriend. She asked me if I could help him. I told her I'd been hired to represent her. She was rather obstinate. 'I don't want your help unless you help him too,' she told me. I almost had to smile. She's a very passionate young woman."

"How serious is this?" Larry asked.

"It could be very serious. The two of them committed a felony. She was driving a car that belonged to neither of them. She parked illegally, at a curb near a neighborhood bodega. The boy—I gather his name is Frank—went inside. Heather claims that he told her he needed cigarettes. He came running out, jumped into the car, and said, 'Drive.' She hit the accelerator and took off. Meanwhile the store clerk sounded the alarm, and in less than a minute a police car was following them. The boy said, 'Go faster,' and there was a brief chase. Luckily, Heather didn't have the nerve, or maybe plain common sense prevailed, and she pulled over before there was an accident. They were both booked for robbery and evading arrest."

"But she didn't know what he was doing." I heard the high-pitched note of hopefulness in my voice even though I was whispering.

"Doesn't matter. We have only her word that she didn't know. She did, however briefly, try to evade the police."

"It was Frank. He made her do it."

"She'll be called soon. She's still a minor. I'm going to move to have her case referred to family court. That will automatically separate her prosecution from his. Also the court will go much easier on her. But Heather won't like it. She wants to suffer his fate, whatever it is, like some heroine in a nineteenth-century novel. Still no Bill?"

"Any minute, I'm sure," I said, willing Heather's father to appear.

Frank stared straight ahead, expressionless. Heather leaned toward him, her eyes trained on his face. It was obvious that she was willing him to glance in her direction.

I raised a hand and wiggled some fingers again, but she was not interested in anyone who might be sitting in the courtroom. All her focus was centered on Frank, who patently ignored her.

She was bedraggled. Her clothes looked as though she'd slept in them. She probably had. Her hair, long now and tangled, had lost its sheen. Remnants of bright red lipstick clung to dry, chapped lips. Her fragile ankles wobbled on impossibly high heels. She wore no hosiery. There was a yellowing bruise on her upper arm.

"Docket number 407132," intoned the bailiff. "State of New York versus Francis X. Murphy." Frank was brought forward.

"Mr. Murphy, do you have an attorney?" Heather was clearly trying to attract Gerald Cook's attention, but he deliberately affected a stone face and didn't glance in her direction.

"No," Frank said.

"No, Your Honor," the judge reprimanded.

"No, Your Honor."

"We'll appoint one for you." She turned to her clerk. "Who's up?"

The clerk consulted a clipboard that lay on a small table near the judge's bench. "Goldstein." He went out through the double doors, returning a moment later with a young man who looked as though he'd graduated from high school a month ago.

"Matthew Goldstein for the defense, Your Honor," he announced as he hurried to the defense table.

The judge scanned her paperwork. "How do you plead?"

Frank squared his shoulders. "Not guilty, Your Honor."

Judge Marshall looked at the young prosecutor. "Bail?"

"The State requests fifty thousand dollars, Your Honor."

Frank whispered to his attorney.

"My client doesn't have access to that amount, Your Honor," Goldstein said.

Goldstein looked at his client, who shrugged. "That's true, Your Honor," he said.

"You're accused of a serious crime."

"My client is innocent, Your Honor. There was a misunderstanding."

"Misunderstanding? How so?"

"The grocery clerk believed he was being robbed. My client intended only to demonstrate to him, with a fake weapon, how easy it might be to rob him."

Beth Arnold stood up. "Oh, please," she said, stepping away from her table, looking sleek in a gray suit and four-inch heels. "What a coincidence that eight hundred forty-three dollars, the exact amount missing from the cash register at the grocery store in question, should be found in Mr. Murphy's possession." She glanced at the hapless defense lawyer. "Don't make me laugh," she said.

Now Heather noticed us, and was begging Larry and me with her eyes. I shook my head ever so slightly in a negative gesture. Larry seemed to ignore the unspoken entreaty.

"Well," Judge Marshall said, "you're with us, Mr. Murphy. We'll get you a court date early next week. Next." Frank was led away. Heather's eyes never left him as he disappeared through the double doors. She was still watching him when she was brought forward and her handcuffs removed. Gerald slid out of our row and joined her at the defense table.

"Gerald Cook for the defense of Heather Brody."

"How does the defendant plead?" Judge Marshall inquired.

"Not guilty, Your Honor," Cook responded. "If Your Honor pleases, I'd like these charges referred to family court on behalf of Ms. Brody," Cook said. "She is seventeen."

"No objection, Your Honor."

"So ordered."

I breathed a sigh of relief.

I saw Gerald Cook glance at his cell phone, which, I suspected, had vibrated in his pocket. "Your Honor," he said, "may I request a moment to respond to a message that has immediate bearing on the case before you?"

"Make it quick, Mr. Cook. Five-minute recess."

"Thank you, Your Honor." Cook rushed toward to back of the room and disappeared out the door.

"Miss Brody, I do hope your attorney will not hold up these proceedings," Judge Marshall commented. "I'm sending you over to family court, but Mr. Cook needs to be here. Please don't misunderstand: the charges remain serious."

At that moment Heather's lawyer came rushing down the center aisle. "Approach, Your Honor?" he called out while still in the center of the room.

The judge beckoned him forward, and the fashionable Ms. Arnold rose to join him. Heather turned once, briefly, and spotted Larry and me sitting a few rows behind her. I wiggled my fingers at her, and she gave a tiny nod. At the front of the courtroom, the judge and the attorneys were deep in discussion. Judge Marshall's hand covered her microphone. I saw her shake her head in a manner that seemed to convey disbelief.

"Because of the extenuating circumstances that have just been presented to me," she announced finally, "I am granting a ninety-minute recess. I will see you back here at 5:00 p.m."

"Your Honor, might I request that Miss Brody's handcuffs not be used? I'll take personal responsibility." Gerald Cook looked agitated.

"Mr. Cook, there's a conference room at the end of the hall," Judge Marshall offered.

"Bailiff, please show Mr. Cook and his client to the conference room, and remain nearby."

Gerald Cook took Heather's elbow as she stood up. He followed the bailiff out of the courtroom. Larry and I tagged along.

"What's going on?" Heather demanded as soon as we'd all entered the room. "I can't believe you let them lock Frank up." Her chin jutted forward. Everything about her small being signaled defiance and aggression. We all took seats around the long wood table.

"I have some very terrible news," Gerald Cook said. He rose, stood behind Heather, and rested his hands gently on her shoulders.

"What?"

"Your mother just called me."

"Oh, great. She probably told you to let them throw the book at me."

"No, Heather. She called to tell me that your father's plane crashed."

"What? That can't be right. He's going to be here any minute."

I realized I was holding my breath. I reached for Larry's hand, and he gave mine a squeeze.

"His shuttle was coming in to LaGuardia Airport, and it overran the runway. It went into Flushing Bay. Your mother just got a phone call from the airline. Your father was one of those who didn't make it. I'm so sorry."

"Dead? My father's dead?" I sank to my knees and wrapped my arms around Heather. Her body was rigid with shock. Then it softened and crumpled in on itself. She folded herself into a tight ball, pulled her knees up to her chest, and dropped her head on to her knees.

"Oh God, oh God, oh no," she moaned. "Daddy. Daddy." I made no effort to control the tears that streamed down my cheeks as I sat down next to her, tightening my arms around the quivering ball of her body. I'd never felt more helpless, not even in the darkest days of Neil's illness. *How I wish I could make this nightmare go away, my sweetheart.* There was nothing I could do for her. I looked over at Larry, whose pain was etched into the lines around his eyes. He pulled out a handkerchief and blew his nose noisily. After that we were all silent, until Heather's weeping subsided into deep shuddery sobs. Then it stopped altogether.

"I killed him, you know." It was a hoarse whisper. Her head was down, her hair falling over her eyes.

"An airplane crash killed him, Heather," Larry said, his tone low and deliberate.

"He was on that plane because of me." She let out one barking laugh. "My mother always said I'd be the death of him. She was right after all."

CHAPTER
20

"When someone dies, we always blame ourselves," I said, stroking Heather's hair. "It's natural. But thinking that way is going to hurt you even more. He loved you. He wouldn't want you to do this to yourself."

Larry reached out and touched the nail-bitten fingers. "We have to call your mother, you know."

"She won't want to talk to me. She's going to blame me. She should blame me. I can't believe he's gone. I'll never see him again. I'll never be able to tell him I'm sorry."

"You two should talk to each other," Larry said. "You need each other now." He reached for his cell phone.

"No. Don't. Please. Not yet. What's going to happen to me?"

The lawyer spoke up. "We have to go back in there in"—he glanced at his Rolex—"forty-five minutes. I'm going to ask for you to be released. But we'll have to show up in family court eventually." He looked at Larry and me. "Bill was hoping he'd be allowed to take her home with him."

"I can't go back there. I could stay at Frank's until he gets out."

"The judge wouldn't approve that."

Larry gave me a long look. I nodded. We didn't need words.

"You need to speak with your mother. But if it can't work out for you to go home, we'd like you to stay with us for a while."

"You'd do that for me?"

"If you'll let us help you," I said, "we want to, very much."

"I don't know what to say." She covered her eyes with her hands.

"Oh God, I can't believe this. My father—I never wanted this to happen to him."

"Of course you didn't. It was a terrible, tragic accident." I ran my fingers gently through her hair, smoothing out some of the tangles.

"Mr. Cook, can you help my friend?" The plea was subdued, the defiance gone.

"First things first, Heather," he answered. "Right now I have to speak with your mother."

"Tell her I'm sorry," Heather said. "She won't believe it, but tell her."

"I'll tell her." He stepped away from us to make the call. Heather continued to sob. Larry and I murmured soothing phrases, which we knew did nothing to soothe.

"It's going to be okay," I said, knowing that it wouldn't.

"You'll get through this," Larry assured her, patting her on her back. *Will she? I wish I could be sure.*

I intercepted Cook as he was headed back to where we stood. "How did it go?"

"Rough. She blames Heather, just as the child predicted. She doesn't want to see her or talk to her. She doesn't want her to come home. She said, and I quote, 'If she has any thoughts of coming to the funeral, tell her not to bother.' Unquote."

"I feel sorry for her, that she lost her husband," I said. "But to be so rejecting of your child—" *Of my child.* I shook my head. "Heather can stay with us for now. But after that, what's going to happen to her?"

"I think we're going to have to take it one step at a time," the lawyer said. "You and Mr. Tobin are being exceptionally kind to the child. She's lucky to have you."

Heather was seated on the bench, drooping like a houseplant in dire need of water. Larry came over to join Cook and me.

"Are you sure you're up for this?" I asked him. "With our wedding so close and everything?"

"I've always known you have a special feeling for this kid. And I do too—if only because she brought us back together. But even if this was just an ordinary case, I can't see us doing anything else, can you?"

"I'm so grateful that you're willing to do this," I told him. "It could make all the difference for Heather."

"I didn't realize you two were getting married," Cook said. We gave him a brief summary of our history, also mentioning Heather's role in our renewed relationship.

"So you see," Larry told him, "we owe a lot to her. Her future hangs in the balance right now. I'd like to prevent her from getting ground up in the system, if it's possible."

"Still," I said, stretching my neck to give him a peck on the lips, "it's very generous of you to be willing to do this. Not many men would go out on a limb, especially just before a wedding."

"She has to feel that she belongs somewhere," Larry said. "She's reached out to you in the past. She feels safe with you. We're not going to let her down now."

The bailiff approached and said something to the lawyer.

"We have to go back," Gerald Cook told us. He reached for Heather's hand and gently pulled her to her feet.

We took seats and waited for the judge to return. The clerk declared the court back in session.

Judge Marshall looked down at Heather, compassion visible on her face.

"Miss Brody, allow me to convey my deep sympathy for your loss. I know you've had a terrible shock, and I am very sorry. I wish we could postpone these proceedings to another day, but the fact remains that you've been charged with a criminal offense, and we need to reach some resolution here and now. We'll try to make this quick. Mr. Cook?"

The lawyer handpicked by Bill Brody stood behind his table. "Heather Brody has never before been in trouble with the law, Your Honor," he said. "It has not been determined that she knew a robbery had taken place. Indeed, she states that she was unaware of what transpired inside the store. This young girl is guilty of naivety more than anything else. We plan to bring her case before family court, but it would be a compassionate kindness not to put her through anything more today. Furthermore, Dr. Rachel Marston, a respected psychotherapist in our city, and Dr. Lawrence Tobin, the author of a highly acclaimed manual on child psychology, have offered to house Ms. Brody until this matter can be resolved. As you know, the defendant's father, William Brody, was killed in a plane crash earlier today while traveling to New York on his daughter's behalf. All things considered, Your Honor, we request that Heather Brody be released without bail and be instructed to remain under the supervision of Dr. Marston and Dr. Tobin."

Heather pivoted in her seat and mouthed a silent thank-you in our direction. I nodded at her and tried to smile, but I felt my lips quiver and I looked away, my heart breaking.

"Under the circumstances," Judge Marshall began, "I cannot in good conscience allow Ms. Brody to leave this courtroom without bail. Having read the file, I'm aware that before being arrested she was a missing person. She had run away from home. This makes her a flight risk. However, I'm not without sympathy for these unusual circumstances."

She turned to the ADA. "Ms. Arnold, as Mr. Cook points out, this is a first offense, if indeed she is guilty of anything at all. Two exemplary citizens have agreed to keep an eye on her. Bail will be set at ten thousand dollars." Heather gasped.

I leaned forward to whisper to her, "It's okay. We only have to put up 10 percent. You'll be out of here very soon."

"See the court clerk to make your arrangements, please. Young lady," the judge said, "you may not leave New York without special permission. Do you understand?"

"Your Honor," Heather said, clearing her throat and starting over: "Your Honor, may I go home for my father's funeral?"

Judge Marshall looked out into the room. "Will someone be accompanying Miss Brody to Washington for the funeral?"

"I'll be glad to, Your Honor," Larry said.

"Permission granted. You may go to Washington on the day of the funeral, stay over one night, and return by 6:00 p.m. the following day. Will that be satisfactory?"

"Yes, Your Honor. Thank you, Your Honor."

"You'll be given a date to appear in family court," the judge continued. "We'll schedule it for after the funeral." Heather was led away by the bailiff.

"Stephanie doesn't want her there," I whispered to Larry as we were led by Gerald Cook to the window where we would post bail for Heather.

"I'll explain it to her. But if she wants to go anyway, I'll take her. She has a right to be there."

"Thank you so much, Mr. Cook," Larry said. "I'm sure Stephanie will agree to retain you to see this case through. If not, then we will."

"Glad to do it. It's a real nice thing you two are doing for the kid."

"She is rather special to us."

"Do you want me to look into the boy's situation?"

I opened my mouth to tell him that it wouldn't be necessary. Larry spoke first. "If you'd do a preliminary check and see what's involved, we'd appreciate it, Gerald. We're certainly not prepared to take responsibility for him, but he's very important to Heather."

"Will do. Gotta run. I'm meeting a new client in my office in twenty minutes. You two can finish the paperwork here; you should have Heather out within an hour. Good luck." He handed each of us a business card. I groped in my purse to find one of mine to give him. Larry flipped open his wallet and produced his own card.

"Thanks again, Gerald," Larry said. "You've been terrific."

While Larry completed the bail arrangements, I called Mrs. Marcus. "We're getting a houseguest," I told her. I gave her an outline of the day's events. "The kid's pretty upset, understandably. She needs some space, but she could also use some of the TLC that's your specialty. Can you get the guest room ready and do something really simple for dinner? Soup and sandwiches would be perfect."

"Of course. The poor child. I'll do everything I can." I found myself smiling at the thought of waiflike Heather engulfed in the warmth of Molly Marcus's generous capacity for love. I envisioned the twins' curiosity as we brought this strange, sad girl into our home. *Oh my God*, I thought as awareness dawned. *Mitch and Ben are going to meet their sister. How I wish I could tell them.* Once again my secret would be my burden as Heather's life incredibly became entwined with ours.

"We're sorry about your father," Mitch said as I introduced Heather to the boys. I was glad Molly had prepared them.

We were a tight little group standing in my foyer. Larry and I flanked Heather, our bodies almost touching her on either side. The boys were somewhat subdued. Mrs. Marcus stood behind them, one hand on each of their shoulders.

"Our dad died too. A long time ago," Ben told her. "But now we're getting a new one."

"I know," Heather said, her voice little more than a whisper. "You're lucky."

"This is Mrs. Marcus," Larry interjected. "She takes care of all of us."

"And you too," Molly said. "You must be exhausted, the day you've had. Come with me, child. We'll fix you up." Too tired to do more than obey, Heather followed her into the kitchen.

"This is a complication, especially so close to the wedding," Larry told the boys. "But I know you'll cooperate. Heather needs help right now."

"I don't know what to say to her," Mitch confessed. "She seems so sad."

"She's had a bad shock. A couple of them, really." Larry led the boys into the living room. He sat on the ottoman. They threw cushions on the floor and sat at his feet. "We all have to give her some time. If she wants to talk, talk to her. If she wants to be quiet, leave her alone. Maybe she'll just want to stay in her room while she's here. That's okay. She needs time to be alone, to think." *He's so great with them. He'd be great with Heather too. His daughter. Their sister.* I felt a pounding behind my eyes. And my hands were killing me. I clenched them into fists, willing the intense pins-and-needles prickle to ease.

"She's real pretty," Ben observed.

"Doesn't she have a mom?" Mitch asked.

"Right now she's having a little problem with her mom," I explained. "Larry and I hope they'll work it out."

"They should stick together when bad things happen. Like we did," Mitch said. I leaned forward to give him a hug.

"I hope they will. I hope they'll find a way."

I knocked on Heather's door at seven o'clock. She emerged looking more haggard than before. Her eyes seemed lost in the center of dark circles that surrounded them. Her pallor was noticeable. At the dinner table, she stared at the sandwich on her plate but didn't touch it.

"May I be excused?" Her voice was flat and weak.

"Of course, Heather. Can we do anything for you?" I asked.

"No thanks. You've been great. Oh—maybe you could find out the funeral arrangements."

Larry cleared his throat. "Boys, would you excuse us for a few minutes?" Ben and Mitch disappeared.

"Heather, your mother has suggested it would be better if you didn't come to the funeral."

"You mean she doesn't want me there."

"He was your dad, honey, and if you want to be there, then you'll be there. But you should know that your mother may not be happy about it."

"I don't blame her," Heather said. "If I were her, I wouldn't want me either."

"I'll find out where and when," Larry said, "and you can decide what you want to do. As I told the judge, if you go, I'll go with you."

"Me too," I said impulsively. *How am I going to do all this with the wedding less than three weeks away? Somehow. I have no choice.* Larry reached across the table and squeezed my hand.

"I don't know how to thank you."

"You don't have to thank us," I assured her. "Try to get some rest. I'll look in on you a little later."

Mrs. Marcus boiled water for tea, and we took our cups into the den. "I could throttle Stephanie Brody," I said when Larry and I were alone.

"She needs a scapegoat for the pain she's in right now."

"Don't excuse her. She's always been concerned with what Heather could do for her—never gave a thought to the kid's needs."

"The way this happened—the terrible circumstances—certainly doesn't help their chance of rebuilding a relationship. But Heather will have to take it one day at a time."

"Where is she going to live in the meantime? We're going away. She needs supervision. What's going to happen?" The full weight of the commitment we'd made was crashing down on me. *What have I done? What did I get us into? Oh, Heather, what are we going to do about you?*

I knocked on Heather's door before heading for our bedroom. Her "Come in" was muffled. She lay across the bed, on top of the spread, an arm flung across her eyes. She wore a pair of my pajamas that Mrs. Marcus had lent her. I sat on the edge of the bed.

"I don't want to intrude. I just wondered if you need anything."

Heather shook her head. She kept her eyes covered. Then she

said, "Could you just stay here for a little while?" I reached out and tentatively stroked her hair. She didn't protest, so I continued the gentle, hypnotic motion until her breathing evened and slowed. I retrieved an afghan from the living room couch and covered her. As she slept, I grazed my lips across her head, careful not to wake her. I felt a giant fist reach inside my chest and squeeze my heart as I tiptoed away and quietly closed the door.

CHAPTER
21

The lead headline in the next morning's *New York Times* screamed, "Fatal Crash at LaGuardia Claims Thirty-Four Lives." The subhead, its point size only slightly smaller, announced, "TV News Exec among Casualties." There was a photograph of the ill-fated plane, its nose in Flushing Bay. The only other picture was a file photo of Bill Brody taken a few years earlier, when his hair was darker and his chin a bit firmer.

Larry and I skimmed the article, after which I carefully folded the paper and buried it under a pile of magazines. The egg Mrs. Marcus had prepared congealed on my plate. My coffee grew cold.

"I'm going with you to Washington," I announced. "When will we know about the funeral?"

"Your family's coming in a couple of days. Maybe you should let me go with Heather. You can stay here and get ready for our wedding."

"No! I have to be there with her." I pushed back my chair and stood up. Larry's cell phone rang.

I heard Stephanie Brody's voice even before Larry punched the speaker button.

"I'm so sorry for your loss," Larry said.

"I'm here too, Stephanie," I added. "It's a terrible tragedy."

"Yes. Well. It need not have happened. However, I'm calling to tell you I've changed my mind about Heather. I want her to be at the funeral."

"She very much wants to be there."

"Frankly, I'm not concerned about what Heather wants. I don't want to have to answer a thousand questions about why she's not there. I want her to be at the service and the cemetery. I want her to come back to the house with me and greet people. And then I want her to leave. Bill's sister Marilyn is willing to take her, at least for a while."

Larry looked at me and shook his head, his lips forming a straight, thin line. I shrugged my shoulders. It was an eloquent silent conversation.

"We'll bring Heather to the funeral," I said. "When is it?"

"The day after tomorrow. I'll see that you get all the information. Thank you for offering to escort her. As long as you're doing that, would you be kind enough to see that she is dressed appropriately?"

"Of course," I answered.

"Where does your sister-in-law live?" Larry asked Stephanie.

"Chicago. Why?"

"Heather won't be permitted to leave New York for a while. Do you have family or friends here in the city?"

"No one on whom I'd inflict my daughter. Well, I have dozens of calls to make. I guess I'll see you at the funeral." The phone clicked, signaling that Stephanie had abruptly hung up. Larry put his phone down, none too gently, next to his coffee cup.

"Mother of the Year," I commented, carrying my plate and cup to the sink, scraping the uneaten remains into the trash and pouring the coffee down the drain.

"He was her whole life," Larry said. I turned to look at him. "I'm not excusing her," he added.

The boys arrived in the kitchen, more subdued than usual. They climbed on to the counter stools and attacked the cold cereal that Mrs. Marcus had laid out for them.

"Where's Heather?" Mitch asked.

"Not up yet."

"How long is she staying with us?" Ben inquired.

"We're not sure yet. First she has to go to her father's funeral. Then we'll see."

"What about the wedding?"

"What about it?" Larry came up behind Mitch and ruffled his hair.

"This is going to ruin everything."

"Don't you worry," Larry said. He stretched his arms wide, hugging both of them around their shoulders. "Your mother and I are getting married. We have to help Heather, but we won't let it spoil things for us."

The boys bounced off their stools, reaching up on tiptoes to plant kisses on my cheek.

"You have a milk mustache," I told Ben, using my index finger to wipe it away. They reached for their backpacks, which sat in readiness near the door.

"Have a good day," I called after them as they left. "I'd better check on Heather," I added, heading for the bedroom.

"Come in," she called when I knocked. She was in bed, staring at the ceiling, hands clasped behind her head.

"Your mother would like you to be at the funeral," I told her, seating myself on the edge of the mattress. "It will be the day after tomorrow."

"It would be *so* not okay if the only daughter didn't show up." I didn't answer. Her comment was devastatingly on-target. There was nothing I could say.

"It's going to be hard to face her. But I have to say goodbye. He was a good dad. It wasn't his fault he had a kid like me."

I'd left the door open. Larry heard Heather's comment as he entered the room.

"You're not a bad kid, Heather," he said. "You wound up in a family that couldn't meet your needs."

"And I sure as hell couldn't meet theirs."

"It wasn't the best fit in the world," Larry acknowledged. "Everyone tried. There's no point blaming yourself."

"Easy for you to say," she mumbled. "He died trying to help me, and now I can't even say I'm sorry." A film covered her eyes; she blinked it away.

"You'll go to the funeral, and you'll tell him then," I said, my voice thick as though I'd swallowed glue. I cleared my throat. "He'll hear you. He loved you, you know."

"I know." She looked up at me with those shockingly blue eyes that only I knew were an inheritance from Larry. "Can you come too?"

"I'm planning on it."

"I don't know how I'm going to get through this."

"You'll get through it. I promise," Larry said.

"How about some breakfast?" I ventured.

"Did you talk to the lawyer?" Heather asked suddenly, switching gears. Her voice changed from heart-stopping sadness to strident anxiety. "Did he talk to the Frankster?"

"You go eat something. I'll call him now. If he's not in court, I'm sure he'll talk to me," I said. "His number's in my purse." I left her with Larry and went to my room, where I rummaged in my pocketbook for the business card Gerald Cook had given me. When I dialed, he came quickly to the phone.

"I had a short meeting with the young man this morning," Cook told me.

"How did it go?"

"He's a tough customer. He has priors, you know. Started out saying he didn't want my help, couldn't afford it, I should go back to milking my rich clients, and so forth and so on. Finally he shut up long enough for me to spell out his situation. I may have gotten through. I'm not really sure."

"And what is his situation?"

"Second offense, he's looking at some serious prison time. Unless he's willing to acknowledge that he's a cocaine addict, that he was stealing to get drug money, and that he wants to be rehabilitated."

It sounded a bit like the story of Larry's transformation. But I couldn't equate Larry with the Frankster. They'd been born on different planets.

"How did you leave it with him?"

"He said he'd think about it. Didn't deny addiction. I'll stick with him a little longer, only because Bill's kid has so much on her plate and he's important to her. But I think he's got a poor prognosis for rehab. Seems fairly hard core to me. However, you never know."

"Thanks, Gerald. Heather will be so relieved that you spoke with him."

"Will she be going to the funeral?"

"We're taking her, Larry and I. It's the day after tomorrow."

"I'm going to try to clear my calendar and get down there as well. Maybe I'll see you there."

Heather and Larry had relocated to the kitchen, where he'd poured more coffee and she was listlessly buttering a slice of whole grain toast. I reported on my conversation with Cook. "It sounds like Frank's best chance is to agree to rehab," I told her. "Even then, we don't know if the judge will go for it. He's been in trouble before."

"I know. Maybe I can convince him. Can I go to see him? Please?"

"I think you should wait until after the funeral. You've got too much going on now. Give yourself a break," Larry said.

I nodded. "Larry's right."

"I'm just so worried about him." Heather took a tentative nibble at her toast.

"I have a good feeling about Gerald Cook," I said. "Frank's in good hands with him, and so are you."

"I don't know what I'm going to do." She pushed away the plate of half-eaten toast. "I guess I'll stay at Frank's place. We have a couple of roommates. They won't mind if I crash there."

"You're going to stay here." There was no point in reminding her that as a minor, she was not in a position to make the choice. I rested the palms of my hands on her blade-thin shoulders.

She turned on the pivoting stool to face me. I saw the silent tears that spilled over her lower lids. "You're getting married." The simple statement was punctuated with a shuddery sob.

"We are going to get married," Larry said, his tone calm and reasonable as it had been when he spoke to the boys. "Nothing will change for us. You can stay here until you have a plan."

"Crashing at Frank's place is *not* a plan," I put in.

She looked at Larry, then at me. The tears had swelled from a trickle to a cascade. "I am such a fuck-up."

"I was a major fuck-up too when I was just a little older than you," Larry said. She raised her head; two pairs of electric blue eyes looked at each other.

"You never killed anyone."

"Dumb luck," Larry said. "I could've. Back then I didn't much care who I hurt. But I got a second chance, and I used it. You're going to be okay, Heather. Right now you need to cut yourself a break."

I went with Heather to the loft space in Brooklyn that Frank shared with an ever-changing cast of roommates. "Hey, Pip, tough break," said one longhaired man wearing a ripped T-shirt with a motorcycle logo. Tattoos, etched up and down both arms, were visible under the tear in the dirty shirt.

"Pip's short for Pipsqueak," Heather explained. "Hi, Joker," she said, stepping over someone's plastic bag of clothes. "I came for my stuff."

"Any idea when I'll get my car back?"

"No."

I followed her as she went to a narrow unmade bed in the far corner. Someone, who I thought was probably a girl, was curled in a fetal position on one of the cots. She was uncovered, one arm hanging down, fingers grazing an empty beer bottle lying on its side. I scanned the bleak room where piles of clothes and blankets were strewn on the filthy floor. Several cots were loaded with more ragtag personal possessions. The bathroom door was open. It hadn't seen a scrub brush or a bottle of Lysol in a very long time. Heather scrambled through the belongings of others in order to identify her own things. Expensive when new, they now were wrinkled and soiled, and some had burn holes or stains.

As she gathered up her possessions, I imagined her bedroom in Washington. Stephanie had probably decorated in pink and white, hung expensive art, and installed the finest of drapes and carpets. But Heather felt more at home in this grungy place occupied by lost souls and used for shooting up, and snorting, and sniffing, and God only knew what else.

"How come you're leaving?" the person she called Joker asked.

"The judge says I have to. Besides, Frankster's not here."

"It's okay if you want to crash."

"Thanks. Maybe when this mess is over."

Mrs. Marcus had not commented when I handed her the plastic bag of clothing and asked her to run an extra load of laundry. A short while later, Heather appeared in the kitchen dressed in her own things. She'd showered and washed her hair. She wore no makeup. Gone were the soft vests and flowing pants that she'd picked out at consignment shops. The arty look she'd cultivated, and which had been so becoming, was no more, replaced by pure grunge. But at least her clothes were clean and pressed. She wore ripped jeans and a tight T-shirt with a swirling abstract design that she might have painted herself.

"So when's the wedding?" She hoisted herself onto a counter stool.

"Two weeks and three days."

"You should be concentrating on that right now."

"Everything's done. I'm just waiting for my family to arrive. Come, I'll show you my dress." I took her into my bedroom and pulled the dress, on its hanger, out of the garment bag. I held it up under my chin and did a little pirouette.

"It's beautiful." She reached out and gently touched the beads at the neckline. "Sparkly. Pretty."

Hanging my lovely dress back up and zipping the bag, I impulsively put my arms around Heather and squeezed. "I'm glad you're going to be there."

"I thought I'd be sitting with my father." Her face fell again. It was going to be a long time before my girl would recover from this tragedy, if she ever did.

CHAPTER

22

Molly Marcus, wizard with a sewing machine, had spent an evening altering my navy-blue skirt for Heather. I lent Heather pantyhose and low-heeled pumps. She found a tailored white blouse among her own newly laundered things. She wore diamond stud earrings, given by Bill on her seventeenth birthday. Her dark hair fell to her shoulders in waves that resembled my own. Her eyes were great pools of misery in her pinched face. We sat three abreast on the flight to Washington, Larry and I flanking the small, pale girl in the center seat. A few rows ahead of us I spotted Gerald Cook. I went up to greet him before the plane taxied.

Heather strained to look down at the airport as we took off. A police barrier remained in place, reminder of the tragedy of a few days before. "Why?" Heather asked, shifting her gaze to my face. "Why did it have to happen to him? He should've stayed in Washington and let me rot in jail. I deserved it."

"It's normal to feel guilty when someone dies," I said. "You don't deserve to rot in jail, and he didn't deserve to die. We don't always get what we deserve."

"I cared about him, you know. It was her I couldn't stand. It got me so mad that he always gave in to her. He'd want to have a quiet evening, just read the papers, maybe watch a little TV, and she always had someplace for him to go. And he always went. He couldn't say no to her. She's such a bitch."

"I think he loved her, Heather." Larry joined the conversation.

"He was proud of her, how elegant and beautiful she is and how people respect her."

"I guess. But if only she'd let him stay home once in a while, maybe we could've gotten to know each other better. I always felt like he was on my side, but he couldn't ever tell me—or show me. He always did whatever *she* wanted. And now he's gone." Her voice had grown husky with unshed tears. Shaking her head and falling silent, she stared steadfastly at the seat back in front of her, occasionally looking past me at the diminishing city and the few puffy clouds that drifted past.

"I've never been to a funeral before," Heather said as we walked up a wide brick stairway and stood outside the double doors of the Georgian mansion–style building. Gerald Cook, who had shared our taxi from the airport, was just behind us.

"Just try to relax," I said. "You won't have to do anything you don't want to do."

"This is William Brody's daughter, Heather," Larry explained to the director, who greeted us at the door. The man extended his hand; Heather grasped it.

"I'm Matthew Keller. Please accept my condolences for your loss."

"Thank you."

"Has Mrs. Brody arrived yet?" Larry asked.

Keller glanced at his handsome watch dial. "It's early still. You're the first to arrive. She should be here any minute. Would any of you like coffee?" We all declined.

"Heather, would you like to spend some time with your father?" he asked. She looked at me, then at Larry.

"I don't know."

"If you have things on your mind that you'd like him to know, this might be a good time," I said. "Before anyone else gets here."

"All right. Will you go with me?"

"Of course." The director opened the door to an adjacent room, where rows of empty chairs faced a closed coffin draped with a velvet cloth. Heather hung back.

"I don't think I can do this."

"Just go up there and say what's in your heart," Larry said. "He'll hear you."

"I hope so." She tiptoed toward the casket and stood before it, her arms hanging rag doll–like at her sides. Hesitantly she lifted one small hand and placed it on the velvet. She stood there with her head bowed for a long time. Larry and I stood to the side, close enough that she could see us. I watched as her shoulders curled in. She removed her hand from the casket. She grasped her upper arms with her opposite hands and began to rock. As she doubled over as though gripped by intense pain, I took a step toward her, every cell in my own body wanting to hold her, comfort her. Larry put out a hand and gently restrained me. Heather returned to an upright posture.

"Daddy," she whispered finally, "I'm so, so sorry." Tears spilled down her cheeks and dampened the front of her blouse. "That's all I can say to you. I'm sorry—for everything. For making you and Mother unhappy. For causing so much trouble. For not being the daughter you needed. For making you die." A huge sob choked off the words. I wept silently. I almost thought I could hear the crack as my heart broke. Larry, groping in his trouser pocket for a handkerchief, blew his nose.

"That's all I have to say," Heather said softly. "I hope you can hear me, Daddy. I'm sorry, and I love you. And I'll miss you. I'm all alone now."

"Heather, please go into the other room. I want to be alone with your father." We all turned toward the door. Stephanie Brody stood there stiff and regal, wearing a black suit and a pillbox hat, from which a fingertip veil hid her eyes. Her greeting to Larry and me was a curt nod. Heather backed away from the coffin, then turned and fled out the double doors.

"It's very painful for me to have her here," Stephanie said to us as she approached the front of the room. "Now, if you'll please excuse me." She walked up to the casket and, bending over, laid her cheek against the dark velvet cloth. We quietly went in search of Heather.

Several people had gathered in the anteroom. We found Heather sitting alone on a bench along the far wall of the room. Conversation swirled around her. We approached her and stood like two sentinels, guarding her from the animosity, which was almost palpable.

"Those guys over there," Heather said, nodding her head toward a stout balding man who was holding a conversation with a too-thin younger person with a pencil-thin mustache and a head of dark hair slicked straight back from his forehead. "The fat one's my uncle Gregory, my mother's brother. He never liked me either. He's talking to Lester Fox, my father's accountant." It seemed to me as if everyone's backs were turned to Heather. No one came over to acknowledge her or offer sympathy. *So these are Stephanie's friends and family. What bastards, every one of them.*

Finally a woman with silver hair, wearing a navy-blue silk dress, bustled over to us. "There you are," she said, relief in her voice. "I've been looking everywhere for you. Stand up, child. Let me give you a hug." Heather allowed herself to be wrapped in a tight embrace. "My poor, poor girl," the woman said. "How dreadful you must feel."

Heather pulled back gently from the hug. "Aunt Marilyn, these are my ... my friends Rachel and Larry. They've been great to me."

The woman put out her hand and shook mine, then Larry's. Her grasp was firm, the handshake vigorous. "I can't thank you both enough," she said. "I'm Marilyn Whitfield, Bill Brody's sister."

"We're so sorry for your loss," I said. *Finally someone in this family I can like.*

"I'm sorry too, Aunt Marilyn. So sorry for everything." Heather looked into the kind brown eyes.

"Sometimes bad things just happen, darling. I want you to come back to Chicago with me. Your mother needs some time alone right now."

"My mother doesn't want me at home. You don't have to pretend."

"She needs a little time, that's all."

"Mrs. Whitfield," Larry broke in, "it's a lovely offer, but Heather is required to stay in New York for the time being."

"Even if she has a relative who's willing to give her a home?"

"Perhaps we could work something out with the judge, but for now she has to go back with us. Her lawyer's here. You might want to speak with him. Meanwhile, she's welcome to stay on with us for as long as necessary."

"Besides, Aunt Marilyn, my boyfriend's there, and he's in trouble. I can't just go off and leave him." The aunt, Larry, and I exchanged glances. None of us chose to comment on Heather's misplaced loyalty.

"Is Chester here?"

"He'll be along with Uncle Drew, dear. They came in a separate car. Chester is my son," Marilyn Whitfield explained. "There was a time when he and Heather were friends."

Stephanie emerged from the chapel and scanned the room. Spotting Heather, she approached us. "Heather, you'll sit with me in the front row." It was a command. "Hello, Marilyn. I guess you should be up there with us as well. They'll be expecting us to go in and sit down very soon."

"Ice princess," Marilyn Whitfield said in the softest of undertones, right into my ear.

The funeral home was rapidly filling with men and women who'd come to pay respects to a man who had made many friends and had achieved success and respect in his career. I recognized the anchor of a Sunday morning news program and the chief political correspondent who worked for Bill Brody's station. Clearly visible whenever the doors opened was a news crew, the photographer holding a camera on his shoulder, pointing it as people walked, in twos and threes, into the building. To my surprise I spotted the president's press secretary in the crowd. William Brody hadn't been in Washington for long, but he had certainly made his mark.

In the chapel I managed to find seats for us almost directly in back of Heather and her mother. As the girl glanced over her shoulder, I was able to give her a small wave and a nod, indicating that we were nearby. Marilyn Whitfield came in and seated herself on Heather's right, resting an arm lightly on the girl's shoulders. I wanted to hug the compassionate woman, who was grieving for her brother but nonetheless was able to comfort his stricken daughter. "Thank God for Aunt Marilyn," I whispered to Larry, who squeezed my hand in affirmative response.

It was a lengthy service, during which notables from Bill's TV station and friends from his New York life came, one by one, to the podium and shared memories. Through their words I got to know Heather's father as brilliant, kind to young reporters and production staffers, with a dry sense of humor and a love for his work. I learned that he had known the names of everyone on the large staff, as well as those of their spouses and children. He had remembered birthdays and was generous with praise.

Christine Nadinsky, anchor of a Sunday afternoon talk program, approached the microphone carrying a large square object. The sleek blonde was a familiar presence. In person, her face communicated a warmth that belied her razor-sharp interview skills. Leaning the bulky item against the podium, she faced Stephanie and Heather. When she spoke, her voice was the husky trademark we knew from television. "Mrs. Brody," she began, "all of us at the station know how proud your husband was of you. He told everyone about your successes in raising money for all the causes and charities you took on. He spoke of you often, and always with admiration. 'She makes me look good,' he told us."

She then turned her attention to Heather, raising the large square object over her head. It was an abstract painting in vibrant primary colors that showed rays of sun streaming from behind a dark gray cloud. The suggestion of mountains, trees, and a crystal-blue lake filled the foreground of the work. "This piece hung behind Bill's desk," Christine told the assembled group. "Whenever a newcomer met with him in his office, he would call attention to the artwork. 'My daughter painted this,' he'd say. Everyone who worked at the station knew that Heather Brody was an artist and that her father believed she would be famous one day. Heather, I want you to know that your father believed in you."

My right hand, tingling painfully, spanned the space between my heart and my emotion-swollen throat. Heather covered her eyes with her hand; her ragged sob freed my own tears. Christine Nadinsky stepped down from the dais and approached the mourners in the front row. She leaned the painting carefully against Stephanie's chair. "I know you'll want to have this," she said. "I hope you'll find some comfort in knowing how fond of it your husband was."

The burial was agony for everyone. Stephanie was a frozen statue in black, supported by her brother Gregory. She held a white rose, stark against her mourning clothes. In a gesture that seemed as melodramatic as it was heartfelt, she tossed the flower onto the casket. "Goodbye, my love," she said, and fell back into her brother's arms. She did not touch her daughter. Aunt Marilyn stood nearby, her hand resting lightly on Heather's shoulder. Larry and I were one step behind.

"Do I have to go back to the house?" Heather seemed done in

by the funeral service and the burial. "Can't we just go back to New York?"

"Hang tough a little longer," Larry said, patting her upper arm. "We'll try to catch the late shuttle."

At Stephanie's house, a catering staff offered drinks and canapés. The gleaming rosewood dining table was laden with platters of hot and cold food. A huge silver coffee urn sat on a wheeled cart in one corner. The mourners gathered in small groups. Without too much difficulty, I was able to identify Bill's workplace associates, Stephanie's contacts from the worlds of music, art, and charity, and family members.

Heather sank into a plush velvet sofa. She declined my suggestion that she eat something. Conversation swirled around us. A young man dropped himself onto the cushion next to hers. His sport jacket spanned an ample stomach. He had red curls and a few pimples on his chin. I moved closer to hear what he was saying.

"How ya doin', Heathie?"

"Not so great, Chester. I've got to get out of here." So this was Marilyn's son, Heather's cousin Chester. His mother came over, nodding to me and bending down to speak with Heather.

"How are you, baby?" The kind words started the girl's tears flowing again.

"I want my dad."

"Sweetie, I want him too. I'm sorry we've all lost him. He was a great guy. And a good brother."

"And a good uncle," Chester added.

"Chester," Heather said, standing abruptly, "come help me pack." Stephanie was standing nearby, holding a martini glass, a group of Bill's employees clustered around her. Heather approached her mother, her cousin trailing in her wake.

"I'm going up to pack my things," Heather announced. I waited for Stephanie's response, hoping that I would hear one note of warmth or regret.

"The suitcases are in the storage closet," she said. "Take what you need, but I'll want them back." Heather and Chester headed for the stairs.

"Excuse me," I said to Marilyn Whitfield. Briefly, Stephanie Brody stood alone. I seized the moment.

"Stephanie, may I speak to you in private for just a minute?" She handed her empty glass to a server and led me through double doors into a room lined with shelves of books. Two leather wing chairs stood in a corner, a round table with claw legs between them. Stephanie sat, gesturing to me to take the other chair.

"Do you want a drink or a cup of coffee?"

"No, thank you. I need to speak with you about Heather."

"I find it hard to understand the interest you and Dr. Tobin have taken in her."

"She came to us for help. Of course we couldn't refuse."

"I advise you to be very careful." She crossed one slender leg over the other. "She'll take whatever you have to give, and she'll give nothing in return. The child has always been a heartache."

"I understand it hasn't been easy."

"You win the Pulitzer for understatement. The child poisoned my life and took my husband in the end. Be careful, or she'll do the same to you."

"Stephanie, Heather needs her mother right now."

"Stephanie doesn't need her." Her brother Greg had entered the room quietly and now stood next to her. "She's a reminder of everything my sister needs to forget."

"She's a thoughtless, ungrateful child," Stephanie added. "We rescued her from God knows what kind of life, gave her every luxury—the best schools, the best clothes—and she made it her life's purpose to embarrass and repudiate us. She didn't want what we had to offer. Well, fine. The offer has been withdrawn." She stood up and took her brother's arm. I remained seated for a moment, speechless in the face of her pain and her rage. Pulling myself together, I stood, dampened my dry lips with my tongue, and smoothened my skirt. As I left the library, I saw Heather descending the staircase dragging a gray leather suitcase with a navy monogram, *sBw*. Chester, behind her, negotiated a larger version of the luggage around the turn of the steps.

Approaching, I saw Heather stiffen, so I turned to follow her gaze. A pair of teenagers were heading toward her. Heather's eyes darted left and right. She found Larry, then me, and her wide eyes and set jaw begged for help. The silent plea was, *Get me out of here.* It was too late. The young people were on top of her.

"Oh, Heather," the girl said, "I just can't believe it. How awful!

How terribly, terribly awful." Heather didn't answer. She reached the bottom of the stairs and set the luggage down. She lowered her head and brushed an imaginary speck of dust from the Persian rug with her toe.

"Hey, Heather, sorry to hear about your dad." The boy who spoke was tall and rangy with a wisp of wannabe mustache darkening his upper lip. "We missed you at school," he added.

"Yeah, right." She raised her head and for a long moment stared directly into his eyes. She seemed very small next to the pair. The girl was easily a head taller than Heather. She had large breasts, and although her gray blouse was appropriate to the occasion, the top button was open and a bit of cleavage was visible.

"Dr. Rachel Marston, Dr. Larry Tobin, I'd like you to meet Chloe Henderson and Jon Bailey." She'd learned the lessons her mother had strived so hard to teach. Her etiquette was impeccable. These were the false friends, the traitors who had set Heather on the path that had led us all to this sad day and this dreadful place. *How dare you show up here?* I didn't trust myself to speak. I inclined my head, acknowledging the introduction. I hoped my look was the glare I intended.

"How do you do?" Larry said. I noticed that he didn't add "pleased to meet you."

"Excuse me." Heather bolted in the direction of the powder room. I followed her, leaving Larry to cope with the two thoughtless high school students who hadn't cared whom they hurt.

Heather hadn't locked the door. I entered the small modern guest bath to find her wiping her lower lids with the side of her index finger and blowing her nose on a wad of toilet paper. I'd heard the sounds of her stomach upheaval as I raced in after her. "Please, *please* can we leave?" she begged.

"Let's go find Larry. We'll head out for the airport." I took her clammy little hand and led her back into the living room. I spotted Marilyn Whitfield in a corner near the buffet table, engaged in animated conversation with Gerald Cook. I imagined she was imploring the lawyer to find a way to allow Heather to come to Chicago.

"Maybe you should say goodbye to your aunt," I suggested.

Heather approached Marilyn. "Thanks for everything," she told her. "You're great, Aunt Marilyn."

Marilyn opened her arms. Heather stepped into them and allowed herself to be squeezed in a long hug. Her aunt laid her cheek against the crown of the girl's head. "You hang in there, sweetie. We're all going to survive this. I'll be in touch." Turning to us, she said, "May I speak to you privately for a moment?" Heather shrugged. We moved out of her line of hearing.

"I know that Stephanie is not being ... Well, she's not being very—how shall I put it?—sensitive where Heather is concerned. Of course she's grief-stricken and not thinking clearly. Still—"

"She's thinking clearly all right," Heather said. She had left the couch and was standing nearby.

"I loved my brother dearly," Marilyn continued as though Heather hadn't spoken. "I certainly don't hold this child responsible for what happened. God knows Bill had taken that shuttle a hundred times or more on business. It could have happened at any time."

"Your support is going to be very important to Heather," Larry said.

"You're the only one I have left," Heather added, moving closer until she stood among us, part of the conversation.

"My niece is lucky to have the two of you," Marilyn said to Larry and me. "Heather," she went on, "I want you to come to us in Chicago as soon as they say you can leave New York." She drew the child into a tight hug and held her for a long time. "You belong with us."

"I don't think I belong anywhere, Aunt Marilyn."

"We'll see," Larry said, placing a protective arm around Heather's shoulders. "You'll have choices, Heather. We'll help you."

"Should I say goodbye to my mother?"

"I think you have to," I told her. "We'll go with you."

Stephanie stood at the center of a small group. "I'll try to get back to work on the auction as soon as possible," she said to a stout gray-haired woman who wore a straw hat with a silly-looking purple feather sticking straight up.

"You take all the time you need, you poor dear," the woman said.

"No, no, I think it will help me," Stephanie insisted. "My days will be so empty now. So lonely."

"Mother, I'm leaving." Several people stepped aside so that Heather could approach Stephanie. The girl raised her eyes to look up at her widowed mother. Stephanie glanced at her then quickly averted her gaze. She stared at the space somewhere between Heather and me.

"Well then, goodbye," she said. "Try to stay out of trouble. If that's possible." Her nod to Larry and me was brisk and businesslike. Then she turned back to the group of men and women with whom she'd been speaking. "As I was saying"—she angled her slim black-clad body so that her back was completely turned to Heather—"I think all minimum bids should be at least a thousand dollars."

"Let's go," Larry said. He picked up one suitcase in each hand. We headed for the door.

"Oh, just one minute," Stephanie called after us. "Wait a moment, please." We all turned to look at her as she disappeared into the library. A moment later she was back, carrying Heather's painting. She extended it toward us, holding it on either side of its frame.

"Heather, I don't have a free wall in the house for this. You take it." Thrusting the oil painting into her daughter's arms, she turned on her heel and walked away.

CHAPTER
23

Larry leaned over me and kissed me awake the next morning. "Eight more days," he said, punctuating the remark with a peck on the tip of my nose. I rolled onto my back and stretched, arms thrown over my head. The fog of sleep dissolved too soon, and my conflicting emotions fought for dominance before my eyes were fully opened. There was a heartbroken teenager in the guest room who happened to be my daughter. She needed attention, support, reassurance. Waiting to board a plane at LAX were my sister and my mother, ready to join me in a flurry of prenuptial festivities. I strongly suspected a bridal shower was to be part of my immediate future. We were planning shopping, catching up, and "girl time," just Annie, Mom, and me. How could I let them know that my heart wasn't in any of it? Surely I couldn't let them know why. Annie, of course, would realize immediately how torn I was. My mother would have no clue, nor should she.

First things first. Larry went to awaken Heather, while I washed my face and padded into the kitchen, where coffee was mercifully brewing. Molly Marcus, who'd given up her bedroom for Heather and gone to stay with her cousin in Brooklyn, was already at work, mixing batter and warming the waffle iron. "It's the boys' last day of school," she reminded me. "I thought they should have a special breakfast." *Damn.* I'd forgotten all about the end of the school year. It was always a big deal at our house. They had only half a day of class, and then they would be here, exploding with eagerness to see their grandmother and their aunt, begging to go with me to the airport.

Suddenly my head hurt. I looked longingly at the coffeepot, willing it to stop dripping so I could pour myself a cup.

"Waffles! Hurray!" Ben shouted, bounding into the kitchen and springing onto the counter stool. "Do we have strawberry syrup, Aunt Mol?"

"Of course, Benjy. But I'm not ready yet. Pour yourself some orange juice."

Mitch and Larry drifted in. Larry headed for the coffeepot. Mitch took juice. We waited for Heather

"Should I start?" Molly asked.

"Yes. The boys are hungry, and they have to get to school. Larry and I will wait for Heather."

"Mom, can we go to the airport with you?" Mitch wore the pleading expression that I found irresistible.

"I don't think so, honey. I have to see a client this afternoon, and then I'm going straight to the airport from work. And Grandma, Aunt Annie, and I are going to go out for dinner together."

"Will you be home before we go to bed? I can't wait to see Grandma."

"We'll be coming back here to drop off their suitcases before we go out. I know they're very anxious to see you too." Everyone was in wedding mode but me. If it were possible, I would have rolled this wedding back a month. I wanted to lavish attention and love on my Heather, making up for the cold, calculated slap in the face she'd received from the woman she'd called Mother.

"Slow down," I urged Ben, whose waffles were disappearing as though he'd inhaled them. "Take time to taste them."

"I can taste them. Yum." His words were muffled by the food still in his mouth.

Mitch savored his breakfast a bit more, but only slightly. Before I'd finished half a cup of coffee, they were at the door, backpacks slung over their shoulders.

"Tell Heather we said g'bye," Mitch he said as he pecked my cheek.

"We'll do that. Have a great last day," Larry put in.

Larry and I sat in companionable silence for a few minutes while we waited for Heather to appear.

"Excited to see your mom and Annie?" Larry asked. He reached for my hand and stroked it with his thumb.

"It'll be great." My flat tone didn't match my words.

"Heather?" I nodded and drew in a deep sigh.

"Sweetheart, you have to let it go. We're doing what we can to help her, but I don't want her problems to spoil this special time for you."

"Oh, Larry. That mother of hers—she's really not a mother at all. Heather is an orphan."

"She has us." He squeezed my hand. I felt love fill my chest as helium fills a balloon. The urge to tell him the truth bubbled to the edge of my lips; I compressed them to keep them silent.

"What?" Larry recognized an unspoken thought.

"Nothing. I love you. You don't have to be doing this, but you are. You're taking responsibility for a child you hardly know."

"I know her enough to realize she doesn't deserve what's happening to her. I know how much you care about her. And I'll always be grateful to her for bringing you back to me." I responded in the only way I could. I leaned forward, took his face in both my hands, and gave him a long, appreciative kiss.

Heather finally shuffled into the kitchen and climbed up on one of the counter stools. She'd tied a short cotton robe loosely over her nightgown. Her hair was tangled, and there were dark circles under her eyes.

"Is there coffee?" Larry gestured toward the pot. She got up and poured a cup for herself. Mrs. Marcus turned on the waffle iron.

"Did you get any sleep?" I asked Heather.

"Not much. Can I see the Frankster today?" I looked at Larry.

"I'll make a call in a little while. If we can get clearance, I'll take you."

"I have to go pick up my mother and sister at the airport. Otherwise I'd go too."

"I am so in the way. Your family's coming and everything. I don't get why you're doing this for me."

"We both feel fine about doing it," Larry said. "You're not in the way. You just need a little time to straighten out your problems and make some plans. We want to help."

"I'd be in a jail cell someplace if it weren't for you guys. Nobody else gives a damn."

"We're going to take this one day at a time," Larry said. "I think you need to talk to your lawyer and find out what's going to happen next. Meantime, you're here with us. You can stay as long as you need to."

"But I can see the Frankster today, right?"

"We'll try." Mrs. Marcus laid a plate of waffles in front of each of us, and we busied ourselves with strawberry preserves and maple syrup. By the time I'd poured myself another half mug of coffee, draining the pot, I felt that I would, after all, make it through the day.

Foster MacCutcheon was the only client on my schedule. I had to see him to make up his interrupted appointment. As always, I took a few deep breaths before the session and switched gears in order to give him my full attention.

"What do you really want, Foster? Really?" I challenged him as he sat straight as a buck private at attention.

"I want her back," he said without hesitation. Suddenly the rigid posture crumbled and the shoulders caved in. With his hands over his eyes, the always-in-control executive began to weep. It was a painful sound to hear, the dry, ragged sobs of a man who long ago had taught himself not to cry. I waited, supportive in my silence, knowing that to speak now would be more than the man could bear.

Finally he pulled an immaculate handkerchief from the pocket of his trousers and blew his nose. "What am I going to do, Rachel?" he asked. "I'm afraid I've blown it—thrown away the best part of my life."

"Call her, Foster."

"What if she won't talk to me?"

"You won't know that until you try."

"I guess I'm afraid—more afraid than I've ever been in my life. Right now I have hope."

"Then you'll know. You'll be able to move on. On the other hand, maybe she'll say yes."

"You're right. I just feel like I've been such a fool."

"Everyone's a fool at times. You're human, Foster. You're not supposed to be perfect."

"But I hurt Norma so badly. I wouldn't blame her if she spit in my face."

"Only one way to find out. First of all, forgive yourself. Then ask her forgiveness. Maybe you'll get it."

"And maybe I won't. You know, I've rarely been in a situation that I couldn't control. I feel so helpless."

"For you, Foster, growth is about giving up control. You'll be a better man regardless of how this turns out."

He glanced at his watch. "Our time's just about up. Thank you, Rachel. I'm going to do it. I'm going to call her."

"As you know, I'm not going to be working for a few weeks. But if you'd like to give me a call after you've spoken to Norma, that's fine. Leave a message and I'll get back to you, okay?"

"Best of luck to you, Rachel. Thanks for everything."

I stood at my window after he left. *We're both struggling, Foster and I. We're both afraid of an unknowable outcome. He needs to approach Norma and face her possible rejection. And I have to share my secret. I can't marry Larry with this deception between us. I'm as fearful of rejection as Foster is.* I turned back to my desk, still unable to take that final step and tell Larry the truth. I knew I had to do it. I just couldn't.

I took the train from Penn Station to Newark airport. Settling back for the half-hour ride, I pulled my cell phone from its slot in my leather bag and accessed my home number, stored as the first one in the phone's memory. Mitch answered. The next few minutes were filled with details about the last day of school, report cards, and which teachers they'd have in the fall. Ben pulled the receiver away from Mitch to share his own version of events. *I should be home for this. Everything's happening too fast. It's too much, too much.*

"Did Larry see your report cards yet?"

"No, he wasn't here when we got home. Neither was Heather." Mrs. Marcus took the phone from the boys.

"Larry went with Heather to the jail to visit her boyfriend," she told me. "Don't worry, everything's fine here. Ben's going to play tennis now, and Mitch and I are going to watch."

"I should be in the house around 5:30. Maybe we'll open a bottle of wine and visit for a while, and then I'm taking my mom and my sister out for dinner."

"I'll have some snacks ready."

"Thanks. You're an angel." Clicking off, I slid the phone back into my handbag, leaned my head against the seat, and ran my fingers through my hair. *Too much. Too much.*

My mother seemed smaller than I remembered. Annie towered over her. They took turns hugging me. My mother grasped my shoulders and stood me at arm's length, giving me a long and thorough look. "You're not getting enough rest," she pronounced.

"You're right. There's been a lot going on." I spotted the driver holding up a sign with my name.

"I'm Vinnie," he told us. "I'll get your bags." The luggage carousel began to turn, spitting out suitcases of all colors and sizes from the central chute. Annie pointed out those belonging to her and Mother. Then we followed Vinnie to our hired car.

Traffic was backed up, as usual, at the Holland Tunnel. As we waited, I filled them in on what had been going on with Heather. "We couldn't abandon her," I explained. Annie pressed her lips into a thin line. Her eyes sought mine; she gave me a penetrating look.

"It's nice of both of you," my mother said, "but you can't be doing all that right now. This is your time to be a bride. There must be someone else who can take care of that girl."

"There's not."

"Well, I hope you know what you're doing. I'm still trying to get used to the idea that you're going to marry Larry Tobin of all people."

"Wait till you see him, Mom. He's not the Larry we used to know. He grew up to be a wonderful man."

"Hard to believe." My mother folded her arms. "I can just imagine what your father would have said."

"Just wait. Dad would have been thrilled. Larry's everything both of you wanted for me." I could understand her skepticism, or Annie's, which I'd also felt. They'd have to see for themselves.

I felt an atmospheric change in the apartment as soon as the door opened. There was an unnatural quiet. The air seemed heavy and oppressive. Mrs. Marcus bustled out to the entryway, her face more telling than any barometer.

"Hello, Molly," my mother said, extending her hand. "It's good to see you again." Molly wiped her hands on her apron before offering them first to my mother, then to Annie. Her glance at me communicated some kind of trouble.

"I'm happy to see both of you on such a wonderful occasion," she said to my family. "Please come and sit. Excuse the mess. I'll have some refreshments ready in a couple of minutes."

I looked beyond her into a room that had obviously been the scene of a recent crisis. Throw pillows littered the floor, two paintings were hanging loosely at a dangerous angle, and a broom leaned against the TV cabinet, with glistening evidence of broken glass on the floor nearby.

"What happened here? Where is everyone?" I asked.

"We're having a bad day. Dr. Tobin took the boys out for pizza."

"He did?" My tone conveyed my surprise. "The boys were so anxious to see their grandmother and their aunt. And Larry was looking forward to it also. I don't understand."

"Dr. Tobin said I should tell you that he thought it was best for Ben and Mitch. It was pretty unpleasant around here for a while."

"What happened?" Mrs. Marcus looked at Annie and my mom and then back at me.

"It's okay, Molly. They know about Heather."

"Well, I know that she went to the jail to visit that no-goodnik who made all the trouble. Dr. Tobin took her. Next thing I know, they're back, and she's screaming and crying and throwing things around. She's yelling words I'm not supposed to know. Mitch and Ben are trying to help, and it's like trying to put out a grease fire with a turkey baster. Then she pushed Mitch hard, and he fell and slid into the wall." My mother gasped and put a hand over her mouth.

"Dr. Tobin got angry," Mrs. Marcus continued. "But even then he was good, like always. He told Heather to go into her room and calm down. He took the boys out for supper. He told me you'd be home soon and said I should leave Heather alone until you got here. I've just been cleaning up the mess."

"Do you know what set her off?"

"She was cursing at that boy—I think she called him Frankster. Whatever happened, he caused it."

"I'd better go check on her." Casting an apologetic glance at Annie and my mom, I headed for the bedroom.

Heather didn't answer my knock. Having found the door unlocked, I walked in quietly. The girl stood motionless in front of the window, gazing out at the courtyard below. Her head was bent forward on her slim neck, and her shoulders were sagging as though her body was too much of a burden to carry. I approached her and touched her arm.

"Heather? Are you okay?" She didn't look around.

"Leave me alone." Her voice was a flat monotone.

"I'd like to help."

"I said, leave me alone." The hostility I was hearing was worse than anything I'd ever experienced from Heather, even in the earliest untrusting days.

"Something's happened. I want to help."

"You can't. Would you please just go away now? I don't want to talk about it."

I was torn. Heather needed to unburden herself, but I knew I couldn't force the issue, not while she was in this mood. I closed the door very quietly on my way out.

Annie and Mom turned to look at me as I returned to the living room. *Why do they have to be here now? Why did this have to happen just when they got here? Who am I supposed to pay attention to?*

"She'll be fine," I said, trying and failing to find a light note on which my voice might land. "It's just teenage stuff. Let's have some wine and cheese and wait for Larry and the boys. Then we'll head out for dinner." Mrs. Marcus brought out a beautifully arranged platter of cheeses with grapes and her own special eggplant dip with pita chips. I found my favorite cabernet in the liquor cabinet. We settled down to begin our visit. More than half my head was in the bedroom with Heather. I was heavy with the oppression of the child's problems and the weight of my secret. The small pink infant a nurse had taken from my arms was now, at last, in my care, under my roof, and she was forlorn, miserable, and feeling totally alone. Annie communicated with me wordlessly, her many glances containing her empathy and concern. In all the world, she was the only one who knew what I was going through.

A burst of energy and tumult signaled the arrival of the twins. They threw themselves on their grandmother and their aunt. The next few minutes were filled with their chatter, each boy eager to talk, the two of them trying hard to take turns as they vied for attention from Annie and Mom. Larry stood quietly, waiting. When finally there was a pause, he pulled an ottoman opposite the couch, sat on it, and smiled warmly.

"Mrs. Green. Annie. It's good to see you. It's been a long, long time."

"Larry, I must confess, I was more than a little surprised by this turn of events." My mother was holding back a small portion of her warmth, waiting to be convinced.

"Hey, Larry, so you got her in the end," Annie said. He responded with a grin.

"Nobody's more surprised than I am."

"You guys haven't seen each other in, like, forever," Ben observed.

"It was worth the wait," Larry said, smiling at my mother as he said it. "Listen, you guys, can you give us a few minutes? We have to catch up on some stuff."

"Yeah, okay." The boys retreated.

"Mitch," Annie called after them, "I'm looking forward to a concert."

"You got it, Aunt Annie." They disappeared into their room.

"Larry, what happened today?" Feeling the tension in my body, I rocked a little as I waited for his answer.

"The boy totally rejected her," he told me. "I'm not sure if he's as callous as he sounded or if he wanted her to give up on him and turn her life around, but he was very cruel."

"What did he say?"

"Called her a rich bitch. Said she was buying her way out of jail with her fancy lawyer. Said she didn't have the guts to face the music."

"That bastard. What was he doing, daring her to go to prison for what he got her into?"

"Who knows? There's more. He called her a baby and said he found a real woman while she was in Washington. He ridiculed her for not doing drugs with him. He told her to get lost and take her fancy lawyer with her."

I jumped to my feet and stood over him. I became aware that my fists were clenched. "That's it. I don't want Gerald Cook to have anything to do with the Frankster. Whatever happens to him, it's too good for him."

"I'm about ready to give up on him too. Unless his motive was to get Heather to walk away. If so, he could almost be forgiven."

"I don't think he has it in him. And I'm not in a forgiving mood. Did he say anything about her father?"

"She asked him if he knew Bill had died. He knew, he said, adding that if she thought he was going to feel guilty for that, she could think again. Bill certainly hadn't flown to New York on Frank's account. Tough break, but that's life, et cetera, et cetera. I mean, he laid it on thick. She was devastated."

"What a terrible night this is going to be for her."

"Let's give her tonight to cope with it on her own. Tomorrow we have to get her to talk to us."

Annie and my mother sat quietly, looking from one of us to the other. My mother shook her head. I knew she was reacting to the sheer sadness and cruelty of the story. I hoped she'd never find out that the suffering child was her granddaughter.

"I think we should stay in tonight," I said. I turned to my mom. "You won't mind if we order something in?"

"Of course not," Mom and Annie said in unison.

"Absolutely not," Larry said. "The three of you are going to go out and have a nice dinner, and catch up and talk about the wedding. I'll be right here if Heather needs anything. I insist."

I felt trapped. I didn't want to be anywhere other than right here, close to my child, ready to run to her if she cried out. "Are you sure?" I tried. "Maybe she'll ask for me."

"I can handle it, sweetheart. You go. This is your time. Enjoy it."

"Okay, ladies," I said as lightly as I could manage, "let's get going. We'll be late for our reservation." I went into the bedroom hallway and called out, "Good night, everyone. See you tomorrow." And I left.

CHAPTER 24

I slept late the next morning. I'd gone back to the Park Lane with Mother and Annie after our lengthy dinner. None of us wanted to say good night. I sat cross-legged on a twin bed in their room until after 1:00. We reminisced, which seemed to make Mother particularly happy.

"Do you remember when you left for college?" she asked Annie. "I couldn't stop crying, and your dad promised me a new fur coat, as if wrapping myself in luxury would make up for losing my daughter."

"You weren't exactly losing me, Mom."

"Annie, you know what I mean. I couldn't imagine life in the house with you not in it."

"And I couldn't wait to move into her bedroom," I added, laughing.

"You say that now," Mother chided, "but you cried too. I remember perfectly well."

"I wish Dad could be here," I said, suddenly wistful for his good common sense, his gentle warmth, the tickle of his mustache when he kissed me good night.

"He'd be so pleased with all his grandchildren," Mother said. "Mitch and Ben are growing up so nicely. It almost killed your father when Neil died."

"Well, I know he'd be pleased that I'm so happy now," I said. "Imagine his surprise if he knew I was marrying Larry."

"I don't have to imagine it," Annie said. "It would have felt just like my surprise. And Mom's."

"Isn't he great?" I couldn't wipe the smile off my face.

"It seems miracles do happen," Mother commented. "And on that note, I'm going to turn in."

"I'm going down to the lobby with Rachel," Annie said. "I'll be back in a few minutes."

The lobby was deserted except for the night-duty clerk behind the check-in desk. "Sit a minute," Annie said. We headed for a brocade couch. "So, how are you really? This business with Heather has to be getting to you."

"It's a terrible strain. I am so glad you're here. No one else knows about Heather and me. I have to act like she's just a young client in trouble and that I'm only a supportive therapist trying to help out. Meanwhile, it's breaking my heart."

"Do you think you can get enough distance from it to enjoy your wedding?"

"Distance? She's living in the next room! But I'm really trying to separate myself. I'm afraid that if I let my guard down, my feelings will show and I won't be able to keep up this charade."

"Well listen, baby, I'm here for you if you need someone to talk to. Just call and I'll come a-runnin'." The hug Annie gave me felt like a lifeline. I held onto her shoulders for an extra moment.

"I'd better go home. It's really late." Annie waited with me until the cab summoned by the uniformed doorman glided to a stop. She bent over as I settled myself in the back seat.

"Remember, I'm here." She blew me a kiss and disappeared into the lobby as the taxi pulled into traffic and I headed back to my life downtown.

It was past 9:30 in the morning when I wandered into the kitchen, rubbing my eyes. "Where is everyone?" Larry sat alone on the kitchen stool, the *Times* spread out in front of him. An empty coffee cup was nearby.

"Molly took the boys down to their summer program."

"Ouch. I should have gone with them for the first day."

"You should have done exactly what you did—rested. They're fine. I'm fine. How was your evening? I never heard you come in."

"It was really late. I couldn't tear myself away. We have only a couple of days of just the three of us, and then Annie's family will be here and we'll be swinging into full wedding mode."

"What's on for today?"

I felt my eyes crinkle as I smiled. "Annie says she has this incredible longing to experience tea at the Peninsula Hotel. But I think there's another agenda."

"Oh yeah? What might that be?" Larry was making an effort to suppress a grin of his own. He wasn't very good at it.

"I suspect I may be walking into a surprise shower."

"Hmm. Well, make sure to act surprised."

"So you're in on it?"

"I'm supposed to put in an appearance at the end. And help cart the presents home. I think that's why I'm really needed."

"It's a little silly, don't you think? A shower for a second marriage?"

"Your sister is having a real blast planning it, so be a good sport. And for heaven's sake, be surprised!"

I hope I looked adequately shocked as I walked into the hotel lounge and allowed Annie to steer me to the far corner. A table for eight had been prepared. Jan, along with four of my closest friends, called out a soft but heartfelt "Surprise!" A waiter snapped photos as I went around the table greeting and hugging Pam, my college roommate; Eleanor, my supervisor from an early field placement; Sandy, my best friend from high school; and my aunt Gloria, who'd flown in from Cleveland and would stay until after the wedding. She sat next to my mother. The two of them had been deep in conversation when I arrived. Her perfect golden curls gleamed as I bent down to offer my cheek for a kiss. It wasn't easy to mask the flush of anger that rose to the surface as her cool dry lips touched my skin. As much as I wanted to confront her, I hadn't been able to do so. My feelings for her, my gratitude at her generosity and amusement at her affectations, had been changed forever. Shaking off the feeling that had been stirred by seeing her, I squeezed her shoulders and offered the other cheek for a kiss.

"Who woulda thunk it?" Sandy whispered in my ear as I gave her a hug.

"Yeah, I know. You'd never know he was the same person."

The women had wisely decided that the theme of this shower should be lingerie, so there were no toasters, no Circulon pots, no Cuisinarts. Instead, I drew gossamer silk nighties from folds of tissue, holding them up against my chest as my friends and family provided the requisite oohs and aahs. Annie's gift was three sets of matching bras and panties, each in a different floral pattern, from the Victoria's Secret collection. My mother's more practical and motherly contribution was a bathrobe of the softest chenille. "To keep you warm when Larry's out of town," she said. Giggles greeted her bon mot. Aunt Gloria's package contained sexy little mules with white pom-poms.

We were having tea and petits fours when Larry arrived, to polite applause from the group. Coming up behind me, he bent over and gave me a serious, meaningful kiss. "Hello, ladies," he greeted the group. "Having fun?"

"Tell Rachel she has to give you a fashion show," Sandy said, laughing.

"Not until our wedding night," I said. "Until then he has to make do with my old pajamas with the rip in the elbow."

Larry produced a box from Bergdorf's. Everyone got quiet as I slid off the ribbon and peeked inside. A small white card lay on top of the decorative tissue.

To my darling,

With supreme gratitude that we found each other again.

All my love,
Your Larry

"Read it out loud," Jan insisted. Polite applause indicated everyone's agreement. I looked at Larry. He took the card from my hand and read it himself, never taking his eyes off me. There was a hush from the women.

My mother broke the silence. "I do believe I'm crying." Annie put her arm around Mother's left shoulder. Aunt Gloria hugged her sister on the right side.

"Aren't you going to look at the gift?" my friend Pam prodded. I drew from the box an elegant knee-length nightgown of peach-colored silk with spaghetti straps and a wide satin band at the waist. There was a matching kimono. Both were from La Perla.

"I love them. Thank you, darling." He kissed me again.

I realized that I'd gotten into the spirit of the occasion in spite of myself. I was surprised at how fast the time had flown, how much I'd enjoyed myself. All at once, chairs were pushed back and goodbyes were being said.

"I'm going to take all these things back to the apartment," Larry said. He'd managed to consolidate the gifts into three large shopping bags. A waiter appeared at his side and took two of them from him. "I'm going to pick up Ben and Mitch from their programs, and we'll hang out together for a while. I think Molly's preparing a special meal for your mother, your sister, Aunt Gloria, and us. Why don't you go back to the hotel with Annie and your mom? I'll see you later."

I invited Sandy to join us at the Park Lane. Aunt Gloria was staying at the hotel; she joined us as well. The five of us sat at the intimate second-floor bar.

"Shall we have drinks?" Annie asked.

"Why not? It's an occasion." I sipped my Bloody Mary, we shared memories, and I answered questions about our plans.

"We're probably going to stay in Manhattan. It'll be a challenge finding a condo that's big enough for all of us and Mrs. Marcus. I'd like a guest room too." I looked pointedly at my mother. "You don't come east often enough. I want you to visit us a couple of times a year."

Sandy drew from her oversized alligator-skin purse an envelope that contained old photographs. She spread them on the table, and we laughed over the way we'd looked in high school. In one picture, we were both making silly faces, tongues hanging out and eyes crossed. In another, I lay on my belly on her bed, propped on my elbows, my legs bent at the knees and crossed at the ankles.

"We had so much fun in high school," Sandy said, scooping up the photos, replacing them in the envelope, and handing it to me. "Until—"

"I know. Until Larry."

"I was *so* glad when you broke up with him," she said.

"You and everyone else," Annie added.

"He's living proof that people can change." It would take them all a while to believe it, I knew. Right now they were hoping for the best. "Excuse me just a minute," I said as my cell phone rang. It was Larry, my caller ID declared. I pushed my chair back and walked through the double doors into the hallway, where stairs curved down to the main floor.

"I hate to disturb the festivities," he said, "but I had to call you. It looks like Heather's taken off again."

"Oh no! When?"

"Earlier today, when Mrs. Marcus stepped out to go to the greengrocer. When she got back, she started cooking and didn't look in on Heather until a short while ago."

"What about her things? Are her clothes gone?"

"As far as I can tell, she didn't pack a bag. The suitcase is here. There are clothes in the closet. I'm not sure how much she had."

I let out the breath I'd been holding. "Well then, she probably had to get out of the apartment for a little while. Maybe she needed fresh air, or maybe she just wanted to take a walk."

"I wish I could agree with you, sweetheart. But she left us a note."

A clutch of dread rose in my throat as Larry read to me. She was gone. She was really gone.

CHAPTER 25

"I have to leave," I announced, returning to the bar. The urgency made my voice shrill. Several people at other tables turned to look at me.

"What's wrong?" my mother asked. She stood, smoothing the skirt of her suit.

Annie made the universal signal to the waiter, scribbling in the air that he should bring the check. She too was on her feet when the tab was delivered, and she bent over the table, signing it to their room.

"It's Heather." I'd given Sandy only a bare-bones account of Heather's tragedy and the reason why my young former client was now staying at my home. One of the hardest things I'd had to do, back in the days when she and I were inseparable, was to keep silent about my pregnancy. I'd done it though. My fear of Larry's finding out was deeper than my need to share my secret. It was ironic, I thought, that after all these years I still couldn't speak freely to my best friend.

"What about her?" Sandy asked now.

"She's taken off. Not for the first time. But she's very depressed and guilty, and she left a scary note. I'm afraid of what she might do."

"It's a matter for the police," my mother said, as though that should be the end of it.

"She'll be fine. I'm sure she will," Aunt Gloria offered.

"You hope," I murmured. I didn't think anyone could hear me. "You four should stay," I said, moving toward the elevators as I spoke.

"I'm coming with you," Annie said.

At the curb I gave Sandy a hug. "See you at the wedding," I

211

told her. One cab pulled up for her, and another arrived for Annie, Mother, and me. Aunt Gloria crowded in with us.

At home Mrs. Marcus was inconsolable. "I should have watched her more carefully," she moaned. "I should have taken her to the market with me. I shouldn't have left her alone."

"It's not your fault," Larry consoled. "You couldn't have known. None of us could have known. We'll find her." He patted her shoulder as she continued to wring her chubby hands.

"I'm glad she left," Ben muttered. "She was spoiling everything."

"If she's going to be missing, she's still spoiling everything," Mitch commented. It was a wise observation, I thought.

"Can I see the note?" Larry produced it for me.

> I'm sorry. Thanks for trying to help. Nothing can help. I have nobody. No parents, no friends, no boyfriend. I killed my dad, the only one who cared about me. I've messed up my life, even though lots of people tried to help me. I'm not going to cause anybody anymore trouble.
>
> Heather

The note was as ominous when I held it in my hand as it had been half an hour ago when Larry had read it to me.

"She's going to do something." I looked up at Larry, hoping to see disagreement. It wasn't there in his eyes.

"I've called the police," he said.

I felt Annie's warm hand on my shoulder. "You've done all you could do for that girl. Let the police handle it. You have a wedding to deal with." I cast a despairing look at my sister. Her eyes were filled with silent compassion.

"I know where she stayed when she was with Frank," I said. "Maybe she went back there."

"Excuse me," Molly said. "I don't know what to do about dinner."

Larry and I exchanged glances. I looked at Mitch and Ben, and then at my sister.

"By all means serve dinner, Mrs. Marcus," Larry said. "There's not much we can do right now."

Molly had gone to great pains to produce a festive meal for our visitors. I hadn't the heart to disappoint the boys, nor could I let my mother know how greatly Heather's problems had affected me. I nodded my agreement, and we trouped into the dining room, where the table had been set with my best china. A gorgeous centerpiece of white roses and freesia created a mood of elegance and celebration. Molly produced, in succession, her fabulous chilled red pepper and leek soup, a salad of Bibb lettuce with scallions and avocado, and a perfect capon.

My mother, my sister, and my aunt were generous with their compliments. Mitch and Ben ate with relish, although Ben poured liberal amounts of ketchup on his capon. I brought my fork to my lips several times in a herculean effort to show appreciation for Molly's talents. Mostly, I moved the food around on my plate, hoping the smile I had pasted on my face looked less artificial than it felt.

Mrs. Marcus served tea. I was so anxious to run off that I felt as if my body hovered over my chair, waiting to be set free. The almond cookies she'd baked last week were undoubtedly as perfect as always. Ben's fingers dipped into the plate for thirds and fourths. I nibbled on one; it felt dry as the desert and was almost impossible to swallow.

"I think Mother and I will spend the day at the Met tomorrow," Annie announced, breaking a silence that had gone on for too long. "There's a costume exhibit that we've really been wanting to see."

"I'm going to the Red Door," Gloria announced. "Hair, mani-pedi, massage, the works. I haven't been there in years."

"If I can, I'll join you at the museum." My voice sounded flat and lifeless to my ears.

"Oh, I hope you will, darling. It's so wonderful to spend time with you." So far, my mother and her sister had managed to be oblivious to the vibes that were clanging around everyone else.

At long last, Annie, Gloria, and Mother said their good nights and headed back to the hotel. "Wonderful meal, Molly," my mother said, manners impeccably in place.

"Yes, thank you so much," Annie added. "I wish I could clone you and take you back to California with me."

"One of me is more than enough, but thank you," Molly said, patting her ample belly.

"To bed, boys!" Larry pronounced almost as soon as the door had closed behind Mom and Annie. "It's late!"

"What're you going to do about Heather?" Mitch asked, as they both headed toward the room they shared.

"We're going to try to find her, of course."

"What about our chapter?" Ben was the twin who most enjoyed the nightly made-up adventures. Larry had become the chief storyteller. His creations were far superior to mine.

"How about we do two tomorrow night? Mom and I think we know where Heather might have gone. We're going to go and check it out right now."

"Okay. I just wish she didn't have to be here at all." On that note Ben followed his brother into the room. I followed Larry to the elevator.

I gave directions as Larry drove his SUV over the Williamsburg Bridge and into the neighborhood where Heather had led me a few days earlier. "I'm not sure I'll recognize the building in the dark," I said, straining for any familiar landmark. I hadn't paid much attention, never imagining that I'd need to find the seedy, run-down apartment again.

"I'll drive slowly. Let me know if you want me to stop."

"Wait a minute. I think this might be it!" I wasn't sure why the building stood out. It had the same number of trash cans on the curb as its neighbors. It was as needy of exterior cleaning as every other apartment house on the street. Perhaps it was the broken window on the second floor. I'd noticed it from the inside and wondered if anyone would repair it before winter. Larry eased the car into a spot a few buildings away. As we mounted the stairs, I noticed the few missing bricks and remembered Heather warning me to watch my step. "This is definitely it."

The apartment door stood partly open. We knocked. A male voice called out, "Who is it?"

"We're Heather's friends," Larry answered.

"C'mon in." We pushed in the door. The man Heather had called Joker was sprawled on the torn and soiled couch, video game controllers in his hands. He made no move to get up. There was a person who seemed to be asleep on one of the cots. I positioned myself so that I could see who it was. It was a girl, but it wasn't Heather. She didn't stir. In the kitchen I heard a sound and went to investigate. Dishes were piled in the sink, which was filling up with water, but nobody was there. The basin was almost overflowing. I reached over and shut the tap. It continued to drip, but slowly.

"Thanks," Joker called, not giving up his game or making a move to stand up.

"We're looking for Heather," Larry said, stepping in front of the TV screen, where noisy, violent animated creatures jumped and flew around.

"Hey, man, move!"

"In a minute. Has Heather Brody been here?"

"Nah. Haven't seen her since Frankster got arrested. Would you *please* get out of my way?"

"Is there any other place she might have gone? Anyplace you can think of?" I forced the words past the lump in my throat.

"Listen, young man," Larry said, bending over to make eye contact, "Heather is in trouble. She's feeling low. You understand what I mean? Real low. She's out there somewhere, and we need to find her. I need your help."

"Okay, okay, I hear you. If I hear anything, I'll get in touch." Larry handed him a card on which he had scribbled our home number and his cell number.

"Ask around, would you? You could be saving her life."

Oh my God. He's thinking what I'm thinking. Heather, please come back to us. You're not alone, sweetheart.

I called Annie in the morning.

"Any news?" she asked.

"None. She could be anywhere. Annie, I'm scared to death for her."

"I know, sweetheart. I feel awful for you. I'd like to be with you every minute, but I have Mom to think about. And Jeff and Brendan and Kim are coming in at 5:30. I told them I'd be at the hotel, waiting for them when they get here."

"There's nothing you can do anyway, Annie. Just take care of Mom. See that she has a nice time."

"Do you want to come to the museum with us?"

"I don't think I can put on a happy face all day long. You're going to bring Brendan and Kim over to my place tonight, right?"

"After dinner. We have to give Mrs. Marcus a break. And they'll be starving when they land."

"Okay. See you tonight. Kiss Mom for me, and tell her I have a lot of running around to do today."

In truth I had no running around to do. I had nothing to do at all. I'd set aside the time to be with my family, and now with the boys at their summer program and every detail already taken care of, I huddled on the living room couch, knees pressed against my chest, and rocked. Feeling chilled despite the warmth of the early July afternoon, I pulled an afghan, knitted by my mother before my marriage to Neil, up around my shoulders.

"I'm going to go back to Brooklyn and drive around," Larry said. He was as concerned as I, and he wasn't trying to hide it.

"I'll go with you."

"No, stay here, sweetheart. Maybe Heather will call or just show up. And the boys will be home in an hour."

"I have to put on a happy face for my mother and for Annie's husband and kids. I don't know how I'm going to do it."

"One step at a time," Larry told me, pulling his car keys off the hook near the door and blowing me a kiss.

Half an hour later I'd unlocked the privacy drawer in my bureau. I held in two hands the journal I'd been keeping for my Julie for the past seventeen years. A ballpoint pen was inserted at the page where I'd written my last entry. I reread it now. "I'm going to marry your dad," I'd written three months earlier. "I wish I could tell you. He's a wonderful man, but you already know that. He's been your therapist in Washington. I hope one day we'll be able to talk about this together."

I held the book in both my hands, rereading my words. I flipped through older entries, begun when Heather was a few months old, already beyond my reach. It was all here, the highlights of the life I couldn't share with her.

Now I clicked open the pen and held it poised over a blank page. My tongue was caught between my front teeth. I pressed down, deep in thought. Finally I began to write:

> You are missing. You are in pain. You are my child. Please, please come back. You believe that you have no one, that nobody cares about you. If you come back, if you find strength to survive your pain, I will tell you the truth. I will tell you how wrong you are. I will tell you that you have a mother who loves you and a father who will love you too, when he knows that you are his longed-for child. Julie—Heather, please come home, darling.

I placed the cloth-covered journal back in its nest of saved printed-out emails, pressed corsages, and the laminated invitation to my first wedding. I returned to the couch, pulled the afghan up over my knees, and waited.

CHAPTER
26

The following day the family gathered in my apartment.

"How do you like parasailing?" Ben asked Kim. His eyes gleamed. I knew he was seeing himself soaring behind a speedboat, suspended by the cords of a parachute.

"It's great," my niece said, popping the last bite of chocolate chip cookie into her mouth. "Can't wait to do it again."

Heather, where are you?

"I'm learning to program in BASIC at camp," Mitch told Brendan. "Cool."

Please come home.

Brendan and Kim had shot up since last summer, and suddenly they seemed much older and more mature than Mitch and Ben. When I was pregnant with Heather, Annie was going steady with Jeff. They were married late the following year, and Kim came along less than two years later. She'd be fourteen around Christmastime, and Brendan was already twelve. Still, the four cousins seemed delighted to be together. My mother sat nodding and smiling as her attention turned from one grandchild to another. "I do so wish that your father was here," she said. "He'd be having the time of his life seeing all his grandchildren together."

Not all his grandchildren, Mom. There's another one, and she's out there somewhere, alone and in pain.

I was working hard at paying attention to my family. They were gathered here for me, to share my joy. I was acutely aware of Annie's long looks of assessment. I could hear the unspoken words behind her sympathetic expression. *How ya doin'?* she asked with her eyes. I answered with a tiny shrug, imperceptible to everyone but her.

Aunt Gloria was glowing, her makeup perfect, her hair newly cut and colored, courtesy of Elizabeth Arden. I worked at trying to ignore her. My resentment of her meddling had grown in proportion to Heather's situation.

"Have you heard anything about that girl?" Mom asked, her words echoing inside my head. *That girl, that girl.*

"Nothing yet," Larry said. "We're concerned, but our focus is on our wedding and our future. Right, sweetheart?" Sitting on the floor cross-legged near my feet, he reached out and touched my knee.

"Right."

"Two more days," Mitch said. "We get to call Larry 'Dad' after they're married," he told Kim. "I've been calling him Dad in my head for a long time."

I jumped up gratefully when Annie announced, "Jeff and the kids have had a really long day. I think we'd better get back to the hotel."

"What's happening tomorrow?" my mother asked, reaching for her handbag.

"I want to sleep late," Brendan announced.

"We're heading up to the inn around five o'clock," Larry said. "We're going to have a short rehearsal, and then we'll all have dinner together."

"Can we go a little earlier?" Ben asked. "Mom says they have tennis courts. Kim and Brendan could play with us." He looked at his cousins expectantly.

When Kim said "That might be fun," he flashed the grin that lit up his face.

"Great!"

As they prepared to leave, I surprised myself by saying, "Aunt Gloria, can I speak to you for a moment?"

"Of course, darling."

"We'll be just a couple of minutes," I told the others as I led Aunt Gloria into my bedroom, where I shut the door.

"I'm not sure I understand why you did why you did," I said as she sat on the edge of my bed and I stood over her. "But your little secret has caused me a huge amount of anxiety and heartbreak."

"I'm not sure I know what you mean."

"Come on, Gloria, I figured it out. You were the puppeteer who pulled all the strings, arranging for me to counsel my own daughter, never saying a word."

She had the decency to look away from me, unable to meet my gaze. "I thought it would be a wonderful surprise when you found out."

"You didn't think at all," I said, cautioning myself to keep my voice down. "I'm the last person on earth who should have been her therapist. If I'd known who she was, I would never have taken her as a client."

"That's why I didn't tell you. When did you figure it out?"

"It doesn't matter," I said, waving my hand dismissively. "What matters is that now she's going to find out, and she's going to feel totally betrayed. She trusted me, and I kept this huge secret from her."

"I'm sorry, Rachel. Really. It seemed so perfect at the time. The Brodys had everything to offer, and they were trying to adopt while you were living in my house, waiting to have your baby. It seemed as if it was meant to be."

"Well, the damage has been done. And it's much worse because of your interference. I'm sorry, Aunt Gloria, but I couldn't keep quiet any longer. I'd appreciate it if you didn't discuss this with my mother. She doesn't know that this unhappy, at-risk teenager is her granddaughter."

Aunt Gloria looked crestfallen. Her eyes pleaded as she looked up at me. "It was supposed to be so wonderful," she said. "When Heather was old enough, you'd reveal who you really are, and it would be joyful because you already had a relationship." She opened her hands, palms out, begging me to recognize the scene she envisioned. "I gave you the chance to be part of your child's life. I was so sure you'd be grateful." All I could do was shake my head.

"You had no right," I told her. "Okay. That's all I have to say to you. Your happy little scheme didn't work out, did it?"

Finally they were gone. Mrs. Marcus left as well, heading for her cousin's apartment. "I'll be back early, to make breakfast," she'd announced at the doorway. "Cheese omelets okay?"

"Fine, Molly," Larry said. "Everything you cook is fine. See you in the morning."

Mitch and Ben disappeared into their room. The sounds of their

Xbox soon echoed down the hall. "Shut the door, guys," I called out, rubbing the spot on my left temple where a headache pulsed behind my eyebrow.

"Maybe we should go back to Frank's place," I suggested to Larry. "It's been four days." It had been four impossibly long days, my heart so divided that I could barely catch my breath. Four days of going through the motions of enjoying prewedding activities with my beloved family. Four days of trying to free my mind of a dreadful vision—Heather lying in a gutter on a filthy street, perhaps only minutes from our comfortable home. "I don't trust that boy to call us, especially if Heather tells him not to."

"Number one: Molly's gone. We can't leave the boys alone. And number two: I'm getting a little weary of Heather and her problems. It's a very sad story, and I feel sorry for her. And yes, she's at risk. But we've done all we can and more, and we have a wedding in two days. I refuse to allow her to spoil it for us, or for Mitch and Ben."

"I just have a really bad feeling."

"I know. You've allowed yourself to get overly caught up in all of this. I should have drawn a line earlier. Now you have to try to put it aside. Heather's going to do what she's going to do. We'll help her if she'll let us. But I want you to think about the two of us applying suntan lotion to each other's backs and sipping chilled sauvignon blanc on the beach at Cannes. I want you to think about shopping in Paris, and eating oysters with shallot vinaigrette and drinking caffe latte at a sidewalk cafe on the Champs-Élysées." He wrapped his arms around me and pulled me close, rocking me as he did so. "Try to relax, sweetheart."

We didn't make love that night. We'd agreed a week earlier to abstain until our wedding night. It had been my suggestion. "I know it's a little silly," I had told him while getting ready for bed, "but if we take a break from sex now, it will feel special the first time we're together as husband and wife."

Larry had laughed. "It will be special to me anyway, I promise. I've waited so long. But if that's what you want, it's okay with me. I'll try to be brave."

I'd given him a deep kiss and then gently pushed him away. "Thank you for understanding. You are so wonderful."

Now we gently kissed good night. Larry fell asleep immediately as he almost always did. I stared at the ceiling. I flipped my pillow to the cool side. I threw off the comforter. Feeling chilly, I pulled it over my body again. Finally I got up and went to the living room window, where I looked down at the street. A few headlights still moved along Hudson Street. The traffic lights turned red, and green, and red again. I looked out over the rooftops, past the water tower on a rooftop nearby. I stared at the jewel of the Chrysler Building twinkling in the distance. *The city is so huge—so dark and frightening. Heather, I'm calling to you with all my strength. Can't you hear me?* I squeezed my eyes closed and pictured my daughter's face: her blue eyes framed by dark lashes, the shock of brunette hair slanting across her forehead, obscuring her right eye, the crevice in her chin that mirrored her grandfather's and her cousins'. I saw her as she stood near my office door, ready to bolt, her black leather tote bag slung over one shoulder, head tilted in an arrogant, try-to-stop-me pose. I saw her as she was the day after her sixteenth birthday, tears streaking through hideous pancake makeup, offering up the thousand-dollar check her parents had written. And there she was in my memory the day we'd said goodbye. She'd looked wholesome, lovely, ready for dinner and theater with her parents. I kept the picture I'd taken of her that day in my little pink journal. Now I resisted the urge to pull out the book and hold it close to my heart. I hugged myself close instead, trying to hang on to the image of the fresh-faced teenager who'd come so far, so fast. I couldn't, however, hold back the thought of the room in Brooklyn, Frank's place, with its filth and its cots and that unknown girl curled up in a ball. *Heather, come back. Come back, come back, come back.* And I couldn't allow my tumultuous mind to imagine Larry's reaction if and when he ever learned the huge secret I'd been keeping for seventeen years, and especially after our love had rekindled.

It was almost dawn when I crept back into bed. Larry sighed and turned over, throwing an arm across my body. The room glowed pink as I fell into a light and restless sleep. When his cell phone rang at 6:45, I jumped, my heart pounding. I didn't know, for the moment, what time it was, what day it was. He groped around on his night table until his hand found the phone. I propped myself on an elbow and realized I was holding my breath.

"Okay, thank you. Did you call 911? Do you know where they're taking her?" He put the phone down and swung his legs off the bed.

"What? Who was that?"

"That kid from the place in Brooklyn. Heather showed up there sometime during the night. Apparently she passed out on the stairs. The boy, the one they call Joker, found her when he went out early to buy cigarettes."

"Where is she now?" I was pulling on a T-shirt and jeans, groping for my sandals, which were in a jumble of shoes, slippers, and sneakers on the closet floor.

"He called 911. The ambulance came. He's not sure which hospital she's going to. I'm going to find out." Larry was buckling his belt and sliding bare feet into loafers. I ran my fingers through my hair. My breathing felt shallow, my head fuzzy from lack of sleep. *Please, God, please, God.* The prayer was an unspoken litany as Larry grabbed the phone.

"I need some information," I heard him say. "A client was picked up in Williamsburg, not far from the bridge. What hospital would she be taken to? Okay, thank you so much." He turned to me. "Let's go."

"Wait. The boys." I stood paralyzed. "You go. What hospital?"

"Maimonides."

"Okay. I'll leave as soon as Molly shows up." Just then I heard the sound of her key in the lock. I ran to the hallway to meet her.

"Molly, thank God you're here early."

"Rachel, what is it? What has happened?"

"It's Heather. She's in the hospital. We're on our way."

"Will she be okay?"

"I don't know. I'll call you."

"Wait. What should I tell the boys?"

"The truth. Tell them the truth. My sister too, if she calls. I've got to go."

Larry was holding the elevator for me. The descent to the street seemed to take forever. What would we find? Would Heather even be alive? If she was, what was I going to do with my heartsick, damaged child while I flew off to honeymoon in Paris? Meanwhile I could only pray, and my prayer consisted of two words, endlessly repeated: *Please, God. Please, God. Please, God.*

The emergency department at Maimonides Hospital was a cauldron of activity. Ambulance sirens pierced the din at irregular intervals. Medical personnel all seemed to be rushing, pushing gurneys, talking on the phone, or arguing with distraught clients or family. Young children wailed from pain or fear. My tension felt almost unbearable as we struggled to get the attention of someone, anyone who could buzz us through the security door so we could find Heather. Finally an overworked receptionist turned to us.

"Name?"

"The client is Heather Brody," Larry said.

"Your name?"

"Dr. Larry Tobin."

"You her physician?"

"No, I'm her, uh—her guardian."

"Okay." Finally she pressed the button as I pushed heavily against the door.

"Where is she?" Larry asked.

"Let's see. Wait a minute. Hey, Roger, where'd you put that overdose? Bed seven, to your right, then a sharp left."

Heather's face and hands were whiter than the bedsheet. Her eyes were closed, and the outline of blue veins under translucent lids made her appear even younger than she was. Two slim tubes extended from her nostrils, delivering precious oxygen. Her breathing was rapid and shallow. She was attached to several pieces of equipment, and above her head a screen with a small blip recorded her heartbeat. It seemed to me to be a little erratic.

I didn't anticipate my tears, and I couldn't control them. She looked so frail and helpless. "Oh God, dear God, why?" I sobbed. Larry came around behind me and placed a firm hand on each of my shoulders until my sobs grew shuddery, like those of a child, finally slowing and stopping. I reached for one small icy hand and clasped it between my own. "Heather, we're here. Larry and I are here." There was no response from the unconscious girl.

Larry didn't touch her, but he added his deep-voiced reassurance to mine. "You'll be fine, kiddo," he said. "I'm going to try to get some information," he told me, and stepped outside the cubicle. He planted himself at the nurses' station nearby. I continued to hold Heather's hand, but I could hear everything that went on outside the curtain.

"Are you Dr. Tobin?"

"Yes, I am. Are you the officer who found Heather?"

"The EMTs called us in. I need some information, sir, if you don't mind."

"I'm happy to cooperate, Officer, but right now I'm trying to get some information about the girl's condition. Isn't there anyone here to talk to?"

"I'm sure someone will be along in a minute. They're watching her very closely. Meanwhile, can you tell me who the girl's parents are?"

"Her mother is Stephanie Brody, of Washington, DC. However, they are estranged. Dr. Rachel Marston and I have been taking responsibility for Heather."

"So her mother doesn't have to be notified?"

"Dr. Marston and I will let her know."

"And her father?"

"Deceased."

"I think I read about that. Recent, wasn't it? Plane crash?"

"That's right."

A white-clad woman entered the cubicle where I still stood by Heather's side, her hand clasped in both of mine.

"Excuse me," Larry said to the policeman, pushing back the curtain to join us.

"We've sent blood work down to the lab," the doctor said. I dabbed my eyes with a shredded piece of tissue. "Nothing is back yet, but you should know the medics found this next to her." In her outstretched palm was a plastic bag with two small pills stuck in one corner.

"What are they?" I asked.

"Looks like oxy."

"Any idea how many she took?"

"We've pumped her stomach. Haven't had time to analyze the contents. We think there was a fairly large quantity of alcohol involved as well. I'll know more in an hour. This could have been accidental, but we can't rule out a suicide attempt."

"She's been depressed," I said. "Doctor, can you tell us if she's going to be all right?"

"It's hard to say. Her heart rate's unsteady, but she's young. She's got that going for her. On the other hand, with the mix of drugs and alcohol, we can't rule out permanent damage."

"Oh God."

Larry squeezed my hand. "Any idea when she might regain consciousness?" he asked.

"It could be hours. You should go home. We have your number."

"We can't leave her alone," I said.

Larry took my shoulders in his hands and looked down at me. He reached out and smoothed my forehead as if to wipe away the worry lines he saw there.

"I'm going to call Stephanie," he said. "And I'm going to call her aunt Marilyn and suggest, strongly, that she get on the next flight to New York. You and I are getting married tomorrow. It's time for Heather's family to take over. I want you to go home now. Try to get some rest. We have a rehearsal dinner tonight. I'll stay here for a while in case she wakes up."

"I can't leave, Larry. I can't."

He stood there for a long time, just looking at me. I felt as though he was studying my heart. I wanted to run, but I held his gaze.

"C'mon, let's get coffee," he said finally. We went into the small space where Heather lay motionless and achingly vulnerable.

"We'll be right back, sweetheart," I said. Larry took my hand and led me through the corridors of the ER. I allowed myself to be led, trailing after him like a child whose father was steering her across a busy street. He found the elevators, he found the cafeteria, and he found a table for us.

"Can't we get married without a rehearsal?" I asked, holding a coffee cup to my lips and waiting for it to cool.

"Rachel, your family is here. Mitch and Ben are looking forward to the day. You can't turn your back on all of them because of Heather. I know you're upset, but you have to keep your priorities straight."

I nibbled at the edges of an English muffin. *I can't explain this to him. I need to postpone this wedding. I have to be here for Heather.* "You're right," I said finally, but my tears betrayed me as they began, once again, to spill over my lids and trickle down my face. I swiped at them angrily with my sleeve. "I have to go back and see her again before I leave."

The ER was, if anything, more frenetic than it had been earlier.

Phones jangled, gurneys blocked the narrow passageways, and in one corner two nurses were having a loud disagreement. I pushed aside the curtain that was meant to give Heather some privacy. Larry and I stood at either side of the narrow bed. I reached again for the small, cold hand.

"Rachel, you should go home," Larry said again. "I'll stay."

I thought I saw movement behind Heather's eyelids. *Is she waking up?*

"A few more minutes. I think she's going to come out of it." As I spoke, her head turned left, then right. "Heather? Heather, it's Rachel. Wake up, sweetheart. Larry and I are both here." I squeezed her hand. She moved her head again. Her lids, still closed, began to flicker, and then I had a glimpse of blue eyes—just a glimpse, before the lids closed again.

"Go away." It was a hoarse whisper. She grimaced at the effort.

"We're not going anywhere," Larry said. He reached for her other hand. We stood there for what felt like endless time. Heather appeared to struggle to keep her eyes closed, but in spite of her will, she finally looked up, first at Larry, then at me. She shook her head again several times. Her chin dropped, shoulders curled in. She looked exhausted and utterly defeated.

"We were so worried," I said. "Thank God you're okay."

"Yeah. I couldn't even do this right," she whispered. "Once a screwup, always a screwup."

"Oh, Heather, I'm so sorry you felt so sad and so alone. Don't you know that we care about you?"

"Maybe you do. Maybe I don't want you to care. Do me a great big favor: stop caring."

"That will never happen," Larry said, his voice deep and calming. Having heard a slight catch in his throat, I looked up to see a mask of pain on his face. Then it was gone.

"I want to die," Heather said. I had to bend close to hear her words. Her eyes looked blankly at the ceiling. "Please let me die. It hurts too much. I ruin everything. My mother hates me. She's right to hate me. I killed my father. Even a loser like the Frankster doesn't want me around. My birth parents must have known right away—they were the first ones to dump me."

"Heather, you couldn't be more wrong." My voice sounded strangled.

A young nurse came in, efficiently feeling for Heather's pulse and checking the numbers on the electronic screen over her head.

"My throat hurts," Heather croaked.

"There was a tube down there. They pumped your stomach. I'll bring you some ice chips," the nurse told her. "I'm going to ask you both to leave," she said to us. "This young lady has to rest."

"See you later," I said. "You're not going to get rid of Larry and me, so you might as well stop trying."

"I was trying to help you to get rid of me," she said to our backs as we left her bedside. "Go, get married. Have a nice life."

"We are going home," Larry insisted, steering me toward the exit. "I'm going to call in Paul Kessler. He's the best psychiatrist I know in New York. I think he has privileges here. He'll take over. Heather needs medication and supervision. He'll handle it. And then we're going to get ourselves together and go to the inn for our rehearsal dinner."

It was a ten-minute walk to where we'd left Larry's car. The sun was beginning to beat down, but I still felt a chill. "She's so unhappy," I said. "She was making such wonderful progress. Larry, do you think she's going to recover from this?"

He clicked open the car doors. The leather seats were hot on my bare legs. I shifted, trying to find a cooler spot.

He started the engine and pulled out into traffic. "She's got an uphill fight. She's been resilient in the past. This is different. She feels that she's lost everything. Think about it." He turned briefly to glance at me. "Her father's gone. Her mother's written her off. Her boyfriend and her best friend in Washington betrayed her. Her New York connection, as miserable as he was, has told her to get lost. She has nobody."

"That's not true," I said, my voice barely audible even to me. "She has us."

Larry patted my hand. "I don't think that means much to her right now. I'm hoping that Paul will hospitalize her for a while. We can get an involuntary commitment because of the suicide attempt."

"I can't go off on a romantic honeymoon and leave her in a hospital. I just can't do it."

"Rachel, you have to detach. You're overinvested. Maybe you should talk to Paul Kessler yourself."

"I can't detach. She's my baby." *Oh my God, I said it.* I felt a cold wave of apprehension as soon as the words were out of my mouth. I hardly dared to look at Larry, but I forced myself to read the expression on his face. It showed concern, nothing more.

"She's not your baby." His voice was soft, tolerant, as if he were speaking to one of his teenaged clients. "She's a kid who's been through a lot. I know you have a special feeling for her, but—"

"Larry, you need to stop the car. Pull over somewhere."

"What? I can't pull over here. What's the matter with you? Are you going to be sick?"

"Just find a place to park. Please." We were still on city streets, and up ahead there was an empty space in front of a fire hydrant. "There. Pull over there." He swerved into the spot. Leaving the car idling, he unfastened his seat belt so that he could turn fully to face me.

"Rachel, you have to get a grip. Our kids are at home waiting for us. This is supposed to be a wonderful day. I can't let this girl spoil it. She is not your baby. She is our client."

"No, Larry, you don't understand." I unsnapped my seat belt as well and turned to him. I put my hand on his arm. Tears began to flow like rivers down my face. "She's mine. My child. I'm her mother. Her birth mother." I made myself look at him. His face showed the blankness of incomprehension.

"What? I don't know what you're talking about." I forced myself to maintain eye contact. My whole body swayed as though the foundation of my life had been built on a fault line that had just tilted.

"Oh, Larry, you're going to be so angry."

"Then I'll be angry. What are you saying? Talk to me!"

When I spoke, the words poured out unplanned, not thought out, not chosen with care. They slipped from me, the effort to contain them suddenly more than I could bear.

"Okay." I took a deep and ragged breath. "Here goes." I reached for his hand and squeezed it gently, whether to give or get support I didn't know. "Heather is our child, Larry. Yours and mine."

CHAPTER
27

"I couldn't have heard you right." Larry's hand turned cold under mine. He stared at me as though I'd spoken in a foreign language.

"I said Heather is our daughter. She was born January tenth, seventeen years ago, in Beechwood, Ohio. I held her in my arms, handed her to a nurse, and never saw her again—until she walked into my office."

"You're saying that you were pregnant with my child, that Heather is ours, that you never told me? I can't believe it. You never told me we had a child together?"

"I couldn't tell you then. We'd just broken up. I didn't want to get back together. I didn't want to marry you. I didn't want you in my life. It had taken all my courage just to end it with you. I found out about the baby a month later. My father wanted me to have an abortion, but I just couldn't do it. So my parents advised me to keep it simple. I'd go to my aunt Gloria in Ohio, have the baby, and let it go to someone who was ready and wanted a child. I just wanted it to be over. I did what they said."

"All these years I've been a father. I've had a child out there." His voice was soft, contemplative. Then it turned hard. "A very unhappy child. A miserable child."

"I know. Oh, Larry, when I realized who she was, the guilt—the guilt was enormous. I was sure I could have given her a better life, even as a single mother. But it was too late."

"And you continued to treat her, knowing you were her mother."

I watched him struggling to take it all in, to understand. I felt the crack in my heart grow larger. "I knew I had to give up the case. Conflict of interest, all that. It was the only thing to do. But I couldn't do it. Give her up again, a second time? I was helping her. She was getting better. And I thought if I kept it a secret, no one would get hurt."

He pivoted in his seat, opened his door, and got out of the car. I sat there and watched as he began to pace up and down on the sidewalk. His eyes were on the pavement, his hands clasped behind his back. Occasionally he shook his head. I finally got out of the car myself. I began to keep pace with him, back and forth, past the fire hydrant, up to the corner, back to the car.

"I can't believe you could do this, Rachel. Not you. It's a side of you I never suspected was there." This was the cold, superior, disdainful voice I remembered. It was as if the young, angry, distant Larry I once knew had appeared at my side. I wrapped my arms around myself. In spite of the July morning heat, I was cold at the core of my being. "And then you referred her to me! What was that, a sick joke? Sent her for treatment to her own father, and not a word to either one of us?"

"Her parents chose you. They read your book. They wanted you. I couldn't think of a good reason to dissuade them."

He stopped pacing and grabbed me by my shoulders, turning me to face him. "Don't give me that. There are hundreds of psychologists in Washington." I thought he might hit me. I almost hoped he would. His blue eyes were the icy color that I remembered from years ago. He looked at me with an expression I hadn't seen since those unhappy days. "Did you enjoy watching me treating her, relating to her, never knowing who she was? Did it give you some kind of a thrill knowing you'd orchestrated this little melodrama?"

"Actually it was Aunt Gloria who orchestrated it. I stayed with her when I was pregnant. I signed the adoption papers while I was living in her house. And then all these years later, she referred the Brodys to me and never said a word."

"And then you found out and never said a word to me." It was as though he'd implicated me in a massive cover-up.

"Larry, I never meant to hurt you. I love you."

"Love." He walked around the front of the car, swung open the driver's door, and sat down. For a moment I thought he planned to drive off and leave me standing there. I hurried to sit down next to him. "I fell in love with you all over again, wanted to be a father to your sons, was ready to spend the rest of my life with you, and still you didn't tell me? Maybe I could understand why you kept the secret when she was born. Maybe. But when we fell in love? When we made our wedding plans? There's no excuse for that. None."

I reached out to touch his thigh, but then thought better of it. He was truly untouchable at this moment. "I was afraid. I was awake most of the night, that first night we made love in Washington. I wanted to tell you. I knew I had to do it then, at the beginning, or not do it at all. You told me how much you'd wanted a child. How could I tell you that my decision had kept you from your daughter for all those years? I thought I'd lose you. I thought you'd never have to know, never have to be hurt like you're hurting now."

"Yes. Well. Too bad. I found out." My tears wouldn't stop flowing. I'd lost him, just as I'd feared I would.

"When were you going to tell me? After we were married?"

"Never. I planned never to tell you."

He stopped asking questions, and I stopped talking. Silence filled the car. The only voice was inside my head. *How could I have messed things up so badly? How many people are going to be hurt now? Larry—he's hurting already. Ben and Mitch? They're going to be devastated. How can I explain it to them? I found them a new father, and now I'm taking him away. Well, he's taking himself away, but it's all my fault. Oh my God, what have I done?*

"Look," Larry said finally, his voice deep and cold. "This is how we're going to do this. We're going to go in there together and tell Heather that she has two parents who love her and want to be part of her life. You can explain why you kept this deep, dark secret. I'll leave that part to you. Our first responsibility is to be there for her, to get her emotionally strong."

I looked up at him. The tears were finally stopping. I sniffed. He reached into his pocket and handed me his handkerchief. I blew my nose. "Okay."

"About us, the wedding, our life—I just don't know. I need some time. Right now I'm more furious than I've been since my father threw me out of the house. I didn't think I'd ever feel this way again."

"I understand. It's just ... oh, Larry, I feel so terrible." His face was as unmoving as granite.

"Do you realize," he said, his voice a controlled monotone, "that if we'd had the chance to tell her this, she might not be here now on her way to a psychiatric unit? If she'd known she had parents who love her and want her, she might not have felt so desperate."

"Maybe. But we tried to make her feel loved and wanted, didn't we?"

"You just don't get it, do you? Heather needed *parents*, not professional friends. And she had parents, but only you knew that. You knew it and you weren't sharing it with anyone."

"Larry, the boys are going to be devastated."

He looked away, staring out of the windshield as if an answer might be written on the license plate of the car parked in front of us. "I'm sorry about the boys. We'll talk to them together. I don't want to hurt them, but I can't go through with a marriage feeling the way I do right now. Not even for them."

"I know that. I just don't know how I'm ever going to explain it."

"Grown-ups make mistakes. They'll understand."

"How can they understand when you don't?"

"You're their mother. They'll forgive you."

"And you won't."

"Rachel, this is a complete and total shock. I don't know. I need time. That's all I can say."

"Larry, are you sure it's best for Heather to learn all this right now? Maybe it will make things worse."

"I'm going to talk to Paul Kessler. I'm certainly not going to tell her anything today. Right now we have to deal with Ben and Mitch."

The drive back to Manhattan seemed to take forever. The roads were clogged, and there was a cacophony of jackhammers, ambulance sirens, and the insistent horns of taxi drivers. I was acutely aware of Larry's stiff back and white knuckles, of the thin line of his mouth and the muscles of his jaw, distended because of his tightly clenched teeth. I hugged the passenger door and tried not to think of the approaching conversation with my boys.

I recalled the night in Washington when I'd lain next to Larry and searched my soul. *If only I'd told him then. Maybe he'd have left me, but Ben and Mitch wouldn't have come to know him and love him. Now he's going to leave them as Neil did. How will they ever be able to trust and love? Oh God, what a mess!*

It was noon when we finally got back to the West Village and found a parking spot. Mrs. Marcus was in the apartment. The boys weren't there.

"Ms. Annie came to pick them up," she explained. "How is Heather?"

"Not great right now," I said, sinking into the couch. "But I think she'll be okay."

Larry had gone into the bedroom. I heard his voice on the phone but couldn't catch the words. I didn't have the strength to stand up and go after him.

"Molly, the wedding's off." Tears filled my eyes again. I didn't know that one pair of ducts could manufacture so many tears.

"Oh, my dear, I am so sorry." She sat down next to me and gathered me up, squeezing me into a tight hug against her bosom. "Larry loves you very much. I'm sure it will get better."

"I don't know, Molly. I really made a big mistake. I did a terrible thing."

"Sh. Sh. Don't talk now. Let me call your sister." I nodded gratefully and let my head fall limp against the pillows.

I don't know how much time passed before Larry emerged from the bedroom. He stood over me, his expression empty. His voice sounded weary.

"Paul Kessler's going to see Heather this afternoon. He thinks she should remain hospitalized, in an adolescent psych unit. I agree." I nodded. "I spoke with Marilyn Whitfield. She'll be here tomorrow. I called Stephanie Brody. She told me to send all the bills to her."

I picked my head up. "How very good of her."

"When will the boys be home?"

"Molly called Annie. They're on their way back from the zoo. I need to talk to my sister before she leaves."

"Does she know about this?"

"She's the only person in the world who knows that Heather is our daughter. She tried to warn me."

"I'm packing. I'll be moving back to the Park Lane. Let me know when the boys get here." He disappeared, leaving me to my growing dread. I was going to lose my boys too. They'd never forgive me for this.

The apartment was suddenly noisy and crowded as Annie came

in with her children and mine. "What's going on?" she demanded, finding me limp and probably pale, stretched out on the couch. "Mrs. Marcus told me I needed to bring the boys back, but she didn't say why."

I pulled myself up and grabbed her hand, steering her into the spare bedroom. I closed the door, threw myself against her, and wept.

"You were right, you were right. It's all fallen apart." I felt her hand patting my back and stroking my hair.

"Sh. Sh. Tell me. I'm here." The story came out punctuated by my shuddery sobs. We sat together on the edge of the bed.

"Will Heather be all right?"

"I think so. Larry's called in a psychiatrist. She'll probably need medication and hospitalization. She's very depressed."

"What will you tell Ben and Mitch?"

"The truth. We're going to tell them together. It's going to be so hard, Annie. I should have listened to you back when I first learned who Heather was. I should have given up the case. I should have walked away. I should have told Larry at the very beginning. There are so many 'should have's.'"

"You followed your heart, sweetie. You thought you could make it work. I'm so sorry."

"Oh, Annie, what am I going to do? I've ruined it for everyone."

"Now you listen to me." She adopted the big sister tone that had seen me through many hard times. "First you're going to talk to the boys and get that over with. Then you and Larry are going to settle things with Heather. And after you've done all that, you and Ben and Mitch are coming back to California with me. We're going to give those nephews of mine a wonderful summer. And you're going to recuperate from all this."

"You'll tell Mom? And Kim and Brendan and Jeff?"

"I'll tell everyone. And I'll call Jan and ask her to make the calls about the wedding. I don't want you to think about any of that. I'm going to get my kids out of here, and you are going to take one step at a time. Put one foot in front of the other, and you'll get through this. I promise."

"There's been a change of plans," Larry told the boys. They sat next to each other on the couch. Larry and I were in the club chairs opposite. The tingling in my hands was painful; I wrung them in my lap. "I'm sorry to tell you that your mother and I are not getting married tomorrow."

Ben and Mitch began talking at once. "What do you mean? Are you postponing it? How come? Is it Heather?"

"I learned something today," Larry went on, "that came as a shock to me. It's such a shock, in fact, that I need time to decide what I want to do."

"You mean you might not want to marry Mom? You might not want to be our dad?" Ben's voice was filled with disbelief.

"I'm going to let your mom explain. Then you can ask me anything you want."

It was my turn. I slipped off the chair to sit cross-legged on the floor at the boys' feet. "I did something many years ago that you may not understand," I said. "It was something I thought I had to do. And then after I met Larry again, I made it worse."

"Mom." Mitch was impatient. "You're not making any sense."

"You're right. I'm just going to tell you this as straight as I can. Larry and I were in love when we were teenagers. But we had a lot of problems, complicated problems. So I broke up with him. He didn't want to break up, but I did. And then I found out that I was going to have a baby. And Larry was the dad. But I didn't want us to get back together again, so I never told him about the baby."

"Did you have an abortion?" Even in the midst of all the turmoil, I felt shocked that Mitch even knew the word.

"No. I couldn't do that. So I had the baby, a little girl, and I gave her up to be adopted by a good family. And I never told Larry."

"So now you told him and he's mad at you?" Ben asked.

"Sort of. But it's more complicated than that. You see, when Heather came to me for help almost two years ago, I had no idea. But then she had a birthday, and I put two and two together—"

"She's the one?" Mitch cried out. "She's the baby you gave away?"

"That's right."

"Holy moly. She's our sister? No wonder you wanted to take care of her."

"Right. But I was getting to know Larry again, and I was falling in love with him, and you boys were nuts about him. I was very afraid he'd be upset if he found out that I'd kept this great big secret from him."

"How could you do that, Mom?" Mitch asked. "I mean, she was living here like part of our family. Why couldn't you just tell us all who she was? She would've been happy, don't you think?"

"Out of the mouths of babes," Larry muttered.

"It was a bad mistake. I wasn't thinking straight. Now Heather's so sick, I felt I had to tell him. And he's very upset about what I did, so now he needs some time to think about whether he still wants to marry me. And I don't blame him. If it happened in reverse, I'd probably need time too."

"How much time?" Mitch directed the question at Larry.

"I don't know. I want you to know that I don't think your mom is a bad person. I understand that she felt afraid. But you see, she didn't trust me, and she thought she had to keep an important secret from me, so that's raised all kinds of questions in my mind."

"But the wedding's tomorrow," Ben said. "Everything's all set."

"I know, sweetheart," I said. "But we can't expect Larry to go ahead with our plans if he's not sure. That wouldn't be fair. We have to wait until he's sure."

"What if you don't ever want to marry Mom?" Ben asked Larry.

"If that happens, then we won't get married. But I'll always care about you guys. And I'll always be there for you if you need me."

"But you won't be our dad." Ben jumped off the couch and stood over me, glaring down. "How could you do this? You always taught us to tell the truth. You're just a hypo—"

"Hypocrite," Mitch interrupted. "You are, Mom. He's right." He turned to Larry, his eyes pleading. "Do you think you're going to change your mind?"

I couldn't handle anymore. I struggled to my feet, unable to hold back a loud sob. I ran into the bedroom. Mrs. Marcus followed me. She'd obviously heard everything. She pulled me into her arms. "Give them all a chance, honey," she said. "I think it will work out in the end."

"Oh, Molly, what if it doesn't?"

CHAPTER
28

I watched the sunrise on what should have been my wedding day. It was a flawless summer morning. I went to the boys' bedroom doorway and stood for a moment watching them sleep, Ben sprawled, Mitch curled up, both of them with their covers thrown off. I tiptoed in and pulled up the comforters. In the kitchen I filled the coffeepot, then dumped out some of the water when I realized I was preparing coffee for only one.

I understood perfectly how Heather felt about the mess she'd made of her life. I too had wrecked everything that was precious to me. I'd hurt the people I cared about most in the world. They were angry with me, but not nearly as angry as I was with myself.

I sipped coffee and recounted in my mind the mistakes I'd made. How many times could I have prevented yesterday's disaster?

I could have informed the Brodys the minute I realized that Heather was my child.

I could have told them that Larry Tobin was the wrong therapist for Heather, that she needed a woman. I could have prevented them from using him.

I should never have allowed myself to get close to Larry.

After I did get close to Larry, I should have told him about Heather. I should have told him that night in Washington at the hotel.

When he asked me to marry him, I should have told him then.

Woulda, coulda, shoulda. It's water under the bridge, over the dam, whatever. I am so sorry. "So, so sorry." I said that last part aloud, and it was a generic apology, meant for Ben, and Mitch, and

Larry, and Heather, and everyone who wouldn't be coming to my wedding today.

I made the shower water as hot as I could stand it, and stayed in it for extra minutes. The steam enclosed me when I stepped out. I wrapped myself in a big towel and went back to my room, throwing myself on the bed. Larry was coming for me at 9:00. This was the day we would tell Heather that she still had two parents. Soon I would add her to the list of those who were angry and resentful at what I'd done. Later, Mrs. Marcus would help me to pack the boys' suitcases. They would be leaving for California this afternoon with Annie, my mom, and their cousins. I had decided to stay in New York. I couldn't run away now, as tempting as the offer was. I had to be here for Heather if she'd let me. It would be painful to cross paths with Larry, but it couldn't be helped.

I dressed carefully for the visit. My face was still puffy, my eyes swollen, and I was certain that they would only be worse later. I applied light makeup, soft pink lipstick, a touch of mascara on the tips of my lashes. *You're being ridiculous. Nobody gives a damn what you look like, especially Heather.* Still, I had a need to be pretty for my child. I put on light blue slacks and a short-sleeved white cotton blouse. I slid my feet into sandals. I waited.

Finally I unlocked the bottom drawer of my desk and drew out the little journal I'd kept for my Julie. Sitting on the edge of my bed, I flipped through the pages. The photograph I'd taken of her at her last session slipped from between the pages and dropped to the floor. I bent to pick it up. It blurred in front of my eyes as the unending cascade of tears began again.

I looked down at the strong slant of my writing. Whenever I wrote in the book, I'd imagined my daughter holding it reverently in her hands. I'd envisioned myself sitting at her side as she discovered, finally, that she had a mother who loved her. *You'll read this and you'll understand. You'll know that I've never forgotten you.* I patted the cloth cover and slipped the book into my purse.

The phone rang at 9:00. "I'm downstairs," Larry said without preliminaries.

Mrs. Marcus's hand lingered a moment on my shoulder as she said goodbye. The boys hadn't yet come out of their room. I paced the gray-carpeted hallway floor as I waited for the elevator. I dreaded facing the angry, disappointed man who was waiting for me.

It was an awkward silent trip into Brooklyn. Everything that needed to be said had been said yesterday. Today, the reality of the distraught suicidal girl who was our daughter dominated the space between us. It drove out even the sadness and disappointment of our canceled wedding.

Again we had to park several blocks away. We walked side by side, not speaking. I couldn't begin to imagine how Heather would react to our news.

"Do you really think she's ready for this?" I asked Larry, more to break through the heavy fog of silence than anything else.

"Paul says it's a good idea. I trust his judgment."

"Yes, but what if he's wrong and she goes deeper into her shell? We're going to tell her this and then send her off to some hospital where she doesn't want to be in the first place."

"We're going to tell her."

"Damn it, Larry, you're not being objective."

"Objective? I guess I'm not. I just found out this kid's my daughter, for Christ's sake. I want to tell her. I want to hold her in my arms and tell her it's going to be okay. And I'm following my instincts on this one."

"I hope your instincts are better than mine were."

Heather had been moved to intensive care. We found her sitting in a recliner at the side of her bed. An intravenous tube ran into her left forearm, the needle covered by a bandage. There was a bulge at her chest where a heart monitor rested. A light blanket lay over her lap. Her bare toes peeked out. A television was on, but she made no pretense of watching. She stared at some invisible spot straight ahead of her, her pretty features immobile, her eyes listless.

"Hi," Larry said, sitting lightly on the edge of the bed. I stood nearby, willing the moment to be over. There was a time when I'd longed to confess to Heather who I was, who she was. I thought it would bring joy to both of us. Now I stood wrapped in the greatest misery I'd ever known.

"Hi."

"How's it going?"

"The same. When do I go to the nuthouse? Nobody tells me anything."

"That'll be up to Dr. Kessler. A day or two, I imagine. Heather, we have something to tell you. Something pretty amazing."

The girl turned her head, including me in her gaze for the first time. "Yeah? What?"

Larry nodded to me. I opened my mouth, but no sound came out. "I can't," I finally said. "I just can't. You tell her." As Larry began to speak, I walked over to the window next to Heather's bed and stared down at the street.

"Rachel and I were talking yesterday. She was very upset. Crying. Worried. Totally miserable. I tried to reassure her that you'd be okay. All of a sudden she blew me away by telling me that she knows who your biological parents are. She's known for a long time."

Heather leaned forward, squeezing her ears closed with her two index fingers. "Shut up. Shut up. I don't want to know. Don't tell me." Tears rolled down her cheeks as she shook her head angrily.

"Larry, please," I begged, turning from the window. "Can't you see this is a bad idea?" Tears were pouring down Heather's face, dripping onto the neckline of the hospital gown she was wearing.

Larry reached over and took Heather's wrists gently. He brought her hands back down to her lap. He held her for a moment, looking down at her with such a compassionate expression that I felt another crack in the region of my heart. He cleared his throat. "Heather, listen to me. This is not bad news. It's very good news. At least I think so."

She looked up at him, shaking her head one last time, but without conviction. He released her hands and leaned forward, commanding her attention with the intensity of his gaze.

"Rachel told me yesterday that she and I are your parents."

A physical jolt ran through Heather as the words registered.

"Yes, I know. That's how I felt too. Rachel is your biological mother, and I'm your father. You know we had a relationship years ago, before college. We broke up, and then Rachel found out she was pregnant. She never told me. She went to live with her aunt in Ohio, where she had you and gave you up for adoption."

Heather's small hands, with the nails bitten to the quick, rose and covered her face. She shook her head slowly from side to side. She leaned forward and dropped her forehead almost to her knees. "That can't be right. Why are you telling me this? I don't want to know. Stop talking about it. It isn't true anyway. Lies. She's telling you lies."

I hadn't known what to expect, but it certainly wasn't this. I moved away from the window and sat on the bed next to Larry.

"I was amazed when I realized who you were and that I'd found you." I reached for her, but she pulled away.

"Shut up! Shut up!" She closed her ears with her fingers again. "Stop talking, Rachel. Just stop."

"Sweetheart, listen to me, please. Don't you know we always had a special understanding for each other? It went beyond just therapist and client. There was something that connected us."

"So that's why you think I'm your kid? Because you felt connected? Get real, Rachel. So you had a kid and gave it away. Well, it wasn't me. Why are you two messing with my head? Don't you think I'm fucked up enough already?"

"We're not trying to do that, Heather," Larry said, squatting down in front of her until he was level with her.

She looked at him, her eyes blazing.

"We know you feel alone right now, but you're not alone. We're not just a couple of psychologists who told the court we'd watch out for you. We're your birth parents, and we love you."

"You can't be. You can't be." Her voice was strangled. "You're just trying to make me feel better." She turned to look at me. "You'd never give away your baby. Your own baby." Tears ran in rivers down her face.

"Larry, please, we have to stop," I begged. "Give her a chance to get used to the idea."

As though he hadn't heard, he leaned over Heather, touching her face gently, taking out his snowy handkerchief, and gently wiping her tears. "Listen, my dear child, if you knew how much I've wanted a child all these years, how sad I was that I'd never been blessed—" His voice broke.

I sobbed aloud.

Heather's face changed. Now it registered amazement. Tentatively she reached out and touched his arm. "Don't cry, Larry."

Then all three of us were sobbing, Heather folded into Larry's arms while I stood, my arms wrapped around my body. I'd never felt so alone in my life.

I don't know how much time had passed while they held each other and Larry whispered words of reassurance. Eventually I said, "I'm going to leave you two alone. I'll be at home if you need me."

Heather looked up at me. "Wait. Don't go. I want to ask you some questions."

"What do you want to know?" I held her gaze, determined not to falter.

"When did you know? And how can you be sure? And why didn't you tell me? I always thought you were straight with me. I trusted you." She sat straight and tall, her legs pressed together. She looked as though she might spring off the chair and bolt at any moment.

"Okay." It came out as a sigh. Pulling over a plastic folding chair that had been propped against the wall, I pushed it open and sat. "Do you remember last year, the day after your birthday? You were so angry, and you had that check you wanted to give me?"

"Yeah. My mother and father had gone out and left me alone on my birthday. They thought a big fat check would make up for it."

"Well, somehow I'd never paid attention to your birthday, which was very unusual. Whenever I knew a child was adopted I always looked, always checked, just like I sometimes walked around the streets of New York and looked at kids' faces and wondered if some girl passing by me could be my daughter. But this time I just missed it. I got caught up in what was bothering you, your whole family situation, and it never occurred to me to check out your birthday.

"I always stayed home from work on January tenth to make the day special, to remember you. I even sent flowers to myself in your honor. So I hadn't been to work the day before, and your appointment was on the eleventh. When you said that the day before had been your sixteenth birthday, I was shocked. Do you remember what I asked you?"

"No. What?"

"I asked you where you'd been born."

"Oh yeah, I thought that was strange. Like, what difference did it make?"

"It made all the difference. You said Beechwood, and I knew. I just knew. I told myself that there could have been more than one little girl born that day in that hospital who was adopted, but I checked, and you were the only one."

"I remember you gave me a big hug, and it was the first time I thought, *Wow, she really does care about me. She's not just another shrink.*"

"And after that, we really started working very well together, didn't we? You relaxed and trusted me."

"I trusted you, and all the time you were keeping this great big secret. You didn't tell my parents—I mean my adoptive parents—either, did you?"

"I couldn't. I would've had to stop seeing you right away. That would have been the right thing to do. It was very wrong of me to keep the secret. Many people would say I could have harmed you because I couldn't be objective anymore."

"But you didn't harm me."

"I hope not. I just couldn't let you walk out of my life a second time.

"And I know I should have told Larry before he started seeing you. But I had this really weird thought that I wanted you to be with someone who had a tie to you, even if neither one of you knew about it. It wasn't rational. It was wrong and it was stupid. I should have sent you to someone else and tried to forget who you were."

"We're all stupid sometimes," my child said to me.

"I kept a journal for you. I named you Julie, and I wrote to you every year on your birthday and some other times when I had big things going on in my life that I wanted to tell you about. I wrote to you when my twins were born, and when my husband died, and when I fell in love with your father all over again." I reached into my purse and drew out the pink clothbound book. Heather reached for it. I placed it gently on her lap.

"Wow. Julie. My name is Julie. I never liked the name Heather." Her thumb ran back and forth across the fabric of the book. A long moment passed while she absorbed the name she'd never known was hers. "Rachel, why didn't you keep me?" Her voice held within it all the sadness of what might have been.

"Things were so different then. Today lots of women are keeping babies without getting married. Back then it didn't happen. Anyway, I was just your age. I was ready to start college. I couldn't ask my parents to raise you. I wasn't ready to be a mother. I thought you'd have a better life with a married couple who really wanted a child."

"Yeah, right. We all know how that worked out." She ran a ragged thumbnail over the journal in her lap. She flipped open the cover to the first page.

"Dear Julie,'" she read aloud, "I hope one day you'll understand that I wanted to bring you home with me, take care of you, and raise you, but it wouldn't have been fair to you. You're going to have parents who can give you everything I can't. You're going to have a wonderful life. I hope one day you'll learn that I love you very much and will know that I will never, ever forget you.'"

She looked up at me then down at the page. She sat for a long moment, her head down, her hair hanging in front of her eyes. I had no idea what thoughts were swirling in her brain as she struggled to take it all in.

Then something occurred to her and she looked up, wide-eyed.

"You're getting married. My mother and father are getting married to each other. Oh my gosh, it's today. You're getting married today!"

"We're postponing it for a while," Larry said.

"Because of me? You can't not get married because of me. It'll be just one more thing I fucked up."

"You didn't cause anything," I said, stroking her hand. "It's just that things are not what we thought they were—what Larry thought, anyway. We need time to adjust to the way things are."

"How are you going to call it off now? It's all set. Jeez, what a mess."

"Everything's being taken care of. You know Jan, my receptionist at the office? She's handling everything."

"So Mitch and Ben are my brothers? I have brothers!" Her voice held awe combined with disbelief.

"They're great kids," Larry told her.

"Can I see them?"

"My sister's taking them home to California with her for a vacation. They're leaving this afternoon. But as soon as they come back, I'll bring them to see you," I told her. "They're pretty amazed that they have a sister, even though they're a little bummed right now. You have a family, sweetheart. We all love you. Your job is to get well and strong so we can have happy times together."

Heather had an unending supply of questions, about her two sets of grandparents, her cousins, my history with Neil, and Larry's brief marriage. Mostly, though, she was concerned about her imminent hospitalization, what would happen to her, and how long she'd have to be there.

"I'm starting to feel better. Maybe I don't have to go after all." The voice held a slim note of hope, tempered by the certainty that this was one commitment she would not escape.

"You need more than a day or two of feeling better to be sure you're on the way to being well," Larry told her. He was calm and reassuring, but the firm note in his voice silenced any thought of protest. "You'll get a weekend pass after a week or two, and then you'll come and stay with me," he said.

"I still can't believe it was you who gave me away," Heather said as she climbed back into the bed. "I can't believe you lied to me, and to Larry, for months and months. Maybe my father would be alive if you'd only told the truth." *Could that be true? How sad, if that's true.*

"We'll never know how it might have been different," Larry told her. "We have to work with the reality of today. We're going to leave now," he told her. "Try to rest. We'll see you soon."

I wanted to take her in my arms. I wanted to crush her slim body against mine and let my love for her seep into her pores and into her heart. I was afraid to touch her, afraid of disturbing some delicate balance that hovered, vibrating, in the room. I bent and brushed my lips lightly against her hair.

I was at the door when she called my name. I crossed the room in three strides.

"Yes, Heather? What is it?"

"Here." She held the journal, her arm stretched out to me. "Take this. I don't want to read it."

"I wanted you to see—" My voice broke.

"I don't want to see. I don't want to know. I want things to go back to the way they were. I want my daddy." As I reached for the journal, she burst into tears. Her sobs were ragged, dragged through the thorns of her pain. The tough little survivor was gone. I wished I could will her back into existence for just a short while, that overly made-up, hostile little clown who claimed to need nobody. Tragedy had wiped her out, and now this girl, my child, was vulnerable and lost.

I took the little book from her. *Will you ever want to read it?* "I understand, sweetheart. Maybe someday."

I bent and placed a soft kiss on her forehead. Was it my imagination that she shrank away from me just a little? I left the room alone, rounding the corner of the corridor before my knees caved in. I leaned against the wall and felt myself slipping downward until I was sitting cross-legged on the floor, the journal clutched against my chest.

What have I done? Oh my God, what have I done?

"Ma'am? Are you all right?" An aide looked down at me, her face soft with concern.

"She's fine." Larry was there, towering over me. He bent down and put a strong hand under my elbow. "Come on, let's go," he said. I put one foot in front of the other and obeyed.

CHAPTER
29

I slept a lot in July. It was an effort to keep my eyes open past 8:30 or 9:00 in the evening. I put away my books and magazines when I realized that I was reading the same paragraph three and four times without absorbing a word. There was nothing on television that interested me. I took a pill and was usually asleep before 10:00, relieved that another empty day was over.

I struggled to get up in the morning. Mrs. Marcus refused to coddle me. She stood in the bedroom doorway at 8:30 every day, hands on her hips. "How do you want your eggs?" she demanded.

"Oh, Molly, I don't care. I'm not hungry."

"I'll have none of that, thank you very much." She'd been the same when Neil died, frequently tender, but very much the drill sergeant when necessary. It was necessary now.

"I'm going to sleep a little longer." I made a big show of rolling over.

"You've slept enough. Breakfast in ten minutes." Somehow I always managed to wrap a light cotton robe around me and shuffle into the kitchen within the allotted time frame.

When Mitch and Ben called, I struggled to make my voice sound normal, alive, interested. I imagined that I could hear their resentment of me through their descriptions of the day's activities.

"No, no," Annie tried to reassure me, "they're doing really well."

"Do they talk to Larry?"

"He calls. In fact, he called last night. They both spoke with him."

"Did you talk to him?"

"For a couple of minutes."

"How is he?"

"Utterly focused on Heather. He's buying her gifts. He's visiting her every day."

"Does he mention me at all?" I heard a note in my voice that I recognized as jealousy. It sounded a little bit like a whine. I certainly wasn't pleased that it was there.

"He asked me how you're doing. He's concerned about you, Rachel."

"He hasn't called me."

"I think he will, honey. Try to be patient. Give him time."

"As if I have a choice."

The boys would be away another two weeks. I didn't know how I was going to make it through the summer. Sandy called and invited me to come out to her vacation house in East Hampton. I told her I'd think about it. If I went, I'd have to talk to her. I'd have to see other people. If Mrs. Marcus would have let me, I'd have pulled my comforter over my head and hibernated until the pain went away. *You survived Neil's death. You'll live through this too!* I pulled on a pair of warm-up pants and one of Neil's old college T-shirts. But it was the guilt that was killing me. *You did this yourself. You have nobody to blame. You made one bad decision after the other. You deserve this, but Larry doesn't deserve it. Ben and Mitch don't deserve it. And Heather certainly doesn't deserve it.*

I considered whether I might need some medication stronger than my trusty sleeping pill, something to get me over the hump. *Maybe I'll ask Dr. Branson for a Xanax prescription.* I remembered the struggle I had getting off Valium after Neil's death. No, I decided, I would tough this one out.

I went to see Heather every day. She asked me to come in the afternoons. "Larry's here almost every morning," she told me.

"You'd rather not see us at the same time?"

"It makes me sad," she said. "It's better this way."

Heather had been moved to the adolescent psych unit at Bellevue. Dr. Kessler was seeing her daily. She was taking an antidepressant. It was challenging to try to determine who she needed me to be. I was no longer her therapist, but I was quite sure she wasn't ready to accept me as her mother. A curtain had dropped between us, more permeable than a wall, but a barrier nonetheless.

"I wonder what it would've been like," she said once as we walked in the hallway together.

"What *what* would have been like?"

"You know, us. You and me. If you'd kept me."

"I wonder too. Different, that's for sure. For both of us."

"Did you think about it? Did you consider it at all?"

How do I answer you? "Of course I did. But remember, darling, I was just about the age that you are now."

"If it was me, I would've kept my baby. If I got pregnant with Frank, I would've kept it." Her eyes were cast down, watching the linoleum tiles as we walked. We turned at the end of the corridor in unison. She didn't look up at me. I didn't take my eyes off her face.

"I was very confused. I'd broken up with Larry—well, you know the story. I didn't think I could give you a decent life."

"And you didn't want to mess up your life. I get it. I really do."

I wanted so much to defend myself. I had to bite back the words of explanation. *I listened to my parents. I wanted a good life for you. It was so hard to be a single parent back then.* I didn't say any of it. "You're in so much pain," I said. "When you're ready to read the journal I kept for you, I think you'll see that I always loved you."

"I don't want to read it. So you wrote in a book once in a while. Did that give you a clear conscience?"

You're so bitter, my poor little girl. These daily visits were hard on both of us. Heather hadn't gained a new mother. She'd lost the therapist she'd trusted.

"Be honest, Heather," I said as we sat in the solarium sipping coffee from paper cups. "Would you rather I didn't visit you?"

She took several heartbeats to answer. When she looked up at me, her eyes were dark and troubled. "I don't know how I feel," she said. "But I don't feel that. You can come if you want."

"I do want—of course I want to see you. I want to take you home with me. I want us to be a family." I stopped myself as I heard the words spilling out, unplanned and uncensored.

"Let's not push it" was all she said.

The only time she was animated during those summer weeks at the hospital was when she spoke of Larry.

"Larry says when I get out of here, he's going to take me to Washington.

"Larry says he wants to adopt me. He says we should get DNA tests to prove he's my father so that he can adopt me.

"Larry says he hopes I go to college in the east so he can see me often."

"He always wanted to be a dad," I said. "That was one of the first things he told me when we connected again. I'm really glad you have each other." I fought back an urge to clear my throat of a lump that threatened my breathing. I turned away and gave a little cough instead.

"And I always wanted brothers or sisters. Will you bring Mitch and Ben to see me when they get back?"

"Of course I will." *Could this heartbroken wreckage ever heal itself and become some kind of family?*

Ben and Mitch, it turned out, were in no hurry to come home. I was pouring a vodka on the rocks, which I'd come to anticipate every afternoon, when Annie called. "The boys would like to stay another ten days or so," she told me. "I wanted to sound you out first, before they asked you. They're having a really nice time with my kids. But I know you've been alone so long already—"

"It's fine, Annie. I'm glad they're having a decent summer. Tell them to call me. I'll say yes."

So the emptiness would stretch a little longer. It felt like penance, and I felt that I deserved it. Anyway, there were plans to be made for Heather. Where would she go after the hospital? What would happen in court? What about Stephanie? Would she make trouble?

Heather's aunt Marilyn was a frequent visitor. She flew in from Chicago most weekends and stayed with her college roommate on the Upper East Side. "We were just talking about my dad," Heather said when I found the two of them in the solarium one afternoon.

"Heather and I both miss him," Marilyn said, patting the seat next to her on the sofa, inviting me to join them. "He was a great brother."

"And a great dad too. I mean, he tried, he really did. I made it so hard for him."

"Oh, my sweet girl, we all have things we wish we'd done differently." I reached over to touch her knee. "We're human beings.

We make mistakes and we have to learn to live with them. Nobody knows that better than I do."

"Rachel, when this court thing is over, if Heather's allowed to leave New York, I'd like to take her to Chicago with me."

"How do you feel about that?"

"I feel like I don't belong anywhere."

"The truth is that you belong everywhere. You belong with Larry. You belong with me. You belong with Stephanie. You belong with your aunt."

"I don't belong with Frank."

"That's very true."

"Rachel, he messed me up *so* bad."

"I know, sweetheart. But that's behind you now. You're going to have a wonderful future."

"I wish I could believe that."

"Can we see Larry?" Ben asked, five minutes after giving me a hug at Newark airport's baggage claim.

"You can call him and work something out. I'm sure he'd like to see you."

It felt almost natural riding home with the twins in the hired car. They competed with each other to tell me about their adventures in California. They challenged each other's memory of events. "No, dum-dum, we saw the polar bear first, and then we went into the birdhouse."

"Did you know Kim's getting her driver's license in less than two years, Mom? She can't wait."

"We went to Disneyland *three* times!"

"Can we call Larry as soon as we get home?"

Every mention of Larry's name pricked my unhealed scar, but I would never let the boys know that. Each time he came to pick the boys up, his voice on the intercom sliced through me. The tingle in my hands always lasted for an hour after they'd left the house. Ben and Mitch seemed reasonably content with seeing Larry for brief outings and excursions. *How long will it last? Heather will get out of the hospital, and he'll want to spend his time with her. He may go back to Washington, to his former life, his friends, his practice. How many separations will my kids have to endure before it's fully and completely over?* I wondered if I should limit the visits, but I didn't have the heart to do it.

It was mid-August before Dr. Kessler pronounced Heather ready to leave the hospital. He asked to see Larry, Marilyn, and me. We met in a conference room on the unit. I tried to read Larry's expression. There was only concern for Heather. His tone was neutral when he greeted me and asked me how I was doing. If he was no longer angry, he was nonetheless devoid of warmth.

"She's stabilized," the doctor reported. "We've got her medication balanced, and the worst of the depression seems to be under control. There's still a whole lot of guilt and sadness, but she's moving forward. It's slow, but it's happening."

"What happens now?" I asked. "What do you recommend, Doctor?"

He folded his hands into a steeple position, resting his two forefingers against his lips. We waited as he organized his thoughts.

"Heather has a court date coming up," he reminded us. "Her lawyer has asked me to testify. It's my hope—actually it's my belief—that she won't get jail time for that fiasco. The boy's going to exonerate her in exchange for a light sentence and a stint in rehab." I heard my own sigh of relief echo in the quiet room.

"The big question, of course, is where Heather should live. We have no shortage of volunteers. Each of you would like to take her home."

"What does Heather want?" Marilyn asked.

"Heather doesn't want to cause anyone any more trouble. But of course she has to live somewhere. At least until she's eighteen."

"That's almost five months from now," I said. "And even then, she's certainly not going to be ready to be on her own. She needs someone to look after her."

"I agree. So I pressed her a bit to make a decision. I told her that none of us wanted to impose one on her."

"What about Stephanie? Doesn't she have a say in this? Shouldn't she be here?" I asked.

"Oh, please," Marilyn commented. "I've been in touch with my sister-in-law. She's quite busy doing all the things she does so well. There's only one thing she doesn't want: to have Heather at home with her. I still think the best thing would be for Heather to come to Chicago with me."

"I agree," Dr. Kessler said. I saw Larry lean hard against the back of his chair. It was not what he'd expected. It wasn't what I'd thought would happen either.

"Why?" Larry's question felt stark.

"I have a couple of reasons. Number one: Marilyn is Heather's closest relative—in her adoptive family, of course. Heather shares a lot of memories of her father with her aunt Marilyn. Number two: Heather believes she's disrupted your lives enough already." He looked first at me, then at Larry across the table. "She feels responsible for the fact that you've postponed your wedding. Number three: she doesn't want to have to choose between the two of you. Need I go on?"

"But I—we," Larry said, "we want to be with her, let her know she has parents who want her."

"She knows that. But, Larry, let me be perfectly frank. Having Heather stay with either one of you would be more for your sakes than hers right now. I believe she'll make a better recovery if she lives with her aunt."

We were silent. I struggled to absorb the reality of another separation from my daughter, about to take place. I could read similar feelings reflected in Larry's eyes.

"You can see her whenever you wish," Marilyn said. "I hope you'll come often. She can visit during school vacations. By the way," she said, her tone becoming more animated, "the school my son Chester goes to has a wonderful art program. I think Heather will fit in beautifully."

"Where will she stay until her court appearance?" I asked.

"We anticipate about a week between discharge and court," the doctor said. "I'm recommending that she stay with you, Dr. Marston. She's used to your home, she knows your children, you have ample support, and it is, after all, for a limited time."

So that was that. I'd have my daughter at home with me for a week or so, and then she'd be gone again.

The only sound in the room was the scraping of chair legs as we all stood.

"Let's go talk to Heather," Dr. Kessler said.

The four of us trouped down the corridor to her room. I thought of all the separations: little Julie, a few days old, carried out of my life; the move to Washington just as we were bonding; her frightening disappearance and the fear that I'd never see her again; and now that she knew at last that I was her mother, a relocation to Chicago to stay with another surrogate. My feet were as heavy as my heart as I followed Dr. Kessler up the hall to give Heather the news.

CHAPTER

30

The extraordinary becomes ordinary over time. School started. Ben and Mitch hoisted backpacks each morning and headed off to school. My caseload grew healthy again, and I found myself working a couple of evenings each week, evenings I welcomed because there were fewer hours in which to feel lonely and unfulfilled. I thought about calling Alan and suggesting dinner with no-strings-attached sex afterward. Although I yearned to be touched in that way, the thought died almost instantly. I wasn't ready for anyone else's touch.

I received emails from Heather, nothing too personal, but it was encouraging that she was willing to reach out to me, even electronically. I knew that she'd friended Mitch and Ben on Facebook, and although I burned with curiosity, I asked them nothing.

I was more than a little surprised that Larry had opted to remain in New York. I was sure that he would have chosen to be as far from me as possible and would move back to Washington as soon as possible, but he remained in the city. "My agent and publisher are here," he said in explanation. "And besides, I really love New York. Anyway, I'm going to wait and see where Heather wants to live when she turns eighteen."

Saturday mornings, the boys knew they had a standing date with Larry. There was an air of excitement as they ate breakfast and waited for the intercom buzzer that would announce his arrival downstairs.

"Bye, Mom," they'd chorus, pecking me on the cheek and racing each other to the door.

"Bye," I'd respond to their backs as they disappeared into the hallway.

"I fucked up *so* bad," I whined to Annie as I spent a lonely Saturday imagining what the boys were doing, imagining what Heather was doing, feeling disgustingly sorry for myself and hating the feeling.

"True." Annie wouldn't coddle me, and I loved her for it. "What is, is," she reminded me. "I know you can move on. C'mon, Rachel," she coaxed, "you had a life before Larry. You have a life now. You have to live it."

"I know, I know," I breathed into the phone. "It's so hard."

"It's hard, baby, but you can do it."

It was late October when Heather called me while I was at the office to ask if she could come to visit the boys and stay at our place the following weekend.

"Of course." I tried not to let my excitement drive my voice above its usual range.

Ben, Mitch, and I picked her up at the airport the first Friday night in November. My eyes drank greedily as I watched her descend the escalator. She'd gotten a haircut. The dark hair curved around her chin and swayed as she walked toward us, a bounce in her step. The ubiquitous black leather bag had been replaced by a canvas tote trimmed in red piping with her initials, HJB, stitched in red. A few books stuck out from the open top, and the corner of a wrapped package was visible. She wore jeans, a T-shirt, and a navy-blue hoodie. Her approach felt somewhat awkward. The boys didn't know whether to run up to her or wait for her to come to them. For that matter, I was unsure myself. Heather got us through the moment. She put down her tote bag, opened her arms, and said, "Well, here I am." There were no hugs and no kisses, but the smile was genuine. Luggage tumbled onto the carousel. When Heather identified her suitcase, Ben and Mitch both scrambled to pull it off.

"I'm so glad you're here," I managed to say as we settled into the limo. The boys sat, facing us, on the jump seats.

"It feels weird to be back."

"You look wonderful. How are things going at Marilyn's?"

"She's so great. She really makes me feel like one of the family."

"You are one of the family."

"Yeah, I know, but—you know what I mean."

"Larry's taking us to the science center tomorrow," Mitch said. "You're coming too, right?"

Heather looked at me. I hadn't been told of the plans. "It's up to you," I told her. "You did come to be with the boys. I know they'd like you to go with them."

"What about you?"

"No, I won't be going. I'll see all of you when you get back. Make sure you take pictures to show me."

The warm aroma of chicken soup engulfed us as we entered the apartment. Molly was beaming. There was no hesitation here. Molly threw open her arms, and Heather stepped into the motherly embrace, wrapping her own slim arms around Molly's ample hips.

"Welcome home, child."

"Something smells yummy. I didn't have much appetite for your great cooking last time I was here."

"Well, you'll make up for it this time. We need to put a little meat on your bones."

"Oh, I hope not." Heather giggled.

Had I ever heard her laugh? Maybe once or twice before she moved to Washington, when the therapy was going well and she was relaxed. Surely not recently.

It was difficult to get Ben and Mitch settled down. Their excitement at spending time with their sister made even Mitch, the quieter twin, hyper. "You have to meet Brandon and Kim," Ben said as we went into their room to say good night. "They're your cousins, you know. You'll like them."

"I'm sure I will, someday. G'night, guys. See you tomorrow."

Mrs. Marcus had wiped the last dish and put away the last pot. "I'll see everyone at breakfast," she announced, before leaving to stay with her cousin in Brooklyn.

Heather and I were alone in the den. She curled up in the corner of my couch, shoes off, legs tucked under her. She fingered the fringe on the chenille throw that Neil's mother had crocheted for us as a first-anniversary gift. The awkwardness was back. I sat in the recliner and pushed it back to elevate my legs. *Who am I now?* I looked at the girl, almost a woman, who'd been through so much sadness and loss. *Am I the first person who ever abandoned you, or am I the therapist who tried to help you? Am I the keeper of a secret that rocked your world? Am I merely the donor of half your DNA?*

"I'm glad you wanted to come," I ventured after we'd been silent for a minute longer than was comfortable.

"I want to get to know my brothers. They're neat kids."

"Yes, they are. They're really excited to have a sister."

"Rachel, I'm still trying to figure things out. I don't know how I feel about you, about everything that happened."

"Heather, there's no deadline. Take all the time you need. I'm just grateful that you're doing well in Chicago. That's all I care about."

"I'm not angry anymore that you gave me up. I've been working with my therapist in Chicago. She's okay—she's helping me. So I get it. I guess it's better than having an abortion, right?" Her smile didn't hold much humor.

"If you're more at peace with it, that's all I can ask for."

"But I still can't believe that you kept this big secret after you knew who I was."

"I wish I'd done it differently. I made a lot of mistakes."

"And then it blew up in your face, didn't it?"

"That's for sure. But you're going to be okay, and that's the main thing."

"I'm working on it. I made mistakes too—really bad ones. And the consequences were so awful, I can hardly stand it. But Marjorie—she's my therapist—she's helping me to move on. I have to move on, or I'll be stuck here forever."

She said good night shortly afterward. I sat in that recliner for a long time. I wasn't consciously thinking of anything, just staring at a crystal cat on my bookshelf, until the light fractured and my eyes blurred, at which point I pushed out of the chair and went to bed.

The three of them trouped out together at 10:00 a.m., leaving me to face another Saturday by myself. I had no ambition to do anything. *He could've invited me to join them. He's still so angry. He'll never get over it. Like Heather said, I have to move on or I'll be stuck forever.*

They got back after dark. To my surprise. Larry stood in the doorway as the boys and Heather greeted me and disappeared down the hall.

"It was a good day," he said. "I'd like to take everyone to brunch tomorrow." He paused. "You too."

I felt a flutter as my heart skipped a beat. I rubbed my palm with my opposite thumb. It had now become a nervous habit. I'd rarely been so nervous. "I have a better idea. Come over in the morning and we'll have brunch here."

"You're on. I was hoping you'd say that. Good night."

Galvanized, I ran into the kitchen and caught up with Molly as she was setting the table. "Molly, can you make your noodle kugel for tomorrow's brunch? Larry's coming."

"I have one in the freezer." Her rosy cheeks puffed out as she beamed at me.

There were moments the next day when we felt like a family. Larry played games with the children; he teased Mrs. Marcus; he was friendly and open with me. Heather and I talked about her school, her art classes, and the medium she was working in.

"I think I'd like to go to Pratt," she said as the subject turned to possible colleges. "I have a whole lot of academic catching-up to do. I really blew the first three years of high school."

"You might want to take a precollege year that some schools offer," Larry suggested. We could have been any family whose oldest child was planning her future. *It could have been this way for us. It could have been.*

Not true, my rational self stepped in to remind me. *If I'd kept my secret, Heather would still be living with Stephanie, and she and Larry would never know that we were a family. Oh, stop it! What's the point of all this "might have been" thinking? It is what it is, like Annie said. Annie was right.*

The day disappeared. Larry took Heather to the airport for her flight back to Chicago, and the boys went down to the third floor to hang out with Billy. I shook the last drops of a bottle of good sauvignon blanc into my wineglass and curled up in the same place where Heather had nestled the night before. I too fingered the fringe on the chenille throw, trying not to let the silence penetrate. *This was good. This was progress. She's going to be fine. Thank God she's going to be fine.*

The boys and I went back to Playa del Mar for the winter holidays. Eduard Montvale was there with Clarisse, who'd matured amazingly in the space of a year. She was going to be a heartbreaker, no doubt about it. She played good-naturedly with Ben and Mitch, although it seemed to me that she felt a little bit above the childish games they'd enjoyed for years.

Eduard and I had a late dinner on the second night of our stay. I knew he was hoping that we'd be a couple for the duration of our stay. *Move on! Move on!* I'd enjoyed Eduard in the past. We'd enjoyed each other and the no-strings freedom that this "same time next year" arrangement afforded both of us.

We clinked glasses. "I almost got married this year," I told him.

"Almost?"

"Last-minute issues. It was traumatic, but it's over."

"I've been seeing Clarisse's mother."

"Really? How's that going?"

"We might give it another try."

Eduard always had booked separate rooms for him and his daughter. Late that night, after dancing, gambling a bit, and drinking several after-dinner drinks, I found myself in his comfortable suite.

"Old times' sake?" he said, pouring champagne from the bottle we'd failed to polish off at the bar.

"Old times' sake." I turned to give him access to the zipper of my little black dress.

He didn't take the opportunity to undress me. Instead, he turned me by my shoulders to face him. "You don't have to do this, you know. You're a delightful dinner companion, and our children are friends. If you'd prefer to leave it there, I understand."

Decision time! "You're a very special man, Eduard."

"Friends?"

"Friends."

"Meet for breakfast?"

"Absolutely."

The boys had a wonderful vacation. I hoped that Eduard would make a go of it with Clarisse's mom. How great for her if her parents were together again.

On New Year's Eve we shared a table with another couple and their three children. The boys and Clarisse were permitted to stay up to see in the New Year. They made the appropriate amount of noise. Eduard and I kissed—the chaste kiss of two friends whose futures lay elsewhere.

CHAPTER
31

On January 5, the boys moaned and groaned, hefted their backpacks, and went off to school. My clients were suffering from the usual post-holiday letdown. Family gatherings hadn't gone as expected. Christmas had not magically wiped out sibling rivalry, parental disappointments, ancient grievances. Snow had turned slushy, and emotions were equally gray and dreary. It was my job to help my clients to remember that the sun would shine again one day. Helping them had the added benefit of helping me to remember as well.

I returned a call from Heather's aunt during a break in my schedule.

"How are you? Is everything okay with Heather?"

"We're all fine here. I hope your holidays were pleasant."

"I took the boys to Puerto Rico—our usual Christmas week getaway. They have a good time there."

"We skied in Utah. Heather loved it. You should have seen her on the expert slopes. She's a natural."

I felt a little surge of pride. "Perhaps one day we'll ski together. Sounds like I couldn't keep up with her though."

"I certainly couldn't. Of course you're aware that her birthday's coming up next week."

"She's turning eighteen. I can hardly believe it."

"I'm hoping that you and the boys can come to Chicago next weekend to help us celebrate."

It took less than a heartbeat for me to answer. "Of course. We'd love to. How nice of you to ask us."

"Great. Heather will be so pleased! Larry will be here too, of course. Will that be a problem for you?"

"No. Of course not. I hope it'll be okay with him."

"I'm sure it will be. We're hosting a little party for Heather on Saturday night at the Hyatt. I'll make a booking for you there. How long can you stay?"

"We can catch a flight Friday after school. And I guess we'll come back to New York Sunday evening."

"Perfect. I'm so glad. See you Friday night. Plan to have dinner with us—my house."

"Looking forward to it. Thanks so much. And, Marilyn, thanks for everything. You've been a godsend."

"Oh, Rachel, it's been wonderful for me too."

I hung up and walked to my windows. I gazed down at the gray winter city, which didn't seem quite as grim as it had a few minutes earlier. Could it really have been two years since a bitter young girl had thrust into my hands the birthday check she didn't want? Could I have played that hand differently? *I'll never know. Probably if I had it to do over again, I'd do the same thing.* I ended my sad little introspection with a sigh and went to call my boys.

"Guess what! We're going to Chicago!"

On the flight, Ben and Mitch settled down with their handheld games, and I stared out at the wintry cloud cover, which hid any hint of the land below. My hands felt icy as I imagined spending a weekend in close proximity to Larry. The warmth I thought we'd experienced at brunch in October had not recurred. It was business as usual when Heather returned to Chicago. Larry had not missed a Saturday with the boys, but he hadn't come up to the apartment with them or reached out to me in any way. I'd begun to think that I'd imagined any change in his attitude toward me. *It's going to be awkward. Maybe we shouldn't have come.* But even as I thought it, I knew that nothing would have kept me away from celebrating my daughter's birthday.

It was Larry who met us at the airport. Ben and Mitch rushed over to him, while I hung back, shifting my shoulder bag from one side to the other. When Larry looked up at me, his smile seemed genuine enough.

He reached out and took my hand. "I'm glad you're here," he said.

"It feels amazing to be here." Did I imagine that his eyes held my gaze longer than necessary? I'd become too good at imagining the things I hoped for. I didn't trust my perceptions anymore.

Larry eased the heavy carry-on from my shoulder and slung it onto his. "Heather's helping Marilyn prepare dinner. Let's get you guys settled at the hotel. Then we'll head over to the house."

Marilyn had arranged a suite for the boys and me. The living room was equipped with a convertible couch and a TV. The bedroom had two double beds. We'd be quite comfortable.

"My room's just down the hall if you need anything," Larry said.

"Can we see it?" Ben asked. The boys followed him as he went to set his bag down in his room. I kicked my shoes off and lay down on top of the comforter, weaving my fingers together behind my head. I couldn't allow myself to think about how this weekend might have been different. *Be grateful. This is more than you expected.* I felt myself begin to drift, fatigue born of tension threatening to overwhelm me. With an effort I got up, unzipped my garment bag, and changed into a seafoam-colored cashmere dress. I draped a double-rope necklace of multicolored stones around my neck, pushed small pearl post earrings into the appropriate holes, and refreshed my lipstick. When the boys and Larry returned a few minutes later, I was ready for the evening.

Larry had rented a car. He drove with confidence through Chicago's Friday night rush-hour traffic. The Whitfields lived in the posh suburb of Aurora. Their home, an elegant Tudor built of weathered-looking stone and wood, had a wide, welcoming circular drive and a double-door entrance with glass panels on both sides. I could see Heather standing near the door as we approached. She flung the door open as we mounted the few stairs.

"They're here," I heard her trill, as she briefly jumped up and down. Marilyn came to join her in the entryway. Heather ran to hug Larry. Marilyn put a motherly arm around my shoulders.

"Hello, everyone. Welcome to our home."

Heather bent to embrace Mitch and Ben, and finally she stretched out her arms to me. "I'm so glad you could come."

"Happy birthday, sweetheart." I held her shoulders and stood her away from me so that I could take a good look at her. Still slim, she had filled out, no longer the wraith she'd been in summer. Her dark hair fell below her chin in waves. Her electric-blue eyes, a gift from her father, flashed with excitement and pleasure. She wore a simple pair of diamond studs in her ears.

"How are you doing?" I lifted her chin so that she looked directly at me.

"Much better, Rachel. I have my moments, but I'm much better. How about you?"

"Me too." I gave her a little squeeze. We all moved into Marilyn's comfortable, spacious living room. Her husband, Arthur, emerged from his study to greet us.

"Good to see you again." We'd met only once, at Bill's funeral. "Nice to have something to celebrate. Drinks?"

We were the only guests at dinner. Heather's cousin Chester clomped down the stairs when called. The two of them exchanged sibling-type banter as Marilyn served the meal, helped by a woman named Lila, whom she introduced as her "right arm." I thought of Molly and understood.

"I got a birthday card from my mother." Heather produced it and reached across the table, offering it to Larry and me.

The printed material read, "Best Wishes on Your Birthday." The handwritten addition said, "I hope you are well." It was signed "Stephanie Brody." I glanced up at Marilyn's face. Her eyes squinted, her nostrils flared, and her jaw went rigid. Her rage was a silent scream.

"Consider it progress," Larry said as he handed the card back to Heather.

"I don't expect to be forgiven. It's okay. I'm dealing with it."

After that small, sad interlude, we settled in to enjoy a gourmet meal, the centerpiece being an exquisitely slow-braised lamb roast. "Lila is a world-class cook," Marilyn said, unable to totally conceal her pride.

"Wait until you taste the birthday cake," Chester said. "Heather picked my favorite."

"Mine too," the birthday girl said. And indeed the flourless chocolate cake was the best I'd ever had. Decorated with pink roses, the calligraphy message read, "To Heather and new beginnings." She scrunched her eyes shut and took an extra few heartbeats to make her wish before blowing out the circle of eighteen candles and the larger, central one—the one "to grow on."

We stayed another hour. Heather, Chester, and the boys sat at a card table in the den, playing a board game I'd never heard of, happy kids laughing and enjoying each other. It made me smile. Marilyn, Arthur, Larry, and I sipped cognac in the living room.

"She seems to be doing so well," I said to Marilyn.

"She is. You're seeing the girl she was always meant to be."

"I saw a glimpse of her once before, but it didn't last." I was remembering her final therapy appointment with me, when I'd dared to hope she had turned the corner.

"She's had some tough blows since then," Larry put in. "But she's coping. I think she'll be okay now."

Finally it was time for us to leave.

"See you tomorrow." There were hugs and kisses all around as we said good night and headed back to the hotel.

"Chester's okay," Ben ventured as we made our way toward the freeway and back to the city.

"He's a nice young man," Larry answered. "It's good for Heather that she has him there."

"Just as long as he remembers that he's not her brother. We are," Mitch declared. Larry glanced at me briefly. We shared a smile.

"Nightcap?" Larry gestured toward the inviting lounge located at the center of the hotel lobby.

"I don't think so. It's been a long day. I have to get the boys settled."

We ascended in the glass-enclosed elevator that afforded a view of the city, rising to the thirty-second floor. "Can we do it one more time?" Mitch asked.

"Tomorrow. Time for bed." Larry came in. He and I chatted about the evening and how well Heather was doing while the twins opened the sofa bed and took turns brushing their teeth. Scrubbed and in pj's, they settled down on the couch. I could tell that after a few minutes of requisite horsing around, they'd both be asleep. It had been a long day.

I stepped out into the hallway with Larry. His eyes were kind, his expression tender as he bent and kissed me on the cheek.

"Good night," I whispered. I stood in front of my hotel room door, my toe preventing it from locking behind me. I watched him all the way down the hall, waiting until he'd inserted his key and stepped into his room before I went back into mine.

My cell phone rang at 9:00. I'd been up for a while but was still in bed. It was quiet in the living room. Like most eleven-year-olds, my boys could sleep through hail and brimstone.

"Hi, Rachel. Good morning." Heather's voice was cheerful. "Guess where I am!"

"Home in bed, looking forward to tonight?"

"You're half right. I am looking forward to tonight. But I'm not home. I'm down here in the hotel lobby. Want to have breakfast with me?"

My feet were already on the floor. "We'll be right down. Give us ten minutes."

"Larry's down here already. We'll get a table."

"Mitch. Ben. Time to get up! We're having breakfast with Heather. And Larry." I heard a groan and saw someone's attempt to pull covers over his head.

I yanked the blanket down as I did on many school mornings. "Let's go. Let's go. They're waiting for us!"

It was going to be a fabulous family Saturday.

"Aunt Marilyn said I could stay and change for the party in your room—if you didn't mind, of course," Heather said once we were settled down for breakfast.

"I don't mind. That will be great!"

"Maybe I could sleep over with you tonight if it gets late?"

"Of course, sweetheart. I'd like that."

"I planned some sightseeing stuff for the boys. You guys can come if you want."

We put ourselves in Heather's hands. She filled our morning and early afternoon with activities—the observatory, the Field Museum, the aquarium. Larry and I watched fondly as the three children enjoyed the sights. Heather was beaming with pride and pleasure as she showed her brothers her adopted town.

"Chicago's great," I commented as we paused for lunch at the museum. "Who knew?"

"I had no idea. And my school is wonderful. I love my art classes."

"So it was a good decision, you coming to stay with Marilyn?"

"She's wonderful. We talk about my dad sometimes. She's so understanding."

"I am so glad things are working out for you." *This is the life I'd imagined for you, my darling. This is what it could have been if Marilyn had adopted you and not Stephanie.*

At 5:00 we were back in our rooms, in time to rest before Heather's birthday dinner. Mitch and Ben took over the living room, competing with video games supplied by the hotel. Larry excused himself to check his emails and make a few phone calls.

Heather took out her dress to show me. I knew she would look lovely and very grown-up in the slim silk sheath. "How are you at eyeliner?" she asked me.

"Probably not as good as you are." We both laughed. I was remembering my first glimpse of her, when liner and mascara had all but hidden her eyes completely. I suspected she was thinking of it as well.

"So I'm on my own?"

"'Fraid so."

She flopped on one bed, I on the other. We wiggled our toes in unison.

"You gave your brothers a wonderful day."

"I was happy today. Really happy. I didn't think I'd ever feel happy again."

I reached across the divide between the beds and stroked her arm. "You're going to have many, many happy days. It's only just beginning."

Marilyn and Arthur hosted a lovely event in Heather's honor. It was held in one of the smaller public rooms of the hotel. Marilyn had invited three or four couples who were their close friends, and about a dozen young people from Heather's school. There was a six-piece orchestra that played the music favored by Heather and her friends.

Heather glowed. Her peach-colored silk dress emphasized the high color in her face. The dress clung, leaving no doubt that she was no longer a child. I removed my smartphone from my evening bag and took a picture. It was the first of many I took during the festivities. Heather danced all evening with her uncle Drew and cousin Chester, with her friends from school, with Larry, and in circle dances with her girlfriends. She pulled Mitch and Ben from their seats and managed to dance with both of them at once, laughing and twirling. She pulled me up for one of the dances. "C'mon, Rachel, let your hair down."

At eleven, Arthur approached the bandleader and negotiated an extra hour. The band played on. It was Marilyn who offered a champagne toast just before the cutting of the cake.

"Heather has had a difficult year and has come through it with flying colors," she said, holding her flute high. "We've been privileged to experience a preview of the woman she is becoming, a woman who is talented, beautiful, and strong. Happy birthday, darling." We all raised the glasses that had been discreetly filled.

"To Heather," one of her classmates called out.

"To Heather," we all responded.

My eighteen-year-old daughter stood, head slightly bowed, a shy smile on her face. "Thank you all for coming. It means a lot to me."

Shortly after midnight all of us were gathered in my bedroom. At Heather's request, Larry joined us. Heather and I sat on the edge of one bed, shoes off. She swung her legs a bit and wiggled her toes. "It was wonderful," she said.

"It felt like an impossible dream come true," I volunteered. "I could never have imagined I'd be sharing in your birthday celebration."

"It's great having a big sister," Mitch offered. The boys sat cross-legged on the second bed.

"It's great having brothers. I hated being an 'only.'" She pivoted to face me. "Rachel, are you going to write about tonight in that journal you kept for me?"

I thought she'd forgotten about the book.

"Of course I am. This is a milestone. It will be a very happy entry. I'm going to write in it tonight."

"You brought the book with you?"

My fingers tingled, a sure sign that my anxiety was peaking. "I did. I knew I'd want to record tonight." I smiled. "In fact, as soon as I can print some of the pictures I took, I'm going to paste them right in."

Heather's comment was almost a whisper. "I think I'm ready."

"Ready to see it? Now?"

"Yes. Yes, I'm ready. I mean, if it's okay with you."

I felt a chill of apprehension. "It's so late. Wouldn't you rather wait until tomorrow?"

"No, I'm not tired. Can we do it now? Please?"

"Sure." I stood up and padded, shoeless, to the night table. Only I was aware that my hand shook as I opened the drawer. Returning with the clothbound book in hand, I saw that Larry and Heather had exchanged places. She now sat in the club chair, her posture erect, expectant. Larry was on the edge of the bed. He patted the spot next to him. I sat.

This is totally surreal. How can this be happening? For eighteen years this little book had stayed hidden in a locked bureau drawer, keeper of the biggest secret of my life. Now I held it in my hands in front of my three children and the man I loved. I reached out to Heather with both hands, the journal resting in them like an offering.

She shook her head. *She's changed her mind.* Disappointment rose to the base of my throat.

"No," Heather said, pushing the book back toward me. "I'd like you to read it to us. Please."

"You want me to read it? Aloud? Now? In front of everyone?"

"Yes, please."

As I opened it, I thought of all the nights when this had been my only way of connecting with my child. For a moment I sat there on the edge of the bed, gently stroking the worn pink cover. Memories flooded, and without warning a hot tear slipped down my cheek. Larry reached over and put an arm around my shoulder. He gave me a supportive squeeze, pulling me gently toward him. "Go ahead," he said softly.

I took a deep breath.

"Dear Julie,'" I began, "I hope one day you'll understand that I wanted to bring you home with me, take care of you, and raise you, but it wouldn't have been fair to you. You're going to have parents who can give you everything I can't. You're going to have a wonderful life. I hope one day you'll learn that I love you very much."

I raised my head to steal a quick glance at my daughter. I caught her in the act of wiping a tear from her cheek with the back of her hand. Next to me, a large warm hand covered my icy one.